Her Sister's Keeper

Leslie McKelvey

ISBN 978-1-936556-63-2

Published 2015
Printed by Black Velvet Seductions Publishing
A division of Savage Publications

Visit us at:
www.blackvelvetseductions.com

This one's for you, Stephanie, my Autumn. You are the second sister I got to choose, but you are not second in my heart. We make each other laugh, we've seen each other cry, and we'll take the other's secrets to the grave.

I love you, and I thank God for bringing you into my life.

Chapter One

A woman's terrified scream pierced the still night air. Juliet Hall stutter-stepped and went absolutely still. Then she chuckled when she realized the unearthly wail had come from the TV, which sat close to the partially opened window inside the quaint bungalow she shared with her sister, Cassie. She saw the telltale bluish light from halfway down the front walk and heard the melodramatic music that was typical background noise for the ending credits of most horror movies.

"Probably watching Friday the 13th again," she muttered. "I love you, Cass, but your taste in films is deplorable."

She sighed softly as she mounted the three narrow porch steps to the cottage. The porch light was out, but the bulb had been flickering when she'd left. Another incandescent gone to an early grave. *Memo to self, ask Mr. Hobbs to use a fluorescent next time, or spring for one on your own.* Juliet pulled her keys from her purse and opened the screen door.

She moved to insert the key and the door whispered open with nary a sound. Juliet froze. An icy claw materialized inside her chest cavity and sharp talons seized her lungs, holding them captive and refusing to give even an inch. The light in the tiny living room was on, casting barely enough light to override the glow from the TV. She paused on the threshold, unmoving and silent, and when nothing jumped out at her those invisible, iron-like fingers released their hold enough for her to draw in a ragged breath. Her heart thumped uncomfortably and a flash of anger warmed her.

"Cassie." She pushed the door open and stepped into the foyer, such as it was. In front of her was the narrow staircase that led up to the two bedrooms and the one full bath. To the right of the staircase was the hall that led back to the kitchen and half bath. To the left of the stairs through an arch constructed during the time her mother had been a tot was the living room. From here all seemed normal, quiet, but normal. Her anger sputtered. Juliet took another breath then closed and locked the door.

"Cassie, you left the door unlocked again. How many times must we go *over* this?"

She moved to the foot of the stairs and looked up, but the second level was dark. A glance down the hall revealed none of the telltale light beneath the swinging door that led to their closet of a kitchen. Chills fanned over her skin and her pulse picked up several notches. She strained to hear something, anything over the steadily increasing beat of her heart.

"In local news, a Seattle man is in custody for . . . ."

Juliet tuned that out. After the noise of the bistro the cottage was quiet, suddenly *too* quiet, *creepy* quiet. Cassie hadn't been feeling well, which was why Juliet had taken her shift at the restaurant, but her sister didn't have laryngitis or anything that would compromise her vocal abilities. No, *those* she possessed in spades, most often to Juliet's dismay and embarrassment. And the fact that the TV was on and Cassie wasn't sitting in front of it was odd. Reruns of the sitcom, *Friends*, came on at 11:00 p.m., and Cassie *never* missed an episode. Even though the show had ended years ago, her sister was still hopelessly in love with Matthew Perry.

"Okay, Cass, this isn't funny anymore." She walked down the narrow hall and through the ancient kitchen door, the hinges moving nearly silently as she flicked on the light. The bungalow had been built in the 1950s, but her landlord was a meticulous man who was quick to respond to any sort of issue with the aging cottage, even squeaky hinges they hadn't complained about. Once in the kitchen a sharp, metallic, singed smell assaulted her nostrils and anger flared back to life when she saw the blue flames beneath the tea kettle. The fact it wasn't whistling told her it was empty, yet the stove continued to burn, gray skeins of smoke curling lazily from the spout and beneath the dented, metal lid. Juliet turned off the burner and turned on the vent fan. "Damn it, Cassie. Are you *trying* to burn the place down?"

The kitchen had two doors, the one that led in from the hall and the other that opened into a small breakfast nook connected to the living room by another graceful wooden archway. The first level of the two-story cottage was basically an oval, with the stairs at the center. Juliet stuck her head through the opposite door and looked around, but the eating area and the living room were empty. With an irritated huff she retraced her steps and mounted the stairs.

When her sneaker-clad foot hit the fourth step it slipped and she shot a hand out to grip the banister, barely preventing a tumble back from whence she'd come. "What the hell?" She looked down at the polished wood. There was a dark splotch on the sturdy oak and in the residual light from the lamp in the living room it looked like chocolate syrup. First the door, now *this*. Heat expanded inside her chest and she didn't bother to hide the irritation in her voice.

"C'mon, Cassie, we agreed no food upstairs. We just got rid of the mice!"

Juliet backed up a step and reached for the switch that would illuminate the second floor landing and thereby the stairs. Nothing. Her anger receded a tiny bit and apprehension shivered through her like a dark mist. She knew it was ridiculous, she'd seen it done a thousand times in movies and had rolled her eyes, yet she couldn't stop herself from flipping the switch several more times. *Nope, you got it right the first time. The light doesn't work.*

That dark mist of apprehension solidified a little, cold tentacles forming and searching through her midsection with icy, menacing intent. She clutched a hand to her stomach, as if by doing so she could dissipate the chill gathering and expanding there. Reaching into her purse she retrieved a miniature flashlight and although the light was small, the illumination it gave off was not. The bright, glaringly white glow from the LED sent shadows scurrying out of the way. It also showed her that it was *not* chocolate syrup on the stairs.

The dark coldness inside her went from fog-like to a solid mass in less than a heartbeat, encasing her heart and lungs. Her eyelids fluttered as she bent down and touched trembling fingers to the sticky, crimson smear bearing the pattern of the sole of her shoe. She looked up several steps and nausea roiled when she saw more of the same. Her diaphragm spasmed, forcefully expelling her pent up breath. She dropped the light and her purse, fear surging through her. Taking the steps two at a time she raced to the second floor, following the blood trail.

"Cassie!"

Juliet crashed through Cassie's door, but the room was empty. Her clothes were scattered about, as they always were, and her bed was unmade. Nothing *looked* amiss, but something was dreadfully wrong.

Juliet could *feel* it, and it was a feeling that was all too familiar. Panic rose, followed by nausea.

"Answer me, Cass!" she called as she flew to the bathroom. The image of Cassie taking a relaxing bubble bath with her headphones on made hope burst in her chest. Cassie could have cut herself shaving, which would explain the blood on the stairs since they kept the first aid kit in the kitchen where it was most often needed. If that was the case she'd first kiss her sister, then throw her damned cell phone and earbuds into the water, and forbid her to ever shave her legs again.

When the bathroom, too, proved empty the wave of reality and dread that stormed over her almost buckled her knees. Juliet braced a hand against the doorframe and stared at the only other door, *her* bedroom door. That was when she noticed the pale, golden glow barely escaping through the narrow crack beneath the panel. It was too faint to be incandescent or even fluorescent, but she knew what it was, and she knew it shouldn't be there.

Despair rose up in her and tears formed as a pained, whispered, "No," escaped her. She took a step and her legs trembled. The light coming from under the door flickered and she gripped the stair railing, her muscles refusing to move. What if he was still here?

Deal with it, Juliet, she told herself. *You've always been the strong one. Now is NOT the time to chicken out. There's still a chance . . . .*

Juliet closed her eyes, her lungs struggling to expand against the ever-tightening band of terror winding around them. Her chest was painfully taut, her heart drumming against her sternum in wild staccato. She started when she heard small, pained whimpers echoing in the hall and her head snapped first in one direction, then the other, her eyes searching frantically for the source. The soft, plaintive cries continued, and she realized they were coming from her own mouth. She pressed her lips together and held her breath. When her throat started to burn she inhaled sharply, then focused on the door and forced herself to move.

The latch hadn't engaged so when she pressed a hand against the heavy panel it swung easily inward. Juliet froze in the doorway. She blinked several times, her brain unwilling and unable to process what she saw. When her synapses finally fired she dropped to her knees, silent sobs clogging her throat. Her jaw worked soundlessly and tears obscured her vision. Grief stormed over her like horses hooves, sharp, cutting, and relentless as she stared, unable to tear her eyes away.

"Oh, Cassie," she whispered. "Oh, God . . . no . . . !"

In the glow from more than a dozen candles Cassie's golden hair glittered like sunlight, her tanned skin burnished and iridescent. Those Caribbean blue eyes that were usually so full of life and laughter were focused on the ceiling, unblinking and unseeing. Juliet doubled over as the pain roared through her like a legion of chainsaws, razor-like teeth ripping mindlessly through flesh, bone, and anything else in their way. Juliet stared at her sister's lifeless body, her eyes taking in the bound hands and ankles, the rose petals scattered over the comforter, the dark splatters on the walls and ceiling, the burgundy blood pooling on the floor beneath the mattress. She couldn't move, she couldn't breathe, and then she saw the words printed so neatly on the wall in what must have been Cassie's blood.

IT SHOULD HAVE BEEN YOU.

It was then she started screaming.

***

The sound of screeching tires drew her attention and she turned her head toward the sound. Detective Daniel Riordan flew out of the nondescript sedan outfitted with blue and red flashing lights. White hot anger boiled in her belly and exploded upwards, nearly blinding her. She launched herself from the porch.

"This is *your* fault!" she screamed. A nearby police officer looped an arm around her waist, but she put up such a struggle that he signaled for help. "You said he wouldn't bother me anymore!" Tears filled her eyes and they slid down her face as she fought against the policemen. "Now Cassie is dead, and it's *your* fault!" She realized the two cops weren't going to let her go and stopped struggling, but the rage continued to seethe. "Wow. That restraining order you suggested did a great job of protecting *me*. Too bad it didn't cover my *sister!*"

Anguish snuffed out her rage and pulled her into a whirlpool of frigid darkness. She sagged against the officers. Unfortunately, the shadows only made her last image of Cassie blaze with Technicolor clarity. The neon pink of the sheer, baby-doll negligee glowed with eerie brightness. She was naked from the waist down and her legs spread wide, each ankle tied to a bedpost. Her hands were tied in a similar fashion at the head of the double bed with colorful scarves, a wide strip of thick silver duct tape covering her mouth. Her throat had been cut from ear to ear, a wound that summoned death in less than a minute. Unfortunately, she knew Cassie's death had not been so quick, and had probably been far more painful. Her sister's body was an angry, bleeding roadmap of cuts and lacerations, purposely inflicted for torture's sake alone. She sank down on the bottom step of the porch, tears obscuring her vision.

"Juliet, I'm *so* sorry . . . ."

She dropped her forehead onto her knees and wrapped her arms around her shins. "Just go away!" she screamed. Sharp, rending pain blossomed in her chest, as if her heart was being ripped slowly and excruciatingly down the middle. "Please . . . !" Her voice broke and sobs erupted. She heard him sigh heavily and then his footsteps took him away.

How had this happened? Why Cassie? For more than a year George Mayfield had stalked and terrorized her, but he'd barely even glanced at her sister. Even when Cassie had gotten in the man's face it was as if she was invisible; his eyes had been for Juliet alone. The knowledge that Cassie wasn't the first to die at Mayfield's hands only amplified her grief. Her diaphragm contracted violently and she fought to breathe as the memory exploded into blazing, Technicolor life in her mind's eye.

"That son of a bitch!"

Juliet glanced up from her latte and was taken aback by the anger in her sister's usually smiling face. She followed the direction of Cassie's gaze and her heart froze. Bright cobalt blue eyes set beneath black, slashing brows watched her with an intensity that was now familiar but still terrifying. He stood across the street, the long overcoat tailored to fit his tall, fit physique, hands clasped neatly in front of him. Most women would find his striking, James Bond-type looks desirable, but the only emotions he inspired in her were cold fear and sheer panic. The restraining order forbade him from getting within 500 yards of her, and across the street from the quaint coffee shop at Pikes's Place Market was well within that distance. She reached for her cell phone but Cassie was already on her feet and striding toward the man.

"What are you doing here?" Cassie demanded. Mayfield didn't even look at her and Cassie stood toe to toe with him. "Answer me, you bastard!"

A faint smile curved his mouth as he continued to look over her sister's head. Swallowing her fear, Juliet forced her feet to move. She ran up behind Cassie and grabbed her arm but Cassie shook her off. Juliet gasped when Cassie planted both hands on Mayfield's chest and shoved for all she was worth.

That's what it finally took to get his attention. He stumbled backwards but quickly regained his balance. His brows rose and eyes widened in surprise, and he looked at Cassie as if she'd just materialized out of thin air. He blinked, stared at her for a few seconds, then his eyes swiveled back to Juliet and his previous expression returned. Juliet felt the blood drain from her face and her heart hit the cement.

That was the only time Mayfield had given Cassie more than a passing glance, and that had been more than three months ago. Now, he'd done more than glance at her sister. He'd killed her. Sorrow wrapped tightly around her middle and forced deeper, harder sobs from the depths of her soul.

"Oh, God, I'm sorry, Cass," she whispered brokenly. "I'm so sorry!"

Not your fault, Juliet. At least now it doesn't hurt anymore.

***

"You should have protected her. She was your baby sister, and she worshiped the ground you walked on! Where *were* you?"

Juliet stared at her mother in shock.

"Helen," her father said, easing down on the edge of the hotel room's king-sized bed, "that's enough."

"Enough?" Her mother gaped at him. "Cassie would never have come here if not for Juliet, Bill!"

Her father rose. "I said *enough.*"

Juliet crossed to the window of the high-rise hotel and pressed her forehead against the cool glass. She had known her mother would blame her; some things never changed. Juliet had been five when Cassie was born, and her mother had told her it was a big sister's duty to watch out for and protect her younger sibling. Oddly, Juliet had never minded the responsibility. While growing up she had not been around enough to do much watching or protecting. Regardless, people often joked that she and Cassie were so close they were like twins born five years apart, and those people were right. She and Cassie finished each other's sentences, they could decipher what the other thought or felt with just a look, and Juliet couldn't remember the last time they'd fought, despite the fact they had lived *and* worked together for nearly four years. Grief scorched through her once more, turning her heart to ash. It was almost more than she could bear.

"I'm sorry, Mom," she whispered. Tears burned and it felt like a cannonball had just punched through her, leaving a gaping, bleeding hole in her torso. "I'm so sorry."

Her father stood at her back and rested his hands on her shoulders.

"Juliet, this is *not* your fault."

She closed her eyes. "Yes, it is, Dad." A strangled sob escaped her and she fought not to remember. "I should have . . . sent her back to California . . . I should have . . . gotten a gun . . . done *something* to make sure she would be safe . . . but I never thought he'd go after her." She covered her face with her hands. "I should *never* have left her alone."

Her mother's voice cut with the cold sharpness of a scalpel. "No, you shouldn't have."

"Helen." Her father's voice had taken on an edge that was in itself a warning.

"We'll be taking Cassie back to San Diego," her mother continued, as if her husband hadn't spoken. "Say your goodbyes now, because I don't want to see you at the funeral."

Juliet heard her father's sharp inhale. She turned and stared at her mother, tears blurring her vision and anguish rushing through her in jagged, radiating waves that shredded her insides.

"Mom . . . !"

"Helen, you don't mean that."

Her mother rose and straightened her spine, tears sliding down her cheeks as she fixed Juliet with a blistering glare. "Yes, I do. Cassie is coming home with us, and you, Juliet, are no longer welcome."

Juliet hadn't thought her heart could hurt anymore, but as her mother's blue eyes bored into hers that shredding sensation grew sharper. Then she felt the freeze. She knew it was her brain's reaction to a perceived deadly threat, but she welcomed the numbness. Still, her throat closed up and for a couple seconds she couldn't draw breath.

A glance at her father only increased the chill. He was shocked, she recognized the anguish in his eyes, but she knew he'd never go against his wife. Her mother wore the pants in the family. She always had. If not for that fact, Juliet would probably have had a more normal upbringing. The tears fell and she wiped them away.

"I love you, Mom," she whispered after several long, taut moments. "You, too, Dad." She walked to the door and grasped the handle. "I'm sorry."

More tears didn't come, much to her surprise. Even after her parent's hotel room door closed behind her, her eyes stayed dry. A heavy sigh escaped her and she started walking.

She hadn't *really* cried since the night Cassie died. Every time she thought of her sister she got teary-eyed, but before the weeping could begin in earnest her brain seized up and choked off the waterworks. Eventually the dam would either burst or she would completely shut down, that much she was sure of. Right now the latter seemed the best option.

I'm sorry, Jules. You didn't deserve that. I love her, but Mom can be a real bitch.

"I know, Cass," Juliet said softly. "I know."

This wasn't your fault. You didn't kill me, Mayfield *did.*

Now the stinging started. "I know, little sister."

Don't let her get to you.

"Easier said than done."

Juliet walked to the elevator, pushed the button, and waited for the car. In movies and TV shows, it would be at this point that one or both of the misguided parents would chase her down, sorrowful and repentant. The mom and/or dad would apologize, everyone would burst into happy tears, and they'd all embrace. Roll joyful music with ending credits here. Juliet didn't even look. Her mother wouldn't apologize, *ever*, and her father might, but not *here* and only if her mom wasn't watching. Juliet loved her dad, but his spine only moved in the direction her mother chose. Cassie was right. Her mom *could* be a bitch.

Juliet walked through the lobby of the hotel without really seeing any of it. Her brain was in tumble-dry mode, meandering, meaningless thoughts spinning to distract her from the emptiness in her soul. She made her way to the elevator that led to the parking structure, knowing Detective Riordan would follow her. Even though she'd left protective custody to see her parents, the man had stayed close. Each time they made eye contact he held her gaze for several seconds before he turned away.

In the week since Cassie's death she had seen him often, but hadn't spoken to him directly. The obligatory post-crime interview he'd conducted had not been pleasant for either of them. Things had left her mouth she'd never thought herself capable of saying, and once her fury was spent she hadn't spoken again. She knew her continued silence ate at him, and even though she realized he was not to blame for her sister's murder she couldn't summon the will to apologize for the awful things she'd said. It just hurt too much.

The parking garage was filled with cars but there was nary a person to be seen. The sun was bright outside, not an everyday occurrence in Seattle, but the light had a difficult time penetrating the narrow open space between the thick, cement slabs. Shadows gathered in corners, between cars, overhead, and behind her like scuttling, whispering specters that shifted with her every step. It sent a shudder through her, and she wrapped her arms around herself. She looked around, eyes darting back and forth, ears alert for any sound. Maybe she should have asked Detective Riordan to follow a little closer.

Her heels tapped rhythmically on the concrete as she reached into her pocket for her keys. She needed to finish packing up the bungalow, although she wasn't sure where she was going once she was done. Maybe she'd visit Amanda in Chicago. They had danced and lived together at the American Ballet Theater in New York until Amanda had blown out an Achilles, but they kept in contact and remained friends. Juliet knew her former roommate would help her however she could, even if that was only giving her a place to stay until she decided what she wanted to do.

A dark cloud of depression settled over her as she contemplated going back to the nearly empty cottage. Thanks to Mr. Hobbs, most of her and Cassie's things were now in storage. What remained were personal items Juliet couldn't bear to part with, and those had been condensed into two large cardboard boxes. A crime scene cleanup crew had finished sanitizing her former bedroom, and the smell of disinfectant and new paint now permeated the air of the quaint house. Her stomach rolled. No, she couldn't go back there, not yet. The few, brief times she'd been there to pack up had been upsetting enough. She choked down the memories that threatened and took a deep breath as she approached her blue Camry.

Her gaze continued to sweep back and forth, searching for any sign of her nemesis. The garage appeared empty. Once she reached her car she tried to slide the key into the lock but couldn't. She bent over to take a closer look and ice gathered in her belly. Something had been shoved into the lock. Juliet inhaled sharply and straightened.

George Mayfield stood behind her, their reflection cast in the driver's window. Where the *hell* had he come from? Her heart stopped, blood freezing in her veins and fear detonating in her chest. Before she could react an arm snaked around her neck and a hand clamped over her mouth. Her scream was cut off as he squeezed her windpipe.

"Time to finish what we started, Juliet," he hissed in her ear. "You will be the proof I need to show him, to show *everyone*, what I am capable of."

For the first time since Mayfield had started harassing her Juliet went into fight mode. She brought the stiletto heel of her shoe down on Mayfield's foot and a surge of exhilaration hit her when a pained cry escaped him. His hold on her loosened and she tried to twist away. She was unsuccessful, so she drove her elbow backwards, hitting him in the gut. A sharp exhale of breath warmed her ear and he stumbled. He fell backwards, dragging her along, more air forced out of his lungs as he collapsed and she landed on top of him. His arms fell to the side. Juliet rolled away, grabbed one of her shoes, and swung the ice-pick-like heel toward him.

He moved out of the way just before the stiletto made contact with his chest. Then another body entered the fray.

"Get out of here!" Riordan shouted. He tackled Mayfield and the two started rolling around. "Go!"

She scuttled backwards against the nearest car, her body and brain out of sync. Her brain was telling her to run but her body wouldn't obey. She stared as they fought, her heart hammering against her sternum. Detective Riordan delivered a blow to Mayfield's jaw, bones cracking together and echoing off the cement structure. Mayfield seemed dazed and Riordan flipped him into his stomach, jerking the man's arms behind him. He had one of Mayfield's hands cuffed when the detective swiveled his eyes her way. As he did, Mayfield seemed to get a second wind and began to struggle again.

"Go, Juliet!" Riordan shouted. "Get the fuck out of here!"

Her brain and body found their rhythm and she shot to her feet. Her keys lay on the ground next to the Camry. She grabbed them, ran around to the passenger side, and less than five seconds later the engine of the Toyota came to life. She jerked the shift lever into reverse, stomped on the accelerator, and shot backwards out of the parking spot. Tires squealed on the concrete, echoing eerily in the garage, and she barely avoided hitting the two wrestling men. After throwing the lever into drive her foot hit the floor and the Camry jumped forward. Without a backwards glance she sped down the ramp and out of the garage.

Chapter Two

The first thing Sheriff Grant Donovan saw when he rounded the curve in the road was the steam coming from under the hood of the blue Camry. He slowed his SUV, and the next thing that registered was the seemingly never-ending pair of tanned, curvy legs that led up to a tight, round backside encased in cut-off jeans. *Holy mother of mile-long*, he thought. *Now* that's *a pair of legs.* The woman's top half was hidden beneath the raised hood as she bent over the engine compartment, heated mist swirling around her and obscuring her from view. After flipping a quick U-turn he pulled to a stop behind the sedan, radioed in, and turned off the engine.

He didn't want to startle her so he made no attempt to move quietly, but apparently the woman didn't hear him as he left the Yukon and walked around the passenger side of the Toyota. Her focus remained on the steam-shrouded engine. Gravel crunched beneath his boots and he smiled when she cursed fluently.

"Excuse me, miss," he said as he rounded the front passenger side. "Having some car trouble?"

She yelped and jerked upright, hitting her head on the hood. "Ouch!" The woman scuttled immediately backwards.

He took one step forward. "Are you all right?"

A gust of wind sent the steam swirling away and he finally got a look at her. He paused and blinked as a pair of wide-set, vivid blue eyes stared back at him. They were the color of tropical seas, a mix of sky blue and Irish-hillside-green, and lined with thick, dark lashes. *Damn, and I thought her legs were gorgeous.* He saw the surprise and the fear there and gave her a reassuring smile as he touched the brim of his hat. She took another step back and her posture tensed.

"Afternoon." He glanced at the engine. "I'm Sheriff Donovan. Are you okay?"

Her face was tight with anxiety but she managed a short nod. "Fine."

Her gaze flicked to the engine and then back to him. "I think it's the radiator hose."

"Mind if I take a look?" He waited until she gave her assent, trying to appear as non-threatening as possible, and then bent over the engine compartment. Sure enough, he could see the ruptured hose through the residual steam. He gave her a sidelong glance. "Well, you're right. Looks like I need to call you a tow truck."

A heavy sigh escaped her. "Just what I need."

He chuckled. "Shouldn't be a problem. Radiator hoses are easy." He started walking back toward the SUV. "You can sit in my car while we wait. It's a mite warm out here and *my* AC, unlike yours, works. It shouldn't take Eddie more than half an hour to get here."

"You're going to stay with me?"

He stopped and looked over one shoulder. He heard the dread in her voice and wondered what was going on with the woman besides a ruptured radiator hose. Most people would be happy to see him if stranded on a deserted road, but she was not. His senses prickled, but when he spoke he kept his voice and expression neutral. "Yes, ma'am."

Her eyes widened slightly. "You don't have to do that. I'm sure you have better things to do than waste your time sitting here with *me*." She took a deep breath and focused on her tennis shoes. "I'll be fine by myself until the tow truck gets here."

Grant faced her. "I'm sure you will, ma'am," he drawled, "but we do things differently here in Montana. Your feminist hackles can get as prickly as they want, but this is going to work one of three ways." Her brows rose and Grant lifted one corner of his mouth in a half smile. "One, we can wait here, together, in my air-conditioned vehicle until Eddie gets here. Two, we can wait here, you outside, and me in my air-conditioned vehicle until Eddie gets here. Or, three, I can drive you into town and drop you at Autumn's Diner, and you can wait for Eddie there until he gets to town with your car." He gave her a pointed look. "Take your pick."

She stared at him, chewing her lower lip. Her brow furrowed and a shadow passed behind her eyes, her fear a palpable thing even with the space between them. He could see her anxiety, evident in her rigid posture and tightly clenched hands. She glanced toward the forest, as if hoping for someone else to come out of the woods and save her, and when no one did she reluctantly turned her gaze back to him.

She was quite pretty, and he hadn't seen a nicer pair of legs . . . *ever*. Her face was heart-shaped, her chin slightly pointed, those amazing eyes set above high cheekbones. Her mouth drew his gaze briefly. It was small with a full bottom lip and a slightly narrower top lip that had a pronounced cupid's bow. She almost appeared to be pouting, but her expression was thoughtful rather than petulant. Finally, she spoke.

"Well, I *am* hungry." She wrapped her arms around herself. "I haven't eaten since dinner last night."

"You're either not a breakfast person, or you're a late riser." He glanced at his watch and sent a wry smile her way. "It's after noon."

Her brows drew together and a spark of annoyance flared in her eyes. "Well, I wasn't hungry when I pulled off the interstate, and apparently there's nothing between the interstate and the closest town, which is where I was *trying* to get to when the hose went." She gave him a scowl. "That sort of limits one's options."

"Yes, it does." He chuckled, walked to the passenger door of the Yukon, and opened it. "Your chariot, madam. Grab your bag. I need to get you to Autumn's before starvation sets in."

She watched him warily for several tense seconds and then sighed and looked at the car. "Should I lock it?"

Grant bit back a laugh because he knew she was serious. *Ah, city folk.* "You can, if it will make you feel better. But out here people barely make the top five list of things you need to worry about." He lifted one brow. "There are several animal species far more dangerous, and unless you have a bunch of food in your car, which I doubt because you said you're hungry, the critters won't bother it."

She didn't move, her gaze fastened on the Camry.

He tried not to roll his eyes. "You've already seen how much traffic we have on this road. How long have you been waiting here?"

She pulled a cell phone from her pocket and glanced at it. Then she frowned and slid her gaze in his direction. "Twenty minutes."

"And how many cars have you seen?"

Her scowl darkened. "Just yours."

"How many cars did you see between here and the interstate?"

She fixed a glare on him. "Just yours."

He tipped his head. "I can pretty much guarantee the next person who sees your car will be Eddie, with his tow truck." He gestured toward the passenger seat. "You ready to go now?"

She started nibbling her bottom lip again. It was nearly a minute before she moved, but Grant just stood there, waiting patiently. At least the fear had faded. That was a plus. Finally, she huffed, opened the driver's door, and reached across to the front passenger seat.

Grant's chest tightened and he slid his hand toward his gun. He watched her carefully, mindful of any untoward movement that would signal she was more than just a stranded motorist. He might be just a small town sheriff, but he was a US military combat veteran and well aware that people were often not what they seemed. When she looped the straps of a leather purse over her shoulder he relaxed just a hair, and when she pulled a large, black duffel bag from the backseat he released the grip of his pistol. After closing the door she moved around to the trunk and opened it. He noted the graceful way she moved, fluid and elegant. She didn't walk, she *flowed*, and he found himself momentarily distracted.

"Could you help me, please?" she asked, looking at him over her shoulder.

He shook himself and refocused on her. He was relatively certain she wasn't going for a weapon so he walked slowly toward her, still alert. "Of course. What do you need?"

There were two large cardboard boxes in the trunk. She grabbed one and looked at him. "Can you get the other one? I'll leave my car here, but I'm *not* leaving these."

He glanced at the box and saw the word "Cassie" written on the side. He wondered if that was her name, but one glance at her face made him think twice about asking. There was a shadow in her eyes and a tightness about her mouth, and he thought he saw the faint sheen of tears. He picked up the box, tucked it beneath one arm, and closed the trunk lid. "Sure thing. Let's put them in the back."

Grant walked around to the back of the Yukon and opened it. He slid his box into the cargo area and reached for the one she carried. She hesitated for a split-second then handed it to him and dropped the black duffel next to the boxes. Without a word she turned on her heel, walked around the side of the Yukon, and slid into the passenger seat. He looked at the back of her head for a moment before he closed the cargo door and walked around to the driver's side.

He got behind the wheel, closed the door, and buckled his seatbelt. She glanced at him and fastened her seatbelt, her expression wary.

"Before we go anywhere I have to ask you one question," he said. Her trepidation was obvious and she shifted in her seat, as if suddenly uncomfortable.

"What?"

Her voice was low, almost fearful, and he wondered where her uneasiness came from. He wondered if it was because he was a cop, or a man. He wondered if she had scars that weren't visible beneath her attractive exterior. He knew about the latter from personal experience. Then again, perhaps that was just her personality. He'd met more than his share of people who were simply overly cautious or afraid of everything. But, people like that didn't usually go driving around the backwoods of Montana, or anywhere else, alone and virtually defenseless. No, people like that usually stayed close to home where everything was familiar and safe.

Grant met her gaze and put on a serious expression. Her eyes widened slightly, and then he smiled. "What's your name?"

She blinked at him. That was obviously *not* what she had expected. He saw the convulsive swallow before she took a breath and extended a hand.

"Juliet. Juliet Hall."

Grant's hand engulfed her much smaller one and he nodded once. Her grip was firm and sure, and he liked the way her fingers fit in his. "Pleased to meet you, Miss Hall, I'm Grant. Now, let's get you something to eat before you waste away."

***

Evergreen Springs was just about the prettiest town Juliet thought she'd ever seen. The downtown area was one giant square centered on a vast park, and it looked like it had been time-warped straight out of the 1940s. The worn brick of the buildings, the colorful awnings and sidewalk signs, and the whitewashed gazebo in the middle of the rolling green lawn reminded her of a bygone era, an era she'd only seen in photographs, history books, and black and white movies. She almost expected Cary Grant or Jimmy Stewart to walk out of one of the buildings and stroll down the sidewalk twirling a cane.

As he drove slowly down the street her eyes were drawn back to Sheriff Grant Donovan. She'd met quite a few law enforcement officers over the past year and a half, but none of them looked like *him*. He had a laid back air and a lazy smile more fit for a satisfied lover after languid

Sunday-morning-sex than a cop. His uniform was a pair of butt-hugging Wranglers, a button-up shirt, and scuffed cowboy boots. The only thing that identified him as law enforcement was the badge over the left front pocket and the gun belt.

He was several inches over six feet tall with a strong, athletic build. Wide shoulders tapered to a narrow waist and hips, and his posture was ramrod straight, almost military in its bearing. This made him appear even bigger than he was. His hands looked as if they could crush fistfuls of walnuts into dust, but his fingers were long and elegant, an artist's hands. Short, curling brown hair peeked from underneath the cowboy hat, and even when he wasn't smiling his eyes were. His eyes were a warm, rich, chocolate brown lined with lashes so thick and dark it almost looked like he was wearing mascara. Juliet chuckled at the thought. He glanced at her then and that lazy smile appeared. Heat climbed into her cheeks and she looked away quickly, mortified to have been caught staring.

He continued to drive, one hand on the wheel.

"So," he said, "you just passing through, or were you planning to stay a few days?"

Until now they'd ridden in silence and Juliet looked at him. "I . . . I hadn't really thought about it."

"Then why were you coming to Evergreen Springs in the first place? We don't get many visitors here unless they're stopping in to see family, stopping on their way to Canada, or they're just plain lost." He gave her a sidelong glance and a grin so sexy it needed a warning label. "Which are you?"

She gulped and turned her gaze out the window to watch the passing storefronts. "None of the above, actually." She took a breath and caught his scent. It was a mix of soap and skin and . . . *warmth*. It was the only description she could come up with. For a moment she lost her train of thought, and that heat in her cheeks intensified when she saw his expression. He looked amused, as if he could read her mind. She took another breath and gathered her wits. "I saw the sign for Evergreen Springs on the interstate and the name caught my attention. It sounded . . . pretty and . . . *serene*. I thought I'd check it out, but I hadn't planned anything beyond that."

"Fair enough." His eyes twinkled. "Although I have to warn you, the place grows on you . . . *fast*. If you've a mind to go somewhere else you may want to do it quickly."

"I'll remember that." His chuckle made her smile. "Thanks for the warning."

"Anytime."

He parked the Yukon in the middle of one of the four long, main streets that bordered the park and turned off the engine. Juliet looked at him and he nodded to her right.

"We're here."

She turned. Large, darkly tinted plate glass windows, with the name "Autumn's" painted in red and white, sparkled, and the gingham curtains screamed "small town" charm and warmth. She reached for the door handle, but before she could move Sheriff Donovan had exited the vehicle and opened her door.

"Thank you," she said, surprised at how swiftly he moved.

He smiled, tipped his hat, and stepped back. A bell on the diner's door signaled it was opening and someone stepped onto the sidewalk.

"Grant Donovan, you handsome devil! *What* are you doing here with another woman?"

Juliet turned toward the owner of the honeyed voice and found herself looking into beautiful, almond shaped brown eyes. The woman was African-American and quite petite, but there was nothing diminutive about her figure. An hourglass would be green with envy. Juliet had no doubt the sheriff would be able to encircle her tiny waist easily with his hands, and probably have room to spare. However, her bosom would overflow just about anything, including the denim shirt she wore so primly buttoned. There was no disguising *that* particular set of assets.

Sheriff Donovan leaned against the vehicle and grinned. "Sorry, Autumn. I forgot."

"It would serve you well not to, Sheriff. You *know* I don't like to share."

He laughed. "Relax. Her car broke down outside of town. She's going to wait here for Eddie, so instead of giving me a hard time you should thank me for bringing you new business."

The woman grinned and kissed his cheek, though she had to stand on tiptoe and he had to lean down for her to do so. "Thank you, handsome." Her grin vanished and she turned to Juliet. The petite woman gave her the once-over and a look she couldn't decipher, the full, generous mouth pursed and one elegant eyebrow lifted imperiously. "At least she's pretty."

Then her face split into a smile and she extended a dainty hand. "Hi, I'm Autumn Idlebird, but you can call me Autumn. This is my place. Are you hungry?"

Juliet blinked, completely taken off guard by the change in demeanor. She glanced at the brawny sheriff then shook Autumn Idlebird's hand. "I'm Juliet, and I'm starving actually."

Autumn put an arm around her shoulders and guided her toward the door. "Then, girl, come on in. Whatever you're craving I probably have it, or I can make it." She paused at the door and glanced over her shoulder. "You coming, pretty boy?"

"Yes, ma'am."

Autumn scowled at him, her brow furrowed. "What did I tell you about that *ma'am* crap?"

Juliet paused as a thought struck her. "Oh, wait, what about the boxes?"

Sheriff Donovan pushed away from the SUV and gave her that lazy smile. "We can leave them in back, as long as you're comfortable with that. I promise I won't open them. When your car is fixed and you're ready to go have Eddie give me a call. I'll drop them by the garage."

His genuine warmth triggered something in her that had been dormant for over a year, and for a few moments she couldn't speak. The blackness that had enveloped her since her sister's murder and her mother's rejection lightened a shade, and it felt like the faintest brush of sunlight on her frozen soul. She met those smiling brown eyes and gulped.

"Are you sure?" she asked.

A flash of white teeth only made him more handsome. "I'm sure. Or I could put them in my office if it's something fragile. The roads around here can be a little rough."

"There's nothing breakable, except some framed pictures but those are easy to replace." She forced herself to maintain his gaze, and was proud of herself for not wavering. Since Mayfield's stalking campaign Juliet had grown wary of people, men especially. Outside of work she shied away from everything but the most impersonal contact. She couldn't do that anymore unless she wanted Mayfield to win. She didn't want him to win, and she didn't want to be an island unto herself for another minute. Sheriff Donovan smiled and, unbidden, she smiled back. "Thanks."

He touched the brim of his hat. "You're welcome. Now, let's get you some lunch before you pass out on the sidewalk. If people see *that* I won't get re-elected."

Juliet laughed and was surprised. She couldn't remember the last time she had laughed.

Autumn Idlebird made an impatient sound. "Come on, you two. The food is *inside*."

Juliet allowed herself to be herded into the diner by the petite force of nature. Sheriff Donovan followed a couple paces behind. She noticed he removed his hat when he entered the small café. *Hmm, old-fashioned manners; I like that.* Autumn steered her toward the counter, which was half full, and then bustled away. The lively chatter softened as people turned to look at her. The sheriff didn't seem to notice.

"Afternoon, Dale," Donovan said to an older gentleman as he eased down on the stool next to her. The man on her left turned, looked past her, and gave Grant a smile.

"Afternoon, Sheriff. Lunch time?"

"Nope," Donovan replied. He looked at Autumn. "I'll just have an iced tea to go, please."

Autumn gaped at him. "You're not staying for lunch?"

"Brought my own today, but I'll probably stop by later," he replied. "With Miss Betty out of town I'm on my own for dinner." He glanced at Juliet. "And her lunch is on me."

A knowing smile curved Autumn's mouth and she retrieved a Styrofoam cup from beneath the counter. "You got it, Grant."

Juliet swiveled on her stool to face him, her nerves prickling. "You don't have to do that, Sheriff. I *can* buy my own lunch." He stood and Juliet had to crane her neck to maintain his gaze.

"I don't do anything I don't *want* to do, Miss Hall," he replied smoothly, the corners of his mouth quirking up just a bit. "Like I said, we do things differently here in Montana. Consider this your welcome to Evergreen Springs." He picked up his hat. "And you can call me Grant. *Sheriff* sounds so formal."

"Which we don't do here," Autumn added as she handed a lidded cup and a straw to the sheriff. "Here it's a first name basis only and if we don't know your business you better start talking because we'll find out anyway." She shrugged and grinned. "Small towns are like that."

Juliet stood and faced him, and it took all her self-confidence to maintain eye contact. "I'll call you Grant only if you call me Juliet."

His gaze wandered over her face for a few moments, and it felt more like a caress than a look. Juliet's cheeks went hot. Finally, he smiled and the heat of that inner sunlight went up a few degrees.

"Deal." He stuck out a hand. "Juliet."

Her name sounded like an endearment when he said it, the rough, velvety tone of his voice sending an unwarranted shiver through her. She slipped her fingers into his. He held her hand for several long moments, then squeezed it and let her go.

"I'll tell Eddie where you are so he can give you an update on your car," he said in a low voice. "When he's done have him or Autumn or, hell, anyone else in town give me a call and I'll swing by."

The words popped out before she even thought them. "Or, you can give me your number and I can . . . call . . . ." Her voice died as she realized everyone within hearing distance had stopped talking and was watching them with guarded interest. She bit her lip and dropped her chin. "Never mind."

"Let me see your cell phone."

Surprised, she glanced up. He wore a ghost of a smile and didn't seem to notice they had everyone's attention. Before she knew what she was doing she had handed him her phone. He put his hat down and started tapping the screen. The heat in her cheeks expanded over her neck and chest as people nearby started looking at each other with knowing, sly smiles. Grant Donovan either didn't care or was unaware. She'd bet on the former.

"There you go." He handed the phone back and she saw his name and number on the display. "Now you can call when you're ready." He picked up his hat again. "Afternoon, Juliet. Enjoy your lunch."

"Thank you, Sheriff . . . I mean, Grant, for everything."

"You're most welcome. I'll see you later."

She watched him as he strode through the diner, nodding to people as he went. He slid his hat onto his head as he exited, and when the door closed behind him she realized she was holding her breath. Juliet returned to her seat, ignoring the amused stares, and slowly exhaled.

"I think he likes you."

Juliet looked at Autumn as the woman handed her a menu. Juliet took it and opened it, her eyes scanning the neat print without really seeing anything. "He doesn't know me."

Autumn laughed. "Honey, you look as sweet and as innocent as they come, but I know even *you* have to understand something of animal attraction." She planted a hand on one lush hip and grinned. "I don't know Chris Hemsworth but I still like him. What I would *do* to that man if I could get him alone in a room for five minutes!" She smacked her lips and closed her eyes with a sigh. After a moment her lids snapped open and she leaned her elbows on the counter. "Now, what can I get you? The special is the cheeseburger with fries or a salad and a drink."

Juliet folded the menu and handed it over. "I'll have that, salad with ranch, and a Coke."

Autumn looked impressed. "So, you actually *eat.*" A sly grin lit up her face. "I like that."

Autumn turned toward the kitchen and relayed her order to the cook. Less than two minutes later she slid a tall, icy Coke and crispy green salad with dressing on the side in front of Juliet.

"There you go, honey. Your burger will be up in a few." Before Juliet could thank her she flitted away, filling coffee cups and chatting and flirting as she went. Juliet watched her for a moment, then sighed and took a long drink.

"So, you're the woman whose car broke down outside of town?"

Juliet looked to her left at the man Grant had called Dale. He was probably in his late fifties or early sixties with silver hair, his blue eyes watching her with a sharpness that made her gulp. "I'm sorry. Did the sheriff take out an ad or something? How do you know that?"

Dale grinned. "Word travels fast around here." He took a drink of his coffee. "Like Autumn said, that's how small towns work. They're fueled by talk, true or not." When she gaped at him he grinned. "And, I have an inside source. My wife is the local dispatcher."

She blinked, chuckled, and took a bite of her salad. "Yes, I'm the woman whose car broke down outside of town. And now, I suppose, I'm dating the sheriff too, right?"

Dale laughed, and it was a warm, gravelly sound that was pleasing to the ears. "More than likely that *is* what will make the beauty parlor circuit before lunch is over."

"Great." She rolled her eyes. "I suppose if I have to stay a while until my car is fixed we'll be engaged before I leave."

Another laugh. "Probably."

Her brain fired off a thought and her mouth let it escape before she could censor herself. "That means the sheriff isn't married, right?"

"That's right." The tone of Dale's voice made Juliet look at him. The man seemed to be enjoying this particular line of conversation, his blue eyes twinkling merrily. "Grant's not married . . . *yet.*"

A strange surge of relief went through her and then she frowned as her brain caught up. "Wait . . . yet? Is he going to be?" Realizing what she'd just asked, her cheeks warmed and she gave herself a mental slap.

Dale merely chuckled, shook his head, and turned his attention back to his pie and coffee. Juliet wondered briefly if that meant Grant Donovan was in a serious relationship, and then she chided herself. *What does it matter? You'll only be in town long enough to get your car fixed and then you're out of here.* Suddenly, she wasn't as anxious to leave as she should have been.

Chapter Three

Grant parked the SUV in front of the sheriff's office, got out of the vehicle, and took the steps two at a time. As he walked through the main doors he smiled and nodded at Roberta, his right-hand woman and the local dispatcher. She sat behind her desk, her headphones on, her fingers tapping rhythmically on the computer's keyboard. Plump, pretty, and sharper than a tack, she smiled and nodded in reply.

Deputy Jackson Branch rose from behind his desk when he saw Grant approaching. The man was a couple inches shorter, but fit and slender with pleasant features that garnered him more than his fair share of female attention. *Damn.* Jackson was supposed to be on patrol. Although the ladies found him appealing, Grant didn't particularly like the man. He ground his teeth together as the deputy walked toward him.

"Hey, Grant, I ran the plates on that blue Camry Eddie is towing back to town."

Grant paused and frowned. "Why did you do that?"

Jackson's blond brows rose sharply. "Eddie called it in and said the tags were expired. You didn't notice?"

"I noticed," Grant shot back, "but I figured being stranded on the road was enough punishment for one day. You didn't write the owner a ticket, did you?"

"Not yet—"

"Good," Grant cut in. *"Don't."*

"Okay." Jackson looked at him uncertainly for a few seconds.

"What, Jackson?"

Jackson walked back to his desk and swiveled the computer monitor Grant's way. "Well, when I ran the plates through the system . . . ." He pointed to a flashing bar at the top of the screen. "Her name is flagged."

Grant took a few steps toward the monitor. "Flagged for what?"

Jackson looked at the screen and shook his head. "It just says to contact a Detective Riordan at Seattle PD."

Grant remembered the fear and trepidation she'd exhibited toward him and wondered if she was running from the law. Uncertainty scraped softly up his spine.

"Send that to my computer." He fixed Jackson with a hard stare. "I'll handle it."

"But—"

Grant cut him off with a glare. "Just do it, and then get back on patrol." He turned toward his office door, paused, and turned back. "And, by the way, if you call in sick again on Friday . . . you're fired." Without another word he walked into his office and closed the door.

Apparently Jackson was quicker with the computer than he was with anything else, and just as Grant sat down at his desk his computer beeped. He opened the window and peered at the screen. There wasn't anything to indicate she was a wanted felon or fugitive, just instructions to contact Detective Riordan at the Seattle Police Department. The number was listed on the flag, and Grant picked up the phone and dialed.

"Seattle Police Department. How may I direct your call?"

"Detective Riordan, please."

"One moment."

Grant waited, but it wasn't a long wait. Only seconds passed before he heard the familiar click.

"This is Riordan."

"Detective, my name is Grant Donovan, and I'm the sheriff in Hill County, Montana. One of my deputies ran the plate on a car that broke down outside of town and the registered owner's name flagged the system with instructions to call you."

There was a brief, taut silence, and when Riordan spoke his voice was low. "The registered owner, is she all right?"

Grant frowned. "If you mean Miss Hall, she's fine."

The detective let out a breath. "Thank God. You've seen her?"

"I spoke with her not ten minutes ago." That uncertainty traversed his back again. "She's probably eating lunch as we speak. May I ask why her name is flagged? She some sort of fugitive?"

"No. No, she's not a fugitive. She's a victim actually."

Grant leaned back in his chair, not liking the direction this was going. "A victim of what?"

Riordan sighed. "Juliet . . . Miss Hall . . . is being stalked by a man named George Mayfield. He's terrorized her for nearly 18 months. Three months ago, she found her sister's body at the house they shared. She'd been murdered."

Air hissed from between Grant's teeth and his abdominals tightened. "God almighty."

"We believe Mayfield is the killer, but the crime scene was clean. In fact, it was so clean that if Juliet hadn't been working a busy café in front of dozens of people *she* would have been the prime suspect."

That explains a few things. Grant rubbed his temples. *With a crazed psychopath on her trail she has a very good reason to be frightened and wary.* "That still doesn't tell me why she's flagged."

"After the coroner released her sister's body, Juliet left protective custody to be with her parents. As she left her parents' hotel Mayfield tried to abduct her. Thankfully, he failed, but Juliet bolted. She cleared out her bank accounts, and her landlord said she came home, threw a couple boxes and a bag in her car, and took off." Riordan sighed again. "This is the first fix I've had on her whereabouts in almost two months."

"Is this guy still after her?" Grant asked. The thought of a vicious sociopath wandering around Evergreen Springs made his stomach knot.

There was another brief silence. "Yes, I believe he is."

Grant pinched the bridge of his nose. He was starting to get a headache. "Weren't you keeping tabs on him? Even if you couldn't prove he was her sister's killer you should have been watching him."

When he spoke next Riordan sounded tired. "We had him under surveillance, but he managed to slip away about a month ago. This guy's father is a former politician, rich, well-connected, and willing to lie to protect his son. Between the father's influence and all the loopholes in stalking laws, we've been pretty much hamstrung here."

Riordan paused, and the concern in the man's voice hinted at a deeper connection between Juliet and the detective. Grant wondered if the feeling went both ways, and then he wondered why he cared.

"Are you sure she's all right?"

Grant glanced through his window across the square, but there was no way he could see Juliet from this distance. "Hold on." He pulled out his cell phone and sent Autumn a text message.

Is Juliet still there?

Just finished her cheeseburger, ALL of it. Why?

Just checking. Thanks. He put the cell phone down. "Yes, I'm sure she's all right."

Riordan exhaled slowly and Grant could almost feel the man's anxiety through the phone line.

"Sheriff, could you do something for me?"

Grant had a feeling he wasn't going to like this. "What?"

"Could you keep an eye on her? Mayfield's obsession with her hasn't just gone away, and he's out there somewhere looking for her. I don't want her to end up like her sister."

A chill went through him as he imagined Juliet dead. Even though he'd just met her, the thought made something inside him recoil. "I can do that, Detective, but I doubt she'll be here come dinner time. The only thing I saw wrong with her car was a ruptured radiator hose, which takes about ten minutes to fix."

"Well, for as long as she is there could you watch out for her? And, if she mentions where she's going, I'd appreciate a heads up. Maybe I can intercept her, convince her to return to protective custody."

Grant immediately thought of his best friend, Laine Wheeler, whom he'd known since kindergarten. Through a twist of fate Laine had found herself in the middle of an undercover Federal investigation into a domestic terror group, and she'd been forced to go into the Witness Protection Program. Thankfully, the Federal agencies involved had managed to neutralize the threat and she had been able to return to her life and her career as an emergency physician. He remembered her telling him what it had been like, first being surrounded by law enforcement 24/7, and then having to start an entirely new existence in a new city with a new name and a fictitious history. Grant wouldn't wish that on anyone.

"As long as she's in Evergreen I'll make sure she's safe, but even if I do manage to find out where she's headed do you think she'll want to go back into protective custody?" Grant rubbed his eyes and felt the familiar weight of responsibility drop around his shoulders like a leaden cloak. "No offense, Detective, but the guy you were supposed to protect her from killed her sister and nearly kidnapped her on your watch. That wouldn't instill *me* with a great sense of confidence."

"Me either," Riordan agreed, "but I have to try. We screwed up and underestimated Mayfield, badly, but that's a mistake we will not make again. The safest place for her is in protective custody, so, from one LEO to another, I'm asking for your help."

Grant exhaled slowly and leaned his head back. "Well, if I'm going to be involved in this I need to know the details."

"I'll e-mail you the case file," Riordan said. For the first time since the conversation started, the man's voice sounded like it had some life. "I'll check with my captain about heading your way, so if you could find a way to keep her there, that would be great."

"I'm not going to force her to stay."

"I didn't ask you to."

Grant frowned. "And I'm not going to lie to her in order to trick her into staying."

"Sheriff Donovan, I don't want to tell you how to do your job—"

"Then don't." Grant straightened in his chair. "I'll do my job, you do yours. You have a nice day, Detective, and let me know when to expect you. I'll be waiting on that case file and I'll call if I have any questions." Before the detective could reply Grant hung up the phone. "Damn city cops."

He waited about 20 minutes, checking his e-mail, but Detective Riordan had yet to send him the case file. Either the detective was messing with him or it was an extensive file. Until Grant interacted with Riordan a little more and got a bead on what kind of man and cop he was, either option was a possibility. When the clock on his wall struck the quarter-hour he decided he'd waited long enough. He got to his feet and left the office.

Roberta wasn't behind her desk and he looked around the office. "Roberta."

The silver-haired woman popped out from behind a filing cabinet. "Yes, Sheriff?"

"I'll be getting an e-mail from the Seattle Police Department with a file attachment." He started walking toward the door. "When it comes in could you download and print out a hard copy of that file, please?"

She bobbed her head once. "Sure thing. Where should I put it?"

"My desk is fine."

"You got it, Grant. You headed back out?"

He tossed her a smile as he pushed through the front door. "Yep. You know how much I *love* sitting behind a desk."

Roberta rolled her eyes and sighed dramatically as she disappeared behind the filing cabinet again. Grant chuckled and made his way to his SUV.

As he passed behind the Yukon his gaze was drawn to Juliet's cardboard boxes. Although Riordan hadn't mentioned the sister's name, Grant had a feeling it was Cassie. He had never lost a sibling, but he had lost several friends in Iraq and Afghanistan he had considered brothers, and he felt the pain of that wound even now. It had dulled over the years, but he doubted it would ever disappear.

As he opened the driver's door he caught a glimpse of a tow truck out of the corner of his eye and paused. Eddie was just getting back to the garage, Juliet's Camry trailing securely behind the shiny red and black vehicle. Grant shut the door and walked toward Eddie's Auto Palace.

He watched from the parking lot as Eddie backed the Camry into the garage. After Eddie released the car and parked the rig Grant walked slowly up to the open bay door and leaned against the cinder block wall. He smiled as Eddie buzzed around the Camry, humming, his movements reminding Grant of a bee as it circled the hive.

As if sensing his presence, Eddie looked his way. Eddie's sharp black eyes peered at him from beneath bushy, salt-and-pepper brows. His face was tanned and leathery, with a beard that reached to his chest. His once black hair was streaked with white and hung past his shoulders. He was about the same height as Juliet, roughly 5'7", and he had a lean, wiry build. A better mechanic Grant had never met. Eddie was a savant with cars, but he had little skill with people. He lived alone on the outskirts of town in a small, isolated cabin, had never married, never even dated as far as Grant knew. Despite his eccentricities however he was well-liked, and once he fixed a car it stayed fixed.

"Afternoon, Grant," Eddie said, giving him a gap-toothed smile as he leaned over the engine compartment. "What can I do for you?"

Grant shook his head. "For me? Nothing. What you *can* do is fix that Toyota so the owner can get back on the road." Detective Riordan's words echoed in his head. *If you could find a way to keep her there . . . .* "So, what's she saying to you?"

Eddie leaned his hands on the frame and peered at the engine. "She's saying she's got a lot of miles on her, but she'll roll the odometer again as long as she receives regular oil changes and service. She says she wishes the owner had noticed the leaking hose back in Missoula, and that she tried to make it to Evergreen." He glanced at Grant over his bony shoulder. "The hose gave up before she did."

Grant smiled. "How long will it take to fix?"

"As long as I have this specific hose . . . ten minutes tops. Where's the driver?"

"At Autumn's."

Eddie nodded slowly and turned his gaze back to the engine. His expression was tender, almost loving as he stared.

"I'll check the part number. If I have to order it from Missoula or Billings it won't be here until tomorrow afternoon. If she can't wait that long I can finagle something that'll work until she reaches the city. It's just a matter of finding the correct diameter hose."

"How do you know the driver is a she?"

Instead of answering Eddie lowered the hood and pointed. The driver's side visor was down and clipped to it was a photo of two young women. It was upside down now, but when the visor was flipped up the driver would be able to see it right-side-up. Grant walked around the side of the car, reached through the open window, and took the picture.

The girls had their arms around each other's shoulders, their cheeks pressed together, and there was no mistaking the familial resemblance. Both of them were grinning, their hair whipping in the wind. Behind them tall masts rose, telling Grant they were standing at a harbor or marina of some sort. He flipped the picture over. *Juliet and Cassie, Summer at Seaside.* They were both beautiful, with the same aquamarine eyes and gorgeous skin. Empathy cut a little sharper this time and his stomach cramped. It angered and saddened him to think of a beautiful young girl having her life cut short. He couldn't even fathom what that must have done to Juliet. In the photo the girls glowed, radiant with life and joy. The woman he'd met on the side of the road was still beautiful, but the vibrancy was gone.

"Damn."

"What?" Eddie asked, buried beneath the hood once more.

"Nothing, Eddie." He looked at the photograph for a few more seconds before carefully putting it back. Sighing softly, he hooked his thumbs through his belt loops. "Hey, could you do me a favor?"

Eddie peered around the edge of the raised hood. "Sure thing, Grant. Whaddya need?"

Grant gestured at the Camry. "Could you give the car a once over, see if there are any other mechanical problems, current or pending?"

When Eddie looked at him quizzically, Grant smiled. "The driver is on a road trip, so until she reaches a more populated part of the country it would be best if her car didn't break down again."

That seemed to satisfy the mechanic. "You got it. If I find something do you want me to fix it or just tell the owner and let her decide?"

Grant thought about it for a few seconds. "If it's easy just fix it and send me the bill. If it's something major, let her decide."

If Eddie thought that was strange he gave no indication, merely nodded his shaggy head. "Will do, Sheriff. Do you want me to head to the diner and let her know her car is here?"

"That's okay, I'll do that. Give me a call when you know about the part."

"Okey dokey."

Eddie walked toward the office part of the auto shop to check the computer, his booted feet shuffling as he went. A twinge of guilt impaled Grant for the possible roadblock he may have just thrown in front of Juliet, but the thought of her stalker finding her on the open road made his stomach curdle. Maybe giving Detective Riordan a little time to work would be a good thing.

Grant stared at the photo for another minute, then turned and headed for the diner.

***

Juliet groaned as Autumn put a piece of peach pie in front of her, the rich, tangy scent of ripe fruit and warm, fragrant crust making her mouth water. The generous scoop of melting ice cream drizzled over the sides of the pastry to puddle on the plate in a mesmerizing pool of liquid vanilla. The lunch crowd had cleared out, leaving only Juliet, Autumn, and Shelby Stewart, another waitress. The quiet was oddly comforting.

"This looks and smells amazing, Autumn, but after that enormous cheeseburger I have nowhere to put it."

Autumn handed her a fork and picked up one of her own. "We'll share." She cut the piece in half, stabbed the tines through her piece, and lifted a generous scoop to her lush mouth. "C'mon, girlfriend. You have to have at least *one* bite."

"She won't let you leave until you try it," Shelby said from down the counter. The gorgeous, blonde twenty-something was filling salt and pepper shakers. A grin that would sell a million tubes of toothpaste flashed and the girl laughed. "Might as well just get it over with." Shelby's emerald eyes shifted toward the door and her grin widened. A moment later the bell on the door tinkled. "Hey, Grant." She stopped what she was doing and skipped across the café to give the sheriff a hug.

Juliet watched with amused interest.

"Hey, Jelly Bean," he said, lifting the girl against his chest. After a few seconds he put her feet back on the floor and looped an arm around her shoulders. "How are you?"

"I'm good." She patted the bulging pocket of her apron. "Made more than $100 in tips today."

Grant chuckled and Juliet gave him a small smile when his gaze slid toward her. "Isn't that about your usual haul? If it gets any bigger I may just have to arrest you for grand theft."

Shelby laughed and gave him another squeeze before returning to her salt and pepper shakers.

"How's your mama?" he asked as he walked toward the counter.

Shelby gave him a wry grin. "You don't really want to know that."

That sensual smile curved his mouth and Juliet found her gaze drawn there. His lips were full and beautifully sculpted, made for the most delicious sort of sin. Juliet stabbed a piece of glaze-drenched peach with her fork and wondered where that totally inappropriate thought had come from.

"If I didn't want to know I wouldn't ask," he replied as he slid onto the barstool next to Juliet. His gun belt creaked softly and he leaned his elbows on the counter. "So, how is she?"

Shelby pursed her pretty mouth and looked at him out of the corner of her eye as she moved on to ketchup bottles. "She's fine. She hates her job and Billings." She put the ketchup container down and faced him. "I told her it was a mistake to break up with you. Said you were the best thing that ever happened to her, *and* me, but she wouldn't listen."

Juliet watched the play of emotions that flashed in his warm, smiling eyes. She saw amusement, regret, and sad resignation. Grant sighed.

"Well, Jelly Bean, if you ever need me you have my number and you know where I live. As for me and your mama . . . it's complicated."

Shelby pouted. "No, it's not. She's always been the jealous type. I told her Laine was just your friend, that there was nothing going on between you but, again, she wouldn't listen." She lifted the ketchup bottle. "Personally, I think *you* should have broken up with *her*."

If the strapping sheriff was uncomfortable with this line of conversation he showed no sign. Juliet glanced at Autumn and even she seemed a little surprised by the frank discussion.

"Well," Grant drawled, "what matters is I love you and always will, and we'll always be friends, right?" His brows drew together slightly as he watched Shelby, and when the girl nodded he grinned. "All right then. Now, speaking of *love* . . . how is David these days?"

Autumn chuckled and Shelby let out a breathy sigh.

"Oh, he's wonderful, Grant. I can't believe we're getting married in a week!" She paused and her jaw dropped as her eyes swiveled to Juliet. "Oh, my gosh! I can't believe I didn't tell you I was getting married!" Her expression was one of dismay, but it quickly morphed into a grin. "I'm getting married, Juliet, a week from Sunday. Do you want to come?"

Juliet blinked, certain the young woman was joking until she saw Shelby's expression. *Holy cow, she's not kidding.* Juliet's jaw dropped and she felt all eyes turn her way as she stared at the vivacious blond. "Um . . . I don't . . . I hadn't . . . well I . . . ." Pausing, she took a deep breath. "Wow. Y'all move really fast around here."

Grant grinned at her. "Welcome to Evergreen Springs, small town America at its finest."

"Mm hmm," Autumn agreed with a nod.

Juliet looked at Grant, then Autumn, and then she turned her gaze back to Shelby. As Shelby watched her, hands clasped beneath her chin, green eyes sparkling, and that look of hopeful expectation on her face, it hit her how much the girl reminded her of Cassie. They didn't resemble each other physically, aside from the blonde hair, but personality wise? In that way Shelby and Cassie were more alike than she and Cassie.

A cold, metallic shaft of sorrow pierced her and it must have registered on her face because everyone's smiles slowly faded. Then she saw something in Grant's eyes that made her throat tighten painfully. Sympathy. She had seen it in the eyes of everyone who knew about what had happened, and nausea roiled as memories spilled forth uncontrolled. Juliet stood, whispered, "Excuse me," and fled the café.

She heard Grant call her name but she didn't stop until she reached the white gazebo in the center of the park, and by then she had a painful stitch in her side. Pressing her fingers into the burning spot below her rib cage she tried to breathe. The tightness in her chest made it nearly impossible. Her lungs burned, her diaphragm contracted violently, and she sank down onto the top step of the decorative, white-washed structure. Juliet blinked when she realized Grant was crouched in front of her, his eyes dark with concern.

He took her hands in his and gently massaged her fingers. "Breathe, Juliet. Breathe."

Her body didn't want to cooperate, but she concentrated on the pressure of his fingers on hers and the deep, resonant voice as he spoke. After nearly a minute her chest opened up enough for her to draw a full breath. When her heart finally stopped hammering against her sternum she met his worried gaze.

"You can really move when you set your mind to it," he said. "It's been a while since I've actually had to work to chase somebody down."

"I'm . . . I'm sorry," she whispered.

His brows drew together. "You have nothing to be sorry for. You didn't do anything wrong."

Juliet sighed and closed her eyes briefly. "All Shelby did was invite me to her wedding and I . . . I acted like a crazy person."

A smile curved his beautiful mouth. "Hey, you should've seen how her mama reacted when Shelby told her I was giving her away at the wedding." He shook his head. "Made Hiroshima look like a party popper."

Unbidden, Juliet chuckled. Grant's smile widened. His fingers continued to stroke hers and she was surprised to realize she didn't mind the simple yet intimate contact.

"You're just not accustomed to being herded into the fold by complete strangers." He looked at their clasped hands and smiled. "Most of us were born and raised here, so we're used to it. Shelby, she . . . well, she loves everybody, even people she's just met. She only sees the best in people."

Her eyes stung but she smiled. "She reminds me of my sister," Juliet whispered. "That's *just* like Cassie." Grief and sorrow ravaged her yet again, like they did every time she thought of her sister. She choked the cold darkness down and took a shaky breath. "I should apologize to Shelby." She stood and Grant did as well. She leaned her head back and looked up at him.

"You don't have to do that," he said softly.

"Yes, I do." She squeezed his fingers and was glad when he didn't let go. "I want to."

He studied her for a few moments, and then he released her. "Okay, then. But, this time let's *walk* across the street. I don't think you realize it, but you almost got hit by a car."

She blinked at him. "I did?"

He nodded. "And, speaking of cars, Eddie says if he has the right hose the fix will take ten minutes tops. If not, he'll have to order it and it won't get here until tomorrow afternoon."

Juliet thought about that. "Oh."

"If you don't want to stick around that long, he says he can manufacture something that will get you to where you're going or at least some place more populated that will have the necessary parts."

She studied him for a moment. His features were elegantly carved, wonderfully masculine without being sharp or heavy. Juliet smiled. "Is this where I take my pick?"

He grinned and stuffed his hands in pockets. "I guess so."

Juliet chuckled again and it struck her that she had laughed more since her car broke down than she had in the last year. She looked toward Autumn's Diner. "Is there a hotel in town?"

His grin seemed to widen just a bit. "Yes, there is. It's just up the street from Autumn's."

"Does Eddie have the right hose?"

"I don't know." Grant pulled out his cell phone. "Let me find out."

She waited as Grant dialed and had a brief conversation with the mechanic, and she was surprised to discover she was sort of hoping the mechanic didn't have the right hose. When he shook his head and put his phone away she smiled. "Then I'll stay until he gets the part. It's not like I was heading anywhere in particular anyway." The look of approval in his eyes made her heart flutter.

"All right." He offered her his arm. "And I'll buy you dinner."

Juliet slid her fingers into the crook of his elbow and fell into step beside him as he walked toward the diner. "No."

He stopped and looked down at her. "Why not?"

"You bought lunch," she replied simply. "Tonight . . . I'm buying."

Grant's brows rose slightly, and the corners of his eyes crinkled attractively as he smiled. "I get off shift at six. Meet you at 6:30?"

"It's a date."

A wicked gleam entered his eyes and he started walking again. "Why, yes it is, Juliet. Yes, it is."

Chapter Four

When Juliet walked back into the diner Autumn gave her a warm smile and gestured at the peach pie as she took another generous bite. Shelby appeared from the back a moment later, and when their eyes met her mouth dropped open. She rushed over and enveloped Juliet in a hug.

"Oh, Juliet! I'm so sorry if I said something wrong!" She pulled back and grasped Juliet's upper arms lightly, her green eyes beseeching. "I know we just met but you seem like a really nice person, and if *Grant* likes you . . . ." Her voice trailed off and color stained her cheeks as she snuck a glance at the sheriff. "I just figured the more the merrier, the whole town's going to be there, and I'm only getting married once. I didn't mean to upset you."

Juliet smiled. "No, Shelby, *I'm* sorry. I shouldn't have freaked out like that. I'm just not accustomed to being treated like family by people I've just met. You don't do that in the city."

Shelby's eyes widened. "Really? Then how do you get to know people?"

"Slowly." Juliet laughed softly. "It takes us city folk a little longer to welcome people into our inner circle."

"Sounds . . . lonely," Shelby observed.

Juliet sobered. The girl was wiser than she looked. "I never really thought about it, but I guess it can be."

Shelby watched her carefully. After a few silent moments she took Juliet's hands. "Well, I'd still like you to come, if you want, but I completely understand if you're not comfortable with that. After all, you just met me. And, if you come don't worry about bringing a gift or anything. Just having you there will be gift enough."

Juliet felt tears sting again but this time it was a good thing. *I know you better than you think. You and Cassie would have loved each other.* She smiled. "How about this . . . if I'm still here, I will *definitely* come to your wedding. If I'm not, then know I wish you and David nothing but happiness."

Shelby grinned and hugged her again. "That works for me. Thank you, Juliet."

"All right, all right," Autumn said, waving her delicate hands in the air, "that's enough of that emotional crap. Come on over here and help me eat this pie before I eat it all myself." She dabbed at her eyes with the corner of her apron and sniffled softly. "You are *not* allowed to make me cry in my own restaurant."

"Aww." Shelby walked around the counter and wrapped Autumn in a hug from behind. "You are such a softie."

"I am not." Autumn tried to scowl and failed. She gave the young woman a sour look. "Aren't you off shift now?"

Shelby giggled and rested her chin on Autumn's shoulder. "Oh, Autumn. Admit it. You're going to miss me."

Autumn's eyes welled and she nodded. "Yes, I am. Now go on." She sniffled again and shooed Shelby away. "Don't you have a date or something?"

Shelby's super-model smile flashed brightly and her cheeks went pink. "I do." She squeezed Autumn once more, then ran up to Grant and embraced him as well. After the sheriff released her she turned to Juliet. "I hope you come to the wedding, Juliet. At least then I know Grant will have a date."

Juliet felt the heat creep up her neck and glanced quickly at Grant. He met her eyes and that slow, languid smile curved his mouth. Before either of them could reply Shelby whirled away and ran toward the back, blond curls bouncing. She reappeared with her purse over her shoulder and a grin on her face.

"See ya!" she said with a wave as she left the café and hurried away.

The three watched her go then Juliet and Grant walked toward the lunch counter.

"I *am* going to miss that girl," Autumn said with a sigh. "Not only does she light up the room, but she's a damned good waitress, too."

Juliet slid onto a barstool and picked up her fork. "Where is she going?"

Grant eased down on the seat next to her. "David got a job in Billings, so after they're married they're moving." He smiled when Autumn handed him a fork. He sliced off a bite of pie and lifted the dessert to his mouth. "It'll be good for Shelby to be closer to her mom, and she's going to start college in the fall."

"I take it you and her mother dated?" Juliet ventured. A flush warmed her cheeks and she squeezed her eyes shut. "I'm sorry. That is *none* of my business."

Grant looked at her, swallowed his mouthful of pie, and put the fork down. "No worries." He leaned his elbows on the counter. "We did, for almost two years."

Autumn huffed and rolled her eyes. "Two years too long, if you ask me." Grant chuckled and Autumn scowled at him. "Well, I'm sorry, Grant, but I always thought you were too good for her."

"Now, Autumn."

"Breaking up with you because you went to your best friend's wedding," Autumn continued as if Grant hadn't spoken. She snorted softly. "Sherri always did have more hair than sense."

Juliet had just swallowed a bite of ice cream and she nearly choked.

"That's rich," Grant observed, "coming from the person who gave me grief for showing up here with *another woman*." He smiled wryly. "What's that saying about people who live in glass houses?"

"Please." Autumn rolled her eyes. "You know I was only teasing about that other woman thing." She looked at Juliet and smiled. "Grant here is a wonderful sheriff and one of the finest men I've ever had the pleasure to know, but his choice in women?" She gave Grant a slanted look. "Let's just say that aspect of his life could use some work."

Grant stood. "And on that note I'd say it's time to head to the Center Hotel and get a room, Miss Hall. Are you finished with your pie?"

"Get a room?" Autumn repeated. A devilish sparkle lit her eyes and she looked between Grant and Juliet with a knowing smile. "Wow. You work fast, Sheriff. I'm impressed."

He rolled his eyes and shook his head, chuckling. "Really, Autumn?"

The woman nodded. "Really." She patted Juliet's hand and grinned mischievously. "You go, girl. And take notes . . . I'm going to want details."

Juliet's cheeks felt like they would spontaneously combust and she imagined she resembled a fully-cooked lobster at the moment, which surprised her. Before Mayfield she would have laughed and promptly parried Autumn's innuendo with a clever, acerbic comeback, but Mayfield's campaign of harassment had changed her. Apparently, socializing was a perishable skill, and it was one she hadn't practiced in more than a year. Unlike riding a bike, it wasn't just coming back to her. Thankfully, Grant rescued her, again.

"Ignore her, Juliet. She's just jealous."

"Damn straight," Autumn shot back, dark eyes glinting merrily. She picked up the now empty pie plate and utensils and sauntered away. "I guess it's a good thing I'm married so I have someone to help me deal with all this sexual tension between you and me."

Juliet's jaw dropped.

"Yes, it is." Grant chuckled and put a hand under her elbow. "C'mon, Juliet. Let's get you settled."

The Center Hotel was an old building, established 1898, or so the elaborate brass sign hanging beside the front doors said. It had an "Old West" look to it, but when she stepped through the front doors the feel was anything but old. The décor and furnishings were bright, warm, and welcoming, the walls painted a pale yellow with beautifully carved wainscoting and crown molding. The floors looked like highly polished maple, the pale wood gleaming. To her left was the front desk, to her right was a gorgeous archway outlined with brilliant stained glass in the style of Tiffany, which led to a small, intimate dining room, and directly in front of her was a wide, graceful staircase.

"Wow. This is beautiful." She looked around, admiring the artwork. Most of the framed paintings were landscapes, with sweeping vistas and rich contrasting colors that looked so lifelike she half expected to be able to smell the wildflowers and feel the wind on her face.

"Yes, it is." Grant leaned against the counter and tapped a bell. The tinkling sound echoed off the walls. "And it's affordable, despite what you might think by just looking around. It's owned and operated by Mike and Nicole Finch, and it's been in Nicole's family since the building was constructed. It's one of the oldest buildings in Evergreen."

A moment later a petite, slender woman entered through a door behind the front desk. She looked to be in her early to mid-sixties, her once flaming red hair faded and streaked with white. Bright blue eyes lit first on Grant, the woman's thin lips widening into a smile that brightened the entire room. She was several inches shorter than Juliet and on the thin side, with translucent skin and a dappling of freckles.

"Grant Donovan," she said, coming around the counter and opening her arms wide. "Come here and give me a hug."

Grant's large body engulfed the woman's much smaller frame and for a second she seemed to disappear in his embrace as his arms wrapped around her. "Afternoon, Miss Nicole."

The woman squeezed him then stepped back. "You're looking handsome as always." Her sharp gaze slid past his broad form and a faint smile lifted the corners of her mouth. "But I don't think you stopped by for afternoon tea."

Grant chuckled and turned to Juliet. "No, ma'am. This is Juliet Hall. Her car broke down outside of town and she's going to need a room for a night."

Nicole Finch extended a hand. Her fingers were long and slender, almost frail looking, but her grip was firm and sure. "Pleasure to meet you, Miss Hall. You can call me Nicole." She turned and walked back behind the counter. "Let's get you checked in."

Juliet filled out the card Nicole slid across the counter then reached for her wallet. She looked up in surprise when the proprietress laid a hand on her arm.

"That's all right, dear. We'll just settle up when you check out."

Juliet stared. *Wow, this really* is *small-town America.* "Are you sure?"

Miss Nicole gave her a gentle smile that sped up the thaw inside her. "I'm sure." An amused glint entered her sapphire eyes and she glanced at Grant. "Besides, if you tear up the room and skip out I'll just have the sheriff here track you down."

"Eddie won't release your car until I let him anyway," Grant added, leaning one elbow on the counter. "Since I called it in, I have to give him the okay before you can drive off, unless you're planning to steal your own vehicle."

The image of him chasing her across rural Montana popped into her head and she smiled. It might almost be worth the grand theft auto charge, but she shook her head. "No. I've never been good at that kind of thing. I tried to steal a candy bar when I was about nine, but I got caught by the store owner. He told my dad and my dad made me stand in front of that store for an entire weekend with a sign around my neck that read 'I tried to steal from this store and got caught.' That humiliation was enough to put me on the straight and narrow and keep me there."

Grant chuckled. "Nice. This country would be in much better condition if more parents disciplined their kids like that."

"Amen," Nicole agreed. "Now, come on, dear. Let's get you settled. I put you in Room Four. It faces south. It overlooks the square, and it gets the most light. I think you'll like it."

Juliet glanced around the beautiful lobby once more. "If it's anything like this . . . I *know* I'll like it."

"Juliet."

Again, an unprovoked quiver vibrated inside her at the sound of his voice and she gulped. She forced herself to meet those smiling eyes. "Yes?"

"Your boxes, if you want I can take them to your room or leave them in the Yukon." When she hesitated a half-grin lifted one corner of his mouth. "Or, I can drop by the garage and put them back in the trunk of your car. They'll be safe there. Eddie may not have locks on his cabin doors, but the security system at the garage rivals Fort Knox."

Juliet thought about it for a moment. "Let me get a couple things out of them and then you can put them in my car, if that's okay?"

He nodded. "Absolutely."

Nicole stepped around the counter and reached for Juliet's bag. "And while you're doing that I'll take your things to your room."

"Oh," Juliet began, "that's not necessary, Miss Nicole."

Nicole smiled and lifted the tote. "Of course it's not *necessary*, dear, but it *is* what I do." She waved a slender hand at them. "You go get what you need to get and I'll meet you upstairs. Take a right when you reach the second floor and it's the last room on your left."

Juliet watched the woman gracefully ascend the stairs and turned when she felt Grant's hand cup her elbow. Tingling pulses traveled up and down her arm and for a moment her chest tightened. It wasn't uncomfortable, just disconcerting. She gulped and forced a smile.

"Let's go then," she said, hoping her voice didn't sound as breathy to him as it did to her. She cleared her throat. "I don't want to take up all your time."

He strode to the front doors, opened them, and quirked an eyebrow. "You're not taking up all my time." His smile widened and she could almost hear the drip of water as that ice around her heart melted a little more. "It's my job to take care of the citizens of Evergreen, and as long as you're here, that includes you."

Unbidden, a surge of warmth enveloped her. She'd been on her own for so long, on guard, wary, and she suddenly realized how tired she was. The idea of letting someone else take care of her, especially if that someone was Grant, made her almost giddy with relief. Her throat tightened as his gaze held hers. Unable to find her voice she merely smiled as they walked back to his SUV.

She waited as he opened the rear hatch and pulled the boxes forward. She stared at the cardboard containers for a moment. Although she'd had them in her trunk for almost two months she hadn't opened them after she'd packed them. She wasn't sure how she felt about having to open them now. The sheriff seemed to sense her uncertainty.

"I'll be in the diner." When she glanced at him he smiled. "Knock on the window when you're ready to go back."

Her cheeks warmed. "I *can* walk two blocks by myself, Grant," she said. "You don't have to escort me to my door."

He hooked his thumbs in his belt loops and smiled. "It is a gentleman's duty to walk the lady home."

Unbidden, a smile blossomed and butterflies stirred in her middle. "We're not on a date, Sheriff."

"I'm just practicing for later," he replied smoothly.

A laugh escaped her. She met those beautiful brown eyes with her own and gulped as warmth started to spread through her. His smile widened. He touched the brim of his hat and stepped around her.

"Take your time, Juliet, and don't forget to knock."

She watched his broad back as he walked into the diner, and when the door closed behind him she felt oddly alone. To her surprise she realized she *liked* being around the strapping sheriff. After what she'd endured at Mayfield's hands, she hadn't been certain she'd *ever* want to be around a man again. She looked at the glass door for a few more moments, then shook herself and turned to the boxes. Taking a deep breath she opened the one labeled *Cassie*.

The first thing she saw was Cassie's toe-shoes and a lump appeared in her throat as if it had catapulted there from the pit of her stomach. Her fingers wrapped around the pink, satin-covered shoes and tears stung. Blinking them back, she put the dance shoes aside and reached for one of several framed photographs lined up against the side of the box.

The first was a shot she'd taken when Cassie had first joined the company. Her sister was dressed in pink leotard and tights with a filmy pink skirt swirling gracefully around her hips. Her hair was pulled into a tight bun at the nape of her neck, but several blonde ringlets had escaped to curl softly around her face. She was in a piqué pose, on tiptoes, arms gracefully curved overhead. She looked beautiful. Tears welled in Juliet's eyes but she smiled as she ran her fingers over Cassie's visage. "I miss you, baby sister." Juliet stared at the picture for another moment before slipping it into her purse.

The second photo was of the two of them, and it had been taken after their first performance together. They were backstage, both still in costume with the heavy theatrical makeup the brightly lit performances required, and in piqué en arabesque, lifted onto one toe with the other leg lifted behind. Nearly mirror images, their bodies faced each other as they smiled into the camera. It was just a snapshot taken by a fellow dancer, but it was one of her favorites. Juliet remembered that night as if had been yesterday.

"Jules, I'm so nervous," Cassie said, staring between the curtains as the dancers twirled around the stage. She flexed and arched her feet in her toe shoes. "How do you *do* this all the time? I feel like I'm going to throw up."

Juliet put a hand on her sister's arm. "You'll be fine, Cass. Now *breathe*. This isn't the first time you've done this; it's just your first time *here*. Have *fun* with it. Pretend there's no one there but you and me, and we're dancing across the living room like we used to."

"How?" Cassie moved one of the velvet curtains about an inch and looked into the packed auditorium. "There were never a thousand people in the living room, or La Jolla."

Juliet faced her sister and grasped her upper arms lightly. "Cassie, think about it. What we do is hard work, but would you want to do *anything* else? How many people get to say they *dance* for a living?"

Cassie pouted and met her gaze. "Strippers. There are *lots* of those."

Juliet laughed softly. "Okay, how many people can say they dance professional ballet?"

"Not many."

"Exactly." Juliet cupped Cassie's face. "You never had a problem performing with the company in La Jolla, so don't get all worked up about it now. Just listen to the music, feel the choreography, and *enjoy* it. This is one of those nights you will *never forget*, Cass. Knock 'em dead, little sister. I know you can do it, and so do you."

"Thanks, Jules." Cassie smiled and embraced her. "Break a leg, my prima ballerina. I can't wait to see your solo."

"You're going to do great, Cassie." Juliet blinked back tears. "Break a leg, little sister, and when the performance is over *we're* going to celebrate."

"I love you, Juliet."

"Love you, too, Cassie. Now get ready, it's almost time. And remember, *have fun.*"

She released Cassie and stepped back. Moments later the music changed and Cassie fluttered onto the stage with the rest of the corps. As Juliet had predicted, she was perfect.

The past faded away and Juliet pressed the snapshot to her heart, feeling the pride and excitement of that night as if it had just happened. And then reality stormed back in like an arctic wind. Tears fell as she put that photo alongside the first. Juliet wiped her cheeks quickly then closed the box, a ragged breath escaping her. She pushed the box back into the cargo area and closed the hatch.

Grant stood inside the door of the diner, watching as Juliet went through the box marked "Cassie." He could feel her pain even from ten feet away with a wall of glass between them. Autumn moved to his side.

"Girl has a lot of hurt inside her," Autumn said softly.

"Yeah," Grant agreed, stuffing his hands in his pockets. "She has good reason to."

"And how do you know that? Did she say something to you?"

"No." He sighed and walked over to the counter. "It's not important."

Autumn moved behind the counter and leaned her elbows on the smooth surface. "Do I sense something else going on here?" she asked. "Is this police business, Grant, or is this more personal?"

Grant looked into the almond-shaped eyes he'd known more than half his life and ran a hand over his forehead. "A little bit of both, if you want to know the truth."

Autumn lifted one perfectly arched brow. "I would say something about keeping professional and private lives separate, but I know I don't have to tell you that."

He gave her a small smile. "No, you don't." A knock on the window made him turn. He rose and chucked Autumn under the chin. "See you for dinner, Autumn, unless Juliet wants to go elsewhere."

"Wait." Autumn looked at him questioningly, both brows lifted in surprise. "You're going *out* with her tonight?" She looked him up and down and shook her head. "Boy, you *do* move fast, Sheriff. I'm beginning to wonder if you're really Grant Donovan or if perhaps I'm in a scene from Invasion of the Body Snatchers."

Grant chuckled. "We're not going *out* out, Autumn. It's just dinner."

Autumn pursed her lips and crossed her arms over her ample chest. "Mm hmm."

"Autumn."

"Go on with your bad self," she said, waving a hand at him. Then a mischievous glint entered her eyes. "About damn time."

Grant rolled his eyes and walked toward the door. He glanced at Autumn and she gave him another dismissive wave before he slid his hat on his head and stepped outside. Juliet stood there, her arms wrapped around herself, her purse over her shoulder. His heart gave a little twinge when he saw the evidence of tears, but she was dry-eyed for now.

"You ready?" he asked.

She nodded and turned toward the hotel. He fell into step beside her.

"After I see you to your room I'll put those boxes in your trunk." He stuffed his hands in his pockets, and searched for something else to say. "So, where are you taking me to dinner?"

She looked at him quickly, guarded, and then a small smile tipped the corners of her mouth. "I don't know any place other than Autumn's, and if you want to go somewhere else you'll have to drive, unless it's within walking distance."

He grinned. "Most places in Evergreen are within walking distance."

"Oh." A soft chuckle escaped her. "Then I guess it's your turn to pick."

Grant laughed. "I guess so. Autumn's is all right with me, unless you'd rather go somewhere else. We *do* have a Mexican place, it's called Casa de Mi Amigo, and it's on the other side of the square."

Juliet seemed to ponder that. "Hmm. Is it any good?"

"Well, I think so but I don't have much of a basis for comparison. You West Coast types have access to a lot more traditional Mexican food than us Montanans." He shrugged. "We could try it, and if you don't like it, I'll buy and we can go elsewhere."

She shook her head and looked at him out of the corner of her eye. "I'm sure it will be fine." A smile twitched about her mouth. "As long as they have margaritas the food won't really matter."

He narrowed his eyes on her. "Are you telling me you'd rather have drinks than dinner?"

Her cheeks flushed slightly and she turned her gaze forward. "I guess you'll just have to find out for yourself."

Grant nodded slowly and grinned. "Looking forward to it. In fact, I may just clock out early. Amigo's offers two-for-one margaritas from four to seven during the week."

They reached the Center Hotel and he stopped, turning to face her. She looked up at him, and thankfully the wariness was absent from her island-sea gaze.

"Are you thinking about getting me drunk, Sheriff?"

He clasped his hands in front of him and shook his head. "No, ma'am. But if you choose to imbibe I will not stop you. I may even have a couple as well."

"Are you the sort to take advantage when a girl has had one too many libations?"

He lifted one brow. "What do you think, Juliet?"

She met his gaze boldly, although color blossomed in her cheeks. "Maybe part of me hopes you are."

He felt both eyebrows shoot north and his stomach lurched. He narrowed his eyes on her and studied her face for a few seconds. Her color brightened and she dropped her chin.

"Well," he drawled, "then I'm sorry to say that part of you will be disappointed." He leaned over to look her in the eye. "You can have as many margaritas as you want. I will make sure you get back to your room in one piece. I'll even tuck you in, but you'll sleep, and wake up, alone."

He thought he saw a flash of disappointment in those blue-green pools and something inside him pulled tight. Her cheeks went scarlet and she turned her face away.

"Thank you," she said. "I don't know why I said that."

Part of me hopes it's because you're attracted to me, too. "Don't worry about it. I've already forgotten what you said." He cupped her elbow with one hand. "Come on. Let's get you settled."

***

Juliet wrapped her hair in a towel and slipped into the oversized t-shirt she always wore when getting ready to go out. Using a dry washcloth she wiped the steam from the mirror and looked at herself.

"What the hell?" she asked her reflection. "Now he probably thinks you're some lush who drinks herself into a stupor and goes home with anyone who looks at her sideways. Nice." With a frustrated sigh she left the bathroom, walked across the polished hardwood floor, and threw herself across the bed. "Aw, hell. What does it matter? You won't be here that long so who cares what he thinks?"

But she *did*. She'd known the brawny sheriff only a few hours, and she *did* care what he thought. Before Mayfield, or BM as she often told herself, she would have been able to easily converse with a handsome man without making a complete fool of herself, although not as easily as her sister. She turned her head and looked at the picture of Cassie in her pink leotard.

"I know what *you'd* say, Cass," she said softly. "You'd tell me to go for it, live a little." Her sister's voice came to life in her head.

You know it, Jules. When was the last time you got laid?

"That's not me, and you know it."

I bet he'd be amazed *at how flexible you are. Go on, show him. I dare you.*

Juliet frowned and rolled onto her stomach.

Cassie had always been the more gregarious of the two of them, and men usually flocked to her sister like moths to a spotlight. Juliet received more than her fair share of male attention, but men seemed to sense she was the more conservative of the two and responded accordingly. Where Cassie could date half a dozen different men within a two-week stretch, Juliet wasn't built that way. She often admired her sister's easy handling of the male animal, but had also chided her for the one night stands she occasionally indulged in. Cassie, in her usual flippant manner, would reply:

"They're *not* one night stands. They're *auditions*, and so far no one has impressed me enough to receive a call back."

Unlike her free-spirited sister, for Juliet sex was something she only shared with someone she truly cared for. Thankfully, her sister practiced safe sex, and she never went out with a man before doing an internet search and background check to find out if he was married, or a felon.

A laugh escaped her and she looked at the photographs leaning against the Tiffany lamp on the nightstand. "Before you went out with someone you knew who they were, at least as well as a background check can help you know someone," she said to her sister's image. "That's something, I guess."

If you spent the night with the Sheriff you'd know him, too.

"I didn't mean in the *Biblical* sense, Cass."

Come on, Jules. It's been nearly two years since your last relationship.

Show Sheriff Donovan the time of his life; you might even enjoy yourself. He certainly looks *like he'd be a lot of fun.* Love *those shoulders. A lot to grab onto with that one.*

Juliet sighed and buried her face in the pristine white duvet cover. She could almost hear Cassie laughing at her.

I know you've already thought about it.

Juliet ground her teeth together and sat up. She glared at Cassie's picture for a moment, and then smiled as sadness burgeoned in a familiar, all-encompassing wave. "You're right, but you know I'll never act on it."

I know, Juliet. I know, and I still love you.

Chapter Five

Grant pulled up in front of the hotel, surprised to see Juliet sitting on the front steps with Nicole. The older woman was talking, her expression lively and animated, and Juliet seemed to be hanging on every word. Nicole made a gesture with her hands of something exploding and Juliet threw her head back as she laughed. Grant smiled, exited the SUV, and walked toward the two women.

"And we were married a week later," Nicole said. "That was 43 years ago."

Juliet's eyes widened. "Wow. Congratulations, that's amazing. My parents have been together 35, but 43? You and your husband deserve a medal or something. Not many people stay together that long these days."

Nicole sighed. "I know, and it's a shame. Personally, I think a lot of couples just give up when things get a little tough. Marriage is a lot of work, but when you find the right person, it's definitely worth it." She glanced at Grant and rose. "Evening, Grant."

He had left his hat in the vehicle so instead of touching the brim he smiled and inclined his head. "Evening, Miss Nicole. I trust Juliet is the model guest?" He glanced at Juliet as she got to her feet. Again he admired the elegance of her movements, like a dancer, smooth and graceful.

"She is," Nicole confirmed with a smile. "We had tea earlier, and decided to step outside and enjoy this delightful evening while waiting for you. She looks lovely, doesn't she?"

Grant gave Juliet a once-over. Dressed in form-fitting black jeans, a square-necked blouse in a deep, chocolate brown satin, and a simple pair of metallic gold ballet flats she looked more than lovely. She looked amazing. He noted the delicate gold chain around her neck with a pendant in the shape of pointe shoes. It was beautiful and unique, the golden ribbons of the shoes twining artfully around the chain as if they'd accidentally gotten tangled there. Hmm. Maybe there was a reason she moved so fluidly.

"She does indeed, Miss Nicole." He grinned when Juliet blushed. "Are you hungry?"

She nodded, a strand of dark hair slipping from behind her ear to brush her cheek. He had to stop himself from tucking the shining tress back where it had been.

Nicole turned to Juliet and gave the younger woman a quick hug. "You two have fun, and I'll see *you* for breakfast."

"You know it," Juliet replied with a smile. "For chocolate croissants I may even get up *early*."

Nicole patted her arm and entered the hotel. Juliet watched the woman leave and then turned her eyes to him. He smiled at her.

"So, do you want to walk or should we drive?"

Juliet glanced around. "Let's walk. This weather is great."

Grant looked across the square and nodded. Dusk was just arriving, shadows lengthening as the sun slowly slipped into the west. It was warm, the sign on the Montana Federal Credit Union reading 71 degrees, with the faintest hint of a breeze. "Yes it is, Juliet. It's just about perfect." He spun to face the square and offered her his arm. "Shall we?"

She hesitated for a second, then smiled up at him and curled her fingers around his bicep. "We shall."

They waited for an old Cadillac to pass then crossed the street to the park. Grant kept the pace leisurely, enjoying the warmth, the sounds of kids playing, dogs barking, and the presence of Juliet at his side. The silence between them was comfortable, oddly familiar, and he glanced at her. She seemed to be taking it all in, her eyes moving from a group of children playing Frisbee, to a woman walking her three dogs, to the old men playing chess at one of the permanent chess/checker tables that dotted the square. As if sensing his perusal she looked at him and smiled.

"This is nice," she said.

"Yeah, the park has always been the heart of Evergreen."

"Nicole mentioned something about a festival tomorrow night?"

He nodded. "During the summer the town holds weekly festivals; arts and crafts, music, whatever they can think up and arrange." He laughed softly. "Not much else to do here to be quite honest. There's no mall, the newest release at our movie theater has been out for a month already, and we have one bar that's open until midnight, but only on Fridays and Saturdays."

"Wow." Juliet chuckled. "That's some night life."

"Yeah, makes New York City look tame."

Her grip on his arm tightened just a bit as a raucous tumble of arms and legs ran past them and one of the youngsters bumped into her. The boy didn't even slow down, but he did spin around and yell:

"Sorry, lady! Sorry, Sheriff!"

Grant shook his head. "Be more careful next time, Tim." He looked down at her. "You okay?"

Juliet rolled her eyes. "I'm fine." Her gaze turned wistful as she watched the gaggle of children race around. "They're just having fun." They started walking again. "Where I come from all the kids have their noses buried in cell phones or handheld game consoles or computers. I feel like I time-warped to Mayberry here." Just then a couple of boys ran past them with fishing poles and she laughed softly. "I rest my case."

"Is that a bad thing?" Grant asked.

"Not at *all*," she replied immediately. She leaned into his arm and rested her head against his shoulder. His abdominals tightened at the close contact, and he had to fight to focus as she added, "I like it, a *lot*."

Warmth invaded his chest cavity at her simple statement and he took a deep, steadying breath. "I like it, too. Even when I went away I always considered Evergreen home, and I always knew I'd eventually come back to stay."

"Where did you go?" she asked. "I think if I'd been born and raised here I'd never have left in the first place."

He chuckled. "I didn't have much of a choice when I decided to go into the Marines. They don't have a boot camp in Evergreen, so San Diego was my first foray into life outside Montana."

"Really?" She looked at him with wide eyes. "How was *that*?"

He thought back to the day he'd flown into San Diego. He'd peered out the tiny window of the 737, his insides knotted as he realized he might have bitten off more than he could chew. He remembered the cold sweat on his brow and the tremor in his hands as if it had happened yesterday rather than two plus decades ago. A chuckle escaped him. "Complete culture shock." He shook his head. "I'd never seen that many buildings or that many people or that many *cars* in one place *ever*. Thank goodness I'm adaptable. There were a few other 'small-town guys' who couldn't hack it and didn't make it through two weeks in boot. They just couldn't adjust."

"I suppose I can understand that." Her expression sobered. "When I moved to New York it was a shock, even though I was born in San Diego. You think when you've seen one big city you've seen them all, but NYC is in a class by itself."

Grant sighed. "It sure is. In California everything is spread out. In New York everyone is stacked on top of each other." He shuddered. "Went there once during Fleet Week and after the first night I decided I'd had my fill. When the buildings start to defy basic laws of physics, it makes me nervous." Juliet laughed, a warm, musical sound that made him smile.

"Y'know? I always felt like the skyscrapers were going to topple over at any moment. It just didn't feel . . . *natural*."

The conversation died as they crossed the street and entered Casa de Mi Amigo. It was a quaint restaurant with interior walls painted in sweeping scenes of what looked like Arizona deserts and Mexican villages. The place was about two-thirds full and, as they stood there, more than one pair of eyes turned their way. Grant pretended not to notice and hoped the attention didn't make Juliet uncomfortable. The place wasn't fancy but the smells wafting out of the kitchen made his mouth water. He glanced down and smiled when she inhaled deeply.

"That smells *amazing*," she said, closing her eyes.

"Good evening, Sheriff."

Grant turned toward the voice and grinned. A short, round man with black hair and dark eyes approached the hostess stand, his swarthy-skinned face split into a bright smile. Grant extended a hand. "Pablo, que pasa, mi amigo?"

"Nada," Pablo replied. They shook and then Pablo grabbed two menus from behind the podium. "Just you and the senorita?"

"Si."

Pablo looked Juliet up and down and then turned to Grant with an approving smile and a knowing look. "Follow me."

He led them to a booth in the back. It was secluded and somewhat dark, the candles in the center of the table doing little to illuminate the area. After they were seated Pablo handed Juliet a menu and then gave Grant his.

"Drinks?" Pablo asked.

Grant looked at Juliet. "Would you like a margarita? They're awfully good."

Despite the lack of light he saw her cheeks flush. She bit her lip, uncertainty clear in her eyes. "Are you going to have one?"

"I am." He smiled when he saw the relief on her delicate features. He turned to Pablo. "Two of your margaritas, por favor."

Pablo nodded. "Patron Silver, correct?"

"Absolutely," he replied. After Pablo hurried away Grant reached across the table and covered her hands with one of his. "Seriously, Juliet, if you want to have a few drinks – knock yourself out. I can't because I still have to drive home later, but if you want to, go ahead. I promise I won't think any less of you if you do."

"Even if I get stupid, slobbering drunk?"

A chuckle escaped him. "Everyone needs to blow off some steam now and then. If you get stupid, slobbering drunk, I promise to hold your hair back while you throw up."

Her brows rose and she stared at him for several seconds. "Thank you, Grant, but one will be plenty." She looked down at their hands, but didn't pull away, a small smile lifting the corners of her mouth. "I don't drink much, and when I do I remember the following day *why* I don't drink much."

Grant gently squeezed her fingers and pulled his hand back. "Okay."

They went quiet as they perused their menus, but Grant already knew what he was having. Every few seconds he slid his gaze to Juliet. She really was beautiful. Candlelight played over her features and darkened her eyes to deeper aqua, like Caribbean seas during a storm. She ran the fingers of one hand over her hair absently and pulled the length over one shoulder, and he wondered if the shining strands were as soft as they looked.

Hold on, bud, he told himself. *She's only passing through, so don't get caught up.*

"Everything looks so good," she said, turning the pages with slender, graceful hands.

"Yes, it does," Grant said, his gaze fixed on her.

Her head came up and her eyes widened slightly. Grant smiled and was rewarded when color glowed in her cheeks and a smile blossomed. She bit her lip and looked away. Her fingers fluttered to her neck and toyed with the ballet shoe pendant.

"Any idea what you want to eat?" he asked. "The carnitas plate is really good."

"I think I want that super burrito."

Grant chuckled. "No, you don't."

Her brows drew together. "Why not?"

"Because it comes on a plate this big," he replied, holding his hands roughly 18 inches apart, "and it fills the entire plate. I ordered one for lunch one time, and it not only served as my dinner later that night, but also my breakfast the following morning." He looked her up and down and gave her a grin. "Unless I'm way off and you're a *huge* eater, go with the regular burrito. It's made the same way, and you'll still end up taking some home."

Juliet nodded and returned to perusing the menu. "Good to know, especially after that *enormous* cheeseburger Autumn fed me this afternoon." A wry grin lit her face. "I better get out of Evergreen fast. At this rate I'll be up two sizes before my car is fixed."

Grant snorted softly. "I doubt that, but if you do, I can help you work some of it off." Her head snapped up and she looked at him, her expression demanding an explanation. For a second he was caught off guard, uncertain what he'd done or said to offend her. Then he replayed the last few sentences in his head. He chuckled when he realized the double entendre he'd just made. "Sorry. What I should have said is I go running along the river every morning. You're welcome to come with, if you like."

She fought a smile and nodded a couple times. "Oh, okay. Thanks for the clarification." Pablo chose that moment to put two enormous margaritas in front of them as a dark-haired woman slid a bowl of tortilla chips and a cup of salsa onto the table. Pablo grinned at Grant and then turned a beaming smile on Juliet. "Is the senorita ready to order?"

Her lips widened in a smile and she gave Grant a knowing look before she turned to the jovial Hispanic gentleman and ordered the burrito.

"Excellent choice." Pablo scribbled and then turned to Grant. "Sheriff?"

"Carnitas plate, Pablo, flour tortillas," Grant replied, his gaze never leaving Juliet's. "And I'd like the spicy salsa with that, please."

More scribbling. "You got it, Grant. I'll be back shortly with your food."

Juliet smiled at the little man and took a chip from the bowl. "He seems nice."

"He is. He and his family moved here about . . . oh, ten years ago." Grant rested one arm along the back of the booth. "It's the first Mexican restaurant ever in Evergreen."

"Well, if the food *tastes* half as good as it *smells*, I may *need* to go on that run with you." She took a bite of the crispy chip and chewed thoughtfully. "Although, this is a million times better than the fast food and pre-packaged sandwiches I've been living on for the last couple of months. It's nice to sit down, relax, and have someone to talk to." She gave him a smile that made his heart constrict. "Thank you."

"You are very welcome."

He almost asked her why she'd been living on food like that, but decided against it. Riordan had told him she'd been off the grid for the past several months, which was answer enough. There would be no time or facilities for home-cooked meals when one was living out of one's car. He briefly thought about telling her he'd been in contact with the detective, but, again, he decided against it. So far the "date" was going well, and he had no desire to bring up anything that would cause her more pain.

"By the way," she said, breaking into his thoughts, "thank you for your service. How long were you in the Marines?"

"Sixteen years active duty and four in the Reserves," he replied. "I would've done the full 20 active but when my dad had a heart attack and had to resign from his position as sheriff, he asked me to run against the undersheriff." Grant shrugged. "I didn't re-enlist when my tour was up, I finished my 20 in the Reserves, and the rest is history."

"Is your dad okay?"

The genuine concern he saw on her face made him smile. "Yes. He and my mom moved to Phoenix a few years ago, wanted to get away from our legendary Montana winters."

She exhaled slowly. "Thank goodness."

He picked up the margarita and took a slow sip. Juliet did the same and he smiled when she said, "Mm, that's good." She took another sip and put the glass down. Her tongue darted out to sweep away the coarse grains of salt stuck to her upper lip and his abdominals tightened. He knew she hadn't intended to be sexy licking her lips, but damned if she hadn't succeeded anyway.

"Did you like it?" she asked, "the Marines?"

Her voice broke into his less-than-pure thoughts. He chided himself and gave her a wry smile. "You don't spend that amount of time in the Corps if you don't like it."

Her fingers wrapped around the stem of the glass. "Did you . . . see any action?"

He nodded slowly, fighting the chill that came with the memories of his time in the service. "I was a Scout Sniper. I did two tours in Iraq and five in Afghanistan, so yeah . . . I saw some action."

Her mouth formed a silent "O" and she dropped her chin. "I'm sorry, I don't mean to pry."

"No worries," he said. Fragmented pictures of his time in the Middle East and Afghanistan zipped across his mind's eye followed by the gut clench and cold wave of sadness that always accompanied those images. He took another drink and mentally swept the memories away. "It is what it is."

"Well," she began in a low voice, her eyes downcast, "I appreciate what you've done, the sacrifices you made, and I'm sorry for any friends you may have lost." A sad smile rounded her mouth. "I've never been in combat . . . but I know how it feels to lose someone you love."

It was at that moment Pablo appeared with their food, and Grant was thankful for the interruption. The conversation had taken a decidedly morose turn, and revisiting old wounds was *not* what he wanted to do. He smiled at the portly gentleman.

"Gracias, Pablo," he said as he laid his napkin over his lap.

Pablo beamed. "Ide nada. Is there anything else you need?"

Grant looked at her. She was staring at the burrito, which was about eight inches long and probably that big around, steam curling lazily from the sauce covered tortilla. "Juliet?"

She looked up. "What?" She blinked and glanced at Pablo. "Oh, no, thank you. I think I'm good . . . for the next three meals, actually."

Pablo chuckled. "I will bring you a box when you are finished, senorita. For now, enjoy."

"Aren't you glad you didn't order the super burrito?" Grant asked as he picked up a fork.

She shook her head and flipped open her napkin. "I can't believe they make them bigger than *this*. *This* one could feed both of us."

He laughed. "Yes, it could." He scooped some pork onto a tortilla.

"Eat what you can and take the rest back. Miss Nicole will let you keep it in the fridge."

"When will I eat it?" she asked as she sliced through the burrito. Melting cheese and sour cream oozed out. She swirled her fork in the mixture and scooped up a bite. "I'm supposed to have breakfast with Miss Nicole and lunch with Autumn." She blew softly on the steaming mouthful.

"Wow, you have your social schedule already mapped out, and you haven't even been in town a full day yet." He lifted one brow. "Am I penciled in there somewhere?"

"Would you like to be?" she asked. She put the food in her mouth and began to chew, and her eyes closed. "Oh, my gosh, this is *delicious.*" She scooped up another mouthful and held it toward him. "Try this."

He smiled and allowed her to feed him. She watched him as he chewed, obviously waiting for confirmation of her declaration. He swallowed and nodded. "It *is* excellent. But remember, I've already had one."

Her mouth rounded into another silent "O" and her cheeks flushed again. She bit her lip and looked down at her plate as she laid her fork across the edge of the porcelain. "Right. That was . . . silly of me."

"Not at all," he assured her. To assuage her embarrassment he added some Spanish rice, sour cream, guacamole, and spicy salsa to the pork, rolled the tortilla, and handed it to her. "Try this. It's braised pork."

A smile twitched about her mouth. "I'm a California girl, remember?" She took the tortilla from him. "I know what carnitas is."

"Now *I'm* the silly one," he replied.

She chuckled and took a healthy bite. Her eyes widened. "Wow. That is amazing." She took another bite and he laughed when sauce dribbled down her chin. Juliet grinned and grabbed her napkin. "And messy."

He grinned. "Always tastes better messy."

"Tell you what, you give me another one of those Grant-made burritos and I'll give you whatever I can't eat of this one to take home. You'll eat it before I will anyway."

Grant studied her for a moment, then grabbed another tortilla and started building. "Deal, with one condition."

Her brows rose. "And what's that?"

He held up the carnitas filled tortilla. "Stay long enough to pencil me into that busy social schedule of yours."

Juliet put her hands in her lap. "Well, I was kind of thinking . . . maybe I'd see you . . . tomorrow night . . . at the festival."

His heart thumped at the look of hopeful expectation on her face. "You will." He smiled. "I'll be working."

"Oh." The disappointment in her eyes was obvious and his heart thumped again. She sighed softly. "Of course. You *are* the sheriff after all."

"I get off at nine." He held the burrito toward her. "The festival goes until eleven."

She looked at him and a smile slowly blossomed as realization dawned. "So," she said as she reached for the rolled tortilla, "I'll see you tomorrow night."

"You'll see me before then." Grant grabbed another tortilla. "I usually have lunch at Autumn's."

A chuckle escaped her. She took a bite of the pork, chewed, and wiped her mouth as she swallowed. "I suppose you and Autumn will just have to share me."

He laughed out loud. "Don't tell Autumn that. Remember? She doesn't like to share."

"Right. How could I forget?" She picked up her fork. "Especially after that welcome she gave me. I wasn't sure if she liked me or not."

"She liked you," Grant assured her. "If not, she wouldn't speak to you at all."

The thaw inside Juliet accelerated again, the slow drip turning into a steady stream. Before she knew what had happened all the carnitas had been eaten, she'd gotten through almost a third of her burrito, and the rest was boxed up and ready to go. A glance at her watch surprised her. She couldn't remember the last time two and a half hours had sped by with such swiftness. Nor could she remember the last time she'd had so much fun on a first "date." Grant was entertaining, intelligent, well-spoken, and she couldn't deny the handsome part. Cassie would've *loved* him, even more than she loved everybody else. Her sister would definitely give the sheriff two enthusiastic thumbs up.

Pablo approached the table and gave her a smile. "I take it the senorita enjoyed her dinner?"

"I did, very much." She reached for her purse. "Now, I'll take care of the check."

Pablo frowned and glanced at Grant. The sheriff watched her

silently with an amused smile twitching around the corners of his mouth.

"She thinks *she* has to pay for her dinner?" Pablo asked, indignant. "Why would you let her think that? You already paid for dinner."

Grant sighed. "I *was* going to tell her myself, Pablo, but thanks for letting the cat out of the bag." He gave the plump man a wry smile. "Muchas gracias."

Pablo's eyes widened. "Lo siento. Disculpeme, por favor." He gave her a short bow and walked quickly away.

Juliet stared after him then looked at Grant. "What just happened?"

"He said he was sorry and excuse me, please." Grant shook his head. He opened his mouth to speak again, but stopped when Pablo returned suddenly. The man clasped his hands in front of him and cleared his throat.

"Senorita," Pablo began, looking at her with the most sincere expression she'd ever seen, "when a man enjoys the pleasure of your company for an evening, the least he can do is pay for your meal. If you value yourself and your time, so will the man you are with." He glanced at Grant. "The sheriff is a little old-fashioned, like me, so do not fault him for wanting to be that gentleman for you." He pulled himself up to his full height of 5'6" and puffed out his chest as he faced Grant. "Perdoname, mi amigo, for speaking out of turn, but I had to say something. These *modern* women . . . they are so complicated." He sighed and walked away muttering, "Aye, Dios mio."

Juliet chuckled when Pablo disappeared through the swinging doors into the kitchen area. "Wow. I've never been scolded by a restaurant owner before."

"Juliet, I'm sorry—"

"No." She looked at him for a moment and then smiled. "It's actually okay." She glanced in the direction of the kitchen and her smile widened. "I needed to hear that." Her eyes narrowed. "You knew you were going to pay for dinner as soon as you suggested this place, didn't you?"

He nodded once, completely unruffled. "I did."

"Why did you let me think otherwise?"

He leaned forward and covered her hands with his much larger ones. His skin was warm and rough, and shivers feathered up her arms as those bedroom eyes caught and held hers.

"So you'd agree to have dinner with me. I didn't think you would otherwise."

Juliet gulped. "And what about my feminist hackles getting all prickly?"

One corner of his mouth shot up and he laced his fingers through hers. "If having me buy you dinner offends your feminist sensibilities, next time I ask you out . . . say *no*."

She gulped again. "And when were you, um, planning . . . to ask me out?"

The lazy smile appeared, his chocolate-brown eyes twinkling. "I don't know. Maybe tomorrow night, after I walk you back to the hotel from the festival."

She felt the heat in her face and could only pray that the dim light hid it from him. However, she highly doubted it, especially when his smile widened. She closed her eyes briefly and tried to think despite the tingles racing up her arms and through the rest of her.

"I'm just passing through, sheriff." She forced herself to meet his gaze and was surprised to see his smile hadn't faltered. A lump formed in her throat. "I may not be here past the festival."

You're hoping he talks you into staying, aren't you?

Juliet ground her teeth together and pushed her sister's voice aside. She stared at him and tried to hide her anxiety, but she knew he was seeing right through her.

"I guess that means I have to work harder," Grant drawled, "get you to extend your stay a little."

Oh, trust me, sheriff. You won't have to work very hard. Not very hard at all.

Chapter Six

Juliet stood on the second step of the gazebo, which put her at eye level with Grant. White Christmas-type lights adorned the painted structure and every tree. The strands of bulbs were arranged so artfully that the effect looked surprisingly natural, like fireflies caught in the wood, leaves, and branches. From what she could see they were the only ones in the park, darkness having sent the other occupants elsewhere. Even though the area was virtually devoid of people it still radiated energy, as if the very land beneath their feet was the source of life in Evergreen. She pulled the lapels of Grant's jacket, which he had chivalrously draped over her shoulders, closer around her neck and smiled at him.

"It's so quiet here."

He took a step toward her and gave her that languid grin. "Yes, it is. It's one of the things people like most about Evergreen. The only time the town is noisy is Fourth of July."

She tucked her hair behind one ear. "Wish I could've been here for that."

"It's a lot of fun," he said, "and you don't have to climb over thousands of people or arrive two days early to get a decent spot to watch the fireworks." He smiled. "People start setting up their smokers and grills on the third, and when they start cooking the smell of roasting meat reaches almost all the way to the Interstate. More than once people have told me they followed the aroma straight to Evergreen."

Juliet eased down on the top step and wrapped her arms around her knees. "Sounds fantastic." She looked around and let the quiet serenity wash over her. "It's so strange. I can't remember the last time I was someplace public like this and was completely alone."

"Hey, *I'm* here."

She rolled her eyes. "You know what I mean."

Grant put the take-out container on the top step, sat down beside her, and leaned back on his hands. "Tell me about San Diego. That was actually my favorite part of California. Must've been nice growing up there."

Memories of her family sprang up but she pushed them away and shrugged. "When I was there to see it, it was."

"What does that mean?"

She tightened the embrace of her knees and shrugged. "It means I wasn't there very much." When she saw his questioning look she sighed. "My mother enrolled me at the School of Ballet at the San Francisco Ballet when I was seven. We went home on the weekends and breaks, but I grew to know San Francisco better than San Diego."

His eyes widened. "Wow. So you *are* a dancer."

She stared at him. "How . . . how did you know that?"

"The way you move." He smiled. "You don't walk. You . . . *flow*, like water."

She blinked a couple of times and her heart did a little spin. "Thank you."

He winked at her and one corner of his mouth lifted in a lopsided grin. "And the pointe shoes hanging around your neck didn't hurt the deductive process."

Grant watched as her hand fluttered to the necklace. She palmed the pendant, dropped her chin, and closed her eyes. He felt the pain, raw and fresh. It passed over her face like a shadow and seemed to chill the very air around them. *Damn. Wrong thing to say.*

"My sister gave me this when I graduated from Juilliard," she whispered. A shaky laugh escaped her and Grant reached for her free hand. He was glad she grasped his fingers tightly instead of pulling away. "That was more than ten years ago, and I've never taken it off except for performances and to replace the chain."

He lifted her hand and pressed a kiss to her fingers, which had gone ice cold. He rubbed them gently. "How long have you been dancing?"

"Since before I was born," she replied with another short laugh. He heard the tears behind the sound and cursed himself for bringing it up. Juliet continued, her sea-green gaze focused on something he couldn't see. "My mother used to tell everyone how even in the womb I spent all my time twirling and spinning and basically making her existence a misery. She enrolled me in formal classes when I was three."

"I'll bet you dance beautifully." He brushed a finger over her cheek and wiped away the lone tear. "You must be talented if you got accepted to and graduated from Juilliard."

"I suppose." Her voice was flat, devoid of emotion, as were her eyes.

He searched for something to say that would lighten the mood. "My Aunt Bea taught me to dance," he offered. "Of course, we're talking the waltz, foxtrot, and the tango, but still . . . . For a country boy like me, that's pretty upscale." He was rewarded when he saw a spark of amusement and a faint smile.

Juliet looked at him uncertainly for a moment then she rose to her feet and slipped out of his jacket. She draped it over the nearby railing and extended a hand. "Dance with me."

Grant laced his fingers through hers, stood, and looked down at her. "What?"

"Dance with me."

He searched her eyes for a few seconds. "Are you sure? I must warn you, I'm not very light on my feet, not like the men you're accustomed to partnering up with." He frowned. "What do they call male ballet dancers, anyway? I mean, you're a ballerina, so what are they? Ballerinos?"

Juliet started laughing, and it seemed to break something free inside her. She kept laughing, her arms wrapped around her middle, and this time when he saw tears they weren't tears of sadness. When she finally stopped chuckling, she shook her head, wiped her eyes, and planted her hands on her hips. "Actually, the technical term is *danseuse* for a female ballet dancer, and *danseur* for a male ballet dancer. *Ballerina* only applies to the principal female soloists in a company. The principal male dancers are just called principals, but at one time they *were* referred to as ballerinos. You don't hear that term anymore."

Grant lifted one brow. "So, you girls get a fancy title but we guys are just called principals?" He snorted. "Sounds a little sexist to me."

She gave him a wry smile. "Ballet is one of the few domains where sexism is still openly practiced, *and* it's one of the few fields where women often make more than their male counterparts."

"In other words, it all balances out?"

Juliet chuckled and took a step toward him. "Who cares? Dance with me."

Grant's insides went taut as he imagined getting closer to her. Slowly, he slid his right hand around her slender waist and fanned his fingers over her back just below her shoulder blades. "I said my aunt taught me to dance. I didn't say I was any good at it."

She put her right hand in his left and rested her left hand on the front of his arm with her fingers draped over his shoulder. When she turned those blue-green eyes on him his breathing hitched.

"If you can count to three you can waltz," she said with a grin.

She settled into his embrace and the faint scent of something, perfume or shampoo he wasn't sure, drifted up to him. It took everything inside of him not to close his eyes and lean closer to find out which. He took a breath and steeled himself.

"There's no music," he pointed out.

She pursed her mouth and he had the sudden urge to kiss her. Juliet released him long enough to pull her cell phone from her pocket, and after a few taps on the screen a slow waltz started to play. She leaned to the side and carefully sat the phone on the railing.

"Are you done?" she asked.

"I'm done."

Her eyes narrowed. "Do you *not* want to dance with me?"

He met her gaze directly. "That's not it at all." He stared at her and his throat constricted. It took more than normal effort to get his vocal chords to function, and her color brightened as the seconds ticked off. "I just don't want to injure you. Your feet are your livelihood, and my size 14s can do serious damage. I know, because I've kicked people into submission before and it only took a couple kicks."

"You'll be fine," she said softly, fighting a smile, "and so will my feet. Now, 1-2-3 . . . ."

It felt like the most natural thing in the world as he waltzed Juliet around the raised wooden floor of the gazebo. She was, as he'd expected, exceptionally light on her feet, and thankfully he avoided stepping on her. Holding her like this was like holding lace. The glow from the overhead lights gave her skin an iridescent shimmer, or maybe that was just her. Her eyes appeared lit from within, and he couldn't take his gaze from her face even when the music ended. They stopped moving and he would have been content to stand there forever and just hold her, until the applause started. Apparently, they weren't as alone as they'd thought.

Juliet looked at him with wide eyes, and he gave her a quick grin as he reluctantly released her. "You've done this before, miss ballerina. Take your bow."

She seemed surprised for a moment, and then the corners of her mouth lifted. She turned toward the sound, gracefully lifted her arms to the side, and bent a knee into the most beautiful curtsy he thought he'd ever seen. When she rose she gestured to him and started clapping. Grant rolled his eyes, took a short bow, and grabbed her phone as the curious onlookers, none of whom he cared to identify, moved on. He handed the cell to her and picked up the take-out container as she shrugged into his jacket. Without waiting for him to offer an arm, her fingers wound through the crook of his elbow and they started walking in the direction of the hotel.

"And that concludes our performance for this evening," he said to no one in particular in what he thought was a stereotypical announcer's voice. Juliet giggled and leaned into him.

"I *told* you you'd be fine." He felt her gaze but kept his eyes forward, and he heard the humor in her voice when she continued. "You did quite well, actually. You're a born leader. I didn't have to correct you once."

"And thank you for not doing so in front of the voting public," he said, "who may very well vote for the other guy come next election now that they've seen me dance."

She laughed and the sound tugged at his heart. There were no tears behind this laugh, and he wished it would always be so.

"Quite the contrary, Sheriff Donovan." She laced her fingers together and gripped his arm a little tighter. "Now that the townspeople have seen your skills off-duty, I think you'll win the next election in a landslide."

"And I will save the victory dance for you," he added. She paused and faced him, and he felt the pull from her aquamarine eyes. It was something he hadn't experienced in a very long time, not even with Sherri. The last time he'd felt anything like this had been with Laine.

"Thank you," she said softly.

He placed one hand over both of hers. "You're welcome."

They walked the rest of the way to the hotel in comfortable silence, Juliet's head on his shoulder, their pace leisurely and relaxed. The streets of downtown Evergreen Springs were empty for the most part. Crickets chirped lazily in the background, the faintest breeze whispering through the trees and cooling the air. When they reached the hotel they stood in front of the building and looked at the façade.

"Well, I guess this is it," Juliet said softly.

She released his arm and stepped away, and Grant fought the urge to pull her back. He watched her as she slipped out of his jacket and held it out to him.

"Thanks," he said.

"No, thank *you*." Her expression turned pensive and a wistful smile rounded her mouth. "Thanks for dinner, for the jacket, for the dance . . . for *everything*."

"It was just a burrito." He tucked a fall of dark hair behind her ear, "and a waltz."

"No." She shook her head. "It was more than that." She paused and looked down at the ground. "I haven't felt like . . . *me* . . . in a long time and tonight . . . ." Her head came up and she lifted her eyes to his. "Tonight I was me again." Tears shimmered. "You have no idea what a gift that is."

His heart twisted and his brows drew together as she dashed a hand across her eyes.

"I'm sorry," she said with a soft laugh. "I don't know why I'm so emotional tonight."

Grant cupped her chin and tipped her face up. "Don't ever apologize for being who you are." He smiled at her and when she smiled back the tightness in his chest expanded. In that second he knew if George Mayfield tried to hurt her again he'd kill the man, and he wouldn't lose a second of sleep over it. "I'm glad you could be yourself with me. I wouldn't want you to be anyone else, because I like Juliet Hall just as she is."

Juliet thought her heart would pound its way out of her chest, it was beating so wildly. The warmth of his gaze, the touch of his hand, that sensual smile, seemed to blot out her past and everything she'd been through. Right now there was no crazy person named George Mayfield, there was just this beautiful hamlet named Evergreen Springs guarded by an even more beautiful man named Grant Donovan. She felt warm, safe, and protected, as if just being near Grant was akin to being surrounded by an impenetrable force field.

His finger dragged slowly over the line of her jaw, sending chills through her. Her breath caught as he lowered his head and she closed her eyes. Disappointment burgeoned inside her when he brushed his lips over her cheek in a chaste kiss and then pulled back.

"You better get inside," he said softly, his voice like rough velvet. "It's getting chilly out here."

Truthfully, she hadn't noticed. Being close to him was warming enough, but as the breeze picked up goose bumps plumped on her arms. "I guess it is."

"You sure you don't want this?" he asked, holding up the take-out box.

She shook her head. "No, you take it. At least then I know it will get eaten. It's too good to waste."

"That's true." His gaze wandered over her face and paused on her mouth. For a second she thought he was going to kiss her again, and this time on the lips. Then he smiled and the moment passed. "I had a great time tonight, and I want to thank your feminist hackles for staying unprickly."

"I don't *have* feminist hackles," she said with a smile. "But if you want to try and rile them again, by all means."

A teasing light entered his eyes. "I'll have to buy you another dinner."

"And that would just be *torturous*," she said with a roll of her eyes. She took a step onto the stairs and waved a hand at him. "Go on. It's getting late."

"I will see you tomorrow, won't I?"

The look he gave her was unabashedly hopeful and it made her heart flip. Immediately Cassie's voice sounded off.

Wow, an alpha male who's actually unafraid to show a girl how he feels. I've never met one of those before, wasn't sure they even existed. Way to pick 'em, Jules.

Juliet ignored her sister and smiled. "You will. Lunch, remember?"

He grinned. "Maybe I'll take a late lunch, that way I can have you to myself."

Her heart double-flipped. She stared at him for a moment then lifted one brow. "Do I get the feeling that Autumn isn't the only one who doesn't like to share?"

"You do."

Juliet hopped up another step. "Whenever you show up I will be there. I'm sure Autumn will understand."

He laughed. "You don't know Autumn." He tossed his jacket over his shoulder. "Good night, Juliet."

"Good night, Grant. Thanks again, for everything."

"You are most welcome. See you tomorrow."

Juliet walked up the final two steps and entered the hotel, closing the door softly behind her. She immediately turned and peeked out the closest window, careful to stay in the shadows. Grant stood on the sidewalk for another few moments, looking at the hotel, and then he turned and walked back to his Yukon.

You should've kissed him, Jules. I know you wanted to.

Juliet sighed and turned toward the stairs when the taillights of his SUV disappeared from sight. "I was hoping *he'd* kiss *me.*"

Chicken. You can dance on stage in front of thousands of people, nail an audition with the confidence and skill of Baryshnikov, and you even helped turn me *into a dancer, but you can't kiss the guy?*

Juliet took the stairs slowly. "I know how to dance, Cass. Flirting? That was always *your* forte."

I know. I was always a better flirt, while you were the better dancer. Everyone has their skills, I suppose.

"I suppose." She walked to her room and took the key from her pocket. "Right now, I wish I had a little more of *your* skill set. Maybe then Grant and I would be on the stoop making out instead of heading our separate ways."

"I'm sorry, Juliet, did you say something?"

Juliet jumped and gasped as Nicole stepped into the hall from the stairs. The woman wore an emerald green satin robe and she was barefoot, her hair braided neatly and laying over one slender shoulder.

"Wow." Juliet pressed a hand to her thudding heart and leaned against the nearest wall. "You startled me."

Nicole smiled and approached her. "I'm sorry, dear. I thought I heard you talking to someone."

Juliet took a shaky breath. "Just myself. I do that sometimes."

"Did you have a nice time with Grant?" Nicole leaned a shoulder into the wall and crossed her arms over her chest.

"I did." Juliet sighed softly and closed her eyes, picturing Grant. "I had a wonderful time."

"I hear the two of you were dancing in the square."

Juliet's eyes snapped open and she gaped at the woman. "I'm sorry, what? How do you *know* that? Do you people have some sort of spy network set up in this town? Let me guess, surveillance cameras on every building, and the monitoring center is right here in the hotel basement."

Nicole chuckled and straightened. "No, dear. It's just a small town." She rested a hand on Juliet's shoulder and looked at her seriously. "Can I ask a favor of you, Juliet?"

"Of course. What?"

Nicole stared at her for several long tense moments, then she said, "Don't break his heart. Grant is well-liked around here, and he's one of the finest young men to walk God's earth. I don't want to see him, or you, get hurt."

"I . . . ." Juliet's voice died and she took a breath. "I just met him, Nicole, *today*."

"I know," Nicole said in a kind, sad voice, "but I can tell by the way he looks at you that he's smitten. He looks at you the way he used to look at Laine."

"Laine?"

"Laine Wheeler. They met when they were four, and they've been best friends ever since." Nicole's hand dropped back to her side. "Grant's been in love with her almost as long, but Laine was destined to walk a different path, one that didn't include the two of them being together. She's happily married now and lives in Denver with her husband." She sighed. "I hoped Grant would be happy with Sherri, but I guess that wasn't meant to be either."

Juliet's brain was spinning. "Wait. Autumn said something today about Sherri breaking up with him because he went to his best friend's wedding. Is Laine that best friend?"

"Yes," Nicole replied with a short nod. "He was Laine's 'man of honor'."

Juliet thought about that and felt the weight of what Grant must have gone through like she'd gone through it herself. "Wow. How hard would *that* be? Watching the person you love marry someone else." She closed her eyes and shuddered. "No, thank you."

Nicole laughed softly. "Grant handled it like he handles everything, with grace and that dreamy smile."

"How did he wind up with Sherri?"

The woman sighed. "Where Grant always had a thing for Laine, Sherri always had a thing for Grant." Nicole shook her head. "I thought Sherri would be happy she finally snagged the most eligible bachelor in Hill County, but she never could control that green-eyed monster. I was actually glad when she finally moved to Billings, and I think Grant was, too. Lord knows he was much happier once she left." Nicole gave her a knowing look. "For some reason, I don't think he's going to be as happy to see *you* go."

Juliet looked at the floor. "That cuts both ways, Nicole."

Nicole's voice softened. "So . . . you're smitten, too."

"I guess I am." It made no sense, but there it was.

The older woman patted her arm and sighed. "You young people these days, so much drama." She smiled and turned to walk back towards the stairs. "Good night, Juliet. I'll see you in the morning."

"Yes, you will, Miss Nicole. Good night."

***

Grant sat down at his desk and flipped the lamp on. The brown folder sat in the center of the blotter and the label read HALL, JULIET in neatly typed letters. A glance out the window across the square showed him Juliet was still up, her windows the only light in the otherwise darkened front of the Center Hotel. As he watched the light went out and he sighed heavily.

He opened his web browser and did a search for Juliet. Within seconds he had several links available, and he clicked on one. His breath caught. It was obviously a publicity shot from the ballet company she danced with, and she looked breathtaking. She wore a white, iridescent bodysuit that showcased her sleek, graceful lines to perfection, and she was lifted high into the air. Her back was elegantly arched, arms curved overhead, her right leg bent and her left leg straight out behind her. Her partner was dressed similarly, muscles bulging as he held her over his head.

"Wow."

He looked at several more shots before he pulled up a You Tube video of one of her performances. The way she moved was absolutely mesmerizing, and when she struck her final pose the audience burst into thunderous applause. Hell, he almost started clapping.

Finally, he accessed a newspaper story about the stalking case. The article had a picture of both her and Mayfield, and explained in almost clinical terms that the former politician's son had developed a fascination for the beautiful ballerina. It stopped just short of saying the man was stalking her. In fact, one could interpret the article to mean that one of Seattle's most handsome bachelors was actively pursuing Juliet, and that she was simply playing coy. With an annoyed huff he exited the web browser and turned his eyes to the file.

"Well, here goes nothing."

He flipped the case file open and started to read. It took him nearly two hours to go through the entire file, and when he came to the pictures from the crime scene of Cassie's murder he blanched and closed his eyes. The girl's body was covered in lacerations that made her look more like a Rand McNally Highway Atlas than a person. To think Juliet had walked in on that sent his stomach rolling and his heart to the floor.

When he was finished he removed the picture of George Mayfield from the file and walked over to the copy machine. He made several dozen copies and put them on his desk. Tomorrow he'd give these out to all his deputies and have Roberta start faxing and e-mailing copies to all the local businesses. If Mayfield stepped foot in his county, he wanted to know about it as it happened so he could get to Mayfield before Mayfield got to Juliet. And if he had to he'd kill the guy, and smile while doing it.

With that picture in his mind Grant smiled, took one of the photocopies, and walked out into the main office. He approached the enormous bulletin board along the wall that faced his door. The board was divided into titled sections – Missing Persons, Upcoming Events, etc. He tacked the photo beneath the BOLO title, be on the lookout. It would be the first thing anyone saw when they entered the Sheriff's Office.

Grant walked back into his private office and stood in front of the window that overlooked the square. He wondered if Juliet was sleeping, and if her sleep was peaceful or troubled by dreams, as his sometimes was. His gaze turned to the gazebo and he smiled, remembering the way she had looked and moved, so elegant and lithe. He hoped he'd get the chance to dance with her again and glanced toward her darkened windows.

"I won't let him hurt you again, Juliet," he said. "I'll kill him first."

***

Juliet sat on the window seat, her knees pulled to her chest, her gaze fixed on the only lighted windows in downtown. Autumn had told her those windows were in Grant's private office. She could see him silhouetted in those large panes and knew he was looking at the hotel. She could almost feel his gaze from all the way across the square. If she turned on the light she realized he'd see her in silhouette as well, but she didn't want to leave her perch long enough to flip the switch.

She'd tried to sleep but dreams of Cassie had woken her. A glance at the clock told her nearly three hours had passed since the Sheriff had walked her home. It was well after midnight.

Better try to sleep if you're going to meet Nicole for coffee and croissants at 8:30. You're not used to staying up so late, big sister.

"I don't want to dream about you again," Juliet said, turning her gaze back to Grant's windows. "I'm sick to death of waking up sweating and crying with those pictures in my head."

Then dream about him.

Juliet thought about that for a moment, and then the lights in Grant's office went out. About a minute later he exited the front of the building and approached his Yukon, tossing one last glance her way before opening the door and sliding behind the wheel. When his taillights disappeared from view she rose from her seat and climbed into the queen-sized bed.

"Okay, Cass, you win." Juliet snuggled into the covers and glanced at her sister's photograph. "I'll try to dream about Grant."

Outstanding, but don't forget to set the alarm. I won't be able to wake you up.

Unbidden, Juliet smiled. "If I'm dreaming about Grant, I won't *want* to wake up." Before her sister could chide her again she reached over and set the alarm. "Good night, little sister. I love you."

Good night, Juliet. Sweet dreams . . . .

***

The DVD of Swan Lake played and George Mayfield sat transfixed as he sipped the 30-year-old scotch. Juliet fluttered across the stage and the familiar longing for her tightened his chest. This recording was one of her last performances of Swan Lake, the last show she'd done before the company released her. A churning cauldron of red anger, hot lust, and ice-cold determination made his abdominal muscles clench.

"So beautiful," he whispered, taking another drink. The cell phone on the coffee table vibrated obnoxiously. With a growl of frustration he hit pause, sat his drink on the table, and picked up the device. "This had better be good."

"I may have a lead."

George sat straight up in his seat, but then he tempered his exuberance. He'd heard this before, and nearly three months had passed since he'd almost laid claim to his prize. "Why do you say that? Where *are* you, anyway?"

"Seattle."

Now he jumped to his feet. "*What?*" He looked at the phone for a second and then put it back to his ear. "Juliet is *not* in Seattle, so why are *you?*"

"I had an idea."

A few seconds of silence passed and George clenched his teeth. "I'm *listening.*"

"Well, all the leads I've followed led nowhere. She's paying cash for everything, laying low, disguising her appearance whenever she goes out in public, so I thought maybe she wasn't the one I should be trying to follow."

Several more seconds ticked off and George made a strangled sound. "Just tell me what the *hell* you're talking about, or I'll find someone else to take over for you."

"Detective Riordan is still looking for her. He has access to resources I don't, and I think I may have something."

"What?"

"When he left his office today . . . he was *smiling.*" There was a brief, sharp laugh. "He hasn't done that since Juliet disappeared."

George sat down, picked up the tumbler, and took a long sip. "So what is it you want to do, exactly?"

"Let me follow the good detective for a few days. He might lead me right to her."

George almost choked. "You think he knows where she is?"

"It's worth a shot. And, if it doesn't pan out, you can still find someone to replace me."

Moving to the window, he stared over the lights of Seattle, and then the image of Juliet once again danced through his brain. He would have her. He *had* to have her. Failure was *not* an option.

"Fine," George replied, "I'll give you until the weekend to make some progress." He paused for effect and lowered his voice to a growl. "You either find her by then or you find other employment, and I *wouldn't* come back to Seattle for your job search."

Without waiting for a response he turned off the phone and tossed it onto the couch. He picked up a framed 8 x 10 of Juliet that sat on a nearby bookshelf and ran his finger over the image.

"Soon, my love," he whispered. "Very soon, we will be together . . . forever."

Chapter Seven

Juliet actually woke up ten minutes before her alarm was set to go off, and thankfully dreams of Cassie hadn't terrorized her again. Sunlight poured through the window to puddle on the foot of the bed. She kicked the covers back and rolled into that illuminated spot, sighing softly as the heat leached into her.

She stayed there until the alarm sounded. The radio turned on to a local station that played country music and instead of turning it off she just let it go. She hummed along, stretched a little, then hopped out of bed and made her way to the bathroom.

After showering and dressing, Juliet straightened her room, stepped into the hallway, and pulled the door closed behind her. As soon as she did the aroma of chocolate and pastry assaulted her. Her mouth started to water and she made a beeline for the stairs, taking them two at a time. The delicious scent led her through the dining room to the kitchen. She stood on tiptoe, looked over the top of the saloon-style swinging doors, and gently tapped the wood. Nicole was just pulling a tray out of the oven, and when she glanced over her shoulder a smile lit her face.

"Ah, there you are." She glanced at the clock. "Right on time. I like a girl who's punctual. Come in, come in."

Juliet pushed through the doors and approached the older woman. Nicole slid the tray of chocolate croissants onto the counter and the smell was almost overwhelming. Juliet closed her eyes and inhaled deeply.

"Those smell *fabulous*," Juliet said.

Nicole tossed her oven mitts aside. "Well, I'm not much of a cook, but I'm one hell of a baker. I can barely boil water, but if you want cookies or cakes or pies or pastries, then I'm your girl." She chuckled and opened a cabinet. "Grab that carafe of coffee and go find us a table. I'll be right behind you with the croissants."

"You got it."

Juliet grabbed the handle of the white ceramic carafe and walked back through the swinging doors into the empty dining room. She picked a table near a window overlooking the square that had almost as good a view of the Sheriff's Office as her room did. Just as she finished pouring the steaming liquid into the delicate china cups Nicole appeared with a plate full of croissants and smaller plates for each of them. Juliet pulled out Nicole's chair, and then sat down across from the older woman.

"Here we are," Nicole said as she put the pastries in the center of the table and then put the smaller plates down. "Help yourself."

Juliet spread her napkin over her lap and used her fork to lift one of the delicate pastries. "These look so good, Nicole. And they're enormous."

"Well, my husband is a large man," Nicole replied with a chuckle, "so dainty food is *not* for him. He says if it's not big enough to fit in his hands then it's not big enough to serve."

Juliet took a bite of the still warm confection and sighed in pleasure. "Oh, my goodness. I don't think I've ever tasted anything so delicious."

Nicole beamed at her. "Try dipping a piece in your coffee. I brewed some of that Sumatran blend just for the two of us."

Juliet tore off a piece of the flaky pastry, dunked it in her coffee, and popped it in her mouth. Another moan of pleasure escaped her and Nicole grinned.

"I take it that means you like it?" Nicole asked as she carefully dipped a piece of croissant in her coffee.

"*Like* it?" Juliet took another bite. "I may just move in with you so I can have these every morning."

"I'm sure Grant would approve of that."

Juliet glanced at the older woman but Nicole wasn't looking at her. Her gaze was focused out the window and Juliet turned her eyes that way. Grant's Yukon was just pulling up in front of the Sheriff's Office, and her heart beat a little faster when he got out of the vehicle. He was so tall and so powerfully built and so unflinchingly *male*. Juliet gulped and picked up her cup as the butterflies started bouncing around her midsection.

"So, have you decided to stay for the festival tonight?"

Juliet took a sip of her coffee and carefully put the cup back on its saucer. "I have." She bit her lip as a thought hit her. "That's all right, isn't it? I suppose I should have checked with you to make sure you still have room for me."

Nicole laughed. It was a delicate, musical sound, and Juliet smiled when the older woman reached across the table to squeeze her hand. "Oh, Juliet, you are a dear. Of course there is room for you." The woman took a sip of coffee, then dabbed at the corners of her mouth with the white linen napkin. "To be totally honest, you're our only guest. The hotel makes more revenue from the dining room, afternoon teas, Sunday brunch, and special events and parties than it does overnight guests." She paused and gazed about the sunny room, her expression wistful. "But, it's been in my family for more than 100 years, and it's my baby."

"It's beautiful. Do you do the decorating?"

"I do." Her cheeks went pink with pride. "I even do the artwork. *That's* my other baby."

Juliet gaped at her. "You painted all those gorgeous landscapes?" When Nicole nodded Juliet put the pastry down and stared at her. "Why are you showing your work here instead of a gallery in Chicago or New York or San Francisco? You are *very* talented."

"And so are you, I hear," Nicole said with a sly glance. "Paulette says you and Grant danced quite well together." One red brow winged skyward. "Now, I know Grant, and while he's a great sheriff he's not known for his dancing abilities, but with you it seems he morphed into a young Fred Astaire."

"Actually, Grant is a wonderful dancer," Juliet replied, somewhat miffed that their every move seemed to be headline news in the tiny hamlet. "He's a born leader, he's quite light on his feet, and he moves with surprising grace for someone his size."

"And it helps to have a first-rate partner," Nicole observed. "Paulette says you move like you *really* know what you're doing."

Juliet wondered who Paulette was, but decided it was probably better she not know. "I've done some dancing in my day."

"What sort?"

Juliet was starting to get annoyed, but she kept it to herself. "Classical ballet."

Nicole heaved a sigh of relief and giggled and Juliet glanced at her, surprised.

"Whew," the older woman said. "I was hoping you didn't say 'exotic'." She popped a bite of croissant into her mouth. "I've made that mistake before. 'So, what do you do?' 'Oh, I'm a dancer.' 'Really? What kind of dancer?'" Nicole rolled her eyes. "It's happened more than once, and even the second and third time I had no ready reply. What do you say to *that?*"

The spark of anger that had briefly flared in her chest fizzled out and Juliet grinned. "Just smile, and say, 'I hear there's a lot of money to be made in that field' and let it go." She glanced down at her chest. "Besides, I don't have the, um, *assets* to be spinning around on a brass pole."

"Nonsense, dear." Nicole gave her a once over. "You're beautiful, and you have a lovely figure."

Juliet felt her cheeks warm. "Thank you, but I've heard girls make *way* more money if they are more heavily endowed, if you know what I mean." She shrugged and took a sip of coffee. "I've never had any complaints, but if that was a field I was looking into, a little cosmetic surgery would probably be necessary to ensure any sort of living wage."

Nicole laughed again. "Oh, Juliet, you are so funny." She took a drink of coffee and carefully placed the cup back on its saucer. "What do you have planned for the rest of your morning?"

"Not much," Juliet replied. "I thought I'd walk around downtown a little, maybe take a stroll through the park and do a little window shopping before lunch with Autumn. Why?"

Nicole eyed her speculatively for a few moments. "Well, I'm going to have a booth at the festival this evening and I need to stock it. I wondered if perhaps you might like to spend a couple hours in the kitchen with me. I can show you how to make these, for starters." She held up another croissant before she slid it onto her plate. "But if you'd rather not I completely understand and I *promise* I won't hold it against you."

Juliet watched her for several seconds and then smiled. "Actually, that sounds like a lot of fun. I'd love to."

"Wonderful." Nicole beamed at her. "It'll be like those times when my girls were younger and used to help me bake." She patted Juliet's hand. "I'm sure you did the same thing with your mother when you were a child."

The thought of her mother brought with it a stab of pain she didn't want to feel. Juliet bit her lip and dropped her gaze. "Once, maybe, a *really* long time ago." Her throat tightened and it took her several seconds to find her voice. "My mother didn't . . . ." She forced a smile. "She didn't spend much time in the kitchen."

"Oh." Nicole seemed a little lost, as if she didn't know what to say to that. Finally, she smiled. "Then this will be even more fun. It'll be my first time teaching a dancer to bake, and it'll be your first time being taught. Firsts all the way around."

Juliet met the woman's gaze and felt the sting of tears. "Sounds like a great way to spend the morning."

Nicole slid another pastry onto Juliet's plate. "Then eat up, young lady. We have some baking to do!"

***

Grant saw the picture of George Mayfield as soon as he entered his domain. The first thing he did was walk into his office to grab the stack of photocopies. He made the rounds, passing out Mayfield's photo to each of the five deputies seated in the outer office, and then he handed the remainder of the stack to Roberta. She gave him a questioning look and a raised brow.

"Hand them out to the rest of the building when we're done here." She nodded and he faced the room. "If I could have your attention, please?" He paused until everyone in the room was focused on him. "The picture you're looking at is one George Mayfield from Seattle, Washington. He spent four years in a mental institution after being tried for the murder of a young girl and found mentally incompetent. He's now the prime suspect in the murder of another young woman and the stalking of the most recent victim's sister." He crossed his arms over his chest and looked at each man and woman in the room. "This guy steps foot in my county, I want to know."

"Why would he be here?"

Grant ground his teeth together. Of course Jackson would ask the obvious question, the one he had hoped to avoid. "Because the woman whose sister he killed, the woman who has a permanent restraining order against him for stalking her, is Juliet Hall."

Deputy Sheridan rose out of her chair. "The woman whose car broke down outside of town?" A small smile twitched about her mouth. "The same woman you were seen, um, *dancing* with last evening?"

A chuckle rippled through the group. Grant pursed his lips and scowled at them. "No, some *other* woman named Juliet Hall." Silence dropped like a stone. "This man isn't allowed within 500 yards of her, so if you see him anywhere in her vicinity, arrest him."

"What's *she* doing here?" Jackson asked. It almost sounded like a whine.

"Passing through," Grant replied, his brows drawing together, annoyance flaring.

Jackson snickered. "Maybe, instead of dancing with her you should encourage her to move on. Then we wouldn't have to worry about this guy."

Grant hooked his thumbs in his gun belt and took a step toward Jackson, no longer annoyed. Now he was getting mad. "You have a problem doing what you're getting paid to do, deputy?"

Jackson blinked. "No, but isn't letting her stay here just encouraging this creep to come looking?"

The anger tightly coiled in his chest expanded until Grant was sure steam would come out his ears. "Last I checked, deputy, American citizens are allowed to move freely about the country as they so choose. If she wants to stay a few days in Evergreen Springs, then she can stay a few days as long as she abides by the law. After all, she's the victim here, not the perpetrator."

"That doesn't mean she's not *trouble*," Jackson said under his breath.

Grant was done. "Enough." His anger came down a notch when Sheridan smacked Jackson in the back of the head and told him to shut up. "As long as Miss Hall is here we have an obligation to protect her just like everyone else who lives in Evergreen." He skewered Jackson with a glare. "You have a problem with that?"

Jackson shrank back in his chair. "No, Sheriff, not at all."

His gaze scoured the group. "Anyone else have any concerns?"

The rest of them knew better. Grant appreciated deputies who took their jobs seriously and asked questions when they were unsure or needed clarification, and thankfully most all of his subordinates were honest, hard-working individuals. Jackson, on the other hand, seemed to need justification to do his job instead of just doing it. As a result he and Grant were always butting heads. Grant often felt like a father of a rebellious teenager who was constantly testing his limits, and Grant was just about at the end of his rope. If it wouldn't have been such a pain in the ass, he'd have fired the guy by now.

"Alright. Take those copies with you when you go on patrol and Roberta . . . ." He looked over his shoulder at the older woman. "Put a caption on it and start faxing and e-mailing that picture to all the local businesses. I want as many people as possible to know what this guy looks like, and to know that he's probably armed and definitely dangerous. If anyone sees him, they need to call us *immediately.*"

Roberta bobbed her head once. "Will do, Sheriff."

He faced the deputies again. "Any questions?" When Jackson's hand shot up Grant almost growled. "In my office, Jackson. *Now.*" Jackson looked surprised but rose and walked into Grant's office. Grant ignored his departure. "Anyone *else?*"

"No, Sheriff," Sheridan said, her green eyes dancing with amusement. "All of *us* know what we're supposed to do."

"Thank you, Jessica," he said with a tight smile. "I appreciate that." He sighed and pinched the bridge of his nose. "And now, for the fun part of my day." He turned toward his office, ignoring the soft laughter from behind him.

He walked through the door and closed it with a little more force than was necessary, but it made Jackson jump and that made him smile. After easing down into his chair he kicked his feet up on the desk, laced his fingers over his abdomen, and fixed Jackson with a scowl. "All right, Jackson. What do you want?"

"I was just wondering if you'd been in contact with that detective from Seattle." Jackson's voice was low, but at least he looked Grant in the eye.

Grant nodded. "I have."

Jackson dropped his gaze for a few seconds, as if searching for something to say. "Well," he drawled, tugging on his shirtsleeves, "did he have any recommendations?"

"None that I care to share," Grant replied. "Why are you so interested?"

Jackson stared at him for several ticks of the clock and then turned his gaze out the window. "Look, Grant, I know we don't get along and we disagree on how to do this job—"

"No, we *don't* disagree. You and I don't *do* the same job." Anger erupted in the pit of Grant's stomach, but he kept his face neutral. He dropped his feet, leaned forward, and planted his elbows on his desk. "I'm the sheriff, you're a deputy. We don't agree on how *you* do *your* job many times, but if you think for one second that *your job* and *mine* are the same, I'm beginning to see where part of the problem lies."

Jackson frowned. "Fine. Permission to speak freely?"

"Knock yourself out, Jackson." Grant leaned back and clamped a lid on his irritation. "I've never stopped you from speaking freely, unless the situation or location would make it inappropriate, and I only do it then because you seem to lack the judgment to make that determination on your own. We're behind closed doors and it's just you and me. Go for it."

It was several seconds before the younger man spoke. "I think you're wrong."

Grant waited a bit, and when Jackson said nothing more he frowned and his fury simmered a little hotter. "Do you want to be more specific, or do you expect me to guess exactly what it is you're talking about?"

Jackson huffed. "I think you're wrong in how you're handling the situation with Juliet Hall." An angry flush crept up the younger man's neck. "You should be convincing her to move on, not . . . *dating* her."

"I'm sorry," Grant began, "did I miss the memo where I asked for your input on how I spend my off-time?" Jackson opened his mouth but Grant silenced him with a look. "Your objections regarding my handling of this situation are noted. Now get back to work."

Jackson came out of his chair. "That's it?"

"That's it."

"You're going to let this guy just *march* into Evergreen and put everyone here at risk?"

Grant rose and came around his desk to stand toe to toe with the younger man. "No. I'm alerting everyone in town so that if he does march into Evergreen I can do what Seattle PD couldn't."

"Like what?"

"Like put him behind bars," Grant replied through clenched teeth. "If he crosses state lines in pursuit of Juliet and violates the restraining *order* that brings *Federal* charges. It won't be so easy for the man's daddy to make *those* allegations disappear."

"You *want* him to come here?"

Grant felt a surge of anger and then his pulse dropped. After his combat tours in the Middle East his commanding officer had recommended him for a study about combat veterans and how they handle stress during battle. The scientists in their little white lab coats had discovered something interesting about him: during the times of highest stress his pulse and blood pressure actually dropped instead of skyrocketing, a phenomenon known as *stress inoculation*. He felt that calm envelope him now, just as it had done each time he took aim at the enemy.

"No, Jackson, I don't *want* him to come here." Jackson started to speak but Grant held up a hand. "However, I am not going to chase

Juliet Hall out of town for no other reason than you don't want to do your job. Therefore, I will prepare as if George Mayfield is on his way, alert my deputies and the townspeople, and do what I need to do."

"You don't need to sleep with her."

Grant stared at the younger man for several long, tense seconds, until Jackson started to fidget. "Get back to work, deputy," he said at last. "And be thankful we're both in uniform right now, or you'd be picking your teeth up off the floor."

Color surged into Jackson's face, and he seemed to understand he'd crossed the line. "Grant, I'm sorry—"

"Save it." Grant walked back around his desk and sat down. "Get out."

"Grant—"

"*Now.*"

"But—"

Grant shot him a glare. "Jackson, if you want to do my job run for it next election. Until you *take* this office it belongs to *me*, so you can either leave *right* now or I will throw you out the window. Take your pick."

Jackson watched him for a few seconds, then sighed and left the office. Grant rubbed his temples. Just when he thought the day couldn't get any worse, his phone rang.

"Sheriff Donovan."

"Sheriff." The voice belonged to Roberta. "I have a Detective Riordan on the phone."

"Aw, hell." Grant closed his eyes and took a long, slow breath. "Thanks, Roberta. Put him through." About a second later the click told him Roberta had done just that. "This is Sheriff Donovan."

"Sheriff Donovan, Detective Riordan," Riordan said. "Have you had a chance to go through the file I sent you?"

Grant leaned back in his chair. "I have."

"Is Juliet . . . I mean, Miss Hall still in town?"

"She is. The part for her car won't come in until this afternoon, so she'll be here at least that long. Beyond that, I don't know."

"Do you think you could get her to stay until tomorrow?"

Uneasiness bubbled up inside him. "Why?"

Riordan paused and then sighed. "I'm taking a redeye out of Seattle tonight, and I'll be in Evergreen Springs by morning."

Grant squeezed his eyes shut and pinched the bridge of his nose.

Damn. He had been hoping to avoid discussing the detective with Juliet, but it looked like he wasn't going to be able to do that. "And what are you planning to do once you get here?"

"I'm going to try and talk her into returning to Seattle."

"Why?" Grant frowned. "There's nothing for her in Seattle. Her parents live in San Diego, her sister is gone, the ballet company let her go because Mayfield's harassment was disrupting rehearsals and performances, and the bastard still lives there. Seattle PD obviously can't keep him away from her, so why the *hell* would she want to go back?"

Riordan made an annoyed sound. "Can you get her to stay or not?"

"I'm not even going to try."

"Sheriff—"

"Detective, she'll probably still be here come morning, as long as I don't tell her you're coming."

"Then don't tell her."

"I'm not going to lie to her."

"You don't have to," Riordan argued. "Just don't tell her."

Grant understood the man's desire to keep Juliet safe, but his conscience recoiled at the idea of lying to her, even if it was by omission. A lie was still a lie. The thought of how she'd look at him once she realized he'd known the detective was coming and hadn't told her solidified his resolve. "I can't do that, Detective. She deserves the opportunity to decide if she *wants* to see you or not. If she does, she'll still be here. If she doesn't, she won't."

Riordan was silent for a couple of seconds, and when he spoke next he sounded angry. "Do you realize what she's facing?"

"I read the file."

"Then you understand if George Mayfield catches up with her, he'll likely kill her."

"If George Mayfield gets within 100 feet of her it'll be *him* on a slab, not Juliet."

The line went quiet, and when the detective spoke again his voice was low.

"So," Riordan began in a low voice, "she's gotten to you, too."

It was Grant's turn to make an annoyed sound. "Detective, I don't know how you do things in the city, but around here when someone threatens someone else we don't just stand around and let the lawyers sort it out. We protect our own."

"Sheriff—"

"Detective, I don't mean to be rude, but do what you have to do. I'll talk to Ms. Hall and morning will determine whether or not *you* get to talk to her." He took a deep breath and reined in his irritation. "Trust me, by lunchtime today everyone in Evergreen will know what George Mayfield looks like and that's he's a dangerous predator. As soon as he steps foot in my town, I'll know. Mayfield won't get near her, and if he does . . . I won't bother to arrest him."

"Works for me."

Grant was surprised. "Really?"

Riordan sighed heavily. "Really. If you get the chance to take that bastard out . . . ." His voice trailed off. "I had the chance and I blew it. If I hadn't Cassie might still be alive."

Grant ran a hand over his face. Thankfully, he had never been in the detective's shoes because whenever he'd had the chance to take the shot, he'd taken it. But, he could imagine how the detective felt. He'd seen it happen to some of his fellow snipers. Often the guilt of *not* killing someone weighed heavier than the opposite. "If I have the chance I'll take it, and I won't miss."

"I know you won't," Riordan said with a chuckle. "I did a little checking on you, Sheriff Donovan. Impressive record. By the time you left the Marines you had a kill count in the low triple digits."

A chill shot up his spine. "I know," Grant replied. "I was there, but thanks for the refresher."

"And you've won every sharpshooting competition you've entered since the tender age of 16." Riordan paused. "Keep that rifle ready, Sheriff. You may need it."

Grant didn't want to entertain that thought just yet. "I always keep my rifle ready, Detective. Now, I'd love to chat but I have a job to do. If you want I can send a deputy to meet your plane in Billings."

"That won't be necessary. If Juliet decides not to speak to me I'm going to need a car to chase her down."

"Very well. I'll see you when you get here." Grant hung up the phone and leaned back in his chair, his gaze fixed on the ceiling. "Shit." He rubbed his eyes and exhaled slowly. Like it or not, he was going to have to tell Juliet that Detective Riordan was coming. But, before that, he had to really get the word out about George Mayfield, and there was one person he knew would be perfect to help him.

Grant left his office and headed for the door. He paused when he saw Roberta as she moved between her desk and the fax machine.

"Roberta, have you sent that over to Paulette's yet?"

Roberta lifted one gray brow and pursed her lips. "You have to ask, Grant? Hers was the first call I made."

"Good. I'll be back in a little bit. Going to make the rounds and see if everyone is getting their notifications."

A sly smile curved Roberta's thin lips and she chuckled. "Of course. Tell Paulette I said hello."

Chapter Eight

Grant strode into Paulette's salon, *Best Tressed*, ten minutes later. The smell of scented candles, hairspray, and other chemicals made for a potent mix after the fresh air outside. He tried not to breathe too deeply as he made his way to Paulette's station. The other hairdressers smiled and nodded at him, and he responded in a like manner until he was standing behind the petite, bottle-blonde. He leaned against the wall and watched as she flitted around her current customer. When she finally noticed him in the mirror she froze, then pasted on her usually bright smile and spun to face him.

Paulette Godwin was a fixture in Evergreen Springs, and the biggest mouth in town. Attractive, whippet slender, and sporting a full head of blonde curls that would look more appropriate on a woman in her 20s rather than a woman in her 50s, she was the heart of Evergreen's rumor mill. Whenever a story made the rounds there was seldom a time where Paulette hadn't started it, and the woman knew even more people in the town than he did. He knew if he wanted word spread about anything all he had to do was tell Paulette. Before the hour was out her gossip network would be running full steam, transmitting as fast as they could dial and text. She was better at disseminating information than the Emergency Broadcasting Network.

"Morning, Sheriff," she said. She spun back to her client. "What can I do for you?"

"Well, after you finish with Mrs. Brown I'd like a minute of your time." He gave Mrs. Brown a smile in the mirror and the elderly woman smiled back.

Paulette grabbed a can of hairspray and started misting Mrs. Brown's head. "Then you're in luck, Grant, because I'm almost finished."

"I'll wait at the reception desk." He nodded at Mrs. Brown. "Looking good, Mrs. Brown. Tell your husband he is one lucky man." He gave the white-haired woman a wink and she grinned at him.

"You are shameless, Grant Donovan," Mrs. Brown said with mock reproach and a twinkle in her eyes. "That's part of the reason I voted for you."

He laughed. "I do appreciate the support. You have a nice day, ma'am."

"You, too, Sheriff. You, too."

Grant approached the reception desk and leaned one elbow on the raised counter. Cindilee Kendrick sat there, her brown hair streaked with vibrant bands of fire-engine red and poppy orange. Plump and rather plain with flat, brown eyes, she was the stereotypical small-town girl who always talked and dreamed of heading to the big city, but never seemed to have the ambition or desire to follow through. She was filing her nails and snapping her gum, and she barely glanced at him.

"Morning, Cindilee," Grant said.

Cindilee tossed him a glance and returned to filing. "Morning, Sheriff. What are you doing here? I thought Bob Granger cut your hair over at the barbershop."

"He does," Grant agreed. "I'm here to see Paulette."

Cindilee's eyes immediately lit up and she sat a little straighter in her chair. "Why? What's going on?"

Grant groaned inwardly but kept his smile firmly in place. "Nothing, Cindilee. Just need a word with your boss, that's all."

"Does it have anything to do with this?" Cindilee put her nail file aside and held up the faxed image of George Mayfield. She glanced at it. "It's hard to believe that anyone as handsome as this guy is dangerous."

Cindilee was only in her mid-twenties and Grant had always thought the girl was a few bushels shy of a load, but she was a trusted minion in Paulette's army of gossips. Regardless, he knew there was a hierarchy in Paulette's world, and to share vital information with Cindilee before sharing it with Paulette would do little more than piss off the older woman and ensure that she'd never speak to him again. Not that that would be a *bad* thing, but sometimes Paulette's propensity to blather everything all over town served his purposes. He had no desire to be at odds with the woman.

"I'm sure Paulette will fill you in if she feels it's necessary." Grant smiled at the girl's annoyed expression. "Sorry."

Cindilee rolled her eyes and picked up her nail file. "Whatever."

Grant checked his watch, and about a minute later Paulette came bustling toward him.

"Here I am, Sheriff," she announced with a twirl and a flourish. "What can I do for you?"

"Cindilee." Grant looked at her and gestured at the fax. Cindilee scowled and practically threw the paper at him. "Thank you." She gave him a snide smile, stood, and walked away. Grant chuckled to himself and handed the picture to Paulette.

"Who is this?" she asked. "Certainly is a looker." She squinted and read the caption Roberta had typed across the bottom. "Armed and dangerous?" She looked at Grant. "Are you serious? He looks like JFK, Junior."

"And *that* is what makes him all the more lethal," Grant replied. "Ted Bundy was supposedly a handsome guy, too, and look how *he* turned out."

Paulette tapped her index finger against her chin as she scrutinized the image. "I suppose appearances *can* be deceiving." Bleached blonde brows rose. "Point in case, who ever knew you could dance? I couldn't believe that was you last night, waltzing around with that pretty young woman whose car broke down."

He smiled. "Yes, that was me, but I didn't come here to talk about my performance last evening." He pointed to Mayfield's face. "This guy is stalking that pretty young woman whose car broke down. Her name is Juliet Hall." He looked around, leaned closer, and lowered his voice. He knew he was being a little melodramatic, but that was Paulette's style and she lapped it up like a cat would cream. Her eyes widened and she leaned in as he said, "He's already been tried for the murder of one young woman, he's the prime suspect in the death of another girl, and the police in Seattle think he may be on his way here."

"Why would he come *here*?"

"Because he wants Miss Hall. He's been stalking her for over a year now, and the second woman he killed was Juliet's sister. Juliet found the body."

Paulette gaped at him. "Oh, my. How awful for her, the poor girl." Her brows drew together. "If they think he murdered Miss Hall's sister, why wasn't he arrested?"

"They can't prove he did it." Grant stared hard at her. "If this guy *does* come here, I need to know about it, preferably *before* he can get to Juliet."

Paulette's eyes narrowed and a meaningful smile brightened her face. "You want me to get the word out."

Grant didn't bother to deny it. "I do."

"And would it be better that Miss Hall *not* hear about this?"

He hadn't considered that, and his gut twisted as he realized what he'd just unwittingly done. If word spread through town, Juliet was bound to hear *something*, and the thought of the kind of pain that would cause her made him grit his teeth. Now he wished he hadn't been so quick to enlist Paulette's help, but he couldn't un-ring the bell.

"It would be preferable, yes," he said with a resigned sigh. "And if you could keep the details that involve Juliet to yourself, I'd really appreciate it. I don't want to traumatize her any more than she's already been."

Paulette patted his arm. "Relax, Sheriff. This town may run on gossip, but the people who live here are, for the most part, a caring, compassionate group. No one wants to hurt our lovely visitor, especially if she can get *you* to dance, so I'll make sure to keep her name out of my broadcast." She gave him a pointed look. "Still, even if people don't know about her they're going to know about Mayfield, and she could overhear them talking about *him*."

"I know." Grant rubbed a hand over his face. "I'm going to speak with her, let her know what's happening so there aren't any *nastier* surprises. If she knows we have her back, maybe that'll ease the sting some."

Paulette gave him a nod. "Hopefully." She leaned behind the reception counter, ripped a piece of Scotch tape from a dispenser, and taped the fax to the backside of the counter where Cindilee and the rest of the staff would see it, but customers wouldn't. "Rest easy, Sheriff. I will not let you down."

***

Juliet walked into Autumn's Diner just after 12:30 p.m. after she and Nicole had pulled the final tray of croissants from the oven and beignets from the fryer. The café was about three-quarters full, and to her surprise Autumn was alone on the floor. The woman darted about like a hummingbird, and Juliet eased onto a stool at the counter. Autumn fluttered past her to return a pot of coffee to the drip machine, and her dark eyes widened.

"Oh, goodness," Autumn said. She glanced at the clock and pulled plates from beneath the heat lamps as the cook slid them toward her. "I'm afraid our lunch date is going to have to wait for a bit. I'm a little behind here."

"Where's Shelby?"

Autumn arranged the plates on a tray. "Shelby is at her final dress fitting, Lucinda called in sick, and my other waitress, Kelly, isn't answering her phone." She flashed a smile as she lifted the tray and rested it on her slender shoulder. "It's just me."

Juliet immediately slid off the stool. "Do you have an extra order pad and an apron?"

Autumn paused and gave her a once-over, her full lips pursed and one brow arched. It was the same expression she'd worn when they'd first met. "Girlfriend, I can take one look at you and tell you're not a waitress."

Juliet smiled. "Do you have an extra order pad and an apron? Unless, of course, you *like* doing everything by yourself?"

Autumn narrowed her eyes on her, and Juliet could almost hear the inner debate. Finally, Autumn sighed. "Underneath the cash register. You can put your purse there."

Juliet nodded and moved behind the counter. As Autumn said there was a stack of aprons and order pads beneath the register, and Juliet tossed her purse onto the bottom shelf. After tying the apron around her waist and pulling her hair into a ponytail, she grabbed a pad and pencil. Autumn brushed past her to grab a large pitcher of iced tea at the same moment the cook slid better than half a dozen plates beneath the warming lights.

"Where do these go?" Juliet asked.

Autumn glanced up, and then returned to filling empty tea glasses at the counter. "The three on the right go to table one, the booth in the far corner on the window. The other four go to table six, back wall underneath that big landscape. The guys at the tables will let you know whose is whose."

Juliet grabbed a tray and started arranging plates. She hadn't been a waitress by choice, but after the ballet company let her go Cassie had gotten her a job at the bistro where she worked part-time. Dancers often had to supplement their incomes, especially when they were just starting out with a company, and while Juliet had chosen to teach private dance lessons to make ends meet before becoming a principal dancer, Cassie had chosen something as far from dancing as she could find. After the bistro hired Juliet the sisters often worked together, and it was one of the only things that made the job bearable for her. Truthfully, she hated waitressing, but at the time she'd had little choice. The company had chosen not to renew her contract for the new season, and although it had hurt she had understood why. Between Mayfield's disruptions of rehearsals and performances and the physical toll that had left her pretty much unable to dance, she was surprised they'd let her stay as long as they had. And then there was the fact that Mayfield's father was a patron of the ballet. The company had had to choose between keeping her and keeping one of their primary financial supporters. She'd lost that fight.

Juliet brushed those memories aside and approached the first table. The men seated there looked surprised to see her, but as soon as she smiled and said, "Okay, fellas, I'm new here so you're going to have to help me out. Who gets what?" they warmed up. She delivered their food then set out for the next table, the tray balanced overhead. Autumn's gaze found her frequently, but Juliet just smiled at her and kept working.

She was taking an order for an elderly couple and their grandchildren when the bell on the door tinkled. Juliet glanced over her shoulder and her breath caught when Grant walked in, sliding his hat off as he did so. Their eyes met and his brows shot north. Juliet gave him a jaunty grin and turned her attention back to her customers.

"Oh," the elderly gentleman said, "make sure you tell that cook I want my burger well done, *not* burnt."

Juliet made a note of that and gave the man a smile. "Absolutely. I don't want you eating burnt burgers today, or any other day for that matter."

"Thank you, dear."

"You bet."

She made her way behind the counter, put her order in, and then filled several glasses with ice. Grant was right behind her, seated at the counter, and she felt his gaze as if it were his hands moving over her and not his eyes. The sensation made goose bumps fan over her skin and set her heart to thumping a little harder than normal.

"What did I miss?" he asked.

Juliet started pouring drinks, and tossed him a glance over her shoulder. "Miss? What do you mean?" His needs-a-warning-label smile made warmth shoot through her and she bit the inside of her lip.

"Did you get a job here between last night and today?"

She arranged the full glasses on her tray and lifted it. "Autumn was short-handed. Should I have just sat on my butt and let her scramble when I could help?"

A strange expression crossed his face as she walked away with her beverages and she saw him pull his cell phone from his pocket. He started texting, but she didn't have time to ask him what was going on. She had customers to take care of.

By the time she returned to the counter the rush seemed to be waning. She grabbed a pitcher of tea and water and made the rounds, then did the same with coffee and decaf. Once that was finished, she took a breath and looked around. Autumn gave her a thumbs up from across the restaurant and mouthed, "Thank you." Juliet nodded and smiled.

She turned to Grant. "So, Sheriff, what can I get you?"

"Nothing." He leaned back on his stool, his gun belt squeaking softly. "I'm waiting for my lunch date."

Juliet fought a grin. "Really? Is she late?"

Those beautiful lips curved into a soft, sensual smile, his chocolate-brown eyes twinkling. "She is."

Juliet grabbed a glass, filled it halfway with ice, and then poured in iced tea. After adding a wedge of lemon she placed it in front of him. "And just how long are you going to wait for her?"

That smile widened, slowly. "Oh, I don't know. I have the strangest feeling I've been waiting for her for a very long time, and an even stranger feeling that she's well worth the wait." His gaze traveled from the top of her head to her feet and back, their eyes locking. "My dad always said there was nothing wrong with waiting on a woman."

Her heart somersaulted and a flush crept up her neck. Before she could say anything the door signaled another customer, and Juliet gave him an apologetic smile as she darted away, thankful for the reprieve. A petite blonde and a girl of about Shelby's age with neon streaks in her dark hair slid into a booth near the window and Juliet approached them with a smile and a pair of menus.

"Afternoon, ladies. I'm Juliet. Can I get you something to drink?"

"Coffee, please, with cream," the blonde woman replied. Her gaze was oddly forthright, even assessing, and Juliet had the strangest feeling she was being measured for something, but she had no idea what. She turned to the brunette.

"And for you?"

The younger woman gave her a sullen look. "Coke."

Juliet jotted that down. "You got it. I'll be right back."

She poured the coffee and the soft drink, retrieving a saucer filled with tiny half-and-half cups from one of the under-the-counter refrigerators. She was acutely aware of Grant's gaze, and she bit the inside of her lip again to keep from smiling. It didn't work. Pleasurable tingles radiated through her and she flashed him a grin as she walked past. He returned it.

When she placed the newcomers' drinks in front of them, Autumn appeared at her side and leaned an arm along the booth behind the blonde.

"Afternoon Paulette," Autumn said, giving the blonde's shoulders a quick squeeze. She looked at the younger woman and smiled, but the warmth stopped just short of her dark eyes. "Cindilee. I see you've both met Juliet."

Juliet recognized Paulette's name and realized the woman with the too-blonde curls was the CEO of Evergreen's gossip network. Having dealt with her share of gossipmongers, she knew enough to keep her smile firmly in place and her mouth shut.

"I have," Paulette said, giving her another lengthy inspection. "You're the young lady whose car broke down, isn't that right?"

"Yes, ma'am," Juliet replied. She snuck a glance at Autumn, who smiled and gave her a wink. "That's me, the woman whose car broke down."

"So, you're just . . . passing through."

"I . . . I suppose I am."

Paulette glanced around the diner. "And yet, you're . . . waitressing?"

Autumn jumped on that. "Lucinda called in sick and I couldn't reach Kelly," she said, placing a hand on Juliet's shoulder. "Juliet just grabbed an apron and an order pad and jumped in. I'd still be drowning if it weren't for her."

"Nonsense." Juliet shook her head. "You weren't drowning, just . . . a little behind."

Autumn laughed. "Right, if by *behind* you mean half the room hadn't ordered and the other half wasn't getting their food." The cook barked out something unintelligible and Autumn glanced his way. "That's my cue. Paulette, Cindilee, enjoy your lunch. Thank you again, Juliet. You *cannot* leave before we have a chance to talk." Autumn pointed a delicate finger in her face and gave her a warning look, but there was a smile beneath it and Juliet smiled back.

"I wouldn't do that." She watched Autumn as the woman darted away, and then focused on Paulette and Cindilee. "Now, are you ladies ready to order, or do you need a few more minutes?"

"Oh, we're ready," Paulette said. She glanced around Juliet toward Grant and a smile slowly blossomed. "We're more than ready."

She took their order and made her way back to counter. After placing the order she refilled Grant's iced tea and took a deep breath. "Well, it seems the storm has passed."

"And it seems you have weathered it just fine," Grant said as he lifted his glass to his mouth. He took a long drink and his gaze flicked over her. "What other talents do you possess, Miss Hall?"

She leaned her elbows on the counter. "Maybe you'll just have to find out for yourself, Sheriff."

His expression sobered. "Maybe you need to hang around long enough for me to do that." A shadow of something she couldn't define passed behind his eyes and he looked down at his tea. "How much longer do you think Autumn will need you?"

Juliet felt his withdrawal and a flicker of uneasiness shivered up her spine. "I don't know. Let me ask her."

"Ask me what?"

Juliet turned and looked down at the petite beauty. "How much longer do you want me to stay? I can stay as long as you need me."

Autumn looked around then gave her a sunny smile. "I think we're good, Juliet. You can retire your apron and order pad. And I'll take care of Paulette and Cindilee."

"What about the dinner rush later?"

"I'm closing at three today," Autumn replied. "Remember? The festival?"

Juliet nodded. "That's right. Nicole said it was New Orleans night."

Autumn grinned. "And I have some jambalaya and gumbo I have to put the finishing touches on before this evening's festivities." She put an arm around Juliet's waist and gave her a squeeze. "Thanks again, girlfriend. Sorry we couldn't have lunch." Her eyes widened. "Oh, I have to pay you for what you did today. How much did you make in tips? If anyone shorted you I'll have a talk with them."

Juliet slipped her arm around the shorter woman's shoulders and squeezed back. "I don't know how much I made in tips and you don't have to pay me anything. I was glad to help, and we can have lunch tomorrow."

Autumn pulled back and looked at her. "Are you going to *be* here tomorrow?"

Juliet thought about it for a few moments, then shrugged and smiled. "I just may be." She slid a glance toward Grant. "We'll see."

Autumn looked between the two of them and then chuckled softly. With a shake of her head she released Juliet and patted Grant's cheek. "Work your magic, Sheriff. Maybe you can talk her into staying permanently." She tossed Juliet a grin as she walked away. "There will be a job here for her if you do."

Speechless, Juliet stared after her for several moments and then turned to face Grant. He was watching her closely and her throat clogged with emotion. Never in her life had she met a more genuine, generous group of people, people who welcomed her with open arms, offering friendship and inviting her to stay. Autumn's simple statement told her that even though she was a virtual stranger they cared about her. She knew it. She *felt* it. She stared at Grant and the obstruction in her esophagus grew. *They're not the only ones who care. I care, too.* Then a shadow danced behind his eyes and that clot of emotion morphed into something cold and apprehensive. She gulped, bit her lip, and took a breath, her hands clasped tightly in front of her. "Well, then. I guess we can have lunch now."

He gave her a small smile, but it was different from his usual smile. There was tension behind this one, as if he was forcing it. Her uncertainty grew but she choked it down. If he wanted to tell her what was bothering him he would and if not, she had no right to pry. A few more seconds ticked off before he stood and gestured toward the door.

"I thought we could have lunch in the park," he said as he waited for her to precede him. "Pizza okay with you?"

Juliet stopped and looked at him over her shoulder. "Pizza? In the park? Are you having it delivered to the gazebo or something?"

This time his smile was genuine. "Unless you don't like pizza."

"Who doesn't like pizza?" She continued walking, not at all surprised when he moved past her to open the diner's door. "Thank you," she said as she stepped onto the sidewalk. "I've just never had pizza delivered to a gazebo in the middle of the park before."

"Well, since there is only one gazebo and one park in Evergreen, I think the pizza guy will be able to handle it without needing a GPS." He chuckled and offered her his arm, which she took. "If that meets with your approval, we shall proceed."

He waited until she nodded before walking her across the street. There were even more people in the park than there had been yesterday, and the energy of it seeped into her.

"This place really *is* the heart of Evergreen," she commented. They ducked as a Frisbee whizzed by their heads and Juliet laughed. "Wow. That was close."

"Sorry, Sheriff!"

Grant laughed softly and they continued their leisurely walk. When they reached the gazebo he led her up the steps and released her. She eased down on the top stair and looked up at him as he pulled out his phone and dialed.

"Yeah, Marco, you can deliver that pizza now. Thanks." He hung up and sat beside her. "Should only be a few minutes."

"I'm sure I'll survive," she said with a wry twist of her lips. "After all the croissants I had this morning *skipping* the pizza is probably a better idea."

"But you cannot live on croissants alone." He closed his eyes and turned his face to the sun. "Besides, after you get your car back you can drive out to my place and go running with me in the morning." One eye opened a fraction. "Or I could come here and dance with you?"

"And whatever would Paulette say?" She rolled her eyes. "You do know that our little waltz last night is the talk of the town."

"I do." He chuckled. "Paulette certainly works fast."

"No, Grant." Juliet pulled her knees to her chest and looked at him out of the corner of her eye. "Nicole mentioned it to me before I even made it to my room last night."

His eyes widened. "What?"

She nodded. "I ran into her in the hallway, and she already knew." She pursed her lips. "Paulette doesn't work *fast*, Grant. She works at the speed of *light*."

Grant exhaled slowly and leaned back on his hands. "Damn."

"Yeah. Wish my cell phone network had that sort of power."

"No doubt."

At that moment a middle-aged man with a bald, shiny skull and an even shinier smile approached them, a pizza box in one hand and a plastic bag with a two-liter bottle of soda, plastic cups, and napkins in the other. He was a few inches shorter than Grant but probably 30 pounds heavier, a white chef's apron tied around his rounded middle. Sharp dark eyes looked at her from beneath bushy brows, his round face folding into pleasant creases as his smile widened. He had beefy arms and large, meaty hands that looked like they could break a person's fingers with little effort. Without the smile he would look every inch the Mob muscleman. The image of him dressed in a pin-striped suit and a fedora with a gun on his hip while twirling pizza dough over his head almost made her laugh.

"Marco," Grant said as he rose and descended the stairs. "That was fast. Thank you, my friend."

"Anytime, Grant." He handed off his burdens and rested meaty hands on his hips. "So, this is your dance partner, eh?" He did a vertical scan and gave Grant an approving look. "You certainly have a good eye." He turned to her and held out a hand. "Afternoon, miss. I'm Marco Angeletti, but you can call me Marco. I own the pizza joint, obviously. It's nice to finally meet the woman everyone is talking about."

Juliet chuckled and shook the man's hand. "It's nice to meet you, Marco. You can call me Juliet."

His eyes lit up. "Ah, a Capulet, eh?" He gave Grant a sly glance. "That make you Romeo, Sheriff?"

Grant put the pizza and bag down close to Juliet and looked at the man in mock annoyance. "Of course it does, because around here it won't matter if I deny it." He took his wallet from his back pocket but Marco put a hand on his arm.

"This one's on the house," Marco said. "Thanks for that e-mail this morning, by the way. I always enjoy a good joke."

The two men exchanged a look that was lost on her.

"Thanks, again," Grant said. "I appreciate it."

"Anytime, Grant. Anytime." Marco turned to her and gave her a wave. "Glad to meet you, Juliet. Hopefully I'll see you around again."

"Well, if you're going to be at the festival tonight you will," Juliet replied. "I'll be helping Miss Nicole."

"Then I will stop by." Marco rubbed his belly. "I need a few more of Miss Nicole's beignets to round out my girlish figure." He gave them a salute and turned. "Enjoy your lunch."

Chapter Nine

Juliet watched Marco go and turned when she heard the rustle of plastic. Grant pulled the soda bottle and cups out of the bag and put them on the wooden floor of the gazebo. He twisted the cap off the bottle and filled both their cups, then gave her a handful of napkins and opened the pizza box.

"Dig in," he said. "Marco makes some of the best pizza I've ever had."

Juliet hesitated and took a drink of her soda instead. Something in the tone of his voice set off alarms in her head, but to look at him nothing appeared amiss. She shook it off and took a piece of pizza.

They ate in silence, and after the second enormous, delicious piece she could eat no more. She leaned against the baluster and sipped her drink slowly. Grant had a third and then a fourth piece, and when he looked at her he seemed surprised to find her watching him. There was a flash of what she clearly recognized as guilt in his eyes before he turned his face away. She was really familiar with that expression because she'd seen that look on Detective Riordan's face, and her own, more times than she could count.

"Okay, what's going on?" she asked at last. She put her cup aside and sat Indian style, leaning toward him. When he turned his eyes back to her the guilt was gone.

"What do you mean?" he asked.

Juliet knew what she'd seen and something cold congealed in her belly. "You're acting weird, apprehensive, like a teenager who crashed mommy and daddy's car and doesn't want to tell them."

He stared at her for several long, silent moments then said, "I crashed your car and I don't want to tell you."

She lifted one brow and pursed her lips as she leaned back against the baluster and crossed her arms over her chest. Grant exhaled slowly and tossed the half-eaten slice of pizza back into the box. Almost half a minute passed before he finally spoke, and when he did his voice was low but clear.

"I spoke to Detective Riordan."

It took her brain a second to process that, and when it did that cold thing in her gut tripled in size. "Wh-what? When?"

"Yesterday, after I dropped you at Autumn's."

That hit her like a brick. Synapses were crackling and firing off until she thought she could smell the smoke. She closed her eyes against the onslaught of memories and emotions that boiled up and threatened to choke her. Finally, she gasped out, "Why?"

He sighed. "When Eddie called in to say he had your car hooked up and was heading back he mentioned the tags were expired. I have an overzealous deputy who ran the plates through the computer and your name flagged the system with instructions to call Seattle PD."

Realization that he'd known about Cassie almost as long as she'd known him and said nothing sent the sharp blade of betrayal scoring through her with cutting precision. It was ridiculous, because he hadn't betrayed her, but logic didn't figure in at the moment. Then another insight hit her, and that blade carved straight through her heart. Her eyes snapped open and she slowly gained her feet, her gaze locked with his.

"So *that's* why," she whispered, cold shafts of pain impaling her.

Grant stood and his brows drew together. "Why what?"

"Why you're spending so much time with me," she replied from between clenched teeth. "Let me guess. He asked you to *keep an eye* on me, try to get me to hang around so he could catch up and convince me to return to police custody."

His eyes flashed and he set his jaw. "That is *not*—"

"So he *didn't* ask?" Juliet interrupted.

"He did." He scowled darkly. "I said *no*." He stepped over the pizza box to stand toe to toe with her, and now the guilt she'd seen in those usually smiling eyes had been replaced with anger. "I already told you . . . I don't do anything I don't *want* to do. If I didn't *want* to spend time with you I'd just assign one of my deputies to follow you around, and I sure as *hell* wouldn't be trying to get you to stay longer."

They battled visually and she felt the rage draining from him. His expression changed to one of regret and frustration, and he planted his fists on his hips.

"The last thing I want to do is hurt you, Juliet, but I'm not going to lie to you. You have a right to know what's happening, no matter how much you may hate me for it."

That dark mist of apprehension she'd experienced the night she'd found Cassie wrapped her in a deceptively transparent embrace before it hardened and tightened around her chest. Her breathing was short, shallow, her lungs barely able to expand. She backed away from him and felt the railing of the gazebo in the small of her back. "What are you talking about?" He took a step toward her, and while she wanted to retreat there was nowhere to go unless she wanted to jump the railing.

"Detective Riordan is taking a redeye from Seattle. He'll be here in the morning."

A contradictory mix of emotions that ran both hot and cold, blended inside her and a wave of nausea burgeoned. Juliet turned her back to him, grasping the railing for support. Anger, sorrow, frustration, and despair curdled in her belly. She gazed over the idyllic scene that was Evergreen Springs and wished with everything inside her that it could be isolated and protected from her life, that somehow her past would be forced to stay outside the city limits. She'd been able to forget while she was here and wrapped in the warm, welcoming embrace of the people she'd met. Unfortunately, life by definition couldn't stay in the past, and the one person she could never get away from was herself. She fought to escape the dread that wanted to suck her into its black vortex and suffocate her, forcing her lungs to expand as she took several deep, necessary breaths.

"I spoke to Eddie a little while ago," Grant said softly, "and he said the hose should be in by three. If you want to head out, your car will be ready to go by about 3:30."

The words popped out before they even registered in her brain. "I don't want to go."

"And I don't want you to." Grant put strong but gentle hands on her shoulders and turned her to face him. When she wouldn't look at him he cupped her chin and tipped her face up. "There's more I need to tell you."

All Juliet could do was nod once. Grant sighed and let go of her long enough to lace his fingers through hers.

"Seattle PD has had George Mayfield under surveillance since Cassie's murder, but about a month ago he gave them the slip." Her eyes flew to his face and he sighed. "They don't know where he is, but Riordan is convinced he's looking for you."

Dread experienced a surge of strength and she felt the whirlpool open up beneath her feet. She tightened her grip on his hands as her knees wobbled. "Oh, God," she whispered. "If he comes here . . . ." Tears welled as she pictured Mayfield doing to her new friends what he'd done to Cassie. She squeezed her eyes shut and dropped to her knees. Grant went with her and pulled her against his chest as her fingers curled into his shirt.

"If he comes here," he said in a low, firm voice, "I'll know about it before he takes two steps across the county line." His hands rubbed slowly up and down her back. "This morning I had my dispatcher fax and e-mail copies of Mayfield's picture to everyone with a fax machine or computer in Evergreen Springs and the rest of the county. My deputies are aware and on the lookout, and I even enlisted Paulette to help spread the word." He pulled back a bit and cupped her head in his hands. "I will *not* let him hurt you, Juliet, do you understand me?"

"But what if he hurts someone else?" she cried, tears sliding unheeded down her cheeks. "If someone here got hurt because of *me*. . .?" That blade pressed deeper into her heart muscle, slicing it cleanly down the middle. The pain was so hot and sharp and intense she nearly doubled over. "If Autumn or Nicole or Shelby got hurt because Mayfield followed me here I'd never forgive myself."

Grant pulled her back into his embrace and wrapped his arms around her. "He's not going to hurt *anyone* here. If George Mayfield comes to Evergreen, trust me when I say *he's* in far more danger than anyone else in town." He pressed a kiss to her temple. "I can pretty much guarantee there's at least one gun beneath every counter of every business here, probably more than one. And, unlike a lot of you city folk, we actually *fire* our weapons." He took a deep breath and ran a hand over her hair. "He gets within 20 feet of you, if *I* don't put a bullet between his eyes someone else *will*."

Tears continued to flow and she looked up at him. "You have no idea how evil that man is," she whispered. "He's not . . . *human*."

Grant framed her face. "I know *exactly* how evil he is. I read the file and saw the crime-scene photographs." He sighed as his thumbs stroked over the tracks of her tears. "And when you've watched a mother hide explosives in her baby's stroller, put the baby in the stroller, and then approach a column of unsuspecting Marines, you learn to identify evil pretty quickly."

Juliet sucked in a breath and searched his eyes. She recognized the regret and the resolve reflected in those warm, brown pools. "Oh, Grant."

"If you want to go I completely understand," he said softly, "but if you stay I promise you you'll be safe." He stood and pulled her with him, looping his arms around her waist. "And if you don't want to talk to Detective Riordan, you don't have to."

Juliet squeezed her eyes shut as she remembered the last time she'd spoken to the detective. It hadn't been a pleasant conversation, and she had vented all of her fury and anguish on him. He'd taken her attack in stride. He'd never once raised his voice, argued with her, or fought back, as if he felt he deserved her venom for what Mayfield had done to Cassie. She knew she'd been unfair to the man and that he didn't deserve the blame she'd placed on him. The thought of seeing him again made her insides curl up in shame.

"I *don't* want to see him," she said, "but not for the reason you think."

"It doesn't matter why."

Suddenly it was all too much. Juliet turned away from him. He stayed where he was, she could feel him, but he made no attempt to touch her. "I need . . . I need to think." She wrapped her arms around herself. "Thanks for lunch, Grant. I'll see you later tonight."

When she started to walk away his voice stopped her.

"Let me walk you . . . wherever it is you're going."

She looked over her shoulder at him and his expression tore at her heart. The silent apology in his gaze sent tears stinging again and she looked away with a quick shake of her head. "I'd like to be alone for a bit." Her voice caught and she dropped her chin. "I'm sorry."

"You have nothing to be sorry for," he replied softly. There was a long pause, and then he said, "I'll see you this evening."

Blinking rapidly she nodded once and started walking.

When she entered the hotel Nicole was sitting behind the front desk talking on the phone. She smiled warmly and raised a hand. Juliet forced a quick smile and bounded up the stairs. Once inside her room she started pacing, her chest heaving with anxiety. She chewed her thumbnail, her body vibrating with restrained frustration. An outlet for all this simmering emotion was what she needed; a place she could forget about what was happening to her life and just *be*. Walking toward the bed her gaze fell on Cassie's picture.

You know what you need to do, Jules. It's what you always do when you're upset.

"And where would you suggest I do it, Cass?"

The yellow pages may give you a clue.

Juliet looked at the narrow writing desk against the wall by the bathroom. In the center drawer was a phone book, one of the smallest she'd ever seen in her life. She walked over to the desk, opened the drawer, pulled the book out, and flipped to the page for health clubs. There were two listings. One advertised a boxing type gym, while the other was a higher-end facility with an aerobics room. It was the 'aerobics room' that caught her eye. From the map shown in the ad the club was only about a mile away.

She changed her clothes, tossed her toe-shoes, a hand towel, and her cell phone in a workout bag, and left her room. As she descended the stairs she heard Nicole ending her phone call and quickened her steps. She wasn't fast enough.

"Oh, Juliet, where are you off to, dear?"

She didn't want to tell the older woman but she couldn't be rude to her. "I thought I'd go out and get some fresh air, enjoy the sunshine before the festival this evening. I've been eating so much since I got here that I figured a little exercise was in order."

Nicole smiled. "Good for you." She leaned her elbows on the marble counter. "Do you still want to help me with the booth this evening? You don't have to, you know. After all, you're a guest, not an employee."

"Oh, no, I *want* to." Juliet walked toward the door and looked at her over her shoulder. "Don't worry, Miss Nicole, I'll be back in time to help you set up."

"And I'll set aside a couple of beignets for you."

Juliet flashed the older woman a grin and stepped outside.

It took her about twenty minutes to walk to the health club, and thankfully the streets away from the main square were nearly empty. When she walked through the front doors of Evergreen Fitness and Racquet Club she was surprised at how modern the place was. For being located in a small town, the club had even more modern equipment than the gym she'd used back in Seattle. But, it wasn't the machines or weights she had come for. Pasting a friendly smile on her face she walked to the desk.

"Excuse me."

A young man who appeared to be in his mid-twenties put his fitness magazine aside and rose. He was close to six feet tall and well-muscled, and a smile warmed his face as he approached her.

"Afternoon, miss, I'm Eric. How can I help you?"

"Your advertisement said you had an aerobics room."

He nodded. "We do, but there aren't any classes right now. Our last aerobics instructor moved to Salt Lake and we haven't been able to find anyone to replace her."

Juliet smiled. "Good. I'm not interested in a class. I'm interested in using the room. How much?"

His eyes narrowed on her face. "You're the woman whose car broke down."

Juliet fought to not roll her eyes and forced a smile. "Yes, that's me. My name is Juliet, and I'd like to use the aerobics room, provided it's big enough."

Eric walked out from behind the counter and gestured to his left. "Well, let's go take a look. If it suits you, I'll give you an introductory pass for $20."

Juliet followed behind the man as he wound his way through the various machines. "And what does an introductory pass get me?"

"Unlimited use of the facilities for a month," Eric replied, giving her a salesman's grin over his shoulder. "Now, I can't guarantee you'll have sole use of the room, a lot of our members use the aerobics room to stretch before or after their workouts, but for the most part it sits empty."

"That's a shame," Juliet said.

"Yes, it is."

She followed him down a narrow hall past the locker rooms. The corridor ended at a large glass double-door, the same type used in department stores. Eric pushed it open and held it for her. Once she was inside he faced away from her.

"Welcome to 1500 square feet of aerobics and dance paradise." He threw his arms wide and gave her that jaunty grin. "The entire room was redone last year: floor, walls, sound system, and lighting, all of it. We have everything one could need for a full body, aerobic workout." He gestured to the racks of hand weights against one wall. Next to the rack was a stack of yoga mats and a cylindrical container with weighted bars used for upper body exercise. But, what caught Juliet's attention was the barre. All four walls were mirrored from floor to ceiling, but the wall with the door had a ballet barre that ran the entire length of the room, broken only by the door itself. There was also a portable barre that could be moved around the room as needed. Juliet leaned over and ran a hand over the floor.

"The floor is specially designed for dancing and aerobics," Eric said, his hands clasped neatly in front of him. He walked toward a cabinet in the corner. "Here is the sound system. It can use CDs, or there is a docking port for an iPod, iPhone, or an MP3. The lighting controls are just behind you."

Juliet glanced over her shoulder at the bank of light switches. She dropped her bag and did a few preliminary turns and a leap, liking the way the floor absorbed the shock, as it should. "Do you allow the use of rosin?"

Eric nodded and pointed down at the floor next to the sound cabinet. A square, squat wooden box sat there. "It's empty now, but I can get you some if you need it."

"I have some, but thanks." Juliet looked around once more and then gave him a smile. "It's perfect. Where do I sign up for this introductory pass?"

***

Grant was just finishing up some paperwork at his desk when his cell phone rang. He glanced at the display, hoping it would be Juliet, and was mildly concerned when he saw Nicole's caller ID.

"Miss Nicole," he said, "what can I do for you this fine afternoon? Are you about ready for the festival?"

"I am." Nicole paused and cleared her throat. "Grant, have you seen or spoken to Juliet since the two of you had lunch?"

Something in his gut tightened. "No. Why, is something wrong?"

Nicole sighed. "I don't know. She took off out of here shortly after two o'clock and said she'd be back to help me set up."

Grant glanced at his watch. "It's nearly five."

"I know. That's why I called. I was hoping she was with you." There was a brief pause, and Grant could almost smell the woman's fear through the phone line. "What if . . . what if that Mayfield person managed to sneak into town?"

Grant closed his eyes and pinched the bridge of his nose. "Boy, Paulette works fast."

"Actually, I got the story from Roberta, not Paulette." Nicole paused and sighed. "I called her when I got the e-mail and she told me what was going on. I guess she figured Mike and I should know because we're the only hotel in the area." She chuckled. "Paulette is actually telling people that Mayfield is wanted for murder and was last seen in Helena heading this way. She's leaving Juliet out of it."

Grant sat straight up in his seat. "She is?"

Nicole laughed. "Yes, Grant. When I talked to her she was still amazed that a city girl would just jump in to help someone like Juliet did with Autumn. It's convenient that Paulette decided to have lunch at that particular time."

"Yes, it is." Grant heaved an inward sigh of relief and then refocused on the reason for Nicole's call. "Now tell me exactly what Juliet said when she left."

***

Music poured through the wall-mounted speakers, bathing the room in waves of Tchaikovsky. She was drenched in sweat but she felt good, her body moving in perfect time to the music. A glance in the mirror showed her that several gym-goers were watching from the doorway, but no one had stepped foot inside the aerobics room. Juliet blocked them out and focused on what she was doing.

Her cell phone had more than an hour of classical numbers from various ballets she'd danced in, and she was nearing the end of her second time through the playlist. Her muscles were fatigued, her breathing heavy, and her left pointe shoe was starting to break down, but she kept going. When she danced everything else melted away. Nothing existed but her, the music, and, on occasion, her partner. Today she needed to disappear, more than almost any other time in her life.

The song ended and the next track immediately started playing. Juliet had done Swan Lake more times than she could count, and the final solo as Odette was second nature. The sound of violins and the crash of cymbals wrapped around her, as if she was part of the music and not just another puppet manipulated by its beauty. It vibrated and echoed inside her, through her, until she felt its imprint on her soul. She fluttered and leapt and spun, and when the final strains faded out tears stung. She'd almost forgotten how much she loved what she did.

She held the ending pose until the playlist started back at track one. Juliet grabbed her hand towel from the barre and walked over to the sound system. After disconnecting her cell phone from the port she tossed it in her bag and wiped the sweat from her brow and chest. She heard the sound of a single person's applause and turned to give the gym-goer a mocking bow. When she saw Grant standing there she froze.

She stared at him for a few moments then shook herself and straightened, winding the towel around her neck. "How long have you been there?"

"A while," he replied. He glanced over his shoulder and gave her that smile. "Sorry if I scared off the rest of your audience."

Juliet took several deep, slow breaths. "Why are you here?"

He took a couple steps into the room and let the door close behind him. "Nicole called me. Said you ran out just after two and hadn't been back yet. She was worried."

Juliet glanced at the clock on the wall and groaned. "Oh, damn it. I promised to help her set up for the festival."

"That's *not* why she was worried." He chuckled. "She was worried that perhaps Mayfield had slipped into town unnoticed."

Juliet sank down on the ground and started to stretch. "Great. So now the *entire* town knows."

Grant crouched down a few feet away. "Not exactly. Roberta thought Nicole and Mike should know because they're the only lodging in town. Paulette is telling a different tale."

"And what's that?" Juliet fanned her legs out into a straddle split and leaned over, laying her chest and stomach flat on the floor, her knees pointing toward the ceiling. She rested her cheek on the backs of her hands and looked at him. To her surprise, his eyes remained glued to her face.

"Apparently, the wire is abuzz with talk of a man wanted for a double murder out of Seattle who was last seen in Helena headed this way. Authorities think he's on his way to Canada."

She rose up onto her elbows. "No mention of me?"

Grant shook his head. "Nope."

"How did you accomplish *that?*"

"I didn't." Grant gave her a pointed look. "*You* did."

Juliet straightened and switched into a front split. "Me? What are you talking about?"

He rubbed his chin then rested his elbows on his knees. "Well, I asked Paulette to leave you out of her broadcast, and she said she would, but I figured if she *knew* you, if she *liked* you, she'd have more incentive to keep that promise." He shrugged. "I had been wracking my brains all morning trying to figure out how I was going to get Paulette to like you, but when I walked into Autumn's you solved my problem for me."

She switched legs. "So *that's* who you were texting."

A grin tugged at his mouth. "Told her there was something at Autumn's she needed to see."

Leaning into the stretch, she laid her chest on her thigh. "I just did what anyone else would have done."

He chuckled. "Funny, but I didn't see anyone else leaving their seat to help Autumn."

Her brows drew together and she looked at him. "Now that you mention it, you're right. What's up with that?"

"Well, unlike you city folk," he drawled, "people around here aren't in such a hurry. If Autumn is behind it just means they'll have to wait longer to order and get their food, but that's okay with them. They're not going to yell or get rude or dock her tip because of it."

Juliet snorted, grabbed an ankle, and rolled onto her back, keeping her leg against her chest, her foot over her head. "Wish everyone was like that." She glanced at him again but his eyes were still on her face.

Wow. You're twisting yourself up like a pretzel and he's not biting. I'm impressed.

Pushing Cassie's voice out of her head she changed legs and met his gaze. "So, now what?"

"As soon as you're done stretching I'll take you back to the hotel," he replied, straightening. "After that, it's up to you what you do, but I have to be in the park by six."

Juliet released the stretch and stood. Moving to the barre, she reached behind her, grabbed an ankle, and pulled until her foot was over her head again. Then she leaned forward, extending the stretch past 180 degrees, and glanced at him when he sucked in a breath.

"Yikes. How do you *do* that?"

He looked to be in pain and she chuckled. "*Lots* of practice."

"Does it hurt?"

"No." She shook her head. "If it hurts it means I'm doing something wrong."

"Well . . . it *looks* like it hurts."

She watched him as she released her leg and did the same with the other. He winced, but that was the only reaction she got. *Hmm. Not a single rude remark or comment. Is he for real?* As if sensing her perusal he moved his eyes to meet hers and something electric cracked sharply between them, at least *she* felt it. Then a slow smile warmed his beautifully carved features.

Juliet straightened and rested her arms along the barre, facing him. She stared at him for a moment, nonplused.

"What?" he asked, hooking his thumbs through his belt loops.

"You are the first male, non-dancer to see me stretch and *not* make some sort of totally inappropriate comment." His gaze was unsettling, so she turned her back to him and placed one ankle on the barre. "I'm impressed."

"Don't be." He chuckled softly. The warm, rough sound crossed the space between them and vibrated through her. "I'm just smart enough to know that sometimes it's better to keep my thoughts to myself."

Juliet met his gaze in the mirror and heat rushed up her neck into her cheeks.

His smile deepened. "I'm really glad you can't read minds right now."

Her flush intensified and her throat closed up. She bit her lip as her mind manufactured images she guessed were similar to what was going on in his head, and heat rushed to other parts of her that, thankfully, he couldn't see. Juliet squeezed her eyes shut and dropped her leg from the barre.

Wow, Jules. You're making me blush.

"Shut up, Cass," she whispered.

"What was that?" Grant asked.

She ground her teeth together and forced herself to face him. "Nothing, Grant." She tossed her things into the workout bag and looped it over her shoulder. "We'd better get going or you're going to be late."

"Don't worry about me," Grant said, opening the door and holding it for her. "I know the guy in charge."

Chapter Ten

Grant strolled around the park, chatting and mingling as the clock neared nine p.m. The festival was in full swing, a jazz band playing lively New Orleans jazz, couples twirling and gyrating on the wooden floor of the gazebo. The aroma of Autumn's jambalaya and Nicole's beignets lent a heady perfume to the cooling night air. He glanced towards Nicole's booth and smiled as Juliet handed out another pastry to an eager young customer. Her Caribbean blue eyes twinkled and she had a laugh on her lips. She was dressed casually in a fitted white t-shirt, a black hoodie, and a pair of jeans that emphasized the length of her legs and her luscious backside. She looked beautiful.

As if she sensed someone watching her she started to look around. Their eyes met and she blinked a couple of times before giving him a small wave and turning her attention to the next customer.

"Nicole is certainly taken with her," Mike Finch said from beside him.

Grant glanced at the older man. Mike was about an inch taller than him and roughly 20 pounds heavier, but there wasn't an ounce of excess body fat on the man. His dark hair was cut short and the neatly trimmed beard was shot through with silver. He had a barrel chest, muscular arms, and legs like tree trunks. While his appearance screamed "lumberjack," Mike was actually the marketing director for an architectural firm with offices from New York to Los Angeles. He did most of his work at home, called it telecommuting. His steely slate-blue eyes could warm or freeze a person, depending on his mood, but Grant had known him all his life and he'd never once seen Mike truly angry. Nicole fondly called him her "gentle giant."

"She seems to rub people the right way," Grant said. He realized his mistake a second too late, a second after a grin split Mike's heavy features.

"So I've heard."

Grant gave him a bored look. "Don't believe *everything* you hear."

Mike laughed and clapped him on the shoulder. "Aw, come on, Grant.

Lighten up." He eyed Juliet speculatively. "Sherri would *hate* her, which is as good as a stamp of approval in my book." He rubbed his beard. "I wonder what Laine would think."

The stab of pain that often accompanied the mention of Laine wasn't nearly as sharp this time. In fact, it almost didn't register. Grant narrowed his eyes on Juliet. "I think Laine and Juliet would get along famously."

"Double-stamp of approval."

Grant looked at him out of the corner of his eye. "Stand down, old man."

"You know she'd want you to move on."

A burning spot of anger flared beneath his sternum but he kept his voice level. "I have."

"So prove it."

Grant scowled. "Y'know, Mike, I think of you like a favorite uncle, but you're starting to piss me off. I don't have to prove anything to *you* or anyone else."

Mike had the decency to blush. "Sorry, Grant, I didn't mean it like that." He glanced at Juliet again. "We all knew your heart wasn't really with Sherri, and it's obvious you like Juliet—"

"I do," Grant said with a huff, "so butt out and let nature take its course, would ya'?" He shot Mike a glare. "Excuse me, but I need to make my rounds before Sheridan gets here to take over."

"Grant, wait!"

"I'll talk to you later, Mike." Grant stuffed his hands in his pockets and stalked away.

Although he loved Evergreen Springs, the situation with Juliet was really starting to bother him. When he and Sherri had been dating no one paid them any mind. In fact, no one had really taken his relationship with Shelby's mom seriously, and when they'd broken up it hadn't even made the rounds of Paulette's network. It was as if the entire town had expected the split and simply waited for it to happen. He wasn't sure how to feel about that.

He deliberately walked in the opposite direction, away from Nicole's booth. He'd never been good at hiding his emotions, and right now fury boiled and bubbled in his gut. He paused near a street light and closed his eyes, taking deep, even breaths.

His position as Sheriff brought with it a sort of notoriety he had always taken in stride before. He never sought the spotlight, but he didn't shy away from it either. Now it seemed he was living under a spotlight, he and Juliet both. Every time they got within 50 feet of each other heads came together, whispers started, and knowing looks were sent their way. While he knew she was accustomed to *dancing* beneath a spotlight, he doubted she was accustomed to *this* particular kind of attention.

Once he reined in his irritation he continued his stroll around the perimeter of the park, eyes alert and ears tuned for anything out of the ordinary. All seemed well. The summer festivals usually went off without a hitch, if you discounted the occasional person who'd had one too many drinks. Even those were handled quickly and quietly, often without the festival attendees even aware something was happening.

His anger had cooled, but a glance Juliet's way again started another sort of heat building inside him. An image of her leaping and spinning across the aerobics room flashed in his mind. He didn't think he'd ever seen anyone dance as beautifully as she. Then a picture of her stretching, her limbs long, shapely, and as flexible as rubber, only tossed gasoline on the flames. The heat turned into a firestorm. His abdominals clenched and he paused, trying to get himself under control. The part of him that wanted her so much it hurt urged him to march across the park, pick her up from her place behind the table in Nicole's booth, and carry her off to someplace they could be alone. Thankfully, he had more self-control than baser urges.

He walked on but his gaze found Juliet every few steps. The closer he got to Nicole's booth the tighter his insides wound, until it felt like his lungs were in a vise. He tried to inhale against the pressure and then Juliet turned and caught sight of him. She gave him a questioning look, smiled, and he felt the corners of his mouth lift in reply. He continued to stare at her and the flush that rose in her cheeks broke something inside him. Grant paused and inhaled deeply as the tightness in his chest loosened.

Movement out of the corner of his eye drew his gaze and he saw Jessica Sheridan walking towards him. He glanced at the clock tower at City Hall a moment before the chimes started to ring, signaling the nine o'clock hour. Glad for the distraction, he turned and moved to meet his deputy.

"Evening, Jessica," he said when they stood facing one another.

"Right on time as always."

Sheridan tucked a strand of red hair behind her ear and gave him a half smile. "Figured it was the least I could do since you volunteered for the bigger chunk of hours." She glanced around, her sharp green gaze missing very little. "How's it been?"

"Quiet," Grant replied. "The Johnson boys got a little rambunctious earlier – too much of Marco's hard cider – so I sent them home with Cousin Bill." His eyes swept over the park. "Other than that, it's been a typical evening. Just be on the lookout in case the Johnsons decide to come back for more cider."

She laughed, a surprisingly feminine sound that belied the uniform and vest that made it almost impossible to determine if she was male or female. One look at her face, however, was enough to prove she was most definitely a woman. Grant often wondered what kept a beauty like Jessica Sheridan in Evergreen where there was a distinct lack of age-appropriate men for her to date.

"I'll do that." She glanced over her shoulder at Juliet and gave Grant a smile. "Why don't you grab your girl and hit the dance floor? I'm sure the rest of the town would love a demonstration of your dancing abilities, now that they've heard the tale."

He rolled his eyes. "Don't start."

Sheridan playfully cuffed his shoulder. "Go on, Sheriff. You're off the clock now, so let me do my job and enjoy the rest of your evening." When he didn't move she shoved him. "*Go.*"

Grant almost didn't want to. Now that he had nothing else to distract him he was going to have to deal with the flurry of strange emotions that swirled through him every time Juliet smiled his way. He hadn't known her even 36 hours, yet he felt like a schoolboy with his first crush. It was ridiculous. He was a sheriff, a combat veteran, *and* a veteran of having his heart broken. How one slender, unassuming woman could send him into such a state was beyond him.

Taking a deep breath he gathered his resolve and spun to face Nicole's booth. Eric, the health-club employee, was engaging Juliet, and Nicole was moving trays of pastries around. Mike was nowhere to be seen. Pasting a serene smile on his face he approached the table.

"Miss Nicole," he drawled, tipping his hat to the woman.

Nicole turned to him and her eyes lit up. "Evening, Grant. Are you here to claim your dance partner?"

The remark fanned the coals of his anger but he let it go. "I am, if you no longer need her."

"Oh, don't you worry about me." Nicole glanced at Juliet. "It's starting to slow down and we only have a few trays of goodies left. I think I can handle it from here, and Mike will be back shortly." Nicole turned. "Juliet, dear, you can go now if you like."

Juliet handed Eric his change and faced the older woman. "Are you sure?"

Nicole nodded. "Of course, dear. You and Grant enjoy the rest of the evening."

Juliet looked at him and the warmth in her gaze was unmistakable. His breath caught.

"Thanks, Eric," she said, her gaze locked on him instead of her customer. "I'll see you around."

Eric glanced at him, glanced at her, and sighed as he pocketed his change. "See you tomorrow, Juliet, hopefully." The younger man walked away, shoulders stooped. Grant smiled.

Juliet removed the apron from her waist and tossed it in a box beneath the table. She gave Nicole a hug and then walked around the table to meet him. "Thanks, Nicole. I'll see you tomorrow."

"No, thank *you*, Juliet." Nicole paused and her brows rose. "Wait, tomorrow?"

Grant chuckled and something inside him clenched when Juliet wound her fingers around his bicep. He forced himself to meet Nicole's gaze. "I'll take good care of her, Miss Nicole, and I'll make sure she gets to her room in one piece. You don't have to wait up for her."

Nicole's eyes narrowed. "You are a fine man, Grant Donovan, but you're still a *man*." She pointed a finger at him, but a smile tugged at the corners of her mouth. "Behave yourself."

"Yes, ma'am, you have my word," he said with a grin. He looked down at Juliet. "Shall we?"

She hugged his arm a little tighter. "We shall."

The two of them strolled along the paved walkways, pausing at booths, examining the vendors' arts and crafts displays, and enjoying each other's company. When people caught sight of the two of them they stopped to watch and the whispers started. His jaw tightened and his abdominals tensed. It was almost comical to watch, but with each pair of eyes that turned their way irritation bubbled a little hotter in his middle. Juliet seemed unaware, but he felt every gaze, heard every hushed comment, and the heated pool in his belly started to swirl outward. He made an effort to tamp down his annoyance. When he felt it growing toward his tolerance limit he just focused on the woman at his side and the rest of the park seemed to fade. Good. He'd rather focus on Juliet than the townspeople anyway.

"So, you're seeing Eric tomorrow?" he asked. "You two have a date or something?" Juliet gave him a look that made him laugh.

"No," she said, indignant. "I just told him I'd probably be using the aerobics room again." Then her eyes narrowed. "Why? Are you the jealous type?"

He pursed his lips and lifted one brow. "Do I seem like the jealous type?"

She studied him for a couple seconds. "No, not really." She dropped her chin and lowered her voice. "Especially if you can stand by and watch the woman you love marry someone else."

He stopped in his tracks and faced her. "What?"

Juliet looked up at him, dismay shadowing her delicate features. "Oh, Grant. I'm sorry. I didn't mean to—"

"It's not your fault, Juliet." He huffed as the heat of anger warmed him again in a red, pulsing surge. Taking a deep breath he looked over the top of her head. "Autumn, or Nicole?"

Her expression turned pained. "Well . . . sort of a combination of the two." He frowned and she ran a hand over her face. "Autumn said yesterday your girlfriend broke up with you because you went to your best friend's wedding, remember? And last night Nicole told me your best friend was a woman named Laine, and that you were her man of honor."

Grant clenched his jaw. "And two and two makes four."

"Grant—"

He pressed a finger to her lips and met her worried gaze. "It's okay." His anger evaporated as those blue eyes searched his, and he fought the urge to trace the outline of her mouth. He let his hand fall to his side. "I'm not mad, not at you."

Anxiety flashed in her eyes. "I don't want to cause trouble between you and your friends."

"You're not." He sighed and shook his head. "I just expected my *friends* to show a little more discretion and *not* give out details of my personal life to anyone who would listen. Not that you're just *anyone*, but I'd prefer to be the one to share those things with you."

She squeezed her eyes shut and dropped her gaze. "Me and my big mouth," she said under her breath.

"This isn't your fault." He curled a finger underneath her chin and tipped her face up. "Why don't we just drop it and forget this little conversation ever took place?"

She looked at him uncertainly and bit her lip. "Are you sure?"

He chuckled. "Yeah, I am." He offered her his arm. "Let's walk."

They started moving again, and after a few minutes of near silence Juliet leaned against him. Before he could stop himself he dropped a kiss on the top of her head. She looked up at him with wide eyes, an expression of surprise on her face. He wondered if he'd pushed it too far and gave her a smile, hoping she'd smile back. After a few seconds she did and her head returned to his shoulder. Grant closed his eyes briefly and held back a sigh of relief.

"You hungry?" he asked absently as they neared Autumn's booth.

"I am," Juliet replied.

"Are you telling me you didn't sneak some of Miss Nicole's beignets when she wasn't looking?"

She laughed softly and the sound washed over him like a warm summer rain. "Goodness, no. I had my fill while we were making them." She inhaled deeply. "That gumbo certainly smells divine, though."

He chuckled. "Gumbo it is then."

They stopped in front of Autumn's booth, but the petite woman had her back to them as she stirred one of several pots bubbling over a portable gas burner. She tasted the soup, added a few shakes of something from an unlabeled spice jar, and stirred again. Obviously satisfied, she wiped her hands on her apron and turned toward them. Her dark eyes widened and a brilliant smile lit up her face.

"Evening you two," she said, planting her hands on her hips. "I was wondering when you'd get over here to see me."

"Yes, well, we've both been working up until a couple of minutes ago," Grant drawled. "But, we're here now, and we'd like two bowls of that fabulous gumbo."

Autumn nodded and grabbed two plastic bowls from a nearby stack. "Coming right up." She ladled the thick, chunky soup into the bowls and sat them on the table.

"Thanks," he said.

That sunny smile brightened her face. "You bet, handsome. Anything else?"

"Nope," Grant replied. He reached for his wallet and pulled some money out.

Autumn crossed her arms over her chest. "Grant Donovan, how many times do I have to tell you your money isn't good here?" She took the bills from him, folded them, and slid them into the front pocket of his shirt. "Now, you two run along and enjoy your gumbo."

"Thank you," Juliet said, wrapping her hands around the steaming bowl.

"Mm hmm," Autumn replied. "You could thank me by getting Grant back out on that dance floor." She arched one patrician brow and handed them each a plastic wrapped spoon, a napkin, and a bottle of water. "I'd like to see for myself what Paulette saw last night."

Grant rolled his eyes and Juliet laughed.

"I can't promise anything," Juliet said, "but I'll do my best."

"You do that." She grinned and waved her hands at them. "Move along, now. I do have other customers to tend to."

Before he could point out that there was no one else in line Autumn fluttered away and returned to tending the various pots simmering on the back table. With a shake of his head and a glance at Juliet, he gestured for her to precede him.

They sat down across from one another at one of the many long tables that had been set up in the middle of the food booths. Globed candles shimmered, casting flickering, golden light along the white, plastic covered lengths. He smiled when Juliet took a healthy bite of gumbo and moaned with pleasure.

"That good?" he asked.

"Better," she replied. "I am going to be *enormous* if I keep eating like this."

"Not if you spend more than two hours dancing your butt off like you did today."

Juliet chuckled. "Oh, that's *nothing*." She took another bite, chewed thoughtfully, and then looked at him. "During performance season we'll spend all day in the studio. Two hours of technique classes, followed by four to six hours of rehearsal, and top it all off with performances." She shook her head. "I can be in my toe-shoes for eight hours a day, so what I did today didn't even qualify as a real workout."

"Wow. That sounds intense."

"It is." She smiled and shrugged. "The up-side is we can eat pretty much what we want, although we have to eat healthy to have enough energy to dance." She stirred her gumbo. "I have *not* been eating healthy since . . . since I left . . . ." Her voice trailed off and that shadow flickered over her delicately carved features. "Never mind."

He felt her pain yet again, but it wasn't as raw as before. They ate their gumbo in silence from that point, and when she was finished Juliet moved to sit next to him. From where they were they had an excellent view of the gazebo. The band was still pumping out lively jazz tunes, the dance floor filled with couples and singles alike. The song the band was playing ended and there was a brief round of applause before the bandleader struck up a slower, more melancholy tune. Grant glanced at her, gave her a smile, and rested his arm along the back of her folding chair.

"Would you look at that?" someone said from behind them.

"They look quite cozy, don't they?"

"They certainly make a handsome couple."

"So . . . do you think it's serious?"

"Oh, come on! She just got here."

Grant ground his teeth together and rose. When Juliet looked at him in silent question he extended a hand. "Dance with me?" He knew that would only start more whispers, but hopefully he wouldn't be able to hear them over the music.

Her brows rose and her mouth opened in a silent "O", but then she smiled and slipped her fingers into his. "I'd love to."

He walked her to the gazebo and up the steps, and they waited until an opening appeared before blending into the slowly undulating circle of bodies. Just as the night before, he fanned his fingers over her back and she rested a hand on his shoulder as he led her in the gentle waltz. Their eyes met and his throat tightened. The pressure expanded outward from his neck across his chest and shoulders until he felt his lungs fighting to inflate. Oddly, the sensation didn't bother him. If he was going to suffocate, let it be because he was drowning in her.

They hadn't made more than a half dozen turns around the dance floor before the murmurs grew to such a degree that even Juliet's closeness and the volume of the music couldn't drown them out. He tried to focus on her, on the shimmer of her skin, the scorching blue eyes, but the muted comments and soft laughs in such close quarters became increasingly difficult to ignore. His annoyance must have registered on his face because Juliet squeezed his shoulder and gave him a questioning look.

"Excuse me, Sheriff," said a familiar male voice. "Mind if I cut in and have a dance with your girlfriend here?"

The two of them stopped dancing and Grant faced Eric Schmidt, health-club employee.

The younger man gave him a sly smile. "I know you two are an item now, but before it becomes official you should let some of us other guys have a dance." He grinned. "It's the least you could do, don't you think, since you stole her before anyone else had a chance?"

Eric had no idea how dangerous was the ground on which he walked.

Juliet must have sensed his ire because she put a hand on his arm and said, "It's all right, Grant. The song is almost over anyway."

Without looking at her he gave a terse nod and stepped back, allowing Eric to move into his place. Unaware of how close to having his teeth knocked in he had just come, Eric spun Juliet away. Grant moved to stand near the band and leaned against the railing.

Now the gazes bestowed on him turned sympathetic. It was as if Eric had somehow wooed Juliet away from him in a sixty-second version of every love-triangle-gone-bad movie he'd ever seen simply by dancing with her. People glanced at him, at her, and then back, and when some of the looks directed her way turned disapproving he'd had enough. Grinding his teeth together he waited for the song to end.

As the last riff faded out he walked toward the bandleader and whispered in his ear. The man gestured for the band to put their instruments down and then he handed Grant a microphone. Facing the crowd, he tapped the head of the device several times and the throng went quiet as they turned to look at him.

"Evening folks." A murmur of acknowledgement went through the gathering. Grant forced a smile and continued. "First, let me thank all of you for coming out tonight. Let's have a round of applause for Nicole Finch and the rest of the town council for putting together another successful summer festival." He paused as applause rippled through the park, and when it died his smile faded.

"Now that's done, I have something else I want to say." He

took a breath, held it for a couple seconds, and then slowly exhaled. "By now I'm sure most of you have heard about our newest visitor to Evergreen, Miss Juliet Hall, the woman whose car broke down. I want to personally thank you for the unbelievably warm welcome you have given her. Your hospitality and kindness are most appreciated, and you've done yourselves, and the town, proud."

Heads began to nod and smiles blossomed.

"That being said," he continued, pulling his brows together, "while I appreciate how you're treating Miss Hall, I *do not* appreciate the sly looks or the behind-my-back whispers, or the betting going on in the basement of Denny's bar as to whether or not Miss Hall and I will head down the aisle with Shelby and David." Someone started to say something but he skewered them with a look. "Don't bother to deny it; I even know what the odds are."

Silence dropped like an executioner's axe. Grant flicked his gaze over the gathering and continued.

"To answer the question that seems to be first and foremost in everyone's mind . . . *yes*, I like her. But, that's between her and me, not her and me and all of *you*." He looked at each face, and there weren't very many who could hold his gaze for more than a nanosecond. "As an elected official in this town I realize my expectation of privacy is not the same as what the average citizen would enjoy, but I am still entitled to a personal life. Therefore, I would appreciate it if, from this point on, everybody would just go about their business and let me go about mine. Believe me, if I decide to get married within the next ten days . . . you'll know."

He glanced at Juliet who watched him with wide eyes, but he couldn't tell from her expression what she felt or what she thought of him at that moment. Grant pinched the bridge of his nose and sighed.

"Sorry for the interruption. Y'all enjoy the rest of your evening."

After handing the microphone to the bandleader Grant made his way down the steps. Without looking back he strode toward the office. Before he'd gone a half-dozen paces the music started back up, but the chatter didn't resume as quickly. It was a pretty safe bet the crowd was watching his departure, but he wasn't about to look over his shoulder to confirm that.

He reached his Yukon and jerked open the door as he fished his keys from his pocket. After sliding behind the wheel and fastening his seatbelt, he jammed the keys in the ignition. Before he could turn the engine over the passenger door popped open and Juliet hopped in.

Grant rested his hands on the wheel. "Juliet, what are you doing?"

"I'm going with you."

He gaped at her. "What? Do you *want* that whirlwind back there to turn into an F-5?"

She met his gaze, her expression solemn. "What you *should* ask me is if I care."

"I promised Nicole—"

"Nicole is *not* my mother," Juliet interrupted, brows drawing down in a frown, "and even if she was I am a grown woman and you wouldn't have to promise her *anything*."

The frustration inside him sputtered out and faded as he looked into those turquoise eyes. While he wished with everything inside him that he could just start his SUV and take her home with him, he couldn't. Not if he really cared about her.

"Juliet," he began in a low voice, "I know that to you Nicole is just a new friend, but to me she's family. I've known her and Mike and most of the residents of Evergreen my entire life. I gave her my word, and while that may not mean much to other people, it means a lot to *me*."

"I don't want to be here without you." She flushed and dropped her gaze. "The only reason I came tonight was to see you."

His heart thumped hard against his sternum and something inside him pulled taut. He couldn't have spoken if he'd had something intelligent to say. His vocal chords were frozen. She glanced up and her eyelids fluttered when he tucked her hair behind one ear. He allowed himself a forbidden pleasure and let his fingers trail down the slender column of her throat. Her skin was like satin, soft and smooth, and he glanced at the pulse fluttering wildly at the base of her neck.

"Juliet . . . ."

She squeezed her eyes shut. "If you really want to go home then just take me back to the hotel, please."

She looked at him then, and what he saw in those blue-green pools almost undid him.

"Please, Grant." Pausing, she took a deep, slow breath. "But, you have to walk me."

"Why?"

Her flush deepened and she ducked her chin. "Because you said something last night about asking me out after you walked me back to the hotel from the festival." She licked her lips. "If you go home, that means you can't walk me back to the hotel, and *that* means you can't ask me out." He saw the convulsive swallow, and then she lifted her eyes to his. "Unless . . . unless you don't *want* to ask me out."

Heat burst inside him and he almost shouted "Yes!" Then something dark and cold burrowed through his middle. Was he really considering doing this again? He'd loved Laine with all his heart, but he'd always known on some level that Evergreen was just a springboard for her, that after high school she'd go out into the world and not return. Now here sat Juliet, the woman whose car broke down, the woman who was just passing through on her way . . . *somewhere else*. His stomach dropped.

He hadn't been this interested in a woman since he'd finally let go of Laine. He had loved Sherri, but Mike was right. His heart *hadn't* been fully engaged. He'd felt more in the past 36 hours for Juliet than he had for Sherri their entire relationship. It was insane. Was he really going to double-down on what was almost certainly a losing hand?

Unable to answer his own question, Grant swallowed hard and faced forward. "I *want* to ask you out, but I don't really see the point if you're leaving tomorrow, do you?" He stared at the windows of his office, pulled in a slow breath, and gradually let it out. *Well, bud, if you're going to play this game, it's time to go all in or fold. Take your pick.* He closed his eyes briefly. *I might as well push that stack to the center of the table and let it ride. I can't win if I don't bet.* His shoulders tightened and he glanced at her. "I guess you didn't notice, but your car is done and parked across the street from the hotel. I had Eddie give it a once over after he replaced the hose. He did an oil change, checked all the fluids and replaced a couple of belts. You don't have to worry about it breaking down, at least not for a while." He fished in his pocket and pulled out her keys. As he handed them over he dared another glance at her and was surprised by the gentle smile on her lips.

"Thank you." She palmed the keys and slipped them into her pocket.

He looked away from her. "Now you can leave before Riordan gets here, if you want."

"What if I wasn't leaving?" she asked softly. "Would you ask me out then?"

"If you were staying, I'd *definitely* ask you out." The words were out before he could fully consider the implications.

Her smile widened and what she said next sent his heart racing.

"Then ask away, Sheriff. I can assure you the answer . . . is *yes*."

He studied her face carefully, searching for any of the indecision and uncertainty that was twining around his heart, but he saw none. Suddenly, what the town would or wouldn't whisper about wasn't nearly so important. And, just as suddenly, doubling-down didn't seem like such an outlandish idea after all.

"Do you want to get out of here?" he asked.

Juliet nodded and fastened her seatbelt. "I do."

Chapter Eleven

"My God," Juliet whispered, "this is *so* beautiful."

She closed her eyes as the gentle rush of the river wrapped around her like a comforting embrace. The air was cool and laden with mist as the water churned and danced over and around the rocks jutting through the undulating surface. With a sigh she looked across the tributary, pale silver light from a three-quarter moon reflected softly back to its lunar source. Tall pines lined the banks and thrust proudly into the sky as if their pointed tops directed the moonlight on its return. She didn't think she'd ever seen anything so breathtaking.

"Yeah," Grant agreed in a low voice. "I come out here when I need to . . . get away."

Those were the first words either of them had spoken since leaving the town square. They sat on the ground against a fallen tree only feet from the water's edge, the temperature several degrees cooler here than away from the softly rushing torrent. Juliet snuggled deeper into the heavy-duty, sheepskin lined jacket Grant had draped over her shoulders. He sat next to her in his jeans and denim jacket, apparently unaffected by the chill.

She'd felt the tension in him earlier and knew it was because of the wagging tongues. His "Evergreen Address" had stunned her, and sent strange, conflicting emotions burgeoning: fear, hope, anxiety, anticipation. The sensation was eerily similar to what she felt after an audition – nervous, excited, optimistic, and pessimistic. The feelings spun inside her, making her chest tighten and her pulse rise as the alternating currents of hot and cold wound together, refusing to be parted from one another.

Juliet looked at his rugged profile, admiring the brazenly masculine yet hauntingly beautiful features. She'd met and partnered with some exceedingly handsome men in her career, but there was something different about Grant. He wore his extraordinary good looks with a relaxed confidence that said he was completely at ease with himself. He had no need for the arrogance that often accompanied external attractiveness, wholly content in his awe-inspiring skin. The fact that he was just as beautiful on the inside as he was on the outside only pulled her closer, and strengthened the contradictory pool bubbling in her middle.

Her pulse started a slow, steady climb and her throat tightened, threatening to cut off her airway. She fought to breathe normally and turned her eyes back to the river.

"Grant, I'm sorry about all of this." She felt him turn toward her, his gaze a tangible caress, but she couldn't summon the courage to look at him.

"What are you sorry for?" He sat up a little straighter. "You haven't done anything wrong, Juliet."

Oh, how she loved the way he said her name! His husky voice seemed to drop several decibels and soften until the sound rasped over her skin like rough velvet. It made her shiver, and she wondered how it would feel to hear her name from his lips while deep in the throes of passion. Heat surged into her cheeks and she closed her eyes.

"How do you deal with being in the spotlight all the time?" she asked.

A low chuckle rumbled in his chest. "You tell me, Miss Prima Ballerina."

She glanced at him, but he was smiling at the moon. "That's different," she said. He turned to her and those warm brown eyes edged her inner thermometer up another few degrees.

"How so?" he asked, one brow lifted in sardonic inquiry.

Her heart started its climb again and she swallowed it down. "My spotlight is fixed," she replied at last. "It only shines when I'm on stage. Once I leave the stage nobody knows me from Adam." She narrowed her eyes on his face. "I suppose being sheriff is kind of like being a doctor. 'Say, doc, I know we're at a cocktail party, but could you take a look at this mole for me?'" Juliet bit her lip and dropped her chin. "And I've only made it worse."

"You're the only one who makes it bearable."

Juliet's head snapped up and she looked at him, surprised. The raw emotion in his voice told her he was as conflicted as she, and when she saw the uncertainty and hope in his eyes the ice encasing her heart split in half and dropped off, shattering into a million melting shards. She sucked in a breath and blinked at him.

"Please don't say anything," he whispered. A flash of pain darkened his expression and he looked away. "I'd rather *not* know that this is all *completely* one-sided." He laughed softly, but there was little humor in the sound. "I know I sound like an idiot right now, but every time I look at you my brain seems to short-circuit."

She started to speak but he gently covered her mouth with one hand and shook his head. His light touch sent heated tingles spiraling downward into her belly.

"Please . . . ." He traced the outline of her mouth and sighed. Warmth fanned over her face and down her neck and she gulped. His eyes narrowed slightly. He stared at her for a few more moments then faced forward and stuffed his hands in his pockets. "I'd like to sit here with you for a while knowing that no one is watching or whispering or laying bets. Is that okay?"

He gave her a sidelong glance and all she could do was nod. He smiled and draped an arm over her shoulders, pulling her against his side. Juliet scooted closer and rested her head in the curve of his neck.

Closing her eyes, she took a shaky breath. She didn't think she'd ever felt so safe or so in danger in her life. Physically she knew she was completely secure, but emotionally she felt like she was walking blindfolded through an active minefield. While Cassie might have fallen for the handsome sheriff in the few hours she'd been in town, Juliet had never even entertained such a thought. She'd always been too busy to foster a truly deep, lasting relationship, and never had she experienced the whirlwind of emotion that Grant roused in her.

The few relationships she'd had ended benignly, although they hadn't been without pain. And she had never experienced infidelity, abuse, or any other sort of male transgression that would jade a woman or make her fearful of intimacy. In truth, she'd always imagined she'd go the way of her mother, even if that wasn't what she really wanted. Her mother had been a dancer also, and she'd left the stage when she became pregnant with Juliet, never to return.

"Juliet?"

The warm, rough sound of his voice broke her racing train of thought. "Yes?"

"What are you going to do when Detective Riordan gets here?"

Her current train of thought derailed. Something cold curled in her belly as fragmented pictures of Mayfield's never-ending harassment assaulted her. She sucked in a breath and fought to turn her thoughts elsewhere.

"I don't know."

"You don't have to talk to him. He's *way* out of his jurisdiction here."

"I know I don't *have* to talk to him." She sighed softly. "I *need* to talk to him."

"Why? Are you thinking of going back into protective custody?"

Despite the circumstances, the note of uneasiness in his voice made her smile. "No."

"Then why do you *need* to talk to him?"

"I . . . I need to apologize." Memories washed over her and she shuddered. "After . . . ." She snuggled against him and he tightened his embrace. "I said some really . . . *awful* . . . things to him, things I should *never* have said."

"He's a cop." Grant rested his chin atop her head. "We get used to the venom people throw at us."

She laughed shortly. "Has anyone in Evergreen ever called *you* a killer?" Several long, silent moments passed.

"You forget, Juliet," he said softly, "I *am* a killer."

Juliet jerked upright and gaped at him. "No, you're not. Why would you say that?"

Those soulful eyes just returned her stare with an expression of sad resignation, and fury bloomed. That he would classify himself in the same category as George Mayfield incensed her, and she felt the red heat of it spiral outward from her core.

"You're *not* a killer, Grant Donovan. Don't you *dare* put yourself alongside the likes of George Mayfield, do you hear me?"

"I was a sniper, Juliet. I've killed more people than he has."

"Like women who put explosives in baby strollers alongside their *babies*?" she asked. "Seems like she got what she deserved." She stood and stared down at him. "You didn't take lives to satisfy some vicious, twisted fantasy, you did it to save others. You fight so I don't have to. You walk where others can't . . . or *won't*. That makes you a *hero* and a *patriot*, not a *killer*."

He rose in one liquid motion, a half-smile playing about his mouth. His apparent humor only fueled her indignation. Angry tears stung and she clenched her teeth.

"George Mayfield is a *killer*," she ground out, "and *you* are *nothing* like him." She glared at him. "I should hit you for saying that."

"That would be assaulting a police officer, ma'am," he said with mock gravity, his twinkling eyes belying the seriousness of his tone. He rubbed her arms gently. "Are you always so quick on the defense?"

"When the situation warrants it." She frowned and moved away, presenting him with her back. "*Don't* compare yourself to him . . . not ever."

"I'm sorry." His voice slithered around her senses like brandy, warm and intoxicating. "I shouldn't have said that."

"No, you shouldn't have." Juliet felt him standing behind her and every molecule of her body wanted to lean against him, to soak in his heat. Even though there was a foot of space between them it was as if he was pressed to her back. She *wanted* him pressed to her front, so she spun to face him. Her heart ricocheted against the inside of her chest as those chocolate-colored eyes devoured her.

It was most unnerving, the electrified current that zipped down her spine and outward until her fingertips tingled. She'd experienced passion before, but not like this. There was an animal sensuality behind Grant's heated gaze that spoke of a beast tightly chained, and something in her responded on a primal level. Before she'd met him her greatest passion had been ballet. However, at this moment, she could barely remember first position. There were several *other* positions jockeying for prominence in her mind's eye, and none of them involved her feet, unless her feet were up past her ears.

Wow, Jules, you shot straight past PG-13 to XXX. Are you channeling me?

His smile told her he knew what she was thinking, or he at least suspected, and heat rocketed all the way to her scalp. Her nipples pebbled and a throb settled low in her belly. With her other lovers, sex had almost been an obligatory act, something that went along with having a "boyfriend". Sometimes it had been fun, sometimes it hadn't. Sometimes she'd experienced an orgasm, but not always. Never had she felt this *craving*, this *need* to get as close as humanly possible to a man, *this* man. Fear raced through her, but instead of diminishing her desire it only added fuel to the fire.

"I should take you back to the hotel now."

His softly spoken words made her heart stop for a few seconds. "What?" She blinked at him as her brain processed what he'd said, and disappointment filled her. "*Why?*" Juliet winced at the plaintive note she heard in her voice, but there was little she could do about it now.

Grant's languid smile widened. "So I can ask you out." He studied her briefly. "Unless you don't *want* me to ask you out."

"You don't have to wait until then to ask me out." Now she sounded breathless instead of whiny, and she groaned inwardly. Couldn't she speak in a normal voice?

"I know," he replied, brushing a windblown lock of hair from her cheek. "But I'm going to do this the right way . . . the old-fashioned way."

His touch set her nerves tingling and the throbbing in her pelvis started to pulse with every beat of her heart. She imagined his hands moving lower, over her breasts, her belly, and elsewhere. Juliet chided herself and took a deep, steadying breath. She wasn't some schoolgirl ripe with blushing virginity. She was a woman, in *every* sense of the word, and part of her was bothered that she couldn't stop drooling over this delicious, audaciously sexy man. He wasn't the first gorgeous male to ever cast a favorable glance her way.

No, but he is the first gorgeous male that you've glanced back at just as favorably, and because you want *to, not because you're* paired up *and it's* expected.

If Cassie had been standing there Juliet would have clapped a hand over her mouth, excused the both of them, and then severely scolded her sister for speaking out of turn. Problem was, Cassie wasn't there and she wasn't speaking out of turn. She really wasn't speaking at all, even if the words in Juliet's head were gospel truth.

Take a walk on the wild side, Jules. You might find you like it there, and that you can still be a good girl.

In that instant, Juliet decided to do something she almost never did: take her sister's advice. She gulped and searched for her voice.

"Let's go, Sheriff," she said at last. "The sooner we get back, the sooner I can say yes."

***

Grant stopped the Yukon in front of the hotel and turned the engine off. Juliet stared at the façade of the building and he followed the direction of her gaze. The windows were dark except for one, telling him the night clerk, or Nicole, was on duty. He hoped it wasn't the latter.

His nerves were wound tighter than bowstrings. It didn't matter that Juliet had already told him her answer was yes, part of him was waiting for the other shoe to drop. He was a small-town sheriff. She had graduated from Juilliard and was a prima ballerina with a prestigious ballet company. He was Evergreen Springs, and she was San Diego, San Francisco, New York, and Seattle all rolled into one beautiful, cultured, elegant package. They couldn't be more different, and yet he felt the pull in her sea-green eyes as if they had been destined to meet. Part of him rebelled at this sense of fate, while yet another part of him hoped for it. He didn't want to feel what he felt, but he didn't want to stop either.

The inside of the SUV was suddenly too small. Grant practically threw the driver's door open and stepped out. Juliet's head snapped around and she watched him with wide eyes as he walked to her door and opened it, much slower and with a smile. She looked at him uncertainly for a couple seconds, then took his extended hand and joined him on the sidewalk.

"Thank you," she said.

"You're welcome."

She clasped her hands in front of her and avoided his gaze, her cheeks going pink. "Well, this is it."

"It is."

"Are you going to ask me out now?"

Her voice was low and he heard the hint of nervousness behind the question.

"If I do, and you say yes, which you already said you'd do, you'll have to stay in town longer." He leaned over and looked her in the eye. "Do you still want me to ask?"

"How much longer will I have to stay?"

Her expression told him she didn't care how much longer she stayed, but he decided to play it cool and gave her a small smile. "Until Saturday at least."

"Go ahead and ask."

Grant hooked his thumbs through his belt loops and glanced at the hotel's front door. "Okay. The county fair starts Friday, and I was wondering if you'd allow me to escort you to opening night."

She chewed her lower lip and he had the urge to kiss the same spot to assuage her self-abuse.

"Will there be corn dogs?" she asked.

"There will."

"Funnel cakes?"

He smiled. "Absolutely."

"Deep-fried Twinkies?"

One brow rose. "I can't say for sure, but I imagine so. If there are no golden, cream-filled Hostess cakes to be found, I'm sure we can find a comparable substitute."

She gave him an indignant look. "There *is* no substitute for Twinkies."

Grant laughed. "Well, if the fair doesn't have any, I have a box at home I will be happy to deep-fry for you." He narrowed his eyes on her. "Provided you go to the fair with me."

Something flashed in her eyes, something he'd seen earlier by the river, something he'd seen when she'd been dancing. Fire. His muscles tensed as his body responded to the unspoken signals she was sending him. He saw it in the shallow breaths, the dilated pupils, and the heightened color.

"Say yes, Juliet."

It was a command, not a plea, and she blinked.

"Yes."

"And spend tomorrow with me, too."

Her brows drew together. "But Detective Riordan—"

"*After.*" He took her hands in his. "You don't plan to spend the whole day with him, do you?"

She shuddered. "No."

"So after you speak with him, spend the rest of the day with me." To his relief her expression was curious, not disinterested.

"Doing what?"

He laced his fingers through hers. "I'll tell you tomorrow."

Those patrician brows arched north. "And I'm just supposed to trust you?"

Grant stepped closer and lifted her hands to his mouth. He pressed his lips to her knuckles in a lingering kiss and then fixed her with a pointed look. "Yes. Tomorrow you're going to do something for me, and then I'm going to do something for you." He watched the play of emotions in her eyes. "Trust me."

He sensed her inner debate and waited patiently, his shoulders tight and his body poised in anticipation of a negative response. This uncertainty wasn't something he was accustomed to, and he braced himself for the sting of disappointment as her silence drew out. Maybe he shouldn't have gone all-in so quickly.

"Okay."

At first her reply didn't register, but when it did a sense of warmth and lightness enveloped him. "Okay?"

"I already said my answer would be yes."

"You said *okay*, not *yes*."

Juliet pursed her mouth and tipped her head to the side. "Fine. *Yes.*"

He grinned and she grinned back.

"I feel much better now," he admitted.

She took a step toward him. "Did you really think I'd turn you down?"

"I try not to be overconfident when it comes to the opposite sex," he replied softly. "Been burned once or twice doing that."

"What stupid girl would say no to *you*?"

His heart twisted. "One I loved almost all my life."

Juliet's mouth formed an "O", but she said nothing, her eyes wide with dismay. She chewed her lip again and once more he wanted to stop her, kiss those lips until she asked him not to. His body reacted violently to the thought and he pulled hard on his inner reins.

She opened her mouth to speak just as the clock tower chimed the midnight hour. She glanced toward the structure entirely reminiscent of the one from the *Back to the Future* movies. It took her several seconds to meet his gaze, almost as if she didn't want to. She looked at him briefly then turned her eyes to the ground.

"I'm sorry, Grant." She squeezed her eyes shut and chuckled softly. "Cassie was always so much better at this."

"What?"

"Flirting . . . interacting with men," Juliet replied. "Cassie could date a dozen different men in a two week stretch, and have even more lined up for the rest of the month." Juliet shook her head and gazed toward the square. "She would *never* say anything to a man she'd have to apologize for."

"You didn't have to apologize." He put a hand under her chin and turned her face to his. "But I appreciate the thought."

Juliet's heart started to thrum against her sternum, the touch of his hand sending heat across her skin like warm breath. His eyes searched hers for several pregnant moments, and then he lowered his head. Juliet closed her eyes and braced herself, every nerve-ending taut and vibrating. The familiar wave of disappointment crested and crashed through her abdomen in a chilling froth when he brushed a kiss over her cheek and straightened.

"I'll call you when Detective Riordan gets here," he said softly.

She looked at him and he took a step back. As earlier, she felt him pulling away, both physically and otherwise. It worried her. "Will you . . . will you be there when I talk to him?" she managed to choke out.

"If you want me there . . . yes."

"I want you there."

A slow smile warmed his face. "Then I will be there. We can do it in my office if you like."

Nervous flutters curdled in her belly. "I don't care where," she replied. "I just want to get it over with."

His eyes narrowed. "What happens is entirely up to you, Juliet. He can't make you do anything you don't want to do."

"I know."

Kiss him, Juliet.

Well, *that* was certainly something she wanted to do.

Grant hooked his thumbs in his gun belt. "I'll see you in the morning then."

Juliet dropped her chin, nodded, and forced a smile. "Yes, you will."

KISS HIM.

"Good night, Juliet."

"Good night, Grant."

She saw the conflict in his eyes, but he remained as still as stone. Burying her frustration she turned and walked up the steps. She felt his gaze on her as she opened the door, stepped into the lobby, and closed the portal behind her. Leaning against the solid oak panel she took a deep, shuddering breath.

Damn it, Juliet. You were supposed *to kiss him.*

Juliet ignored her sister's voice and went to the window. Grant stood on the sidewalk staring up at the front of the hotel. She read the indecision and frustration in his expressive eyes, a mirror for what she felt, and it was nearly a minute before he walked back to the Yukon. Her heart thumped uncomfortably and she turned from the window, but Cassie's voice stopped her.

Wait for it, Jules.

"Wait for *what?*"

Trust me.

Juliet peered out the window again, careful to stay hidden. He opened the car door and slid behind the wheel. A sad sigh escaped her when she heard the engine turn over and the lights came on.

Listen to me, Juliet. Wait.

Something sparked deep inside her, so faint it almost sputtered out and died right there, but as the seconds ticked off the snap of light grew. The Yukon sat at the curb, engine idling, lights on, but Grant's gaze remained fixed on the hotel. She stood up a little straighter and her fingers touched the pendant at her neck. Nearly another minute passed but the SUV remained where it was. It wasn't until her lungs started to burn that she realized she was holding her breath.

When the lights went off and the engine died that barely-there spark flared to vibrant, blinding life. Her heart nearly burst as the driver's door came open and Grant stepped out. He walked toward the front of the hotel with long, purposeful strides, a scowl of determination on his brow. Juliet ran for the front door, jerked it open, and leapt off the top step.

He caught her easily and their mouths came together as if magnetized. Heat spun like a supernova in her chest, her heart fluttering violently as he held her aloft. She wound one leg around his muscular thigh and sighed softly. His embrace tightened. Pulsing heat settled low in her belly as his lips moved over hers with exquisite, delicate skill, stealing what little breath and conscious thought she had left.

His tongue made cautious entrance into her mouth and a low moan was pulled from somewhere deep inside her. He tasted her, softly, slowly, and fire throbbed through her veins. Her limbs went warm and rubbery, as if he was a narcotic. She already knew she was addicted, and the realization didn't frighten her a bit. She needed more.

Her breasts ached as he slid her slowly down his body to put her back on her feet. Juliet wound her fingers through his hair, relishing the feel of the soft curls against her palms. Grant fanned one large hand over her back as the other moved to cup her head, and when he deepened the kiss her knees wobbled. He pressed her closer.

Time stopped and her awareness narrowed. Somewhere in her brain she knew a cool breeze was picking up but she couldn't feel it. All she felt was him, the heat of his body, the pressure of his mouth, the taste of his tongue as it danced with hers. She dragged her hands over his shoulders and down his chest, a dizzying euphoria washing over her at the warm steel of the muscles corded there. His masculinity overwhelmed her, and she was helpless to do anything but submit to it.

When he finally ended the kiss a whimper of protest escaped her and she fisted her fingers in the front of his shirt. Her breathing was ragged, shallow, and fast, her heart racing. Juliet rested her brow against his chest and noted, with no small amount of pleasure, that his breathing was just as labored as hers. He put his chin on top of her head, his hands moving slowly over her back in wide, sweeping circles.

"*Damn.*"

Juliet smiled as he uttered that single, whispered word.

"I have wanted to do that since the first time I walked you home," he said.

She lifted her head and looked at him. "Why didn't you?"

His expression was pensive and he framed her face. "I wasn't sure I should."

Warmth fanned over her skin as his thumbs stroked her cheekbones. "You should," she said with a small nod. Her breath caught. "You *really* should." Her fingers curled around his neck and she lifted onto her tiptoes. "Again."

That now familiar smile curved those sinful lips. "Yes, ma'am."

Chapter Twelve

Grant covered her mouth with his again and everything inside of him vibrated as his heart beat a rapid staccato against his sternum. Heat pooled in his midsection, radiating slowly outward until his entire body was warm and tingling. Her lips were soft and tasted like strawberries. He threaded his fingers into her hair and cupped her head, the silken threads cool and slippery in his hands.

He slid his tongue over her lower lip and she gasped. Grant took advantage of the opening and deepened the kiss, exploring her mouth carefully, deliberately, and fully. His pulse began to climb as the heat from her kiss and her proximity invaded parts of his body that would soon tell her just how much he wanted her. Given what she'd been through he knew he needed to rein himself in, to go slowly. Problem was he didn't want to rein himself in or go slowly. He wanted to throw caution to the winds, throw her across his king-sized bed, and drown in her.

He couldn't remember the last time he'd felt like this, and the awareness startled him. Even with Laine there had never been this *visceral* rush of emotion, sensations that invaded even the most closely guarded parts of him and urged him to release the reins he kept in such tight control. The few kisses he'd shared with Laine, the ones that *hadn't* been friendly and chaste, had been passionate. However, the passion he'd experienced with Laine and the blazing, combustible fervor Juliet roused in him were vastly different, taking *passion* to an entirely new level. A chill of fear fanned through him as he realized he was in uncharted territory. Up until now he had thought the life he'd lived had prepared him for *everything*. He had been wrong.

"Ahem."

Grant jerked away from her and Juliet let out a soft yelp of surprise. He immediately pushed her behind him and reached for his gun, his protective instincts in full gear. When he realized it was just Mike standing on top of the hotel steps he dropped his chin, planted his hands on his hips, and exhaled sharply.

"Damn it," he said. "You should know better than to sneak up on me like that. I could've shot your ass, and then Miss Nicole would tear me a new one."

Mike chuckled. "Sorry. I was in the kitchen getting some hot cocoa when I heard the door open and close . . . twice." A wry grin warmed his face and lit a twinkle in his eyes. "Gabe is on his break so I thought I should check it out."

Grant grinned and shook his head. Juliet stood behind him, her face pressed into the spot between his shoulder blades, her fingers hooked through his belt loops.

"It's okay, Juliet," he said, "it's just Big Mike."

Juliet didn't move. "Sorry we bothered you, Mike," she said, her voice muffled against his shirt.

"It's no bother, Juliet," Mike replied, laughter rumbling in his chest. "I'm going back to bed now and you two . . . *carry on.*"

Grant waited until Mike closed the door behind him, and then he turned to face Juliet. Her arms wound around his waist and she laid her head on his chest.

"Well, that was . . . *embarrassing,*" she said softly.

He chuckled and wrapped his arms around her. "Just be glad it was Big Mike and not Paulette. At least that way the town won't be gearing up for a double-wedding."

"Hear, hear."

Grant rested his chin atop her head and they stood like this. The tranquility of night in Evergreen enfolded them like a comforting mantle, heavy and warm, but not suffocating. He closed his eyes, let the stillness soak in, and tried to wrap his head around what was happening between them.

The fact that Juliet was shaking the cornerstones of his foundations made him nervous. She challenged the very fabric of who he was: levelheaded, even-keeled, logical, and by-the-book. He had never believed in fairy-tales, had even scoffed at them as a child. The diametric opposition between the mantras of *love-at-first-sight* and *love-is-blind* had always bothered him, and happily-ever-after was something that only happened in books. His parents had a wonderful marriage, had been married more than 40 years, but even in that rock-solid relationship reality had intruded to dispel the myths of childhood fables.

And yet, he couldn't deny what he felt. He'd known Juliet not even two full days, but he knew if it came to it he would sacrifice himself for her. It made no sense logically, or even practically, but there it was. Was he in love with her? He wasn't sure, but what bothered him more was the fact that he could not reply with an unequivocal *no.*

"Grant?"

"Hmm?"

"What are you thinking?"

He smiled. He couldn't count how many times Sherri had asked him that very question and he had replied, in all honesty, "Nothing." That had frustrated his ex no end. Now, however, he couldn't reply the same and still be honest. Always preferring truth to fiction, Grant decided to just put it out there.

"I'm thinking about how crazy this all is."

"How crazy what is? My life or what's happening between us?"

He chuckled softly and laid his cheek against her hair. "Both, but more the latter." He felt her breath on his skin as she sighed softly, and shivers coursed through him.

"Good," she whispered. "Then I'm not the only one."

"No, ma'am."

He tried to concentrate on something other than the feel of her pressed against him, the scent of her hair, and the warmth of her breath on the skin exposed by the open neck of his button-down shirt. Heat shot through him and he felt it in his groin. Grant gulped and fought it. He had no desire to embarrass himself . . . or her.

"It's late," he finally said, unable to think of anything better. "You're going to need some rest before tomorrow, so you should probably go inside."

"I'm happy right here, thank you."

She snuggled closer and he groaned inwardly as his body responded with enthusiasm. It had been a while since he'd been with a woman, and his libido roared to the forefront to remind him just how long. Grant ground his teeth together. He took several deep breaths and tried not to tense up with her in his arms. He knew she would ask him what was wrong, and he didn't want to have to explain it, not right now.

"I'm happy where you are, too," he admitted, "but you're not the only one who needs some sleep. Didn't get much last night and today was a pretty long day for me, for you as well."

She lifted her eyes to his and his gaze was drawn to those beautiful lips against his will. They were skillfully chiseled, delicate but ripe and made to be kissed. He wanted to kiss her again, to explore the warmth of her mouth and hear her sigh as she leaned into him. Truth be told, he wanted to do *way* more than kiss her.

He forced himself to look her in the eyes, but what he saw there did nothing to put out the firestorm inside him. Quite the opposite in fact. Those blue-green pools called to him the way sirens called to sailors, and he felt his will wavering. *Come lose yourself in me . . . I want you to. Surrender to my song and crash upon my rocks.* Grant dragged his gaze from those shimmering turquoise orbs, although he almost didn't have the strength to do so.

"Juliet—"

She pressed a hand to his cheek and turned his face to hers. "One more kiss," she whispered, "then I'll go inside."

He steeled himself. "Without Mike to interrupt us . . . one more kiss could be dangerous."

Her expression was solemn. "I know," she said in a low, honeyed voice, "but aren't these the moments we live for?" She traced the line of his jaw and her gaze wandered to his mouth. "The times our hearts race and our minds blank out and we want to just go with it, consequences be damned?"

"What about possible repercussions of 'just going with it'?" He forced himself to meet her eyes. "My father taught me a long time ago that a few moments of pleasure are rarely worth the price, no matter how much we want that pleasure in the moment."

Pink surged into her cheeks and she ducked her chin. "I seriously doubt you're going to ravish me on the steps of the hotel if we share one more kiss."

He chuckled. "No, but if we share one more kiss I may very well toss you over my shoulder, carry you upstairs, and ravish you in your room." He paused. "I know *exactly* which one it is."

Her head snapped up. "Mike and Nicole—"

"Wouldn't stop me," he interrupted, "unless you gave them some indication you didn't *want* to be carried up those stairs." He brushed a wind-caught tendril of hair from her face and tucked it securely behind her ear. His fingers moved slowly from the sensitive lobe downward over her throat, and he smiled at her indrawn breath. "They might not think as highly of me afterwards, but we're both adults."

Her color deepened, but she met his gaze boldly. "And if I *want* you to carry me upstairs?"

The draw was instantaneous and he had to struggle to pull in the surge of lust that threatened to overwhelm him. He was not the kind of man who let passion cloud his better judgment, but she was damn close to turning him into one.

He shook his head slowly and stepped back from her. "Bull*shit* your sister is better at this."

She blinked at him.

"You have no idea how much I want you, how much I want to take you upstairs right now," he said to her unspoken question, "but I won't." He thrust his hands in his pockets and forced his libido back into its place behind his common sense and fortitude. Closing his eyes briefly, he took a deep breath. "There's only one first time with a woman, Juliet. Call it pride, call it ego, call it whatever you want, but I like to know that when a woman I've made love to remembers me, she does so with a smile and the burning desire to see me again."

She only stared at him, those beautiful blue eyes wide and incredulous.

Grant choked down his frustration and looked over the square. "Sorry if that disappoints you."

"Wow." When he looked at her a small smile curved her mouth, her expression pensive. "Where have you *been* all my life?"

He didn't want to smile but his face didn't care. "Waitin' on you."

She bit her lip and although he wanted to kiss her to make her stop he held himself in check. Her eyelids fluttered and then she did something that completely floored him.

Juliet rose on her tiptoes, grabbed his head, and pressed her mouth to his in a kiss that seared him to his soul. Before he could stop himself his arms enfolded her. He closed his eyes and lifted her against his chest. Then, just as suddenly as it had started, it ended.

"Good night, Grant," she said in a hushed voice as she pushed out of his embrace.

He was too startled to move. It wasn't until the hotel's main door closed with a soft *thump* that he came back to reality. He shook his head to clear it, then turned and looked at the hotel's façade.

"I don't know your sister," he said to the brick building, "but I seriously doubt she's better at *that* than you are." With another shake of his head he walked back to the Yukon.

Juliet leaned against the door and took several long, gulping breaths. Her pulse pattered uncomfortably against her esophagus and her insides quivered uncontrollably, lips tingling and aching for more.

Way to go, Juliet. And here I didn't think you had it in you.

"Give it a rest, Cass," Juliet said under her breath. "Just stop."

Thankfully, Cassie said nothing else. Juliet heard the Yukon's engine roar to life and tears stung. She didn't want to go upstairs to her room; she wanted to go home with *him.* Closing her eyes she pressed her hands into the carved wood and waited until she could no longer hear the SUV. Drawing in a ragged breath, she glanced at the night clerk. The man named Gabe was watching her with far too much interest, and she scowled as she pushed away from the door.

Juliet bounded up the stairs, as if by running she could outrun what had just happened on the sidewalk in front of the Center Hotel. It didn't work, and it took all she had not to call him and beg him to come back. It was crazy, but he'd only been gone a couple of minutes and already she missed him.

Relax, big sister. You'll see him in the morning.

She opened her door and slipped inside the brightly appointed room.

"I know," she said as she tossed herself across the bed, "but I'd rather wake up to him in the morning . . . *every* morning."

Whoa, hold on. Are you falling for this guy? You, Juliet Hall, whose only loves are ballet and the beach, is falling for a small-town sheriff? Granted, he's more appetizing than a plate of hot chocolate chip cookies, but oh. My. Gosh. Now I've seen everything.

Juliet ignored the imaginary voice of her dead sister and got ready for bed. After slipping between the sheets she turned her extra pillow and pretended it was Grant's chest. She laid there, her fingers stroking over the soft, cotton pillowcase, wishing with everything inside her it was him, but there was simply no substitute. The plush cushion was *far* too soft to be Grant's chest, it didn't smell like him, it wasn't warm, and it didn't have hands that could stroke her skin in return. The pillow was Pepsi and she wanted Coca-Cola - the *real* thing.

Frustrated, she rolled over and turned her back on her pillow Grant. A glance at the digital clock told her it was nearly 12:30 a.m.

Even though she was tired, she knew she would lay awake staring at the ceiling for hours.

Her cell phone rang and she jumped. Frowning, she grabbed the gadget from the bedside table and her heart rocketed into her throat when she saw Grant's caller ID. She blinked several times, certain she was imagining things. She wasn't. She pushed the button and held the device to her ear.

"Hello?"

"Did I wake you?"

She couldn't stop the smile and settled into the pillows. "No. I wasn't even close to asleep."

"Yeah." He sighed. "I have a feeling it'll be a while before the sandman visits my house."

"Me, too."

"We could talk for a bit."

Juliet giggled. "That sounds like something lovesick teenagers do, talk on the phone all night until they fall asleep."

"I don't know about you . . . but I sort of feel like a lovesick teenager." He chuckled softly and the sound traveled through the phone and her. "Crazy, huh?"

Her throat closed up and it took her a moment to free her voice. "I, um, I wouldn't know. Cassie had plenty of experience with that, but I've never actually *been* a lovesick teenager."

"That's right," he said with another soft laugh, "you were too busy with ballet lessons and Juilliard for things like puppy love weren't you?"

"I was." She squeezed her eyes shut and for the first time in her life wished she'd grown up differently. Maybe if she'd had a normal childhood and teenage experience, she wouldn't feel so out of sorts. "However, I'm beginning to understand the appeal. And here I thought only performing gave me butterflies and tingles."

"I give you butterflies and tingles?"

Her heart thumped. "You do." She frowned. "But, shouldn't that worry me? I mean, if this *is* just puppy love, doesn't that mean it's doomed?"

"God, I hope not."

She smiled so widely it felt like her face would crack. "Me, too."

The line was quiet for a few moments.

"I suppose the lightning fast way you came out that door means you were watching me through the window."

"I was." She rolled onto her side and pulled her pillow Grant closer. "I was wondering what I did wrong, why you didn't want to kiss me."

He laughed. "Believe me, that was *not* the problem. I *wanted* to kiss you . . . more than I've wanted to kiss any woman in my life."

The words popped out. "Even Laine?" She winced and cursed herself. "Grant, I'm sorry—"

"Even Laine."

That brought her up short. "Really?" The single word came out in a breathless rush.

"Really." His voice was low, but there was no mistaking the quiet conviction in his tone. "Laine set the bar, Juliet, but you leapt right over it, with skillful ease and unparalleled grace I might add."

She gulped. "Well . . . nobody's really set the bar in *my* life . . . until now." Her heart started a steady *ka-thump* against her breastbone. "But, I don't think even my best partner would be able to clear that height." Her cheeks flamed. "When you set the bar, Grant, you set it *really* high. It would probably be easier if they just jumped out of an airplane to get over it rather than trying to do that from the ground."

Another brief silence passed.

"Thank you."

"You're welcome."

"I'm glad you decided to go with me to the fair," he said after a short pause.

She laughed softly. "The way things are going I just may be your date for Shelby's wedding."

"If I thought you'd say yes I'd have already asked."

That *ka-thump* picked up its pace. "Why don't we wait until after the fair? I'll be much more agreeable with a funnel cake under my belt."

"I'll buy you ten."

A chuckle escaped her. "Don't do *that*. I have enough trouble dancing on my toes being as tall and as heavy as I am."

"I'm sorry, did you say *heavy*?" His incredulity was apparent, even if she couldn't see his face. "What do you weigh . . . about 120?"

Juliet rolled her eyes. "Yeah, and I'm 5'7"."

"In case you were unaware, that actually makes you *underweight* for your height by *normal* standards."

"I don't live by *normal* standards," she replied. "For your information, most ballerinas are between 5'2" and 5'6", and weigh 90-110 pounds." She pouted. "I actually weigh in at about 112 during performance season. Dancers who weigh less are lighter on their feet and are easier for their partners to lift."

He whistled softly. "Well, don't take this the wrong way, but I think you're perfect just like you are and if you put on a few pounds . . . ? *I* could still lift you, and you'd *still* be perfect."

Warmth enveloped her and she closed her eyes. "No, *you're* perfect."

The line went quiet for about ten seconds, and then they both said: "I wish you were here right now."

They laughed and when the chuckles died down Juliet sighed softly. "Tell me about yourself, Grant."

"What do you want to know?"

"Everything."

"Hmm." He paused. "That's a lot of territory to cover."

"Then you'd better start talking."

When they finally said goodbye it was after 2 a.m. Among other things she now knew he had an older sister and brother. The former was a school teacher and the latter worked for the county planning commission. They all lived just outside of town, on opposite sides, but their respective careers kept them from seeing each other as often as they would have liked. He had a half-dozen nieces and nephews and numerous cousins, all of whom lived within a few hours of Evergreen. Juliet envied their familial closeness, and their proximity to each other.

After she left for Juilliard nearly 10 years passed before she returned to the West Coast. Seeing her parents and Cassie had been a twice-a-year thing at most during her stint in New York, and only if they came to see her. That was part of the reason she'd left the Big Apple to become a principal at Ballet Northwest in Seattle. It was an easy flight to Seattle from San Diego, and once Cassie was accepted at the company she and Juliet were inseparable. The sisters saw their parents every few months, but having Cassie as her roommate had been the cherry on top of her career-in-Seattle sundae. Not once had she regretted the move.

Grant had promised to introduce her to his siblings the first chance he had. It was obvious family meant a lot to him, just as it did to her. She didn't think it was possible, but she liked him even more than she had before their late night phone call. And they'd already made a date to do it again the following evening, and it would be *her* turn to talk.

Juliet smiled and snuggled against her pillow Grant. It wasn't him, but she could pretend.

I have to say, Jules, I envy you.

She yawned. "*You . . .* envy *me?* How so?"

Oh, I don't know. You went to Juilliard and danced with the American Ballet Theater while I stayed in Cali and danced with a small ballet company in La Jolla.

"That was your choice, Cass. You didn't *want* to go to Juilliard and, unlike me, Mom didn't *make* you audition."

I know, but still. You were a principal at Northwest while I stayed in the ensemble. You perform like you were born to the stage, you never lose a jump competition, and it all comes naturally. You don't even have to practice.

Juliet's eyes snapped open. "Hey! I practice. I practice all the time."

I know, I'm just giving you a hard time, but now you've really *outdone me. You've got yourself a keeper with Sheriff Donovan, sister. Out of all the auditions I held, I never met a man worthy to clean his gun. Tell me, would you be willing to give up dancing to stay with him?*

Juliet thought about that for a moment. "I don't know."

You may want to think about it, Jules. That choice may head your way faster than you know.

"I can't think about that now, okay? I don't *want* to think about that."

Completely understandable. Good night, Juliet.

"Good night, Cass."

Sleep well and dream of your man. I love you.

"Love you too, little sister."

Chapter Thirteen

Grant's phone went off at 8:03 a.m. He growled, rolled over, and grabbed his cell from the nightstand. "Yeah, what?"

"Sheriff Donovan. It's Detective Riordan."

Grant sat straight up in bed. "Where are you?"

"I should be in Evergreen by about 10 a.m." The detective sighed. "Would've been in sooner, but the best flight I could get was from Seattle to Billings with a two-hour layover in *Portland*. What kind of shit is that? I leave *Seattle* and have to fly to *Portland* first. And we wonder why the airlines are bleeding money."

In spite of himself Grant chuckled. "Yeah, doesn't make a lot of sense. Do you need directions to my office? Miss Hall indicated she'd prefer to meet there."

"No, Google Maps can tell me how to get there, as long as you have cell coverage out that way. You guys are a little far off the grid."

"Google should be just fine," Grant replied. "At least, it works on my phone. Personally, it creeps me out that Google knows where I am all the time."

Riordan laughed, and it was a warm, genuine sound. "I hear you. I'll see you and Miss Hall soon." The line was quiet for a few seconds. "Thanks for convincing her to talk to me, by the way. I know you didn't want to."

"I *didn't* convince her. I told her you were coming and she decided for herself to talk to you."

"Really?" Riordan sucked in a breath. "*That's* a surprise."

"Sometimes people do that, they surprise you." Grant cleared his throat. "Just . . . don't be surprised if the conversation doesn't go the way you hope. I don't think she agreed to talk to you so you could arrange secure transport back to Seattle."

"What *do* you think?"

"That's between the two of you but prepare yourself for the worst."

"Okay." Riordan sighed. "Thanks for the warning, but you'll forgive me if I still try."

"Knock yourself out," Grant replied. "I don't think you're going to succeed no matter how hard you try, but I'm not going to stop you from giving it your best shot."

"My best shot." He laughed, and this time it was a short, sharp sound. "Yeah, that wasn't enough last time either."

Grant had no idea what that meant, but he kept his mouth shut and Riordan sighed again.

"All right, Sheriff. I'll see you and Ms. Hall in a couple of hours."

"We'll be waiting on you." Grant hung up and flopped back on his bed. "Well, at least I have another hour to sleep." He rolled onto his side and set his alarm, then rolled onto his back and drifted off, images of Juliet dancing in his head.

***

The sound of a soft knock pulled Juliet from sleep, a sleep that had been, surprisingly, dreamless. Or, at least, she hadn't dreamed of Cassie. That was plus enough. She pushed her hair out of her eyes and swung her legs off the side of the bed.

Sunlight fought to enter the room, finding every crack and crevice between the blinds and curtains to paint thin skeins of bright illumination on the floor. The clock read 8:45 and her eyes widened. Normally she was up at seven. Then again, she didn't usually stay up until after two in the morning talking to handsome men who gave her butterflies and tingles. A smile blossomed. Another knock broke into her thoughts of Grant and the smile vanished.

"Just a minute." She slipped into her robe and approached the door. "Who is it?"

"It's Nicole, dear. Could I speak to you for a minute?"

Juliet opened the door and smiled. "Morning, Miss Nicole. How are you this fine day?"

"I'm well, thank you. Did I wake you?"

"I was just getting up," Juliet lied.

Nicole peeked around her into the room, a curious look in her eyes. "Are you . . . alone?"

"Should I . . . *not* be?" Juliet asked.

The older woman's cheeks colored prettily. "Well, it's just that Mike said he saw you and Grant on the stoop last night . . . ."

Juliet fought a grin and leaned against the doorframe. "Grant left shortly thereafter, Miss Nicole."

"Oh."

Nicole looked and sounded disappointed, and Juliet bit the inside of her cheek to keep from smiling. "Is that what you wanted to talk to me about?"

"Oh, no dear." She shook her head and smiled. "I was just wondering . . . do you have any idea how long you're going to stay in town?"

"Not really. Why? Do you need the room?"

Nicole laughed softly. "Oh, no, Juliet. I already told you you're our only guest, and I don't have any reservations until the week of Thanksgiving, which is *several* months away." She patted her hair. "I just thought that if you're going to be here for a while . . . maybe you'd not be averse to spending some time with me in the kitchen a few days a week." A sly gleam entered her eyes. "You do some baking with me, and I give you the friends and family discount on your room."

While Juliet wasn't cash-strapped, she didn't have unlimited funds. Until she settled somewhere and found a job she had to be judicious with her money. "And what is the friends and family discount?"

"Ten dollars a day, what it costs to have Iris clean the room."

Iris was Nicole's housekeeper, a dour, middle-aged woman Juliet had met the previous morning. She was tall, sturdily built, with sharp black eyes and white haired pulled into a severe bun at the nape of her neck. Iris and Nicole were opposite ends of the personality spectrum from what she could see, and Juliet wondered how the two managed to work together.

"Ten dollars a day?" Juliet gasped. "I can't do that, Miss Nicole. I'm not going to take advantage of your hospitality and generosity." She shook her head. "I've stayed in rooms that weren't half as nice as this that cost ten times as much. It wouldn't be right."

Nicole actually laughed and patted her arm. "Oh, Juliet, you are a dear."

"Miss Nicole—"

"Child," Nicole began in a patient, motherly voice, "ten dollars a day is ten dollars more than I would make off this room if you weren't here, and it's a *fraction* of what I would pay you if you actually *worked* in my kitchen." She grinned. "I'm getting the better end of the deal, if you want the truth and besides . . . I'll get to spend time with you." Her expression turned wistful. "Baking with you yesterday reminded me of when my girls were younger. Now that they're grown and have families of their own, they don't have time to help their mama in the kitchen as often."

Helen Hall had never been the maternal type, and Juliet had learned to survive without the praise, affection, and love she saw other mothers bestow on their children. Her father had more than made up for that loss, or so she thought. Now, with Nicole standing there, asking her to help her in the kitchen like other mothers would, Juliet couldn't say no. She grasped the older woman's hand and squeezed lightly.

"I'd *love* to work in the kitchen with you, even if I have to pay $10 a day to do it."

Nicole's gaped at her. "You would?"

Juliet grinned and nodded. "I would."

Nicole clapped her hands together and laughed. "Oh, Juliet, this will be so much fun! We'll have to start early . . . around five a.m., but you'll be done by nine and the rest of the day will be yours." One brow slowly rose and a mischievous twinkle brightened her blue eyes. "I'm sure Grant will like that."

Juliet groaned. "I may only be here a few more days, another week *tops*."

A smug smile curved Nicole's thin lips. "That's enough time."

"Enough time for what?"

"For Grant to convince you to stay," Nicole replied. "Not that it'll take much convincing. Evergreen works its magic fast, but the Sheriff? He works *his* magic even faster."

Juliet stared after the woman as she turned and started to walk away.

Nicole took two steps, then stopped and turned back. "Oh, I won't need you until Monday. Have a lovely weekend, Juliet, you and Grant both. I hope you enjoy the fair."

***

Grant pulled up in front of the office at 9:27 a.m. He bounded up the stairs and went straight for Roberta's desk. The silver-haired woman looked at him and blinked.

"Morning, Sheriff. Aren't you supposed to be off?"

"Yep," Grant replied. "But that detective from Seattle should be here within the next hour so I thought I should make an appearance."

A smile curved Roberta's mouth. "Do you *ever* rest? I don't recall your daddy being in this office as much as you are."

"Yeah, well Dad had Mom to keep him occupied outside of work." He gave her a wry grin. "I don't have that excuse."

One silver brow arched. "Really? After what went on last night I'd say that statement isn't entirely true."

Grant gaped at her. "Seriously? How do you know what went on last night?" He planted his hands on his hips. "Did Mike say something to you or do I need to start checking this town for surveillance cameras?" His brows drew down. "I am *really* getting tired of my every move being made public before *I* even know what I'm doing. Can't even kiss a pretty girl without it being headline news."

Silver brows shot north. "I *was* referring to the dancing and your public address last night, but kissing, eh? Way to go, Grant." She chuckled and turned her gaze back to her computer screen. "About damn time."

Grant squeezed his eyes shut and ran a hand over his face.

"Don't worry, Sheriff," Roberta said, her fingers flying over the keys, "*I* won't tell anyone." She shot him a wry glance. "As far as I'm concerned, if I didn't see it, it didn't happen."

He huffed and looked at the wall over her head. "Thanks, Roberta."

"You're welcome."

Turning on his heel he headed for the front door.

"Where are you going?" Roberta asked.

"To get Juliet." He tossed her a wave. "If the detective gets here before we get back offer him a cup of coffee and have him make himself comfortable in my office."

Roberta nodded. "Will do."

Grant crossed the street and had just entered the park when a figure walking toward him caught his eye. The graceful way she moved, the dark hair, it could be no one but Juliet. He smiled and allowed himself to drink in the sight of her. She wore a simple white cotton sundress with a pale blue lightweight sweater tossed over her shoulders, her hair hung loose and shining around her face. She hadn't noticed him, her gaze focused downward as she put one foot in front of the other. When he reached the gazebo he leaned against it and just watched her, warmth filling his chest cavity. She got within 20 feet and still hadn't noticed him so he let out a low whistle.

Her head snapped up and her brows drew together as she looked for the source of the sound. She stopped in her tracks when she spotted him, and then a slow smile tipped up the corners of her alluring mouth. Grant felt his heart thud and his pulse pick up as she walked slowly toward him.

"Morning, Sheriff," she said, her cheeks going pink.

He tipped his hat. "Miss Hall."

She looked up at him through her lashes. "Did you get enough sleep last night?"

"You mean this morning?" He smiled. "I could do with a couple more hours, but I'm good. You?"

"I could use a little more sleep, too, but I'm fine." An elegant shrug lifted her shoulders. "I can always sleep in tomorrow."

"Mm hmm," he replied. His gaze swept over her. "You look beautiful, by the way. Dressing up for Detective Riordan?" Her gaze sharpened and he saw the flash of indignation.

"No." She dropped her chin and fingered the sleeve of her cardigan. "I was dressing up for . . . *you*, actually."

A tingle shot up his spine. He leaned over to look her in the eye. "You don't have to dress up for me, Juliet. I don't care what you wear. You'll always be beautiful to me but I do appreciate the effort. Thank you." He saw the convulsive swallow and her cheeks brightened a couple shades.

"You're welcome," she whispered.

He chuckled and tucked a lock of hair behind her ear. "Come on, darlin'. Your detective will be here shortly." He offered her his arm. "Let's head back to my office so we can greet him properly."

She shot him a glare even as she wrapped her fingers around his bicep. "He's not *my* detective."

"So your association with Detective Riordan is strictly professional?" He tried to appear nonchalant, but he kept his gaze forward just in case. If she saw in his eyes what he was feeling it would open up a totally different conversation, one he didn't want to have.

"Yes." She stopped and tugged on his arm. "Why?"

Grant faced her and looked over the top of her head. "Just the way he talked about you. It sounded like there was something else there, something deeper than a simple cop/crime victim relationship."

A puzzled frown marred her brow as they started walking again.

"Well, if there is I don't know about it. I was so busy trying to hold my life together and stay out of Mayfield's grasp that I really didn't notice much, if anything, outside of those efforts." She bit her lip. "I always thought he had a thing for Cassie, which was *typical*, so I didn't pay much attention."

He fought the surge of relief. "Hmm." Grant rubbed his chin. "Well, maybe I'm right, maybe I'm wrong. We'll see when he gets here, won't we?"

"I hope not," she said with a shake of her head. "An apology is about as deep as I want to take this conversation."

He draped an arm over her shoulders. "This conversation only goes the way you want it. If it goes any other way, you let me know and I'll send Detective Riordan right back to Seattle." His insides tightened when she wound an arm around his waist and hooked her thumb through his belt loop.

"Thank you," she said softly.

She leaned into his side and exhilaration rose inside him. He grinned, kept walking, and said, "You're welcome."

They paused on the sidewalk in front of the Sheriff's Office and Juliet looked up at the pale brick façade. Like the Center Hotel, it had an Old West look and feel to it. Grant released her and gestured for her to precede him. Nervous flutters danced in her belly, but she took a deep breath and mounted the stairs. She wanted to hold his hand, let his touch reassure her, but she realized that would be inappropriate in this particular setting.

The Sheriff's offices were on the second floor and she gripped the wide, square railing as the aged stairs creaked beneath her feet. When she walked through the open double doors a pretty, plump woman with silver hair and intelligent brown eyes that crinkled pleasantly at the corners when she smiled turned to her. The woman removed her headset, came out from behind the desk, and walked toward her with her hand extended.

"Hi there," she said, closing Juliet's fingers in a strong, warm grip. "I'm Roberta. I've seen you around," she paused and gave Grant a look Juliet couldn't decipher, "but it's about time we were formally introduced."

Grant chuckled and gestured at Juliet. "Roberta, this is Juliet," he drawled. Then he swept an arm toward Roberta. "Juliet, Roberta."

Juliet laughed softly. "Pleasure to meet you."

Roberta smiled back. "Oh, honey, the pleasure is all mine. We've been hoping and praying that Grant would--"

"Roberta," he said in a softly warning tone.

Roberta's eyes moved past her to land on Grant. "Yes, Sheriff?"

"Please show Detective Riordan in when he gets here."

"Yes, sir."

Juliet's gaze was drawn from the older woman back to Grant when he placed a hand in the small of her back.

"Do you want a cup of coffee or something?" he asked.

"I'm fine, thanks."

"Okay, then." He hung his hat on a nearby rack and gestured toward an open doorway. "This way."

Juliet started toward the office door when something in her periphery caught her attention and she stopped in her tracks. Her head slowly turned to her right and she looked into the eyes of George Mayfield. Something cold and chillingly familiar coiled below her heart. It didn't matter that it was only a picture. He had the same look on his face in the mugshot that he'd had every time he'd looked at her, an expression of complete contradiction. He appeared at once intensely focused yet apathetic, as if every person his gaze landed on was just another bug under glass for him to study. They were interesting as long as he was interested, yet he cared nothing for them and would squish them without a thought. She squeezed her eyes shut and fought to rein in the panic sneaking up her throat.

"Juliet."

Her eyes snapped open and Grant's face swam into view. She blinked several times and the sound of her own labored breathing reached her ears. His brows drew together and he grasped her upper arms lightly. Juliet focused on his beautiful chocolate-colored eyes and tried to take long, slow breaths.

"Juliet, are you alright?"

The panic receded and she nodded. "I'm . . . I'm fine." Her gaze flicked toward the wall again. "I just didn't expect to see . . . *him.*"

A look of self-reproach shadowed Grant's features. "I'm sorry. I should've warned you."

"That *wouldn't* have helped, believe me. Even after I realized he was stalking me and I *expected* to see his face every time I turned around, it still startled me when I did." A shudder ran through her and his grip on her arms tightened just a bit. "You grow up hearing about the boogeyman, but you expect monsters to look like *monsters*, not *angels*."

His eyes were dark with concern. "Let's go in my office." He glanced over his left shoulder. "Roberta, I think maybe a cup of coffee would be in order after all."

"You got it, Grant."

Juliet fought the urge to turn and stare at Mayfield's image as she allowed Grant to lead her to his office. Once inside he steered her to one of the chairs that faced his desk while he sat in the one at her elbow.

"Maybe we should do this meet another time," he suggested. "I'll send Riordan to the diner and we can arrange something for later today, or even tomorrow. Or never."

She shook her head. "No." She met his worried gaze and laid a hand over his. "I just want to get this over with, so we can get on with the rest of our day."

His brows drew together. "I'd understand if you didn't want to do anything." He laced his fingers through hers and rubbed the back of her hand with his thumb. "Maybe when this is done you should go back to the hotel and just get some rest."

The friction of his skin against hers was distracting but in the most pleasant way. Juliet let the warmth of his touch travel up her arm and through the rest of her. "Not on your life, Sheriff. I've been waiting . . . ." She paused and glanced at the clock on the wall, "more than nine hours to see you."

Roberta entered the office at that moment, a steaming cup of coffee in her hands. Juliet was surprised when Grant didn't pull his hand from hers or break eye contact. Roberta handed the cup to her.

"Thank you," Juliet said.

"You're welcome." Roberta gave her a wink and exited without saying another word, closing the door behind her.

Juliet took a sip of the hot brew. It was surprisingly good. The coffee at Seattle PD had always been thick, dark, and tasted burnt. After another careful drink, she put the cup on his desk and faced him.

"I'm fine, Grant, I promise."

"*You* didn't see your face." His thumb continued the soft, soothing strokes. "You went white as a sheet and I thought for a second you were going to pass out."

Her jaw tightened. "If I didn't pass out when I found Cassie's body I'm sure as hell not going to pass out because I see a photograph tacked to a wall."

He winced and dropped his gaze. "I am so sorry you had to find your sister like that."

She squeezed her eyes shut and frowned. "Better me than a stranger I suppose."

Before he could reply there was a light rap on the door. He gently slipped his fingers from hers and rose to open the heavy, oak panel. Roberta stood there.

"He's here," she said in a low voice. "Do you ... need another minute?"

He glanced at Juliet, and when she shook her head he looked at Roberta. "Send him in."

Detective Daniel Riordan strode in and Juliet sucked in a breath at the barrage of memories that came flooding back: yellow crime scene tape that changed color with each pulse of the red and blue patrol car lights, dozens of voices that seemed to drop to whispers when they passed by, and the gurney. The gurney that carried her sister's body from the house to the waiting ambulance. She gulped and willed the mental pictures away.

It was odd that a man who would awaken lust and longing in almost every woman he met only stirred bad memories, fear, and mild nausea in her. He was a couple inches shorter than Grant which still put him over six feet, and he had the physique of someone who kept in top physical shape. Blonde hair was cut short in a military style, and bright hazel eyes looked out from a face that was intelligent, masculine, and well-sculpted. He was dressed in dark jeans, a button-up shirt with no tie, and a dark brown blazer. The triangle of skin exposed by the open neck of his shirt gave a tantalizing hint to the musculature that lay beneath it. She'd known him for more than a year, but she'd never really noticed his physicality until now. Not that it mattered. His handsomeness paled for her when he stood next to Grant.

Riordan shook Grant's hand. When his eyes swiveled to his right and caught sight of her the relief that swept his features made her wonder if perhaps Grant was correct to ask if there was something deeper than a professional relationship. The detective immediately dropped down into the chair Grant had vacated and grabbed her hands.

"Thank God," he said. "You're safe."

"Did you expect her not to be?" Grant drawled as he moved behind the desk and sat down.

Riordan threw a glance at the sheriff and then went on the offensive. "Juliet, I want you to come back to Seattle. Mayfield is out there somewhere, and I'd never forgive myself if something happened to you." His eyes pleaded with her. "Please. We can keep you safe."

Juliet felt the sincerity behind his words, knew he truly desired to protect her, but she shook her head and disentangled her hands from his. "No."

He blinked at her, but he wasn't done yet. "You're in danger."

A short, sharp laugh escaped her and she stood. "*You're* telling *me* that?"

"Juliet—"

She squeezed her eyes shut and sliced the air with both hands. "No." Taking several deep breaths, she looked at him and met his beseeching gaze. "This is *not* why I came here."

"I can't protect you from him if you stay in Montana."

She gaped at him, her insides spinning in fierce, frantic circles. "You couldn't protect me from him in *Seattle*." A frown darkened his brow and he stood. Before he could speak she pressed a hand to his mouth. "Please, Daniel. I didn't agree to meet with you so you could talk me into returning to Seattle."

"Then why *did* you agree to meet with me?"

Memories of what had happened that night – what she'd seen and the things she'd said – launched to the forefront of her mind, and shafts of pain pierced her like arrows of pure ice. Tears stung and she blinked rapidly. "The night I found . . . ." She gulped and closed her eyes briefly. "I said some awful things to you that night." The last thing she wanted to do was cry, but the well behind her eyes overflowed and tears gathered. She took a hitching breath and plunged on before her nerve deserted her completely. "You didn't kill Cassie, you did everything short of breaking the law yourself to protect me, and her, and I am so sorry for blaming you." Her throat closed up and the tears finally fell, trickling slowly over her cheeks. "You couldn't have prevented what happened and I had no right to take out my anger on you. Please . . . please forgive me."

The pain and disbelief in his eyes knifed through her and she couldn't take anymore. The images she had managed to keep at bay since arriving in Evergreen assaulted her in what felt like a rape of her soul. No matter how she fought them, they were stronger than her and determined to have their way. The pictures gathered and loomed in her mind's eye, faded black and white images amongst the blazing Technicolor flashes: glossy, liquid blood on the pale maple floor, the pink baby-doll negligee, Cassie's bright, blue, lifeless eyes, and the dark, vulgar splatters and block letters on the smooth white wall. Panic tightened around her heart and lungs and suddenly she couldn't breathe. She glanced at Grant, looked at Riordan again, and the movie started to play. She fought it, but she wasn't strong enough, not with *him* here. The office closed in on her, pressed down on her heart and lungs, and the overwhelming urge to run spurred her to her feet. She needed to get away from him, from the memories he roused in her, from the guilt that gnawed at her from the inside. Without a word she spun and raced out of the office as if Mayfield himself was chasing her.

Chapter Fourteen

Grant sighed heavily and rubbed his eyes. Riordan looked every bit as devastated as Juliet, a muscle in his cheek twitching. He moved to go after her but Grant rose quickly and interposed himself between the detective and the door.

"Don't."

"But—"

Grant cut him off. "*No.* Give her some space."

Riordan stared at him, and the warring emotions on his face brought back Grant's own memories of being torn emotionally asunder by people he loved and circumstances he couldn't control. He tamped those feelings down and focused on what was happening right in front of him instead of what lay in his past.

The man looked exhausted, both mentally and physically, and Grant could well imagine the sleepless nights he'd probably spent. Riordan backed up several paces, and after about half a minute his shoulders slumped. He walked to the window overlooking the square, rubbed his brow, and stared through the tinted glass.

"Sorry, Detective," Grant said softly, "but I *did* warn you."

"I know, but I still had to come," the man replied in a hushed voice. "I don't think I've slept a wink since she dropped off the grid." He clenched his jaw. "I had to see for myself that she was all right."

Grant moved to the man's side. Juliet sat on the steps of the gazebo, and although he couldn't make out her face from this distance, the stoop of her shoulders told him much of how she felt.

"She looks a hell of a lot better than she did last time I saw her," Riordan commented softly. "Before she lit out from Seattle she was hovering at about 100 pounds . . . *barely* . . . pale, gaunt. She couldn't sleep, she couldn't eat, she couldn't dance . . . she could hardly function."

A pained smile lifted the corners of his mouth. "At least she's put on a few pounds and has some color."

Grant stuffed his hands in his pockets. "Your relationship with Miss Hall goes deeper than simply professional, doesn't it?"

Riordan pressed his thumb and forefinger into his eyes and laughed shortly. "It does, but it only flows one way, from *me* to *her*."

So he'd been right. The knowledge gave him no pleasure; it only made him sad for the detective. He knew *exactly* how it felt to be in love with someone who didn't feel the same way. "She doesn't know."

"No," Riordan said with a shake of his head. "How could she? She was so bound up by what Mayfield was doing to her, and I certainly wasn't going to say anything, not in the middle of everything that was happening. When Cassie was alive I could play it off, flirt back when Cassie flirted with me, but then . . . ." He rubbed his brow and took a deep, shuddering breath. "Then everything went straight to hell."

Both men went quiet and the silence stretched out.

"Why would Mayfield go after Cassie?" Grant asked at last, more of himself than the detective. "She wasn't his type."

Riordan glanced at him, blonde brows drawn together. "What do you mean?"

Grant gave him a sidelong glance. "You didn't notice how much Wendy Braxton and Juliet resemble each other? Both are dark-haired, blue-eyed, slender, and pretty." He rubbed his chin. "The mother, too, Mayfield's mother, she also had dark hair and blue eyes. She died when Mayfield was a teenager, didn't she?" He walked back behind his desk and picked up the file. After flipping through it he came to a photo of the Mayfield family and tapped the image with his index finger.

Riordan moved to his side and looked at the picture. "There is a resemblance, but Mayfield's mother drowned in the bathtub when he was . . . ." Riordan turned the pages quickly until he found what he was looking for, "Fifteen."

Grant sifted through a few more pages. "Mrs. Mayfield was 5'3" and 105 pounds. Her son, at 15, was 6'3" and 195." He rubbed his chin. "Maybe she had some help . . . drowning in the bathtub."

Riordan looked at Grant out of the corner of his eye, and it was as if he read Grant's mind. "You think he's a serial."

"Makes more sense than the theory that all these attractive, slender, blue-eyed brunettes dying around him is just coincidence, don't you think?" He frowned and eased down in his chair. "But, Cassie doesn't fit."

Riordan sat on the corner of his desk, his gaze vague. "Actually, she kind of does." When Grant looked at him in silent question Riordan turned toward him. "When Mayfield went to Juliet and Cassie's that night he had committed himself to a specific course of action. He must have planned it for weeks, so when he entered that house . . . *someone* was going to die."

Grant sat up a little straighter. "Cassie was *supposed* to be working. I read in the file that the manager at the restaurant said someone called a couple of days before the murder, asking about the sisters' schedules. That *had* to be Mayfield, so he fully expected Cassie to be gone and Juliet to be home."

"By the time he realized it was Cassie and not Juliet, it was too late for him to turn back."

"Hence the tagline he left on the bedroom wall."

"It should have been you." Riordan sighed heavily. "Fuck me. If you're right about this, it opens up a whole new can of worms; you know that, don't you?"

"Yeah," Grant agreed. "It means you need to start digging a little deeper. You know what they say about a serial's first kill."

Their eyes met and Riordan nodded. "It's usually the closest to home." He got up and moved back to the window, hands in his pockets. "Forgive me for changing the subject, but the relationship between you and Juliet is deeper than just professional, isn't it?"

"It is."

"And it goes both ways, doesn't it?"

Grant sighed softly. "It does."

"I could tell. The way she looked at you . . . ." Riordan faced him and he saw the blatant envy in the man's eyes. "If you care about her, Sheriff, I mean *really* care about her, don't do what I did."

"And what is that?"

"Don't let your feelings get in the way of taking that bastard out."

Grant winced. He'd read in the file how Riordan had almost shot Mayfield when the man attacked Juliet outside of the theater after rehearsal one night. Riordan hadn't taken the shot because he had been afraid he might miss Mayfield and hit Juliet instead. It was a perfectly legitimate reason to not fire, but he knew it did little to assuage the detective's guilt.

"I'm a good shot, Sheriff," Riordan said, moving to sit on a chair facing the desk. A wry grin twisted his lips for a split-second. "I'm not as good as *you*, but better than most." His expression turned introspective. "That night, outside the theater when he grabbed her and I confronted him, he let her go. He held up his hands as if surrendering, that *smug* smile on his face." His expression darkened and he slammed one fist against the arm of the chair. "Once Juliet darted away I could've shot him and it would've been a good shoot. He'd already killed one woman, he was threatening Juliet, she feared for her life, and he attacked her in a darkened alley. I could've put a bullet in his brain and been hailed a hero. Instead . . . I arrested him."

Grant sympathized with the decision the detective had faced that night. The only advantage he'd had in the decisions he made to shoot people was his location. He'd been in a war zone, which was subject to far less analysis and liability than the average cop on the street had to deal with. Law enforcement officers were under constant scrutiny and were often held to ridiculous standards even when a civilian's life, or their own life, was in danger. It was an impossible situation, one that he, thankfully, had never faced outside of the Marine Corps.

"If you could go back would you do things differently?" Grant asked.

Riordan huffed. "Absolutely."

"Don't do that, Detective," Grant told him. He rose and moved to the window. "If Juliet doesn't blame you for what happened, which we both know she *doesn't*, it's just masochistic to blame yourself."

"How do you not?" Riordan asked in a low voice, rising and walking to Grant's side. He stared toward the gazebo. "How do you get the image of a beautiful, 26-year-old girl, whose life was brutally ended, out of your head?"

"Nail the guy who did it."

Grant followed the direction of Riordan's gaze. Juliet still sat on the steps of the gazebo, but Mike and Nicole had stopped to chat. The couple was obviously out delivering Nicole's baked goods, a cart filled with pink boxes sitting nearby.

"I hope you don't mind, but I'm going to stick around for a few days," Riordan said.

The last thing he wanted was for the detective to stay in Evergreen, a reminder to Juliet of what she'd been through, but there was little he could do about it. A flash of annoyance warmed him. He choked it down.

"I'm the Sheriff here, not the king, so it wouldn't matter if I *did* mind," Grant replied. "Unless you break the law or piss off the locals I have no valid reason to chase you out of town." He gave Riordan a sidelong glance. "There's only one hotel, however, and Juliet is staying there."

"I don't plan to spy on her," Riordan said flatly.

"Then why do you plan to stay at all?"

"I can't just leave." He gave Grant a level look. "Tell me *you* could walk away."

He thought about it for a few seconds and sighed. "She won't want you here," Grant said.

"I know." Riordan nodded and turned his gaze back to the square. "I'll stay out of your way."

"Going to be hard to do that in a town Evergreen's size." Grant glanced out the window. Mike and Nicole had moved on and Juliet rose. She looked in their direction, then squared her shoulders and started walking. He leaned a shoulder into the glass. "Unless you plan to lock yourself in your room for the foreseeable future, you're *going* to run into her."

Riordan simply repeated, "I'll stay out of your way."

"You could stay here," Grant suggested. "There's a bunkroom in back, and showers in the locker room. It's not as comfortable as the hotel, but you won't have to work so hard to stay out of sight."

Riordan seemed to ponder that. "Would you have a computer I could use?"

Grant was following the detective's line of thought. "Deputy Tiller is on vacation for the next couple of weeks. You can use his desk and computer while you're here. I'll have Roberta set you up and get you a password."

Riordan nodded and then was quiet for several seconds. "Sheriff, I feel ridiculous even asking you this but . . . ."

The look on the detective's face made him distinctly uneasy. "What?"

"Mayfield has a juvenile record that we've been trying to unseal for almost a year." Riordan faced him, his expression skeptical. "I don't know why you would, but if you have any ideas as to how we could get our hands on those files I'd be anxious to hear them. It might give us some more insight into the man, something we have precious little of."

His insides relaxed. "Actually," Grant began, his mind working quickly, "I may be able to help you, Detective." He met Riordan's eyes.

"Let me make a call and I'll get back to you."

"Great," Riordan said with a small sigh as he extended his hand, "and since we're going to be working together maybe you should call me Daniel, or Danny."

The sad acceptance Grant saw in Riordan's eyes was achingly familiar. It was the same look he'd seen in his own reflection when he'd realized Laine was in love with Jack and lost to him forever. Despite the differences between them, he was beginning to feel a sort of kinship with the Seattle cop. Grant gripped the man's hand firmly. "All right, Daniel. Call me Grant."

Sensing another presence in the room Grant released Riordan's hand and turned. Juliet stood in the doorway, her expression uncertain, and her teeth worrying her lower lip. Her hands were clasped in front of her, and Grant thought if she chewed her lip any harder she'd draw blood.

"Sorry I ran out of here like that," she said in a low voice, her fingers tugging self-consciously on the sleeve of her cardigan. "I . . . needed some air."

Riordan took several steps toward her, obviously hesitant, but he was the first to reply. "I'm sorry if me being here hurts you, Juliet, but I had to see for myself that you were all right."

She shrugged. "Seeing you does bring up a few memories I'd rather not think about, but *none* of this is your fault."

"I should've done more. I let you down, you and Cassie both."

Her brows drew together and Grant saw the concern reflected in those amazing eyes. That she could put aside her own pain to consider another's only heightened his esteem for her.

"You didn't let us down, Daniel," she said, crossing the distance between them and taking his hands in hers. "The *system* let me down." She sighed and closed her eyes briefly. "Criminals seem to have more rights than victims these days."

The detective's next words were hushed, and Grant felt a little uncomfortable, as if he was intruding on a couple's intimate moments together.

"I wish things were different."

A sad smile curved Juliet's mouth. "So do I, but wishing won't make it so." Her smile faded and a glint of steel entered her eyes. "And, I'm sorry you wasted your time coming here, but I'm not going back to Seattle with you. There's nothing left for me there."

Grant winced as he imagined the wound Juliet had unknowingly inflicted on the lovesick detective. Part of him wanted to teleport out of the room, but he decided to remain mute and motionless and let things play out. If Juliet wanted to say something she didn't want him to hear she'd no doubt ask him to leave. He would comply with that request happily.

"I didn't waste my time." Riordan shrugged. "At least now I might get some sleep." He held Juliet's gaze for several long, silent seconds then said, "What if he finds you?"

Juliet's reply was immediate. "Then he finds me." She released his hands, sighed, and sat down in the nearest chair. "He's already taken my career, my family, and my sister." She looked up at him. "I don't have a whole lot left to lose."

He sat opposite her. "You could lose your life."

She thought about that for a bit. "Well, if I *have* to make a last stand . . . ." Her voice trailed off and she looked at Grant. "I'd rather do it here where I know I'll have backup." Grant gave her a small nod.

Riordan looked over his shoulder. "And this is okay with you?"

Grant lifted one brow in mocking reply. "I'll do my job, and it's really not my decision to make."

"It's mine," Juliet said. There was a distinct frost in her tone and she stood. "I'm going to stay here."

Riordan looked up at her. "For how long?"

"I don't know. I haven't decided and it's really none of your business."

Grant watched as Riordan seemed to deflate before his eyes. The detective rested an elbow on the arm of the chair he sat in and dropped his forehead into his cupped palm. Grant focused on the toes of his cowboy boots because seeing the detective realize imminent defeat hit a little close to home. A little too close.

Silence prevailed for a bit and then Grant heard Riordan inhale deeply. He looked up as the detective rose, straightened his spine, and faced Juliet.

"Okay then," Riordan said. "If you're staying here, so am I."

She blinked at him and her mouth dropped open. "What?"

"I can't make you come back to Seattle, and you can't force me to leave Evergreen Springs."

She stared at the detective.

Riordan clenched his hands at his sides. "Until I get a bead on

Mayfield's whereabouts, I'm staying where I can keep an eye on you. But don't worry, you won't see me." He glanced over his shoulder at Grant. "Grant."

Grant nodded. "Daniel."

Riordan strode out of the office without looking back. Juliet watched him go with wide, disbelieving eyes, and then she turned to look at him. "He's staying?"

"That's what he said."

"Where? The hotel?"

"No." He crossed his arms over his chest. "We have a bunkroom in back. He'll be staying here."

"Why?"

Grant studied her face carefully. "If he doesn't stay here the hotel is his only other choice."

"Why let him stay at all?"

"He wants to help, Juliet, and I can't force him to leave any more than I can force you to stay." She sank back down in the chair and clasped her hands in her lap. He moved to sit on the edge of his desk. "Give him a break. He cares about you."

Her gaze flew in his direction. "He *said* that?"

He gave her a curt nod. "But rest easy, he knows you don't feel the same."

She squeezed her eyes shut and pressed her fingers to her temples. "I just hurt him again, didn't I?"

Grant took a deep breath. "Yeah." When he saw the distress in her eyes something inside him lurched. "Sometimes love hurts," he said softly. "Sometimes we fall in love with people who, for whatever reason, can't return those feelings. Does it suck? Yeah, but there's nothing anyone can do. People can't make themselves feel something they don't." He sighed. "It's a part of life, and I think it's those experiences that give us a truer appreciation of what real love is when we finally find it."

"That doesn't make it any easier."

"No, it doesn't," he agreed. "You don't have to like it; you just have to deal with it."

She looked at him uncertainly for a few moments. "I suppose." A shuddering breath escaped her. "What doesn't kill us makes us stronger, right?"

He shrugged. "Personally, I've always been of the mindset that whatever doesn't kill me had better start running, in a zigzag pattern if they know what's good for 'em."

A chuckle escaped her and then she looked at him in surprise. "Only you could make me laugh in the middle of something like this." A smile curved her mouth. "Thank you."

"You are most welcome."

"Can we get out of here?"

He nodded. "Absolutely. Where do you want to go?"

Delicate brows rose. "I thought you already had this day planned out."

"I did," he replied, "but if you want to go back to your room and be alone for a while I completely understand." He searched her eyes. "It's been a rough morning."

"The last thing I want right now is to be alone." She reached for his hand and laced her fingers through his. "I'd much rather be with you."

Warmth enveloped him and his heart flipped. He lifted her hand and brushed his lips over her knuckles. "Works for me."

Jackson chose that moment to walk into his office without knocking, his nose buried in a stack of papers. Juliet tried to pull her hand from his but he tightened his grip just enough to keep hold of her. When she looked at him questioningly he only smiled and cleared his throat. Jackson froze. His head snapped up and his jaw went slack.

"Grant," he said, his eyes going wide. "I thought you were off until Monday."

Grant saw the deputy's gaze slide to their joined hands, and he saw the flash of disapproval before it was carefully masked. Anger flared briefly, but Grant pulled it in and gave the younger man a bland smile. "Do you always make yourself at home in my office when I'm off-duty?"

Jackson's mouth opened and closed a couple times and color stained his cheeks. "Um, no, of course not." He flapped the sheaf of papers at him. "Just had some paperwork I was going to leave on your desk."

"Mm hmm," Grant replied. "I *do* have a cubby in the main office."

"Which I will utilize right now." Jackson nodded to Juliet. "Miss Hall."

She nodded back. "Deputy." After Jackson retreated she looked at Grant out of the corner of her eye. "Do I sense a little tension here?"

"You do."

"Because of me?"

He shook his head. "No."

She didn't appear convinced. "Okay."

"Don't you worry about him," he said. "Now, I have a couple quick things I have to do before I can go. Will you be okay here for a few minutes?"

"I'll be fine," she said with a nod.

Grant rose. "All right then. I'll be back shortly."

When he stepped out of his office the sound of hushed chatter reached him. Grant glanced toward the deputies' work area and felt a surge of angry heat as he saw Jackson leaning on the edge of Simmons' desk. The rest of the deputies, except for Sheridan who was working at her desk, were gathered around and listening intently. Simmons happened to notice him and gave Jackson a look. The group went oddly silent and a guilty flush stained Jackson's face when he turned and saw Grant standing there.

"Shouldn't a couple of you be out on patrol?" Grant asked in a bored voice.

Epps and Barnick shot to their feet.

"Leaving now, Sheriff," Barnick said. He and Epps walked quickly toward the exit without a single backward glance.

Simmons and Jackson remained where they were, looking like naughty children who'd just been caught doing something they oughtn't.

"Is there a problem here?" Grant asked, hooking his thumbs through his belt loops.

"No more than usual, Sheriff," Sheridan said with a roll of her eyes. She went back to her computer, but not before tossing a caustic glance Jackson's way.

Grant looked at Simmons, who shook his head and started tapping on his keyboard. When Grant moved his gaze to Jackson the younger man colored again, but shook his head and returned to his workstation. Damn it. Firing Jackson seemed to be more and more inevitable, no matter how much of a pain in the ass it was.

He turned to Roberta, who watched this exchange with a completely neutral expression. Their eyes locked.

"What do you need, Sheriff?"

"I need you to set up system access for Detective Riordan. He'll need a password, and he'll be using Tiller's workstation while he's here."

Roberta frowned. "How long is he going to be here?"

"Don't know," Grant replied. "Just get him up and running and . . . keep an eye out."

She gave him a grim smile. "Will do."

Grant walked toward the bunkroom in the back, pulling his cell out as he went. Pausing in the hallway, he dialed an all-too-familiar number. Laine answered after the second ring.

"Hey, Grant!"

"Hey, Lainey," he said, leaning against the wall.

"I was just thinking about you."

"You were? Why?"

"Well, we haven't talked in about a week." Laine paused. "Is everything okay?"

"Everything's fine. Why wouldn't it be?"

"I don't know. You just sound . . . upset."

He sighed. "Problems with Jackson."

"Again?"

"Again."

She laughed softly. "Why don't you just fire him and get it over with? You've been butting heads with that man since you took office."

"I know, but the paperwork is a real bitch."

"So have Roberta do it for you."

A chuckle escaped him. "Maybe I will."

"Let me know if you do, and I'll come up so we can celebrate."

"I'll do that." He paused as his stomach clenched uncomfortably. "Is Jack there?"

The line was silent for almost five seconds.

"Um, no . . . he's at the office. Why?"

"Could you text me his office number? I need to speak with him."

"Really? *You* want to talk to *Jack*?"

He rubbed his eyes. "I said *need*, not *want*. There's a difference."

Laine made an annoyed sound. "It would be really great if the two most important men in my life could find a way to be friends. You *can't* still be pissed at him for what happened."

"Yes, I can."

"Grant."

It had already been a hell of a morning and between Riordan, Jackson, and this, he was just about at the end of his rope. Frustration roiled and he tried to keep it out of his voice. "I'm working on it, Laine.

Can you text me his number?"

"Sure," she said in a subdued tone. "Is that the only reason you called?"

You're an asshole, he thought to himself. "I'd love to talk but I'm in the middle of something here, and I'm hoping your husband can help me. How about I call you later this evening and we can catch up?"

"Whenever you have the time," she replied. "I miss you, Grant."

"I miss you, too, Lainey. I'll talk to you soon."

"Okay. Love you."

"Love you, too."

Less than 10 seconds after he hung up he received a text message from Laine. He dialed the number, followed the automatic prompts, and all too soon a familiar male voice answered.

"Special Agent Vaughn."

"Jack, it's Grant." There was no reply and for a moment he thought the line had disconnected. "Jack?"

"Um, yeah, Grant, hi. Sorry, I'm just surprised to hear from you."

"Believe me, when I got up this morning this is *not* a phone call I thought I'd make." Grant sighed. "Look, I know things between us are . . . *tense,* but I have a problem I'm hoping you can help me with."

"What kind of problem?"

Grant tapped on the bunkroom door. "Let me get a third party in on this call and we'll explain it to you."

Jack was quiet for a few seconds. "I'll help however I can, Grant. I have no desire to be at odds with you. I'd like to be friends, if possible. I hope someday you can forgive me."

It felt like a band of wire was tightening around his middle. This was *not* a conversation he wanted to have. "You don't need my forgiveness, Jack. You didn't do anything wrong. Laine fell in love with you and that's not an offense against me. It was just hard."

Riordan opened the bunkroom door and looked at him in silent question. Grant motioned for him to get his cell phone.

"I can imagine." Jack sighed. "If this helps mend fences I'm all in."

In spite of the tautness in his belly Grant smiled. "Well, I don't believe friendship is contingent on doing someone favors, although I appreciate your willingness to help. This is work-related, so I'll owe you one. We'll sort the rest out later, all right?"

"Fair enough," Jack replied. "Now, how may I be of service?"

Chapter Fifteen

"So, what are we doing?"

Grant gave her a languid smile as he opened the door of the Yukon. "I'll tell you when we get there."

Juliet pursed her lips and climbed into the passenger seat. "It's a surprise?"

"Sort of." He closed her door and walked around to his. After sliding behind the wheel and buckling his seatbelt he put the keys in the ignition and started the engine. "I just don't want to give you a chance to say no."

"Haven't we already gone over this?" she asked with a quick grin.

"Like I said before," Grant began as he backed out of the parking spot, "I try not to be overconfident when it comes to the opposite sex."

"You'd be perfectly justified," Juliet said under her breath.

"What?"

"Nothing," she lied. "Nothing at all."

The look he gave her sent tingles fanning over her skin. A soft chuckle rumbled in his chest and he put the Yukon in drive. When they pulled in front of the hotel and parked Juliet looked at him.

"What are we doing here?"

He rested one hand on the steering wheel and stared at the façade of the hotel. "Well, you need to put on your workout gear and grab your toe shoes. You're also going to need two additional changes of clothes, jeans and t-shirts and the like, sneakers, and toiletries, whatever you need to shower."

She blinked at him and a tingle of uncertainty shivered up her back. "Okay. Why?"

That sensual grin widened. "I'll tell you when we get there." She didn't move and he got out of the Yukon. After opening her door, he leaned against the frame. "Come on now, unless you want to sit here all afternoon."

Juliet briefly entertained the thought of being stubborn, but when he held out a hand she couldn't stop herself. Before she realized it she'd slipped her fingers into his and allowed him to escort her to the lobby. Nicole was behind the front desk with the phone to her ear, and she gave them a wave and a smile. Grant leaned against the counter and gestured toward the stairs.

"Go on, Juliet. Daylight's a wastin'."

The warmth in those bedroom eyes made her pulse move a little faster, and suddenly she wanted to run to her room. She forced herself to walk until she was out of his line of sight, then she sprinted the rest of the way.

She changed quickly, choosing a dark blue leotard, nude tights, and pair of black yoga pants. The rest of the requested clothing and toiletries she tossed into a duffel bag alongside her pointe shoes.

Don't forget some perfume, Jules, and some sexy underwear. You know where this day might lead.

Juliet rolled her eyes. "Give me a break, Cass. We're just spending the day together."

Mm hmm. I'm sure that's all you're going to do.

"Stop it." Juliet tossed a glare at the photo on the nightstand. "Besides, I don't have any sexy underwear."

Then make sure your bra and panties match. I'm sure that'll be sexy enough for your sheriff.

"He's not *my* sheriff."

Oh, yes, he is. And you're the only one who doesn't seem to understand that.

Juliet zipped the bag shut and slung it over her shoulder, not bothering to reply as she left the room. Thankfully, Cassie's voice didn't follow her downstairs.

"All right, Grant," she said as she approached him, "I have my toe shoes, two extra changes of clothes, and toiletries." She put her hands on her hips. "This is your show. What now?"

Grant gave Nicole a wink and a smile. "Don't wait up, Miss Nicole. Juliet may be late."

"Good," Nicole said under her breath. "About time." Juliet gasped and the older woman smiled widely. "I'm sorry. Did I say that out loud?"

"You did, Miss Nicole." Grant laughed and reached for Juliet's hand. "C'mon, darlin', let's go."

Nicole giggled as Grant led Juliet outside. She let Grant open her door and climbed into the passenger seat, dropping her bag on the floorboard at her feet. He jogged around to his side, slid behind the wheel, and started the engine.

Neither of them said a word as he drove to the end of the block, turned left, and drove about halfway down that block. He pulled up in front of a blank storefront and parked. The enormous plate glass windows showed a large, rectangular interior space, and when Juliet saw the mirrors and ballet barres she gave Grant a quick glance. At one time there had probably been a wall about 10 feet inside the main windows but the drywall had been removed, leaving the studs bare and the space beyond open to the view of anyone who walked by.

"A dance studio?" Juliet asked.

"It was my Aunt Bea's until her arthritis got the better of her and she had to retire." He looked at the glass. "I bought it from her, but I have no idea what to do with it. Sherri wanted to turn the place into a boutique, but tearing down the waiting room wall was as far as we got."

"Why are we here?"

"Well," he drawled, rubbing his chin, "I want you to do something for me, and then I'm going to do something for you."

Juliet watched his face carefully, and the uncertainty was clear in his eyes. He obviously knew what he *wanted* to do, but he was also obviously unsure she would cooperate. "Okay, I'll bite. What do you want me to do for you?"

"I want you to dance with me."

That simple statement brought her up short and butterflies launched against the inside of her stomach. She blinked at him. "Grant, we danced last night, and the night before, and we can dance every night as long as I'm here. We can dance on the stoop of the hotel for all I care. You don't need to take me someplace like this to dance with me."

"Not *that* kind of dance." He met her eyes and the fire banked there made her breath catch. "I want to dance *your* kind of dance."

It took a couple seconds for that to register, and she gaped at him. "You want to learn *ballet?*" Her brows shot north. "Why?"

"Because it's something you love," he replied simply, "and if I want to know you, I need to know that part of you, too." A mischievous twinkle entered his smiling eyes. "Besides, it'll give me a chance to get close and put my hands on you."

"You don't need an excuse to do that, Sheriff." The words fell out in a breathless rush before she could stop them. Heat blossomed in her cheeks again, hotter this time, and she tore her gaze from his.

Way to go, Jules. Aren't you glad your panties and bra match now?

She bit her lip to keep from replying to the voice in her head.

Grant cupped her chin and turned her face to his. His thumb stroked over the spot she'd been chewing on with a feather light touch that sent her heart racing.

"In case you hadn't noticed," he began with a small smile, "I'm trying to slow-play this hand."

Juliet took a shaky breath, which was harder than normal as invisible fingers took hold of her heart and lungs and squeezed. The sensation wasn't unpleasant, just unfamiliar. "I noticed," she whispered.

His eyes narrowed. "Is that bad?"

Warmth fanned out from where he touched her face and neck, and for a moment she couldn't concentrate. She imagined those hands moving elsewhere and the heat that would no doubt follow. Juliet gulped and forced herself to focus.

"Um, no, not at all," she replied. "It's just . . . surprising."

One dark brow quirked upward. "I'm happy to surprise you." He released her and opened his door. "C'mon, Miss Prima Ballerina. Let's dance."

After he opened her door he walked around to the back of the SUV, opened the tailgate, and pulled a large duffel bag from within the cargo area. Juliet left the Yukon and leaned against the plate glass window. Grant gave her a boyish grin as he walked toward her, pulled a key ring from his pocket, and unlocked the door. He held it open and gestured for her to precede him.

The inside of the studio was cool, the high ceiling lending itself more to an industrial space than a dance studio, but at least the floor was good. In one corner stood a cabinet with racks of vinyl records and CDs, the sound system hidden behind pressboard doors. Juliet walked to the center of the barre along one wall, dropped her bag, and slipped out of her yoga pants. She glanced at Grant when she heard his sharp intake of breath. He was staring, and tingles shivered over her skin at the look in his eyes. He blinked a couple of times, cleared his throat, and then strode over to the cabinet and opened the doors. To her surprise, in additional to the CD player and the turntable, there was also a docking port for an iPhone or MP3 player. When he saw her expression he smiled and shrugged.

"I figured if I was going to refurbish this place I was going to need some music." He held out a hand. "I think for this evolution we're going to need your phone. I don't have anything ballet-worthy on mine."

Juliet fished her cell phone from her bag and walked toward him. She handed the device off and his fingers brushed hers. Electricity shot up her arm and crackled through the rest of her, and she sucked in a breath.

"There's a warm-up mix in my music library," she said in a low voice, backing away from him. "That should work. Just put it on replay."

She stared at the floor until the music started playing. His nearness did strange things to her heartbeat and she moved back to the barre, hoping some distance would help. If being within arm's reach did this to her senses, she couldn't imagine the effect being held by him, draping herself around his body, and having his hands on her, would have.

"I'm going to change into something more appropriate," he said softly.

Juliet could only nod, her throat tight and her breathing rapid and shallow. She wasn't sure how much time passed before she heard his voice again, but her heart was still thudding against her sternum.

"Um, I wasn't sure what type of footwear I was going to need."

She glanced at him and smiled when she saw he wore socks, a pair of running shoes in one hand and his bag in the other. Once she looked past the shoes her heart nearly stopped. He had on a pair of black sweatpants that hugged his body in all the right places and a white wife-beater tee. His shoulders and arms were muscular and magnificently shaped; the white cotton barely able to contain his pectorals as it hugged his ridged abdomen tightly. He was, truly, a beautiful sight to behold. Juliet gulped. The men she had danced with had all been handsome and wonderfully built specimens, ballet demanded it, but she'd never been sexually attracted to any of her partners. It was her unwritten rule. Professional and private lives were strictly separated, for self-preservation if nothing else. This would be an exceptionally difficult dance.

"So, what do I wear?" he asked. He lifted the shoes and then lifted one sock-clad foot, waiting for her decision.

Juliet cleared her throat. "Well, the first thing we need to do is warm up." She glanced at him but quickly looked away as heat speared through her again. "I have a specific routine I do to warm up, but what do you want to do?"

He was quiet for a few moments and she looked at him. It took all of her willpower not to salivate.

"I could run to the high school and back," he said. "Take me about 15 minutes. Will that do?"

Juliet remembered driving by the school on the way into town. "That's a pretty fast pace, Sheriff."

"I'm quick . . . at some things." A devilish sparkle lit his eyes. "Other things, not so much."

She wanted to peruse his musculature, but focused on his face instead. "A run will work. Just make sure to stretch beforehand. We don't want any injuries."

"And after the run?"

His eyes said things his mouth didn't, and Juliet's body responded with gusto. She took a quick breath and rummaged through her bag for her pointe shoes. "Bare feet will work."

"All right, then."

He balanced on one foot as he donned first one shoe, and then the other without bothering to untie and retie them. Juliet was impressed. Taller people, especially men, had a harder time balancing because of their higher center of gravity, but he stayed upright as if he was a human flamingo. He flashed her a grin.

"I'll be back in about 15. Be ready."

Juliet gave him what she hoped was a bland look. "I'm always ready."

"Glad to hear it." He walked toward the door. "See you soon."

When he disappeared Juliet sank down on the floor and put her head in her hands.

Wow, he's got you jumping like a long-tailed cat in a room full of rocking chairs, sis. Have you ever felt like this before?

"No," Juliet said in a shaky voice. "No, I haven't, Cass. Thanks for pointing that out."

Don't you think it's about time? You're 31, for Pete's sake, Jules. It's your turn to dance through the minefield of human emotion like the rest of us, no pun intended.

"Sorry if I was too busy to fall in love with every guy who looked my way," Juliet shot back. She instantly regretted the words, even though she knew Cassie wasn't really there and wasn't really listening. There was a brief pause.

Nice one. I always knew you had some fight in you, outside of the studio, I mean. You just don't show it very often.

Juliet took a deep breath. "I don't know how to do this, Cass. Even Doug never made me feel like this."

Which says a lot about his *skills. Dodged a bullet there.*

With a growl of frustration Juliet taped her toes, put on her toe shoes, walked over to the sound system, and cranked the volume. She wound her hair into a tight bun at her nape, secured it, and inhaled deeply, and then let the music wash over her. Her body began to move as if she was on autopilot rather than consciously aware. Cassie didn't say another word.

After going through the initial warm up, she let go and let the music take over. She didn't do anything choreographed or any dance she'd previously learned, she just moved in time with the violins, woodwinds, and drums. Dancing like this was almost like flying.

She was unaware of the passage of time. Her heart beat in rhythm with the music. When the song ended and another didn't immediately start, she looked toward the sound system, and her stomach flipped. Grant stood there, a towel around his neck, a look of complete awe on his face. Her heart immediately started pounding a different rhythm, one much faster than the Beethoven previously coming through the speakers.

"I could watch you do that all day," he said softly. "You move like nobody I've ever seen before."

Heat warmed her cheeks and she looked at her toes. "Then you haven't seen much ballet. We pretty much all move like that."

"No." At his negation, her head snapped up and she was instantly captured by that warm, brown gaze. He shook his head once. "My Aunt Bea took me to see the Chicago Ballet twice a year starting when I was ten, and I've taken her to see the Bolshoi, the Joffrey, and even the Moscow Ballet when they made a stop in Chicago a few years back." He took several steps toward her. "When you dance I can't look away, Juliet. It's just not possible."

"Well . . . that's good." She gulped. "When we partner up you need to focus on me."

A sensual grin warmed his features. "*Not* going to be a problem."

Juliet blinked at that and wondered how on earth she was going to get through this. Taking a deep breath, she put on her dance instructor's hat and forced herself to focus.

"All right, then." She put her hands on her hips. "What do you want to learn?"

"I thought you could teach me some of those fancy lifts you do with a partner," he replied, his eyes glinting suggestively. "At least, some of the *easier* ones."

Juliet bit the inside of her cheek and tried to peruse him the way a costume designer does a mannequin. She wasn't entirely sure she'd been successful. "Well, you're definitely strong enough, and you seem pretty flexible . . . ."

"Flexibility is helpful when you're a sniper," he said. "It makes it easier to move around after holding one position for hours on end if one is flexible."

"I imagine so," she said in a low voice. "I already know you have excellent timing and rhythm." The thought of having his hands on her in the intimate fashion required for *pas de deux*, steps of two, started heat swirling in her belly, and she closed her eyes briefly. "Okay. Let's get started."

Thankfully, Grant was all business as she instructed him in the finer points of basic ballet partnering. He was attentive, thoughtful, did what she asked without question, and asked questions when he had them. It made being so close to him much easier, and more like working with a first-time partner than some elaborate mating dance with a potential lover. To her surprise, he was very graceful, despite his height and build, and had a natural ability she knew would be the envy of many of her previous partners.

Unfortunately for her, once he started to get the hang of the technique the mood shifted dramatically. He moved with the enthusiasm that distinguished true *dancers* from those who simply danced. It was something of the heart, something spiritual that translated through movement to touch the people watching in profound and indescribable ways. Every time his hand curled around her upper thigh or hip or rested at her waist her lungs constricted. There was chemistry here, chemistry any choreographer would kill to capture and present on stage, chemistry that was turning those butterflies in her stomach into flying Molotov cocktails.

They were practicing a cambré press lift in which the male grips his partner's waist from behind, lifts the ballerina straight up, and she arches her back at the peak of the lift. To exit the lift the male dancer slowly slides his partner down his body until she is back en pointe. It was during these moments, the slower, drawn out moments that she became acutely aware of the hardness of the body at her back, the strength of his arms, and the effortless way he seemed to lift her. It made her heart quiver, and when she was firmly back on the ground it was all she could do not to turn, throw her arms around his neck, and kiss him until she couldn't breathe. Like the true professional she was, however, she managed to maintain the final pose before taking a graceful step away. Grant grabbed her hand and pulled her back. She didn't fight it.

"You realize we have an audience, don't you?" he whispered in her ear.

His breath feathered warmly against her nape and goose bumps plumped on her skin. After taking a deep breath she looked out of the corner of her eye and realized he was correct. She recognized Paulette and Cindilee, but the rest were unfamiliar to her. "Great." Grant was silent for several seconds and she felt his heartbeat against her shoulder blade.

"You wouldn't have anything more . . . *risqué* . . . in your repertoire, would you?"

Juliet spun to face him, her arms in second position, and his hands on her waist. She knew to the onlookers it was just another dance move, but when her eyes met his it became far more to her.

"What are you thinking?" she asked in a breathless voice.

A boyish grin lit up his face. "Are you sure you want me to answer that?"

Her pulse leapt even as she gave him a reproachful look. "Grant."

"Okay, okay." His eyes narrowed slightly. "I'm thinking if they're going to watch, we might as well give them a good show."

The conspiratorial twinkle in that brown gaze sparked something in her. She gave the onlookers a covert, sidelong glance, and then grinned at him. "I have the perfect piece."

A flicker of uncertainty passed over his finely hewn features. "How hard is it?"

She shook her head almost imperceptibly. "No harder than what you've already learned, and for most of it . . . all you have to do is stand there and look good." Juliet spun away and presented him with her back, arms curved overhead. "Just . . . pretend I'm not even here."

He grunted. "Not sure I can do *that*."

She laughed softly as she came off pointe and walked over to the sound system. "I have faith in you, Sheriff." She tossed him a glance over her shoulder. "Like I said, stand there and pretend I'm invisible.

I'll talk you through the rest of it."

"What's this piece called?"

Juliet grabbed her cell phone and started scrolling through the music library. "It's called *Fall of an Angel.* It's about an angel who falls in love with a human, but until she agrees to sacrifice her wings and her immortality, he can't even see her."

"How does it end?"

He sounded wary and that made her smile. She chuckled. "Well, the choreographer did two endings, one happy, one not so much." She hit play and walked over to him. "But we're not doing the ending. We're doing the part where she falls in love and sheds her wings so he can finally see and touch her."

"Will it give these biddies a good show?" he asked, one dark brow lifted imperiously.

"It will." She gave him a pointed look. "It's a *very* sensual piece, but . . . ." She paused and gulped as heat flooded her face, and other parts of her. "No kissing allowed."

Both his brows rose and he fought a smile. "Are you reading my mind?"

"No." Juliet ducked her chin. "But I want to kiss you *now*, so once we get into this—"

"You *are* reading my mind."

She glared at him. "Grant."

He chuckled and shrugged. "Sorry."

Juliet clenched her teeth. "Look, just stand there, feet shoulder width apart, hands clasped behind you, and eyes focused on the wall. Remember, you can't see me."

He pursed his lips and gave her a sarcastic look.

Her brows drew together. "You wanted to learn ballet, and this is part of it. It's not some elaborate mating dance—"

"I know," he interrupted. "Feels more like foreplay to me."

Juliet stared at him. She knew her jaw was hanging slack, but she couldn't close her mouth as images of their bodies, naked and sweating, wound together in the most intimate fashion, blazed to life in her mind's eye. A coiling ache settled between her thighs, and she was suddenly unsure she could pull this off. It didn't matter that half of Paulette's salon was standing on the sidewalk watching through the plate glass window. She wanted him. Now.

So, make him want you just as much. I doubt he's wearing a dance belt, so it will be obvious to anyone with eyes. Turnabout is fair play, after all.

Cassie had remained silent until now, but her sister's words struck a chord. Juliet steeled herself, calling on the reservoir of calm she used to combat stage fright and pre-audition jitters.

"Do you want to do this, or not?" she asked flatly. "I'll take my pointe shoes off right now."

He had the decency to look sheepish. "I'm sorry, Juliet." He met her gaze and smiled. "Let's do this."

Juliet moved to the opening pose when his voice drew her attention.

"How will I know when I, I mean my character, can see you?"

"I'll let you know," she said. "Now, focus, Sheriff."

To his credit, he focused on the wall as she flitted, twirled, and moved around him. Her angel tried to get the attention of her human, rubbing her body suggestively against his and touching him the way only a lover would. For the better part of five minutes she teased, flirted, and tried to seduce but he remained as solid as an oak. In fact, he was so good at being a statue she was starting to get insulted. Even her most experienced partner had joked about fighting an erection during the course of this particular dance. Apparently, Grant had more fortitude than any man she'd ever partnered with.

Damn it.

Focus, Juliet. Trust me, he's just playing the part. When the human can finally see his fallen angel, you'll see a whole different Grant.

Juliet heeded her sister's advice and lost herself in the choreography. By the time she came to the section where the angel bows before her maker and surrenders her wings her body was singing. Her breasts ached, her vulva throbbed, and all she wanted was to yank Grant's shirt off and touch him . . . *everywhere.* She steeled herself and knelt, went through the motions of removing the mark of her angelic lineage, then slowly rose onto pointe and turned to face him.

"You can see me now," she whispered.

The change was so dramatic and fast that she was momentarily stunned. Fire was banked in those chocolate depths and the naked desire on his face called to her on an animal level.

"Reach for me," she said softly. Both his arms came forward, and she took several delicate steps into his embrace. "Rest your hands at my waist."

He did as she commanded, but his expression told her he wanted to do so much more. She performed several pirouettes, spinning on one toe, his hands steadying her. Each time she returned to face him her breathing hitched. She did a final pirouette and stopped facing away from him. Slowly, she bent forward, her right leg lifting behind her and curling around his body until her right heel touched his left shoulder blade. It was a position that would easily facilitate intercourse, were they not clothed. Juliet pushed the not entirely unwelcome thought aside and returned to her original position.

She pirouetted away from him and back, facing him once more. "Now, we're going to do a cambré lift, but with me facing you instead of facing away. It's a little awkward, but just focus on pushing me straight up and you'll be fine. And don't let me down until I tell you."

He performed the lift flawlessly, and she looked upside-down at their reflection in the mirror. They really did look good together. She felt his breath against her mid-thigh and closed her eyes at the barrage of feelings and images that assaulted her.

She gulped and fought to find her voice. When she finally found it, she could speak in little more than a husky whisper. "Now, slowly, bring me down until the tops of my thighs are even with your shoulders, and hold me there."

As she started her descent she straightened her spine and returned to the upright position. When her progress stopped she placed her hands on his shoulders and looked down at him, her breathing rapid and shallow. They stared at each other for what seemed minutes. A wicked gleam entered his eyes and he pressed a kiss to her lower belly. Juliet sucked in a breath.

"Hey," she hissed, "I said no kissing."

"I thought you meant on the mouth," was his blasé response.

Juliet ground her teeth together. "Put me back en pointe . . . slowly."

The scrape of his body against hers was thrilling and her nipples tingled in response. She closed her eyes. *Damn.*

"Bend me back over your left arm and press your face into my cleavage."

"Boy, if I had a nickel for every time a woman told me to do *that* . . . ."

His breath was hot on her skin, his lips barely brushing the curve of one breast. *Double damn.*

"I'd have a nickel," he finished.

"Back en pointe," Juliet whispered, her breathing ragged, her pulse surging through her veins in a languid, sensual rhythm. Grant followed her instructions and she fought to focus. "Other arm, same movement." This time his mouth deliberately grazed her skin, and she felt the shock of it to her womb. "God help me."

If Grant had heard her whispered plea he gave no sign as he draped her over his arm, and then returned her to the upright position. Juliet could barely drag her eyes open long enough to look at him.

"I'm going to pirouette away," she told him.

"Okay."

"When I finish the second turn, grab my hand and pull me back . . . *hard.*"

A smile tipped the corners of his mouth. "Gladly."

Juliet did her turns and even though she knew it was coming, she still gasped when he grabbed her and pulled her roughly against his chest. One leg wound around his waist. It wasn't part of the choreography, but it seemed a natural outcome.

Her eyelids fluttered. "Press your face into the curve of my neck."

His grin said he was happy to obey. Her insides turned to liquid when his tongue darted out to taste her. Juliet tried to calm her racing heart.

"I'm going to lean back," she whispered. "Keep your face against my skin and follow the line of my chest until your head is between my breasts."

"Like I'm listening to your heart?"

The clinical nature of the question helped to steady her. "Exactly."

She curved her arms overhead in fifth position and slowly arched her back. The steadiness she'd felt vanished as his skin rasped against hers. She licked her lips and tried to concentrate on the choreography, but all she wanted was to rip her leotard off and throw herself against him.

"Your heart is pounding," he said softly.

It was just a statement; she heard neither triumph nor humor in his voice.

"And yours isn't?" she managed to reply, barely.

"Oh, it is, *believe* me it is."

She let her arms dangle at her sides and just held the pose, trying to get her pulse under control. "Reverse the movement," she said at last, "and stay close."

The stubble on his chin abraded the tender skin on her chest, and it sent shivers coursing through her. Her leg was still around his waist, and she was suddenly aware that he was aroused, very much so if the hardness pressed intimately against her was any indication. The knowledge sent a shock of desire spiraling through her. Again, they were in a position that would be perfect for lovemaking, if it weren't for their damned clothes. Juliet took a shuddering breath and tried to focus.

When they were face-to-face his breath warmed her cheek, his nose nearly touching hers. His eyes held hers captive, but when she licked her lips his gaze landed there. She slowly lowered her leg and leaned into him.

"Please tell me we're done," he said in a low, husky voice, "because I don't know how much more of this I can take."

"Did they enjoy the performance?"

His eyes slid to his left and a slow grin spread over his face. "Oh, yeah. I'm surprised they haven't fainted on the sidewalk."

"Then we're done."

"Thank God. Just . . . don't move for a minute. If you do, they probably *will* faint on the sidewalk."

Heat surged into her cheeks when she realized to what he was referring. He was hard against her stomach and she squeezed her eyes shut as lust roared through her.

I told you, Juliet, totally different Grant. Can I call 'em, or what?

Juliet fought to slow and deepen her breathing. The thick hardness of his erection gradually waned and she was disappointed when it did. Nevertheless, it brought her no small measure of satisfaction to know she affected him as much as he did her.

She looked at him and was immediately caught and held by that warm, smiling gaze.

"You said no kissing during the dance," he said softly.

"I did."

"The dance is over, right?"

Juliet gulped. "Right."

That now-familiar lazy smile curved his mouth. "Good."

Chapter Sixteen

Grant swooped in and she melted against him. His mouth covered hers with blatant masculine possession. The sound of giggles, gasps, and clapping from the front of the studio barely penetrated the sensual fog that wrapped around him. He held nothing back this time. He was demanding, almost arrogant in his claim of her. Her arms wound around his neck and elation burgeoned inside him when he felt her let go.

He recalled the feel of her body, the way she'd wound around him and touched him so intimately. If it weren't for the enormous windows and the delighted onlookers he would have taken her on the floor of his aunt's dance studio. His control wavered and he ended the kiss, his forehead resting against hers.

"God almighty," he breathed. "How does a man dance with you and *not* embarrass himself?"

A low chuckle escaped her. "It's called a dance belt. It's like a cross between an athletic cup and a pair of thong underwear. They were invented because it was believed the sight of male genitalia outlined in such stark relief by tights would prove distracting to the audience."

"To say nothing of the guy sporting the hard-on," he added. "But . . . aren't most *danseurs* gay?"

"No," she replied with a soft laugh. "There *are* gay men in the ballet world, but the majority of *ballerinos* are straight." Her fingers draped over the nape of his neck and sifted through his hair. "Personally, I think most of them get into ballet specifically *for* the girls."

"Guess I missed my calling."

"You *do* have a natural ability most dancers I know would envy," she said. "Are you good at everything?"

His heart thumped against his sternum. "I certainly hope so."

Pink bathed her cheeks. Her skin glistened with perspiration, which only intensified her natural glow and he fought the urge to kiss her again. His fingers fanned over her lower back and pressed her closer. Her flush deepened.

"Aren't you worried you'll give someone in our audience a heart attack?" she asked softly.

"Actually . . . I'm more worried about giving myself one." He smiled at her. "It's been a while since I've been this . . . *interested* in a woman."

"The feeling is mutual," she replied in a breathless voice. "Consider yourself lucky, Sheriff. I don't usually partner with someone I'm attracted to."

Warmth spread through his middle. "You're attracted to me?"

The flash of annoyance in her eyes only made her more beautiful.

"No. I *always* go around kissing every handsome man who looks my way."

"Wow." He leaned toward her. "You must spend all your off-time kissing."

She glared at him and pushed out of his embrace. "*Not* funny."

He pulled her back. "I wasn't *being* funny."

Before she could speak again he kissed her. She was stiff and unyielding for several seconds, and then his insides tightened when she sighed and looped her arms around his neck. He explored her mouth slowly, thoroughly, and deeply. She met his tongue with her own and heat spiraled out from low in his belly through the rest of him. When his libido started to aggressively assert itself he pulled back. To his secret delight she whimpered in protest.

"Come on, darlin'," he said softly. "We need to cool down so we can get out of here."

"Where are we going?"

Her voice was breathless, sultry, and he had to force himself not to kiss her again.

"Well, you've done something for me," he replied, "and now it's my turn." The look she gave him made his groin tighten, especially when her gaze drifted to his mouth.

"And what exactly are you going to do for me?"

There were at least a dozen things that leapt to the front of his mind, but he managed to keep those to himself. He laced his fingers behind her back and fixed her with a lazy-lidded stare. "Well, first I'm going to give you a gun and teach you how to shoot. After that, I was planning to make you dinner . . . at my place." His gaze wandered over her finely sculpted features. "Anything beyond that . . . I figured we'd improvise."

She nodded once. "Okay."

Her acquiescence only sharpened his need. They were going to have to get close when he taught her to shoot, and he wondered if perhaps it was too much physical contact for one day. The past two hours had flown by for his brain, but his body was still reeling from the effect she had on him. Grant cleared his throat. "That was easy."

"You'll find I'm good at no-brainers."

"I thought you might balk at the gun thing."

Her expression turned pensive and she looked away. "Had I bought a gun when the thought first crossed my mind Cassie might be alive today."

"Don't," Grant said. He curled a finger under her chin and turned her face to his. His teeth ground together at the self-recrimination and guilt he saw there. "*Don't* put that on yourself."

She eased out of his embrace and walked over to the barre. "It's hard not to, Sheriff," she said, lifting one ankle onto the barre and leaning into the stretch. When she went to change legs she faltered and rested her hands on the polished wood, shoulders bowed. "God, I feel so guilty."

He wanted to hold her, reassure her, but something in her posture kept him back. Taking several steps toward her, he clasped his hands in front of him. "What do you feel guilty for?"

"*Breathing*," she said in a gasp. Almost half a minute passed before she faced him and draped her arms over the barre. "Here I am in this charming little town, welcomed in by all these warm, wonderful people, I'm dancing with *you* and loving *every* minute of it . . . ." Her expression fell and tears shimmered. "Cassie hasn't even been buried three months yet, and here I am acting like I haven't a care in the world."

Misplaced guilt, as far as Grant was concerned, was the most useless emotion in the world. It served no one, neither the person who felt it nor the person who was the basis for it. Anger flared to life inside him.

"That's because that is what is *supposed* to happen." He approached her slowly. "You lose someone, you grieve, and then you move on, because it's what you're *supposed* to do. What purpose does it serve to spend all your time wallowing in guilt? You do that and you'll waste the rest of your life, and *that* would be something to feel guilty about." He stood toe to toe with her. "Is that what Cassie would want for you?"

Juliet sucked in a breath and two tears slid slowly over her cheeks.

Grant framed her face and wiped the tracks with his thumbs.

"What would Cassie say to you in this moment, Juliet?" he asked. "If she was here, right now, what would she tell you to do?"

She looked up at him and the naked emotion in her turquoise gaze caught him off guard. She studied his face, as if memorizing him, then rose onto her tiptoes and kissed him. Fire traveled from where their lips were joined to the rest of him, every nerve-ending crackling and sizzling in the flames. Her movements were tentative, but as the seconds passed her timidity was replaced with something far more volatile and intoxicating. He tasted her tears, the strawberry lip balm she used, and deepened the kiss. Her fingers curled around his forearms and she leaned into him.

Juliet was the first to pull away and it took his brain several seconds to catch up. He looked at her in disbelief and she blushed.

"Sorry," she said, "but you *did* ask."

"Your sister would tell you to kiss me?"

"Yes," she said with a faint scowl. "And *that's* just for starters."

Grant fought the grin and failed. "I think I like your sister."

The scowl vanished and she ran her fingers over her jaw. "Cassie would *adore* you."

He slid his hands around her waist and pulled her closer. "It's not Cassie's adoration I want." His body went stiff as long-dormant feelings and sensations threatened to overwhelm him. Even the feelings he'd harbored for Laine hadn't been this intense and fear-inspiring. Those feelings had built over years of time and friendship. This? This was new, but he wasn't the type to live in denial. He narrowed his eyes on her face. "Her *sister's* adoration . . . ? Now *that's* something I'd fight for."

A wistful smile rounded her mouth and he found his gaze drawn there.

"You don't have to fight for it, Grant." Her fingers tightened on his arms. "You have it. Now, take me out of here before we *really* put on a show."

A strange euphoria washed over him and suddenly it was as if there was no such thing as gravity. He grinned down at her and fought to keep his feet anchored to the ground. "Yes, ma'am."

***

Juliet absently rubbed her left shoulder as Grant pulled into the driveway of a log cabin and parked the Yukon. They had discovered that even though she was right-handed she was left-eye-dominant, which meant she fired pistols right-handed, but she had to shoot long guns left-handed. It was a bit of an adjustment, but Grant had been patient and attentive. She had never imagined shooting could be so much fun, and having him pressed against her for the better part of three hours had been a plus.

From the front of the house it was hard to tell how big it was. Behind the log structure was a gentle slope that ended about a hundred yards away at the river where tall grass rippled like water. The front lawn was manicured and fenced, nary a weed to be seen. Tall trees surrounded the property and moved gently in the early evening breeze. They'd left the studio just after two, but now the sun was dancing atop the mountains to the west. A glance at the clock on the radio told her it was 5:38 p.m. It was then her stomach growled.

Grant threw her a quick grin. "Hungry?"

"All I've had since breakfast is water," she replied.

"Then we need to fix that." He left the SUV and came around to her side to open the door. "I'll give you the nickel tour, take a quick shower, and get dinner started while you get cleaned up."

Juliet got out of the Yukon and looked up at him. "You're quite the renaissance man, Sheriff Donovan."

He snorted and closed her door. "Hardly."

They started walking toward the house and Juliet watched him out of the corner of her eye. "You're a sheriff, a war veteran, you shoot, you dance, and you cook." A giggle escaped her. "Do you sew?"

"I can do a button." He paused at the foot of the porch steps and narrowed his eyes on her. "That does *not* mean I can sew."

Juliet fought the grin. "Okay."

"And if you're a bachelor you either learn to cook, or you learn to love frozen dinners." He mounted the stairs two at a time and pulled a key ring from his pocket. After unlocking the door he stood to the side and gestured for her to precede him. "I stopped liking frozen dinners pretty quick, so it was cook or starve. I chose the former."

Juliet stepped through the door. "Lucky for me."

"Mm hmm."

Juliet's eyes widened as she took in the room before her. What looked cozy and quaint from the outside was actually quite spacious and airy. The living area was directly in front of her, punctuated by a large river-rock fireplace that ran from floor to ceiling along the rear wall, a wall made up almost entirely of windows. Through those windows she saw a wide redwood deck that ran the length of the house. The furnishings were large and cushy and looked so comfortable she wanted to throw herself on the sofa and sleep for days. To her right was a large eat-in kitchen with a breakfast bar that separated the living room from the cooking area. The appliances were modern, the counters done in what looked like granite.

"Wow."

"Yeah," Grant said, hanging his hat on a hook near the door. "Doesn't look like much from the outside, but my parents were big on entertaining, so they needed the space." He chuckled softly. "I used to get so sick of people being over here almost *every* weekend, but now I must admit . . . I sort of miss it."

Juliet couldn't even imagine growing up like that. Grant tapped her on the shoulder and walked down a hallway to her left, crooking his finger at her as he went.

"There are three bedrooms," he said. He gestured to the door on the left and Juliet peeked through the opening as he continued. "My brother and I shared this room and my sister was in the room across the hall."

Juliet stared at the large desk and the built-in bookcases. It was neat, almost austere, but it felt like Grant. "There's no bedroom furniture." A peek in the other door revealed a set of weights, a treadmill, a futon, and stacks of unlabeled boxes. "Where do you sleep?"

"The master," he replied. "I gave my sister all the bedroom furniture when her brood outgrew their toddler beds. I certainly didn't need bunks and a pink canopy bed." He moved down the hall. "Here's the guest bath, and there's another half bath off the kitchen between the pantry and the door to the garage."

Juliet stood in the bathroom doorway. She had expected a completely masculine motif, given who lived in the house, but the décor so far had been surprisingly gender neutral. It wasn't a man's house, and it wasn't a woman's house. This was a *family's* house, and just about anyone would be comfortable here.

He waited for her at the end of the hall in front of the only closed door. She moved to his side and looked up at him. "Let me guess," she ventured, "the master bedroom."

He wiggled his eyebrows and pushed open the door. The first thing to catch her eye was the enormous bed. It was a Cal King with a large, square wooden headboard and no footboard. At the foot of the mattress sat a large, unadorned wooden chest made of what looked like red and white oak. A set of dressers topped with a mirror sat along the wall to her left, and there was nary a stray sock or t-shirt to be seen. Through an open door to her right she saw a huge ball-and-claw bathtub and a glassed-in shower.

"It's awfully neat," she commented. "I always thought bachelors were the messy sort. Did you clean all this up for me?"

"I wish I could say yes," he began, stuffing his hands in his pockets, "but being a Marine tends to shape one's habits." He shrugged. "And Iris comes in once a week."

"Right." She smiled. "I'm still impressed."

He rolled his eyes and steered her back down the hall. "Don't be." When they reached the living room he released her and walked into the kitchen. "Now, why don't you sit down, have a glass of wine while I hop into the shower real quick." He opened the refrigerator. "I have some chilled white, or there's some red in the pantry."

Juliet walked to the breakfast bar and hopped onto one of the tall bar stools there. "Are you trying to get me drunk, Sheriff?"

He peered around the refrigerator door at her, and then returned to his perusal of the contents. "We've had this conversation before I believe."

"True," she conceded, "but we had that conversation in front of the hotel, not in your house."

He closed the door, faced her, and leaned his hands on the edge of the counter. "If you want to get drunk, go ahead. If you do I will tuck you into my bed and sleep on the couch."

His gaze was direct and Juliet's stomach started to spin. She gulped. "Always the gentleman."

"Not always," he replied, his expression solemn, dark fire lighting his eyes, "but I try. Besides, when I make love to a woman I want to know she's going to remember it afterward."

"So she'll have the burning desire to see you again?"

He stared at her for several long, tense seconds. "Exactly."

Heat coiled low in her belly, gradually furling outward. Part of her wanted to look away from his penetrating gaze but she found herself unable, or perhaps unwilling, to break the stare. She loved looking at him, the finely hewn features, the lips made for sin, the eyes that warmed her and gave her chills at the same time. Moments ago she'd been hungry for food. Now, food was the last thing on her mind.

"White, or red?" he asked in a low voice.

Juliet blinked at him and warmth bloomed in her cheeks. She bit her lip and dropped her chin. "White will be fine."

Less than half a minute later a glass of white wine slid across the counter toward her.

"Make yourself comfortable," he said. "I'll be back in ten."

Juliet wrapped her fingers around the crystal stem and nodded mutely. When the sound of his footsteps disappeared down the hall she moved to a couch by the fireplace. Sinking into the thick, plush cushions, she sipped the wine and tried to remember when she'd become such a bumbling buffoon. She couldn't recall acting like this around a man, *ever*. Usually, she played a *little* harder to get.

It's because you like him. You really like him.

"I barely know him, Cass."

Sometimes love grows over time, other times it smacks you upside the head and says hello! *Take it when you find it, regardless of when or how it shows up.*

Love. Juliet shook her head and got to her feet. She moved to stand in front of the enormous windows, her gaze taking in the idyllic scene before her. After another sip of wine, she opened the sliding glass door and stepped onto the deck.

Was she in love? She had to admit there was *definitely* a physical attraction between her and the broad-shouldered sheriff. She also found herself thinking about him pretty much all the time. He invaded her thoughts when he shouldn't have, like when she was mixing dough for beignets, or filling soda cups at the diner. She loved so many things about him, his eyes, his voice, that super-sexy smile, the way he smelled, the way he treated her, but was that enough to say definitively that she was *in love?*

"More like in lust," she said under her breath as she leaned her elbows on the deck railing and stared toward the river.

A few quiet minutes passed, her gaze wandering over the beautiful scenery. She straightened when her eyes fell on a short staircase that led into the grass from the end of the deck, and she saw a narrow trail leading from those stairs toward the waterway. That was when she noticed the short, narrow dock jutting into the rapids.

"Wow, Juliet," she said to herself. "Not only are you a hussy and an exhibitionist, you're also blind." With a shake of her head, she walked over to the steps, descended them, and strolled toward the dock.

Grant had just finished toweling his hair when movement through the window caught his eye. He stuck two fingers through the slats of the blinds and pushed them farther apart to get a better view. His heart constricted painfully when he saw Juliet walking slowly toward the river, her wineglass in hand. With a sigh he let go of the blinds and cursed himself.

He had seen the obvious longing in her turquoise eyes and his body had responded aggressively to her silent invitation. The two of them needed to talk, and soon. Although he *wanted* to take her up on what she was, perhaps unknowingly, offering him, he *didn't* want to be just another stop on her cross-country tour. A one-night-stand did *not* interest him.

His phone rang and he wrapped the towel around his waist. Walking into the bedroom he fished it out his pants' pocket. Autumn's caller ID was displayed, along with a picture of the petite beauty.

"Hey, Autumn. What's up?"

"Grant, you need to get down here, *now.*"

The tone of her voice, and the low volume, immediately put him on alert that something was *very* wrong. "What is it?"

"There's some guy here with a picture of Juliet asking questions," Autumn replied.

Grant's heart rate skyrocketed, and then fell as he pulled in a long, slow breath. "Has anyone said anything to him?"

"The only people in here right now are Dale and the Johnson boys, and we both know how *they* feel about talking to strangers." Autumn sighed. "But, if he keeps it up he's *going* to run into someone who unwittingly gives Juliet up . . . someone like Shelby."

"Is she working?"

"Not today, but you get my meaning, don't you? Blondie's not the only one in town who talks too much."

Grant eased down on the edge of his bed, his mind spinning. "Can you get me a picture of him, without him knowing?"

Autumn snorted. "Hello, have we met? Of course I can."

"Good. Then chat him up, flirt with him a little. See if you can find out where he's from, get a name, you know what to do. You watch all those Law & Order shows."

"Mm hmm," she replied. "You can count on me, Grant. Does this mean I'm an unofficial deputy or something?"

He laughed in spite of the dread curling in his gut. "Yes, Autumn. You are now my unofficial deputy. So, get to work."

"You got it, Sheriff. Deputy Idlebird over and out."

Grant tossed the phone aside, lay back on the bed, and thrust his fingers into his hair. "Shit."

Before he could even start to think his phone dinged, telling him he had a text. There was a photo attached and he opened it. Again, in spite of circumstances, he laughed. The photo was of Autumn and the newcomer, cheek to cheek. The accompanying text read, I *said I take pictures with all the newcomers to Evergreen. I think he bought it. Says he's passing through on his way to Canada. I haven't gotten a name yet, but I think he likes me so give me a few.* Judging from the older man's smiling visage, Grant guessed Autumn was right. Then again, when Autumn started flirting Grant didn't know a man, married or otherwise, who could resist her charms except, maybe, for him. Thankfully, she was quite content with her husband, Landon, a football coach at the University of Montana. They'd met when she was the head cheerleading coach, and the rest was history. Grant looked at the picture for a few seconds, but the man was unfamiliar to him. He tossed the phone aside and dressed.

The brief time he spent putting on his clothes was enough for him to think. Once he was dressed he grabbed his phone and dialed. Nicole answered after the second ring.

"Center Hotel."

"Nicole, I need to ask a favor, and then I need to talk to Mike."

"Of course, Grant, ask away, and Mike is right here."

Less than three minutes later he was walking toward the river. Juliet sat on the end of the dock, her feet dangling in the water. Despite the fact it was August, that river was formed from snow run-off and he knew it was cold. When his boots hit the wood she turned her head and glanced at him over her shoulder.

"Hey," she said. She kicked one leg and sent a cold spray his way.

"Hey, yourself," he said, stopping just short of the splash zone. "And I already had a shower, but thanks."

She laughed softly and leaned back on her hands. "Sorry. I guess it's my turn?"

"In a minute." His expression must have alerted her that something was up because her brows drew together and she pulled her feet out of the water.

"What's wrong?"

His instincts said to lie. Say he was going to the grocery store and that he'd be back in a while. But he very well knew that a while could turn into all night and longer, and what would he tell her then? He eased down beside her and leaned against a piling.

"I need you to do something for me, but I'm not going to force you." She blinked. "Okay."

"I need to run into town for a little while, and I'd like you to stay here. You can take a bath, relax, and I'll start dinner when I get back."

She faced him and sat cross-legged on the dock. "Why?"

Grant stared at her and although his instincts were still telling him to lie, he couldn't. Not to her. He took a deep breath. "There's a man in town showing your picture around and asking questions."

Her eyes widened and she straightened her spine. "Mayfield?"

"No." He reached for her hand. "But I'll bet that's who he works for."

"And you want to leave me here . . . *alone?*"

The note of hurt in her voice made him wince inwardly, but he steeled himself. "I'd rather leave you here where you're surrounded by available firearms than take you into town where he might see you." He wound his fingers through hers. "Nobody in town knows where you are right now, and even if they know you're with me, they're not going to give out my address. It's safer for you here."

"And if I'd rather go with you?"

"Then you can," he replied without hesitation. "I'd prefer it if you stayed here, but it's your choice. It *is* your life, after all." He watched her carefully, the play of emotions so clear in her eyes: fear, anxiety, and then determination.

"Well," she began, her voice low, "in TV shows or movies the girl would insist on going with you. Even *then* I thought they were being impractical, although now that I'm in it I can understand their position." She looked at their intertwined fingers. "Although I'd rather go with you, I'll stay here."

He grabbed the back of her head and gently pulled her closer, pressing his lips to her forehead. "Thank you." He rested his brow against hers.

She wrapped her hands around his forearms and closed her eyes.

"Just make sure you come back."

"I'll be back," he replied. "There's no place else I'd rather be."

She smiled, but her eyes remained closed.

"Look at me, Juliet." It took her several seconds and when her eyelids fluttered up his heart thumped hard against his sternum. "I will *not* let him hurt you, do you understand me?"

"I know, Grant," she whispered. "I know."

He intended just to kiss her lightly, but once his lips brushed hers a charged current shot through him and his body betrayed him. He threaded his fingers into her hair and molded them to her head. His mouth slanted over hers. She sighed and leaned into him, her grip on his arms tightening. He touched his tongue to hers and fire surged through him as she responded. He deepened the kiss and she went with him, heat scorching his insides in gold and red waves of tingling sensation.

When he felt his control falter he ended the kiss, his lips a hair's breadth from hers. Her breathing was fast and shallow and warm on his skin. Grant released her and pulled back. Her hands dropped from his arms and he stood before he could kiss her again.

"C'mon, darlin'," he said softly, extending his hands to her. "I need to get to town."

Juliet grasped his fingers and allowed him to pull her to her feet. She bent to retrieve her shoes and then insinuated herself under his arm. She fit perfectly against his side, and wound an arm around his waist as they made their way back to the house.

Once inside he locked the door and led her to a barstool. He then walked to one of the gun cabinets in the large room and opened a drawer. She watched him, her expression completely neutral, as he opened the pistol safe, and pulled out a Sig Sauer .45 and a hip holster. He moved to stand in front of her.

"You know how to use this," he said, handing her the gun. "Quite effectively, I might add." Her fingers wrapped around the grip with a surety that was heartening, her trigger finger straight along the barrel. He met her gaze. "Check and see if it's loaded."

She moved the slide back to reveal that the gun was indeed loaded and let it return to its original position. He handed her a second magazine and she slid it into her back pocket.

"I want you to keep this close," he said, "even when you're showering. After you've cleaned up and changed clothes I want you to wear the holster and the gun until I get back."

Juliet slid the pistol into the holster and nodded. "Okay. You really think I'll need it?"

"No, but it's better to be prepared than not," he replied. "And remember, if you have to draw your weapon—"

"Empty the magazine," she interrupted. She put the holstered pistol on the counter and faced him. "I remember."

He narrowed his eyes on her and she returned his gaze with one of cool composure. "You sure you're okay with this?" he asked.

She dropped her chin. "Well . . . I'll be alone, but not defenseless." She lifted her eyes to his and he saw the steel in those blue-green depths. "Not this time."

Grant smiled. "That's my girl." She blinked and her brows rose. He dove in for a quick kiss and then walked to the sideboard in the foyer to grab his badge and gun. "Now, once I leave, lock this door, and if anyone but me or Mike tries to get in, *put them down.*"

Her expression turned questioning. "Mike?"

He approached her and planted a hand on either side of the bar behind her, effectively penning her in. "I called Miss Nicole and asked her to gather all your things. Mike's going to bring your stuff and drive your car out here. He'll put it in the garage where no one can see it." His gaze wandered slowly over her face. "Sorry, ma'am, but you are now in protective custody. I hope you like my house." He kissed her again, not so quickly this time. When he pulled away she was breathless and pink-cheeked, and his smile widened. "Make yourself at home."

Chapter Seventeen

Grant pulled up in front of the Sheriff's Office, flew out of the Yukon and bounded up the stairs. At this time of night there were two deputies on duty, but Roberta had gone home for the day. The night dispatcher, Andrea Marsal gave him a nod. He nodded in reply, ignored the questioning looks from Atwater and Mills, and made his way to the bunkroom.

Daniel opened the door after the second knock. "Grant."

"Daniel." Grant held up his phone that displayed the picture of Autumn and the visitor. "Recognize this guy?"

Daniel scrutinized the photograph. "No, should I?"

"He was at the diner with Juliet's picture asking questions." Grant fixed him with a hard stare. "Tell me there's another explanation as to why he's *here* other than he followed you from Seattle."

Riordan blinked several times, then ran his hands through his hair and looked up at the ceiling. "Shit." Air hissed out from between his teeth and he met Grant's gaze. "I don't *think* I was followed, but I *was* distracted. If the guy is good, he could've slipped under my radar."

"We need to find out who he is," Grant said.

"Get me his prints and I will." Daniel glared at him. "I have a field forensics kit, so if he's in the system somewhere, I can get an ID."

Grant glared back. "I *do* have a fingerprint kit, but thanks." He turned on his heel and stalked away several paces as he texted Autumn.

Hey, I need our new friend's fingerprints. Think you can help me out?

Autumn texted back. *One step ahead of you, Sheriff. Already saved his coffee cup and put it in a Ziploc bag. He never even noticed. By the way, he said his name is Charles. I'm not buying it, but that's what he said.*

Is he still there?

Really? Do you know any man who can turn down my peach pie?

He chuckled. *I don't think pie is the reason he's sticking around, at least not the peach kind. Just don't lay it on too thick or he may get suspicious.*

Honey, this is not my first rodeo. Now do your job and get your cute butt over here.

Grant smiled. *Yes, ma'am. I'll be there in five.*

He slid his phone back into his pocket and wiped off the smile as he faced Riordan. "I'm heading over to the diner to collect our visitor's prints, maybe get a read on who he is. Do you want to come with or stay here?"

"I'd rather go with you, but if the guy recognizes me?"

"My thoughts exactly, although he already followed you this far so he knows you're here somewhere," Grant said. "You stay and I'll be back as soon as I can."

"Where is Juliet?"

The plaintive note in the detective's voice wasn't obvious, but Grant heard it. "She's safe. And I don't know if you're aware, but she's also an excellent shot."

Riordan gave him a thoughtful look. "I suggested she get a gun shortly after I first met her, but I wasn't at all sure she could handle it. When she declined I didn't press it." He shook his head. "She was so skittish and jumpy I was afraid she'd shoot herself before she'd shoot anybody else."

"Well," Grant drawled, "I guess some things have changed between here and Seattle."

"Thank goodness." He shrugged. "Doesn't surprise me, actually. Women are naturally better shooters than men, and Juliet's grace, physical strength, and balance will just enhance her innate abilities."

"She was a little nervous at first, but after she'd put a few hundred rounds down range she was fine." Grant gave him a grim smile. "She knows what she needs to do, and I have no doubt she'll do it."

"Good. If Mayfield shows his face here I hope she puts the bastard down." Riordan stuffed his hands in his pockets and watched Grant carefully. "It won't bring Cassie back, but it will definitely close this particular chapter of her life."

And then she'll be moving on. Grant pushed the unwelcome thought aside, gave the detective a nod, and turned. "I'll be back shortly."

"I'll get hooked up with my partner in Seattle so he can run the print through our databases."

Grant only nodded as he made his way outside.

He walked through the park to the diner. A glance down the block told him Mike had already left in Juliet's car, and he could only hope the nosy newcomer hadn't seen it.

The café was about half full and it was easy to pick out the stranger from among the familiar faces. The stranger sat in a booth by the front window, and Grant gave him a nod and a smile as the door closed behind him. The tables around the stranger were empty, the other diners preferring to leave defensible space between them and him. It was as if they sensed there was something underhanded about the man and didn't want to get close. After removing his hat, Grant walked toward an open seat at the counter.

"Evening, Sheriff," Autumn said as she grabbed a coffee cup and a pot from a warmer. "Here for your nightly java?"

"Yes, Autumn, but make it decaf," Grant replied, sitting down on the swivel stool. "And could you wrap me up a piece of peach pie to go? I need to get back to the office." He gave her a wink and she grinned.

"Absolutely. I'll be back in a jiffy."

Grant sipped his coffee and glanced at the stranger out of the corner of his eye. The man sat stiffly in his seat, but he kept his eyes forward as he finished off what looked to be his second piece of peach pie. Autumn reappeared about a minute later with a white take-out bag and a winning smile.

"There you go, handsome. Put it on your tab?"

Grant removed a $20, tossed it on the counter, and grabbed the bag. "Keep the change."

Autumn scowled at him. "Grant Donovan—"

"Just keep it . . . for *once*." Without waiting to see if she would keep the money he spun on his heel and walked toward the newcomer. The man looked up when he stood at the end of the booth.

"Can I help you?" the man asked flatly.

He was about 50, with black hair combed over a balding scalp. His eyes were small and close-set, dark and intelligent, and there was a severity to his features that usually came from a life lived fast and hard. Grant saw parts of several tattoos over the collar of his button-up shirt, but other than that he blended in. After all, the guy wouldn't want to draw unwarranted attention if he was what Grant suspected he was.

"Well, hey there, I'm Sheriff Donovan. You're new in town, aren't you?"

The man gave him a nod, and Grant grinned.

"Welcome to our little haven. I like to greet newcomers to Evergreen whenever I can, although I don't get the opportunity near as often as I'd like." He extended his hand, and the man reluctantly grasped his fingers.

"I'm Charles . . . Schulz."

So, you do Charlie Brown cartoons. Right. Grant pumped Schulz's hand once and put on his simpering "Don Knotts from Mayberry" persona. "I'm pleased to meet you, Mr. Schulz. What brings you to Evergreen?"

Schulz smiled, but it looked forced. "I'm just passing through, actually."

Grant put a semi-dismayed expression on his face. "Aw, that's too bad. Evergreen is a right nice place if you stay a while. The county fair starts tomorrow night and it's one of the biggest events of the summer. Best funnel cakes this side of Amish country." The flicker of annoyance in the man's eyes made Grant smile inwardly.

"I'll bet."

"You should check it out, if you're still in the area." Grant extended his hand and again they shook briefly. "Well, I must be off, but hopefully I'll see you around. Enjoy your stay."

"Thank you, I'm sure I will."

The dismissive look in the man's eyes assured Grant he'd accomplished his goal. He didn't want Schulz thinking he was anything other than a simple-minded, small-town sheriff. When he reached the door he put on his hat and turned toward the interior of the restaurant.

"Evening, Autumn, folks."

A chorus of, "Evening, Sheriff," went up and he pushed through the door.

He didn't open the bag until he and Daniel were snugly ensconced in his office. He pulled out the Ziploc bag that contained the precious coffee cup, and he chuckled when he saw the white, Styrofoam take-out container beneath the cup.

"Do you like peach pie?" he asked as Daniel opened the Ziploc and removed the cup with gloved hands.

Daniel gave him a look and put the mug down on a paper towel. The fingerprint kit was already out and ready. He dipped one brush in a container of fine, black powder, and began swirling the soft bristles slowly over the surface of the porcelain. Two sets of prints were revealed, one small like a child's, the other larger.

"The small ones must be Autumn's," Grant commented as Daniel grabbed a piece of clear tape and covered the larger print. "She owns the diner."

"Hmm." Daniel pressed the tape down onto a white index card. The black whorls and lines contrasted sharply. "One of your deputies was kind enough to bring me a chicken-fried steak dinner from Autumn's Diner. Some damn good food."

"Yes, it is."

Grant watched as Daniel took a picture of the print with his cell phone and e-mailed it. Once the e-mail went through Daniel dialed the phone and put it on speaker. About ten seconds later a male voice reached them.

"I've got it, Danny. Running it now."

"Can you link up with us here?" Daniel asked. "Sheriff Donovan is with me."

"Evening, Sheriff. I'm Detective Steve Nguyen, but you can call me Steve."

"And you can call me Grant," Grant replied. He sat down at his computer and started typing. "Go ahead and dial in, Steve. You should be able to hook up with my system now." Mere seconds later an image of the fingerprint appeared on half of the screen, and the other half showed the quickly changing images of database prints as the computer did its search.

"Do you have it?" Steve asked.

"We do." Grant watched the blindingly fast shift of prints as the computer worked. He was so intent on the screen that when a match popped up he jumped. "Wow. That was quick."

"Usually doesn't work that way," Steve said, "but we got lucky with this one. The print belongs to a James Coulter. He's a licensed private investigator out of Tacoma. No criminal record that I can find, *yet*, but I'll keep digging."

"Ten to one he works for Mayfield," Grant said.

"I could verify that if I had a subpoena for his financials," Steve said, "but I don't and Mayfield probably paid cash anyway. I do have something else, however."

"What?" Daniel and Grant said in unison. They glanced at each other and then turned their attention back to the phone.

"I started looking deeper into Mayfield's background. I cross-referenced missing persons' reports with his known locations and, *shocker*, I found several connections."

"Like what?" Daniel asked.

"Well, when he was getting his undergrad degree at UCLA, six women that match Juliet and Wendy Braxton's descriptions went missing over that four-year period. Several were prostitutes, so there wasn't much investigating done, but a couple of them were also students at the University."

Grant looked at Daniel, whose brows rose as he eased down on the edge of the desk. Steve continued.

"Then Mayfield attended Columbia for his graduate degree." There was the sound of a keyboard in the background. "During his two years there three slender, blue-eyed brunettes were reported missing from the local area."

"Any bodies?" Grant asked.

"Only three between both locales, and they were all murdered the same way Wendy Braxton and Cassie were, tortured and bled out."

"Mayfield's signature," Daniel said softly.

"Right-o." Steve snorted. "I can't believe nobody made a connection before now."

"Is that it?" Grant asked.

"Nope, and thank you for asking, Sheriff. Because my partner is out of town and I'm all caught up on paperwork and bored, I decided to go down a rabbit hole and see if I found anything else interesting."

Daniel leaned in. "What did you find, Alice?"

"Well," Steve began, "not only was George Mayfield in the general vicinity when the women went missing, dear old dad, Gregory Mayfield, spent quite a bit of time in both locations, either visiting his son or in town on business."

Daniel swore. "Shit."

Grant rubbed his temples as they started to throb. "If they both become suspects, they can alibi each other, or both of them can claim to have committed the crimes."

"And *that* could create enough reasonable doubt to get them both off," Steve added with a sigh. "Coincidence? I think not."

Daniel ran a hand over his face. "We have to find definitive evidence that ties one or the other to multiple crimes, in multiple jurisdictions, or they could *both* walk."

Grant's gut was heaving. He was having a premonition, as he'd often had in battle. He wasn't psychic, but he had finely tuned instincts that had usually proved to be dead on, and those instincts were humming. "Won't happen. Mayfield will come after Juliet then I'll kill him."

"And I did *not* hear that," Steve said. "Glad no one else in the squad room is close enough to listen in."

"Thankfully," Daniel added.

The detective shot him a look that said he should know better, but Grant didn't care. He knew a confrontation with Juliet's stalker was imminent. It was just a question of *when*. First thing tomorrow he would ask Roberta to resend Mayfield's picture, father *and* son, throughout the county. He wanted to be doubly sure that when Mayfield showed up, he and Riordan would have advance notice. The best way to win a battle was to fire the first shot. And Grant didn't intend to miss.

Suddenly his brain spit out a thought and he stood abruptly, the rolling chair sliding backwards into the wall.

"What is it?" Daniel asked.

"Maybe we're looking at this all wrong," Grant said. He met Daniel's eyes. "Maybe George Mayfield isn't a serial killer."

"But he's stalking Juliet," Daniel argued, "just like he did Wendy Braxton before killing her. There's a definite pattern here."

"Yeah, but for most people the step from stalking to premeditated murder is quite a step," Grant said. "I mean, there are tens of thousands of stalkers out there, but how many of them are killers?" His mind was whirling, synapses firing almost audibly in his brain. "Steve, can you find out where Mayfield senior was when Wendy Braxton was killed?"

There were some serious keystrokes on the other end of the phone line and Grant met Daniel's eyes when Steve exhaled sharply. "He was in Portland at a business conference." More typing. "Braxton's body was found in Seaside, less than an hour's drive from Portland." He paused and whistled softly. "According to Braxton's case file, the detectives investigating did only a cursory check on Gregory Mayfield's alibi. He *was* a registered guest at the hotel in Portland, but that's as far as they went because all the forensics pointed to his son. Jesus."

Grant rubbed his forehead. "Maybe . . . maybe *Daddy* is the killer, and he's using his son as a patsy. Hell, maybe they're *both* in on it, and father-dearest is passing on more than his good looks. Hey, Steve?"

"Yeah?"

"You may want to take another look at Mrs. Mayfield's untimely death, start talking to the people who knew her." He fixed Daniel with a stare. "If she was planning to leave or divorce her husband . . . ? Wives have been murdered for less."

"We don't know Mayfield's wife was murdered," Steve pointed out.

"Can you get the file?" Daniel asked.

Steve gave a mirthless chuckle. "What do *you* think, Danny?" More typing ensued. "That's like asking if an Asian is good at math."

"Then do it," Daniel replied. "I still like George for this, but it wouldn't hurt to widen the net a little."

Steve sighed. "At least I'll have something to do." "You work from here," Grant said to Daniel. "Feel free to use my office, and I'll make sure the rest of the department is aware."

Daniel stood. "What are you going to do?"

"I'm going to make certain Mayfield doesn't get anywhere near her," Grant replied. "Keep me in the loop."

"Are you sure your deputies are going to be happy with me stepping in here?"

Grant frowned. "They'll do their jobs, or they can find other employment."

Daniel cast a speculative eye his way. "You're certainly not what I expected, Sheriff."

Grant gave him a tight smile and headed for the door. "I will take that as a compliment."

***

Juliet chewed her thumbnail as she paced in front of the fireplace. Heat emanated from the blaze Mike had started there. Her insides were curled into tight, undulating knots that seemed to relax and then contract tighter with every breath. She'd taken a hot bath, changed her clothes, started a load of laundry, and had a second glass of wine, but nothing could dispel the dread pooling in her belly. Not even the .45 on her hip bolstered her spirits.

"Juliet, honey, you should sit down," Mike said from the couch behind her. "You're going to wear a path clean through that floor."

Before she could reply a rectangle of light danced across the wall. She sucked in a breath, spun, and looked toward windows that lined the front door. Mike was on his feet instantly, but she was faster. She felt the older man's considerable presence behind her as she practically leapt to the foyer and pressed her nose to the glass. Grant's Yukon was just pulling into the driveway. A patrol car also pulled up and parked along the front fence.

"Oh, thank God," she breathed. She threw open the door and raced across the porch. Her feet barely touched the ground as she jumped to the grass, foregoing the steps completely, and raced across the lawn. Just as he shut the SUV's door she threw herself against him.

"Whoa," he said with a laugh. "Easy, darlin'."

Juliet buried her face in his chest as his arms closed around her, her hands fisting in his shirt. He rested his chin atop her head, his warmth and strength soaking into her like a soothing tonic. She drank him in and the tension drained away.

"She's been pacing ever since I got here," Mike said from behind her.

"Thanks for staying, Mike," Grant said, his hands moving slowly up and down her back in soft, comforting strokes. "I appreciate it."

"Don't mention it," Mike replied. "Nicole and I are happy to help. We shredded her registration card and got rid of anything that would show Juliet was ever at the hotel."

"Did you take her out of the computer?"

"Didn't have to," Mike replied. "Nicole hadn't gotten around to putting her info in yet."

Grant sighed softly. "Good."

"Is there anything else you want us to do?"

"Be careful. The guy will probably stay at the hotel so keep an eye out, but don't be obvious about it," Grant said. "Above all I want you and Miss Nicole to be safe, and call if *anything* happens."

"You got it." There was a brief pause. "By the way . . . I'm sorry about what I said last night. You were right, I was out of line. You don't have to prove anything to anyone."

There was a brief silence. "Thanks, Mike. Apology accepted. Now, you should get back to your blushing bride. Mills will drive you home."

"You'll let us know if you need anything?" Mike asked.

She felt Grant nod.

"Absolutely," he said.

"All right then." Gravel crunched underneath Mike's shoes as he walked toward the patrol car. "I'll see y'all soon."

Juliet pulled out of Grant's embrace. "Mike, wait." The big man turned and looked at her. She took a hesitant step toward him, and then walked up to him and hugged him. He seemed surprised at first, but then his strong arms closed around her. He smelled like her father: masculine, clean, with a hint of Old Spice. Her heart twisted as she thought of the last conversation she'd had with her dad, but she swallowed her pain and whispered, "Thank you."

"You are more than welcome, honey," Mike said softly. "And don't you worry, Juliet. We've got your back."

Tears stung and she nodded against his brawny chest. "Tell Nicole I said thanks, too."

"I will." He dropped a kiss atop her head and released her. "She's grown quite fond of you, you know that? So have I."

She smiled and looked up at him. "The feeling is mutual."

Mike pressed a hand to her cheek briefly, then grinned and stepped back. Juliet watched him walk to the patrol car and looked up at Grant when he moved to her side and draped an arm around her shoulders. He gave them a wave as he opened the door. Juliet leaned into Grant and waved back. The two of them stood there until the patrol car's taillights were no longer visible.

"Glad to see you're wearing the Sig," Grant said. "I half expected you not to."

"It made me feel better about what would happen if the guy came after me *here*," Juliet admitted. She gave him a sidelong glance. "It didn't stop me from worrying about *you* at all."

"You don't need to worry about me," Grant said. "I'm fine." He looked down his nose at her and smiled. "Now, it's time to cook you some dinner."

Juliet pulled away and stared at him, incredulous. "Are you kidding me?"

"What?"

She crossed her arms over her chest. "You're not going to tell me what happened?"

He chuckled and held out a hand. "I will. Do you mind if I do it while I'm making dinner, or do you prefer to stand out here in the dark and talk? Take your pick." When she didn't take his hand he reached over and laced his fingers through hers. "I don't know about you, but I'm hungry. And, I could use a beer."

Her indignant sails deflated at the same moment her stomach growled.

Grant grinned. "I guess that means you're hungry, too."

"I am," she admitted. "And another glass of wine doesn't sound half bad."

He pulled her arm through his and started walking. "You haven't had any more since I've been gone?"

"Just one glass." When she saw his smile she frowned. "One more in addition to the one you poured me earlier."

"Ah."

Juliet tossed him a scowl. "I *can* handle two glasses of wine, Sheriff."

"Did I say you couldn't?"

She felt the pout, but for some reason she couldn't rid herself of it. "No, but ending up in bed alone with you on the couch is *not* where I want this night to go."

The deep chuckle that rumbled in his chest sent chills skittering over her skin. He pulled her closer and pressed his lips to her temple as they walked toward the house.

"Me either."

Chapter Eighteen

Grant started pulling pots and pans from beneath the stove, his eyes straying to her every few seconds. Each time he looked at her something in his chest pulled taut. "Do you mind if I get things started before we talk?"

Juliet slid onto a barstool across from him and shook her head. "Not at all, unless you're trying to dodge the conversation."

He grinned. "No dodging here." He opened the refrigerator and grabbed butter, cream, and several other ingredients. "How does grilled chicken and penne in a garlic cream sauce sound to you?"

Her brows rose and she smiled. "Sounds like I should've come straight to Evergreen from Seattle instead of wasting all that time and money at truck stop cafés."

"But then you would have missed all the gorgeous country in between here and there."

"Hmm." Her expression turned introspective. "Didn't see much of it anyway. I spent too much time looking in my rearview."

Regret pooled beneath his heart. "That's a shame," he said in a low voice. "No one should have to go through life looking over their shoulder, especially when what's around you . . . ." He paused and met her gaze, ". . . is so beautiful." She colored and he saw the convulsive swallow before she dropped her chin.

"You're right." She took a deep breath, lifted her eyes, and focused on him. "But, I don't have to do that here."

His insides clenched. "No, ma'am, you do not."

A faint smile curved her mouth. "Do you need any help?"

"Nope." He pulled out a plastic covered dish and put it on the counter. "Already had chicken breasts marinating and, unlike Miss Nicole, *I can* boil water."

A mischievous twinkle entered her eyes. "Maybe, but can you prepare chocolate croissants that make people sigh with pleasure?" she asked.

Grant leaned his hands on the edge of the counter. One dark brow quirked up and he fought a grin. "Personally, I prefer to use *other* methods to elicit sighs of pleasure."

A hint of pink bathed her cheeks and she bit her lip, but she continued to meet his gaze, the Caribbean blue of her eyes darkening a few shades. "Well . . . I guess we'll have to wait and see if you're as good at . . . *other* things as Nicole is at . . . *baking.*"

The insinuation was clear and the naked longing he saw in her eyes made his breath catch. Fire burned low in his belly, warm enough to let him know an inferno was headed his way. The image of Juliet with her leg stretched over her head intruded into his thoughts. The flames went up several degrees. He shook his head and turned his attention to the chicken, although at the moment he couldn't even remember what he had planned to cook.

He cleared his throat. "I suppose we will," he replied.

They chatted about mundane things – the dietary preferences of Autumn's customers, the inclusion of three kinds of pepper in his marinade, the use of butter versus margarine – while he prepared dinner. They avoided the subject of the man at the diner as if it would bring the plague down on them. After he had the pasta boiling and the chicken on the grill, he started the garlic cream sauce and the conversation died down as Juliet sipped her third and final, so she said, glass of wine.

"Are you sure you're not avoiding the conversation about what happened in town?" Juliet asked as she put her empty glass aside.

"Positive, and I'll prove it right now." He stirred the sauce ingredients together, took his cell from his pocket, pulled up the detective's picture, and handed the device to her. "His name is James Coulter." At her sharp intake of breath he looked up. "What?"

Her eyes were glued to the phone. "I've seen this guy."

He stopped stirring. "Where? When?"

She blinked and he saw the pain that flashed in her eyes. "Um, he started coming into the bistro a couple months before Cassie was killed." She put the phone on the counter and slid it toward him, almost as if she didn't want to touch it. "He came in almost every night I worked. The only reason I remember him is because each time he asked to be put in my section."

Grant pocketed the phone. "What's so unusual about that?" He gave her a quick grin. "I'd ask to be put in your section, too, if I got to choose *my* server."

She lifted one patrician brow and crossed her arms on the counter. "People paid good money to see me *dance*, Grant. They did *not* request me as their waitress."

He adjusted the heat on the sauce and continued to stir. "Why not? You seemed right at home at Autumn's."

She rolled her eyes. "Yeah, which seats *maybe* 80 people who aren't in such a hurry and who won't dock their waitress's tip if she's not perfect." She sighed. "I know how to dance, and I'm good at it. When it came to waitressing . . . let's just say if they held auditions I would *never* get a callback."

"Did you two interact at all?"

Her gaze went vague. "No, other than hi, what can I get you, and how was your meal. He was always polite, but he wasn't a talker, just a healthy eater."

"That explains how he powered through two pieces of Autumn's peach pie." Grant checked the chicken, but his mind was focused elsewhere. "Was he there the night Cassie was killed?"

Her eyes widened slightly and she sat up straighter in her chair. "Yes. Yes, he was."

The questions in his head only multiplied at her simple statement. "If he was working for Mayfield . . . and Mayfield had him watching *you*, why didn't he tell his boss that you went to work in Cassie's place?"

"Maybe he doesn't work for Mayfield."

He heard the tremor of fear in her voice and wanted to kick himself. This was *not* the direction he wanted this evening to take. Reaching across the island, he laced his fingers through hers. "Don't worry, Juliet. I'll find out exactly who he is and who he works for."

Her eyelids fluttered. "And, if he's dangerous?"

Grant smiled and squeezed her hand. "Then he just tussled with the wrong small-town Sheriff." He released her and stirred the sauce. "Want a taste?"

She gave him a reproachful look. "You're changing the subject and trying to distract me."

"I am." He grabbed a spoon and dipped it in the cream. "So, want a taste?"

She pursed her lips and stared at him for a few seconds, and then a smile tugged at the corners of her mouth. "Give me that spoon."

Grant wiggled his eyebrows and handed over the utensil. She popped it in her mouth and her brows rose. He smiled. "You seem surprised." He checked the pasta, and then looked at her again. Her expression said volumes.

"That's really delicious," she said.

He checked the chicken once more and continued to stir the bubbling sauce. "I told you, bachelors either learn to cook or starve."

"No, I mean that's *really* delicious." She put the spoon in the sink. "That's better than the chef at the bistro could cook up, and he trained at the Culinary Institute of San Francisco."

"It's not so hard." He shrugged. "I like food. Most everybody in town has been a victim of my culinary experiments, and this was one of the winners. It's all in the spices. Now, can you give me a hand here?"

Juliet hopped off her stool and came around the end of the counter. "What do you need?"

You, was his first thought, but he managed *not* to say it. "Can you cut the chicken?" He pointed to a butcher block and a knife on the counter. "Just slice it into strips while I drain the pasta."

"You got it."

Grant turned the heat on the sauce off, grabbed a pair of potholders, and lifted the bubbling pot. After draining the water he put the pasta back on the stove, watching her covertly as he poured the sauce over the penne. She even cut chicken gracefully, and Grant felt the pull inside him. He stirred the noodles then put the spoon aside and stood behind her, his hands on the counter on either side of her hips.

"You do that well," he said softly, his lips near her ear.

Juliet hesitated for a moment. "Lots of practice," she said in a breathless voice. "M-my mother wasn't much of a cook, so, like you bachelors it was either learn or go hungry."

He took the knife from her hand, put it in the sink, then spun her to face him and penned her in again. "I'd kiss you right now, but I have the feeling we'd miss dinner if I did. And, since the sauce is only good when it's fresh . . . ."

"Then we'd better eat . . . dinner," she whispered, color washing over her skin in darkening shades of pink.

"Mm hmm." He really, *really* wanted to kiss her, and she was so close he could feel her breath on his cheek. "We better eat . . . *dinner.*" He watched her closely, noting the deepening of her blush, her fast, shallow breathing, but her eyes remained locked with his. "I'll get the plates."

She only nodded as he turned. After he heaped steaming mounds of pasta on the plates she laid a sliced chicken breast over each. She smiled when he gave both plates a dusting of chopped parsley with a flourish that would gain him entrance to any gay pride event. He then led the way to the four-person table situated in the nook off the kitchen. After placing the plates on the polished wood surface, he lit the candles and pulled out her chair.

"Madam, your dinner," he said with a bad French accent and a short bow.

"Merci," she replied as she sat down. She looked up at him through her lashes as he flipped out a napkin and laid it over her lap. "Merci beaucoup."

"Soyez le bienvenu," he replied. Her wide-eyed stare made him chuckle. "Oui, je parle en peu Francais."

She blinked at him. "How much is a *little* French?"

"Enough to get by," he replied as he sat down. "I spent some time at Camp Panzer in Germany, and we did a few liberty trips to Paris." He gave her a sly smile. "For some reason those French girls *love* Marines."

"I'll bet," she said with a laugh and a shake of her head. "There *is* something about a man in uniform."

He sat straight up in his chair. "Hey, I want you to like me for *me*, not my uniform."

One arched brow rose. "I would say I like you out of uniform, too, but since the only difference between your civilian attire and your work attire is the presence of a badge, I'm not sure I've ever *seen* you out of uniform, except for earlier when we were dancing."

He fought the smile but he wasn't entirely successful, and her cheeks went pink as if she knew what was coming. Nevertheless, he couldn't stop himself from saying, "Then perhaps I'll have to remove *all* my clothes, just so you know for certain I'm not in uniform anymore."

When she smiled and responded with, "Can't wait," his jaw hit the table. She reached over, put a finger under his chin, and closed his mouth as she laughed softly. "Eat, Sheriff. The sauce is only good when it's fresh."

Grant wasn't sure he'd be able to swallow anything even if he *did* manage to successfully maneuver a fork to his mouth. Suddenly the candles seemed like a very bad idea. All he could see were pictures of Juliet naked, bathed in candlelight, those Caribbean blue eyes lit from within. It made his mouth water, and not for chicken.

He forced a smile and started to eat, although it was several minutes before he could really relax, or enjoy his food. She seemed to understand his discomfiture and kept the conversation light. They were back to the mindless chatter, the pleasant dialogue people resorted to while "dating" and on their best behavior. The problem was he didn't want to be on his best behavior. He wanted to behave badly, with her, and he wanted her to want the same thing as much as he did.

Keep it together, Grant, he told himself. *If you do this right you just might get what you're after.*

His brain spit out a question. *Maybe, but will I get to keep her?*

You'll never know until you try. You've never been the type to quit, so don't start now.

"Grant?"

"I'm sorry, what?" He blinked at her then smiled when he saw her concerned frown. "Sorry, Juliet. Lost in thought for a few seconds there."

"I asked you if you were finished."

He looked down at his plate and was surprised to see his food was gone, as was hers. She rose, took her plate, and reached for his. He handed it over. "Thanks."

She smiled. "You're welcome."

He watched her as she put the plates and other dirty dishes in the sink and began to run hot water. "What are you doing?"

She glanced at him and shrugged. "I figured since you cooked I'd clean up." She pointed at the fridge. "Do you mind?"

"I told you to make yourself at home," he replied. "That includes the fridge."

"Right." She opened the appliance, retrieved a bottle of beer from the shelf, and turned to him as the door closed on its own. "Here. Have another beer, relax, and I'll be done in ten minutes."

He took the bottle, frowned, and rose. "You're a guest here. You don't have to do dishes."

"What is that line you're so fond of saying?" She paused, leaned one hip into the counter, and tipped her head. "Oh, yeah. I don't do anything I don't *want* to do." She waved an elegant hand at him. "I'm sure you have a report to finish, or a briefing to write up, or a phone call to make." She squirted some dish soap into the flow. "Call and check on Detective Riordan."

Grant scowled. "I saw him before I left town. He's fine."

"So, you have *nothing* to occupy yourself with for the next ten minutes?" She rolled her eyes and finished clearing the table. "Fine. Stand there and be bored while I wash dishes."

"You wash and I'll dry."

Juliet frowned at him. "No."

"Juliet—"

She placed her hands on his chest and he was surprised by the shock that traveled through him. It had apparently hit her as well because she sucked in a breath, and it was nearly half a minute before she forced her gaze upward.

"Grant, go sit down."

"And if I don't?"

Juliet shivered. His voice was a silky challenge, as was the sparkle in his eyes, and she felt a hedonistic thrill vibrate between her legs at what that voice promised.

"If I *don't* go sit down, what are you going to do to me?"

Unbidden, heat bloomed inside her and she gulped as erotic images started to play in her head. She felt the warmth in her cheeks and more pictures sprang to life, fueled by his nearness and his warm, woodsy scent. Her heart started to pound, which only increased blood flow to certain parts of her body and upped the rating on her mental movie. Juliet closed her eyes and tried not to groan.

Whoa, Jules, you're making me *blush.*

"Shut up."

"Why?" Grant asked. He leaned against the end of the counter, his brows drawn together.

She covered her face with her hands. "I wasn't talking to you."

He looked around the kitchen and the living room. "There's no one else here, Juliet."

"I know."

"So, you're talking to . . . ?"

She sighed, braced her hands on the edge of the counter, and dropped her chin until it touched her chest. "You're going to think I'm crazy."

He chuckled. "I've never met anyone who is *completely* normal, thank

God. Try me."

She heard the humor in his voice, but it did little to restore her confidence. "You really want to know?"

"I do," he said, "but if you don't want to tell me I could guess."

Juliet groaned. "Can we just forget it? I promise not to talk to any other invisible people as long as I'm here."

"And how would Cassie feel about that?"

Her head snapped around and she gaped at him.

A half-smile lifted the corners of his mouth. "It was my first guess."

She blinked.

He eased up onto the nearest barstool. "You seem to forget I've been *exactly* where you are. I just . . . I just have more than one voice in *my* head."

Juliet straightened, her heart thumping against the inside of her chest. "You do?"

He nodded. Juliet bit her lip. His expression hadn't changed, but the air around him certainly had. It was cooler, almost damp, and heavy with sorrow that seemed to dim even the bright overhead lights.

"Do you still hear them?" she asked in a whisper.

He leaned his elbows on the counter. "Every once in a while, though the volume seems to fade with time." A pained smile appeared. "For most of them anyway. E doesn't talk to me as much anymore, but his voice is as clear and as loud as it was the first time I met him." A wistful chuckle escaped him. "You should've heard him when I first saw *you*. There was an *ay caramba* and several *muy calientes* in there."

Juliet leaned toward him. "Who's E?"

"Elian Martinez, known by his buddies as E. His parents were from Oaxaca, came to the US in the 70s. Born and raised in East LA, he somehow managed to avoid gang-life and wound up a US Marine." A shadow passed briefly over his striking features. "We met in Sniper School. He was my best friend."

"What happened?" The words fell out before she could stop them. Grant froze for a moment and she saw the pain in his eyes, a pain she was well acquainted with. "Grant, I'm sorry—"

"We were on our way back to base after a routine patrol," he said softly. "Isn't that how it always goes?" He leaned back in his chair and crossed his arms over his chest, his eyes focused on the opposite wall. "We were about 10 miles out, and E had been bugging me for the last 20 minutes." He chuckled. "I was the better shot so I was up top manning the .50 cal and he kept asking me to let him take over. He said I was hogging all the heavy weaponry, that I got to have all the fun, and that he needed some fresh air and sunshine before he wilted inside the armored transport."

Juliet gulped and braced herself for what was surely coming.

His eyes went vague. "I finally got sick of him tugging on my pant leg and agreed to switch places. He was as happy as a pig in shit and climbed into the turret. About two seconds later we started taking fire, and about a second after that I realized E wasn't shooting back."

Her breath caught and her lungs refused to draw air.

He closed his eyes and grimaced. "I pulled him back into the AT but it was too late. Half his head was gone. He never knew what hit him."

Tears stung and Juliet's jaw dropped. "Oh, my God."

Grant took a deep, slow breath and met her gaze. "If I'd waited three more seconds to change places with him it would have been *me*, and E would have been escorting *my* flag-draped casket home. It would have been E meeting with my folks, telling my story at the local VFW, and saluting at my funeral." His eyes were filled not only with sadness, but also resolve. "Three heartbeats, Juliet, and he'd still be alive."

An ache filled her chest, expanding with each passing second until she had the sensation of being internally strangled. Her heart labored to beat, her lungs fought to inflate, and tears slid down her cheeks. Her stomach clamped into a tight, fist-sized knot in her belly. Grant left his barstool and walked around the counter, moving to stand in front of her. He laced his fingers through hers and held them to his chest.

"I know how you feel, Juliet, as if every . . . *heartbeat* is a betrayal." His eyes searched hers. "It took me *months* to realize that not once had E's voice blamed me for what happened."

She closed her eyes against the pain clawing its way up her throat. "But it *wasn't* E's voice, not really, just like it's not really Cassie's voice." She pulled her hands from his. "I'm grieving, Grant, not nuts."

"I know," he said, "and I know it's not really E's voice. But somewhere in *here*," he paused and tapped a finger against her chest, "and *here*," he paused again and touched her temple, "you *know* you're not to blame for Cassie's death."

"I should have been home," she choked out, grief darkening the edges of her vision.

"And I should've been up in that turret."

Something cold and sharp shot through her chest as that scenario played out in her head. Imagining Grant laid out in a box covered with Old Glory made her insides seize up in protest. She knew it was ridiculous; if Grant had died she'd never have met him and she couldn't miss someone she'd never met. Nevertheless, the very thought made her recoil. When he slipped a hand around her neck she sucked in a breath.

"Grieve, however you need to," he said softly, "but dump the guilt. It serves nothing and no one, and it will eat you alive." He pulled her against his chest and she went willingly. His fingers sifted slowly through her hair. "There's nothing I could have done to prevent what happened to E except die in his place. I would gladly make that sacrifice to bring him back, but I can't. Neither can you."

Sorrow welled up from the bottom of her soul and found its way out her eyes and mouth. Tears ran unchecked and great gasping sobs were muffled against his shirt. He tightened his embrace and she leaned into him, her hands gripping his waist. It was the first time since finding Cassie's body that she'd cried, *really* cried. She wept for Cassie, for a life stolen and cut short, for what might have been, and for what she and her parents had lost. Time seemed to slow, distorted and amplified through the lens of grief. Finally, after what seemed hours, she gasped.

"God, I miss her!"

Grant rested his cheek atop her head. "And you always will," he said softly, "but as long as you remember her, she'll always be with you."

Her lungs felt heavy, as if they were filled with something other than air, and she tightened her grip on him. "Does it ever go away?"

"I don't know." His breathing hitched, and when he spoke again his voice was low and pained. "Ask me in ten more years."

The sound of his sorrow was more than she could handle. Tears started afresh. Deep wrenching sobs were pulled from within her until she had the sensation of being hollow and empty. She trembled and he slipped an arm behind her knees. He lifted her and cradled her against his chest. Her arms wound around his neck as he walked to the couch and sat down. Juliet tucked in beneath his jaw. She pressed a hand to his cheek and when she realized she wasn't the only one shedding tears she pulled back to look at him. The shimmer in his eyes nearly undid her and her eyes welled again.

"You're not alone, Juliet," he whispered. He pressed his brow to hers and cupped her head. "You don't ever have to be alone again."

He closed his eyes and the tears fell. Juliet ran her thumbs over the wet tracks and pressed her lips to his eyelids. "Neither do you, Grant." She framed his face and willed him to look at her. When he did she couldn't stop the smile. "I'm here." His expression tore at her insides.

"For how long?"

Her heart wrenched. Evergreen had never been part of her plan. Grant wasn't part of her plan. Truth be told, she didn't *have* a plan outside of getting out of Seattle and luring Mayfield away from what was left of her family. Now *that* plan seemed incredibly selfish as she contemplated the danger she'd put her new friends in. People she'd only just met had welcomed her as if they were blood relations, promising to stand behind her in a manner no one else, not the police, not even her parents had been able to do.

"I don't know, but I'll stay as long as I can."

She knew Cassie would speak up, and she didn't have long to wait.

You know you want to stay. The people here have shown you more love in three days than Mom ever did, and Grant? Why on earth would you want to leave him? Damn, Jules. If I was still alive I'd do my best to lure him away from you, if we weren't sisters, that is.

"Does E always speak when you wish he wouldn't?" she asked softly.

Grant nodded. "He says really inappropriate things, too, just like when he was alive."

Juliet sighed and pressed her face into the crook of his neck. "He and Cassie should meet in the afterlife, go out. Maybe then they'd leave us alone."

Hmm, I like me a spicy Mexican dish.

He was quiet for a few seconds, and then he chuckled. "E says he's good with that."

"Cassie, too."

Okay, I'll say one more thing and then I'll leave you two alone. You love him, Juliet, and denying it will not *make it go away. And, before you start protesting, yes, you deserve someone as wonderful as Grant, and he deserves someone as wonderful as you. You may have just landed the role of a lifetime, sister. Don't let it go without a fight.*

Grant's pocket started to vibrate and Juliet jumped. He sighed, fished his phone out, and glanced at the display. His head fell back against the cushions and he stuffed the cell back in his pocket with a groan.

"What is it?"

"Remember when you asked me if I had a call to make?"

"Yeah."

"Well, that's my calendar reminding me I have a call to make."

Juliet chuckled and relaxed against him, enjoying the feel of his arms around her for another few seconds. "Go make your call," she said. She extricated herself from his embrace and rose, somewhat unsteadily. When she had her feet beneath her she smiled at him. "Go on. I'll do the dishes and be done before you've finished talking to Laine. Tell her I said hello, and that I hope we meet soon."

Chapter Nineteen

"So, who is she?" Laine asked.

Grant leaned against the deck railing. "Who?"

"Grant, this is *me* you're talking to."

He frowned. "Did Jack say something?"

"No. He doesn't talk to me about work." There was a brief pause. "You just sound . . . different, happier. So, who is she?"

Grant looked through the sliding glass door into the kitchen. He and Laine had been catching up for about 10 minutes and Juliet was almost finished with the final pot. He sighed.

"Her name is Juliet."

"Pretty name."

"She's a dancer."

"Ooh." Laine chuckled. "I never figured you for the brass pole type, but hey, if she floats your boat who am I to judge?"

Grant growled softly. "She's a ballerina, Laine. She graduated from Juilliard, danced with the American Ballet Theater for more than five years, then moved to Seattle and danced with a company there called Ballet Northwest."

"Wow. Impressive résumé."

"I didn't ask for her job history when we met."

Laine laughed. "I know, big guy. I'm just giving you a hard time. As your best friend it is my duty and obligation to do so."

"And it helps that you enjoy it," Grant said.

"There's that." Silence reigned for a few seconds and then Laine asked, "Is she in some kind of trouble?"

He didn't bother to lie. "Yeah."

"Dangerous kind of trouble?"

"Could be."

Laine sighed. "Promise me you'll be careful."

"I'm always careful."

She snorted. "You sound like Bear."

He chuckled. "How is the newly married Mr. Bristol?"

"He and Beth are well. They went on a photo safari in Africa for their honeymoon and just got back."

"And here you were worried he'd never find a woman to put up with him."

"Yeah, well, now it's your turn, mister."

"Don't go putting the cart before the horse, Laine."

"Grant, I know you. You're not the type to get involved unless you're . . . *involved*." She paused. "Does she not return your feelings?"

Grant rubbed his eyes and wished for the first time in his life that Laine didn't know him so well. "I've only known her a few days, Lainey. That's not a subject we've broached yet."

"Then get on it, Sheriff. I *love* December weddings."

He laughed. "And on that note I think I'll say good night."

Laine laughed as well. "All right, I'll let you go. You have a nice rest of your evening, Grant, and thanks for calling. I've missed our chats."

"Bullshit. With Jack and Bear to keep you busy I doubt you think about me at all."

"That's *not* true."

He heard the pout and smiled. "My turn to give *you* a hard time."

"And, thankfully, you enjoy it even less than I do."

"It's a tough job, but *somebody* has to do it."

A chuckle escaped her. "Good night, Grant. I love you."

"I love you, too, Lainey. Tell Jack I'll be talking to him soon."

"I will. Go get your girl, Sheriff. I can't wait to meet her."

Grant rolled his eyes. "Good night, Laine."

She laughed and hung up the phone.

Grant turned toward the river and watched the gently rushing water as it glowed beneath the three-quarter moon. About a minute later he heard the sound of the sliding glass door and glanced to his left when Juliet appeared at his side.

"Thank you for washing the dishes," he said softly. "You didn't have to do that."

She gave him a quick smile and leaned her elbows on the railing. "Thank *you* for cooking dinner, and for everything else." She turned a speculative eye on him. "You're going to make some girl very happy someday."

Uncertainty scraped his spine and his chest tightened. "Hmm." He faced her. "I wouldn't mind making a particular girl very happy right *now*."

He heard her sharp intake of breath and her eyes widened just a bit. "And who might that be?" she asked softly.

He put a hand on her neck, his thumb sliding slowly over her jaw. "I think you know her."

A small whimper escaped her when he covered her mouth with his. A strange rushing sensation filled him, as if the river had been transplanted from its rocky bed to his chest cavity. A chill shuddered through his body followed by a swell of heat, and his muscles tensed. He slid his arm around her waist and jerked her against him. Her hands flattened on his chest and she gasped softly, which gave him the entrance he wanted. His tongue touched hers and she wound her arms around his neck, lifting onto her tiptoes. The length of her body pressed against his.

Fire built low in his belly as his lips moved over hers. The feel of her in his arms, the scent of her shampoo, the taste of her mouth made his body sing with need and desire. Earlier he had thought they needed to talk about what was happening between them. At this moment he knew there was no way he could even string words together to form a coherent sentence, so talking was *out*. That was okay. He would rather kiss her anyway.

When Juliet pulled away his eyes snapped open and he looked at her in surprise, until she grabbed his hand. She turned and made for the house, dragging him behind her as she went. He grinned and didn't fight it.

She led him inside, and once the door slid shut she spun to face him. Her hand slid around his neck and pulled his head down, her mouth opening beneath his. Grant inhaled sharply but took what she was offering. Sparks crackled along every nerve-ending as their tongues melded together and the kiss deepened. A shock of sensation settled in his groin and he hardened.

Realizing he was fighting a losing battle he dragged his mouth from hers and trailed his lips down her neck. It gave him the barest distance, enough that he could rein himself in, and he smiled when she gasped softly. He pressed a kiss to the pulse throbbing in her throat. His tongue flicked over the same spot and she moaned. Her fingers wound through his hair, pulling him closer, and he left a wet, warm trail over her collarbone.

"Grant," she said in a gasp.

"Hmm?"

"In case you're wondering whether or not you should," she whispered, "you should."

He smiled and cupped her breasts. They weren't large, but they weren't small, perfect for his hands. Her nipples were hard and she sucked in a breath when his thumbs grazed them lightly. "Should I?"

"Yes. *What* are you waiting for?"

He pulled back and looked at her through lazy-lidded eyes. "Making love to you in my kitchen wasn't exactly what I had in mind."

Her eyelids fluttered and she licked her lips, an inadvertently sensuous mannerism that made his groin throb.

"What *did* you have in mind?"

His gaze wandered over her face for a few seconds, and he was again struck by her classic beauty. The thought of having her naked in his arms, their bodies joined intimately, sent a bolt of searing heat to his very soul.

With a low growl he captured her lips in a savage kiss, pushing her backward until she was pressed against the nearest wall. He planted his hands on either side of her and plundered her mouth with ruthless purpose. She trembled, her breathing ragged and shallow. He jerked away from her.

"*Don't* move."

Juliet knew if she did move her knees would not support her. She couldn't even find the strength to open her eyes. Bracing her hands against the wall she fought to simply remain upright, her blood boiling in her veins. Her lips felt bruised and abraded, but she knew she'd give anything to have him kiss her like that again. She heard her own rapid breathing, felt her chest rise and fall quickly as unfamiliar and frightening sensations thrummed through her.

The sound of Grant's footsteps grew fainter as he walked away from her, and if she hadn't been so overwhelmed she would've cried out for him to come back. Her body ached to have him touch her, to have him pillage the rest of her as he'd done her mouth. A pulsating, coiling tension settled between her legs, her vulva throbbed with each labored heartbeat.

She didn't know if seconds or hours had passed before she heard his returning footsteps. There was a soft thump, a rustling, and then silence. Still, she couldn't open her eyes. Fear and anticipation sent warmth and chills through her in alternating waves. Her pulse jumped and then she realized he had returned.

She felt his heat a split-second before he pressed her against the wall. Her breasts throbbed and she automatically tipped her face up. His lips brushed hers with a barely-there touch and her heart rate rose again. Unbidden, her hands flattened on his chest and moved slowly upward, her fingers lacing behind his neck. His erection was hard against her belly and that ache between her legs intensified.

His mouth crashed down on hers, turning what would normally be sweet and loving into something carnal and primitive. Juliet felt as if he was pulling her soul from the depths of her being. Oddly, the thought didn't frighten her, it excited her. She surrendered to his unspoken demand and let herself fall. She knew he would catch her.

Grant cupped her backside in his hands and lifted her. Her legs automatically wound around his waist and she nearly cried as she felt his hardness pressed so intimately against her. That ache began to pulsate with every beat of her heart. He moved away from the wall and took several long strides, holding her as easily as if she weighed nothing.

He ended the kiss and bit down gently on her lower lip as she tried to take a full breath. Her head spun, but she gradually became aware of heat and the crack of burning logs. Her eyes snapped open as Grant dropped to his knees in front of the living room fireplace. Golden light bathed the room. Eyes locked, he leaned forward onto his elbows and carefully laid her down. Something soft cushioned her back and she felt the luxurious brush of micro-fleece against her upper arms. His body covered hers, his weight a welcome pressure. He framed her face and his gaze wandered over her features, as if committing them to memory.

"*This* is more what I had in mind," he said softly. "You are beautiful, but . . . *damn* you look good by firelight."

Juliet gulped. Her heart beat briskly against her sternum as he continued to stare at her. She felt him swell and throb and her body responded with such ferocity that she gasped. He must have read the surprise and desire in her eyes, because that lazy smile appeared even as fire sprang to life in those warm, brown pools.

He slowly lowered his head and kissed her, softly, gently, and with such restraint that her lungs refused to draw air. This time he didn't demand entrance to her mouth, he coaxed it out of her. Her lips parted as if they had their own will, but he didn't invade, he *explored*. Heat spread through her and she had the sensation of flying, as she often did when she danced. He stretched out beside her and she moaned in protest. She didn't want him beside her, she wanted him *inside* her.

She needed to touch him . . . *now*. Her fingers quickly worked the buttons of his shirt loose and her womb contracted as she came in contact with warm, smooth skin. His muscles rippled as she stroked his pectorals, the ridged abdomen, and lower. When she brushed his groin his mouth left hers. A twinge of fear wormed through her as he stared at her and then pulled away.

Juliet's fingers curled into the ultra-soft blanket as he stood. From her position on the floor he looked huge, half his face cast in shadow as firelight glinted off his hair in gilded highlights. One at a time he kicked out of his boots then pulled off his socks, tugged his shirt from his jeans, and unfastened the final two buttons. He shrugged out of the garment and dropped it on the floor. Her breath caught as her gaze wandered over the chiseled torso. She had imagined what he looked like, but the reality of him blew her away. She had never seen a man more beautifully crafted.

His eyes caught and held hers, and heat climbed through her until every part of her, even her ears, burned. He unfastened his belt and then his jeans, and she struggled to breathe as need surged through her. She couldn't look away as he divested himself of his trousers and his shorts. The deep clefts that ran from his hips to his pelvis, known as Apollo's belt, drew her gaze downward. When she saw the evidence of his masculinity standing so large and proud from the dark thatch of hair her heart somersaulted.

Twice.

"Oh, God," she whispered. She closed her eyes and pressed her hands against her belly, as if that would somehow stop those Molotov cocktails in her stomach from setting her on fire. A whimper escaped her as he stretched out beside her again.

His lips feathered over her cheek, her nose, her brow, and finally her mouth. When he deepened the kiss, it felt like he was drinking her, the pull of his mouth on hers turning her bones to liquid. Her abdominals contracted violently when his hand fanned over her belly, his fingers slithering inside the waistband of her jeans. As his lips dominated hers, sending spiraling, infuriating tension through her, he worked the button loose, and then the zipper. He slowly pushed the trousers past her hips, massaging her derrière as he did so. Her panties were already damp, and as her jeans slid down her thighs the rasp of material and the feel of his calloused hands only made her wetter. Her aggravation grew and she kicked her legs until she was free of the restrictive denim. She sighed softly as Grant hooked one hand behind her right knee and pulled it up to his waist. Juliet turned onto her side and pressed herself as close to him as possible.

His kiss turned possessive, his tongue winding with hers. It was maddening. She could feel him, hot and hard against her pelvis, only the thin fabric of her underwear separated them. He seemed oblivious. He tasted her, like she was a confection, taking his time, rolling her tongue with his. His hand curved around her hip then slowly dipped, his fingers following the cleft of her buttocks downward. Juliet sucked in a breath as he delved a little deeper, pressing against the damp crotch of her panties, but he went no farther. A groan of frustration rose in her throat and she moved her hips against his.

She was rewarded when he pulled back sharply, air hissing from between his teeth. Emboldened by his reaction, she slid one hand down his chest and closed her fingers around his erection. Her breathing hitched as his hips jerked. She stroked the throbbing shaft and met his burning gaze with her own.

A glint of determination entered those bedroom eyes. His lids dropped to half-mast as he flattened one hand on her belly and slipped his fingers inside her panties. Juliet bit her lip. He carefully parted the damp, swollen folds of flesh between her legs, grazing his thumb over her clit. A cry of pleasure was wrenched from her and he began a slow, methodical massage, each feather-light touch tightening the spiral between her legs until she was quivering uncontrollably. Unable to concentrate on anything else she released him, her hand braced against his rock-hard stomach.

She was panting, eyes closed, and she felt him watching her. Her hips began to move in time with his stroking of her flesh, and when he slipped a finger inside her she moaned. Tingles built beneath his hand, gradually spiraling outward and sharpening as he continued to caress the tiny bundle of nerve endings that was the center of a woman's pleasure. She felt as if she was hurtling toward a cliff, and just before gravity thrust her off he stopped. It was like hitting a wall.

Her eyes snapped open and she stared at him, her breath coming out in sharp, protesting gasps. "Wh-what's wrong?"

He dipped his head and kissed her, then trailed his lips over her jaw and downward. "Nothing's wrong, except you're still half-dressed." He covered her breast and lightly pinched her nipple, sending a flurry of fluttering sensations to her vulva and back. "I want to see you, *all* of you."

He leaned on one elbow and his fingers found the hem of her T-shirt. Juliet lay back and lifted her arms, arching so he could pull the garment up and over her head. His hand slipped behind her and he deftly worked the clasp of her bra loose. Slowly, reverently, he pulled the garment from her, and the darkening of his eyes told her more than words ever could. His gaze was hot on her body, traveling slowly over her breasts and the rest of her. His breathing quickened.

"*Damn.*"

Juliet pushed her panties down, drawing her knees to her chest to facilitate their removal. His sharp intake of breath made her give him a slanted look, and then she straightened both her legs so her feet were up over her head.

"Holy shit," he breathed, his brows shooting up.

She tossed the panties aside, gracefully lowered her legs, and rolled toward him. "You can see me now . . . *all* of me."

A silken chuckle escaped him and he narrowed his eyes. "Tease."

Her brows rose. "*Me?* Sounds like the pot calling the kettle black. You bring me right to the edge and then stop so you can finish undressing me." She pouted. "That was *not* well done of you."

"And this morning you spent the better part of two hours rubbing yourself all over me and I wasn't allowed to do a damn thing about it." The sensual smile curved his mouth and she touched a finger to his lips. He nipped at the digit and gave her a wicked look. "Now, I can do something about it, and I intend to make *every* minute count."

He swooped in for a kiss and her toes curled as that warm tingling gathered in her belly again and started to spin.

"Not only am I going to *look* at you," he said against her mouth, "I am going to *touch* you, and *taste* you . . . *all* of you."

She could only sigh in acknowledgment and press closer to him, her fingers winding through his hair. It was soft against her palms and she fisted her hands in the thick waves. The brush of his skin against hers sent sparks flying and she swore she heard them snapping as his tongue trailed liquid fire down her throat and over her collarbone. He cupped her breast and she tensed in anticipation.

Grant took his time, kissing his way downward, until she was vibrating with need. His breath was hot on her breast, fanning over her nipple, and after what seemed like days he flicked the budding peak once with his tongue. Her hands clutched at his head and a ragged moan was pulled from deep within her. Fire banked in her loins, her womb quivered, her legs shook, and as his tongue rasped once more over the taut nub her lungs spasmed. It was all she could do to draw a breath.

His hand slipped between her legs and his finger dipped into her heat, rubbing her swollen clit with gentle, circular strokes. The coil inside her contracted, relaxed, and contracted again. Grant suckled her, pulling her nipple into his mouth and the fuse was lit. The tension built, expanding through her as the seconds turned into minutes, until the roar in her body drowned out the sound of her moans. Everything else faded into the background. All she was aware of was the feel of his hands on her flesh, his tongue on her breasts, and the orgasm building.

"God, you're so tight," he said in between soft bites on her nipples. "I'm almost afraid I'll hurt you."

Juliet groaned as he sucked one nipple, hard. The ache traveled from beneath his mouth to her clitoris. "You won't hurt me," she replied in a hoarse voice, "but I'll definitely hurt *you* if you stop."

He chuckled and pulled the other rosy bud to the roof of his mouth. Juliet gasped as pleasure sizzled through her.

"Are you threatening a peace officer, ma'am?" he asked, his breath hot on her skin.

"Why, yes I am, Sheriff," she gasped out. "Does that mean you're going to . . . arrest me?"

"That remains to be seen." His finger probed deeper and he growled. "Do I need to restrain you first?"

Juliet couldn't respond, awash with dizzying sensations that spiraled out from beneath his hand until her entire body tingled. The wave was cresting, and when he pressed the heel of his palm against her clit as his fingers laid firm strokes on the sensitive interior walls of her vagina, that wave burst up like sea foam hitting a breaker. A strangled cry escaped her and her body bowed as her climax exploded and spun outward, flashes of bright color dancing behind her tightly closed eyelids. She clutched his shoulders as the spasms rocked her, his fingers working their magic and drawing her orgasm out. The supernova whirling through her body blotted out everything except the intense, electric sensations. Surely, the human body wasn't designed for this. He continued to massage her and she continued to come. Gradually the last ripples of pleasure left her and she collapsed against him, her breathing sharp and ragged.

"That was payback for this morning," he said, nuzzling her ear.

She gave a short, breathless laugh. "I think you have this whole *payback* thing wrong." Her hand slithered down his torso and around his erection. "Payback isn't *supposed* to be . . . *enjoyable*." She stroked the velvety, pulsing shaft, her fingers unable to fully close around him. "Payback is supposed to cause pain." The head of his penis was large and flared, and she found herself transfixed as it throbbed beneath her touch.

"I want you so much I ache," he bit out. "Does that count?"

She slid her tongue over his lower lip. "No."

He chuckled. "So, how much must I suffer before it's enough for you?"

Juliet gave him a wicked grin. "I want you to want me so much you either take what you want, or beg me to stop." She kissed his chest then pushed him onto his back.

"The former might happen," he said, "but the latter? I don't think so."

She rose onto all fours, her knees cushioned by the thick carpet and the super-soft fleece, and kissed her way down his torso, stopping every few inches to taste his skin. He sucked in a breath and his abdominals clenched when she circled his navel with her tongue.

"Are you sure about that?" she asked.

He focused on the ceiling and clenched his jaw.

"I'm damn sure I'll take what I want before I *ever* ask you to stop." He looked at her through lazy-lidded eyes, the warm brown darkened to near black. "But . . . that's what you *want*, isn't it?"

A thrill of excitement shot through her and settled between her thighs with a throb. The thought of him taking her forcefully started warmth that radiated from her center outward. She gripped his penis with one hand and started a slow, gentle stroking as she lowered her head and swirled her tongue around the tip. His hips jerked in response and she smiled.

"Why, yes it is, Sheriff," she replied softly. "Yes, it is."

She took him into her mouth and smiled when he groaned. Juliet licked and caressed him, relaxing her throat as she slid her lips down his hardness. Even so she couldn't take all of him, but she took all she could. His hands fisted in the blanket and his breathing turned ragged.

"My God, Juliet," he said in a guttural whisper.

The ache between her thighs sprang back to full, coiling life. She had wondered what her name would sound like from his lips while he was deep in passion, and now she knew. It stoked the blaze inside her, taking it from a wildfire to an inferno, and all she wanted was to hear her name again as he reached orgasm. She took him deeper, smiling inwardly as his hips arched toward her.

"Damn, girl," he rasped. "One more thing your sister *isn't* better at than you are, I'll bet."

She reached between his legs and gently fondled his scrotum, pulling another moan from him. His hips started to move in rhythm with the bobbing of her head. Her lips were still bruised from his kiss, but they warmed and stretched as he thrust up to meet her mouth. She watched his face, the clenched jaw, the half-closed eyes that were filled with heat. He grew thicker and harder with each passing second, and Juliet purposely slowed her pace. Grant groaned and pressed his head back against the carpet. A fierce expression of primal pleasure etched his features, and the animal excitement she saw there made him seem wild and wholly sexual. The considerate, laid-back, old-fashioned man was morphing into a beast, and Juliet felt the rush of heat and moisture as the female in her responded. His breathing grated in and out, his muscled chest rising and falling quickly.

"You *are* trying to hurt me," he ground out.

Juliet wrapped one fist around the base of his shaft and pumped up as her mouth moved down. His penis started to throb and twitch and she locked her lips around him, sucking harder, faster, and deeper. Although she hadn't been as sexually active as Cassie, she'd done a *lot* of reading, and her last boyfriend had enjoyed being the guinea pig for her oral explorations. It was in her nature to practice whatever she did until she did it well, whether that was dancing or performing fellatio. If the rough moans coming from between Grant's clenched teeth were any indication, her investment was paying off big.

She was so immersed in pleasuring him that when he hooked his hands beneath her arms and tossed her onto her back she cried out in surprise. He pushed up onto all fours and stared down at her. His eyes bored into hers, desire tinged with a little bit of anger, and she gulped.

"Have it your way," he said in a growl. "I'm taking what I want."

Her mouth was already open so he didn't need to find a way in. His tongue wrapped around hers and turned up the flame. As if it could get any hotter. Every cell in her body vibrated with anticipation, her limbs were fluid with desire, her head spun as he sucked the oxygen from her lungs. She wanted him so much her womb was shuddering and contracting. His lips trailed fire down her throat and over her chest, and when he bit down lightly on one taut nipple she arched her back and moaned.

"Grant . . . !"

He ignored her. With agonizing slowness he slid a finger inside her and started a languid, deliberate stroking. Her hips began to move against his hand and when his thumb found her clit with a feather-light touch she almost came off the floor.

"Mmm . . . so hot," he whispered against her breast. He sucked one nipple into his mouth. "So wet for me. I can't wait to taste you, Juliet."

The husky vocalization only added to her arousal. Her pulse went into high gear, her chest heaving with each sharp breath as he continued to torment her. Ripples of pleasure built and expanded, pushing higher with each stroke of his finger and his thumb.

"Tell me you want me, darlin'," he said, the potent sexuality in his voice sending her higher. "You want me inside you, don't you?" Another finger joined the first.

"Oh, God," she gasped as his fingers hit something deep and high within her, something that nearly sent her over the edge. Tingling pulses began to radiate outward from low in her belly. "Yes, Grant. Please, oh please. I need you."

She didn't care that she was begging. Never before had she felt such a profound need to be one with a man, to have him deep and hard inside her, taking her and making her his. The ache was so intense and forceful it hurt.

"I don't believe you," he said. She wound her fingers into the blanket, twisting the fabric as his tongue laid a hot swath over her abdomen downward. A gasp was forcefully expelled from her lungs when he placed his hands on the insides of her knees and pushed her thighs apart. Cool air met heated flesh and goose bumps skittered over her skin. A chill traversed her spine.

He chuckled, and the dark, sensuous sound wrapped around her. "*This* is what I want . . . for starters."

Juliet cried out in pleasure as his mouth covered her, his tongue moving in slow, luxurious circles around her engorged clitoris without touching it. She shuddered with each long, slow lap of his tongue, the familiar tingling building again but from a deeper place this time. Her body cried out for release as the tightening in her clit expanded until she ached.

"Please, Grant," she gasped, "please . . . ."

The pressure inside her reached dizzying heights, the walls of her vagina tightened and clamped, longing to feel the stroke of his hard, throbbing erection. His soft, liquid laugh was the equivalent of tossing gas on an open flame and a sharp pang of desire speared her.

"I still don't believe you."

All Juliet could do was moan, her head thrashing back and forth. He continued to lick her swollen flesh while ignoring her clit. The throbbing between her legs grew until she could hear it. When his tongue finally grazed the swollen nub she nearly screamed, her back arching and her hips bucking against his mouth. Then he enveloped her with his lips and sucked.

This time she did scream, pleasure ripping through her until she was sure she would come apart and shatter. She thrashed beneath him as agonizing shards of ecstasy radiated outward from beneath the heat of his mouth and tongue, but he held her down with little trouble. He continued to suckle her, his hands gripping her hips as her orgasm rocked her. Her brain went numb, her body shuddering violently as the wave crested and pushed higher. Never had she experienced anything so acutely intense, so all-consuming that she was reduced to little more than a quivering, moaning mass without the ability to think, reason, or do anything other than *feel*. Her climax pinnacled, lingered there, and then rushed into the stratosphere as she splintered in one final, mind-blowing explosion of pure, carnal pleasure.

Bliss wrapped around her and her body hummed, her skin flashing hot and cold as she slowly floated back to earth. About halfway between the summit and the ground however, she became coherent enough to realize his mouth was still fixed on her flesh. His assault on her clit had softened but it hadn't stopped, and as he continued to lave his tongue over the throbbing bundle of nerve endings the pressure started to build again.

"Grant Donovan," she bit out, "if you *don't* make love to me *now*, I'm leaving."

When he pulled away her clit protested with a violent twinge and she bit back a moan of protest. Grant pressed a kiss to the inside of her thigh and laughed softly.

"Bullshit."

Chapter Twenty

Grant sat back on his haunches, and even though every fiber of his body wanted to plunge into her wet sex he merely looked at her. Her body glistened with a faint sheen of perspiration, those blazing Caribbean blue eyes locked with his, her breasts heaving with each labored breath. Need surged through him, making his penis throb.

"You said to take what I wanted, darlin'," he said. He stroked her clit with one finger and smiled when she mewled softly and closed her eyes. "That's what I'm doing."

"And what about what *I* want?" she gasped.

He chuckled and continued to torment her swollen flesh. "Two orgasms aren't enough for you? Greedy."

"I never said . . . I wanted . . . two orgasms." Her breath caught as he rolled her clit gently between his thumb and forefinger. "I *said* I wanted *you* . . . inside me."

"And if that's not what *I* want yet?"

Her eyes opened and she glanced down at his rock-hard erection. "Really?"

He leaned over and flicked her clit with his tongue. She groaned.

"Oh, I want you, darlin'," he said. "That's no secret. I just want to make sure *you* want *me* just as much." He licked her again.

"Oh . . . *God.*" She writhed against his tender onslaught. "If I wanted you any more my head would explode."

He loved her taste, her scent, a mix of fully aroused woman and something citrus and floral, no doubt her body wash or lotion. The way her clit bunched and hardened beneath his tongue sent heat through him like no woman before her had. He was so hard he could pound railroad spikes.

"Damn, Juliet," he breathed as he slid a finger inside her hot, wet channel, "I think I finally believe you." Her muscles clamped down on the digit and he sucked in a breath. If she was this tight around his finger he realized he probably wouldn't last a hot minute once he put another part of his anatomy inside her. "Yeah, you're ready for me."

"Then do something about it, dammit," she growled. *"Now."*

He laughed softly and retrieved a condom from his shirt pocket.

"You keep condoms in your shirt pocket?" she asked.

"Not usually," he chuckled. "But tonight, I was hoping . . . ."

She watched him as he ripped open the foil packet, her gaze hot and hungry. The primitive lust in her eyes called to the animal in him, and his heart pounded in response. Desire morphed into unyielding need; he didn't just *want* her, he *had* to have her. He slid the rubber down the length of his shaft. She licked her lips and the flame in her eyes burned even brighter. He felt the heat coming off of her in waves. This was a woman brimming with passion. He saw it when she danced, when she spoke of her sister, and he saw it now as she trembled. Oh, yeah, this was going to be incredible.

He braced his arms, one hand planted on either side of her shoulders and lowered his hips. Air hissed out from between his teeth when she lifted her pelvis and he felt her heat bathe the head of his erection. She whimpered and dug her fingers into his back.

"Grant."

With one powerful, driving thrust he speared her to the womb and froze. Her muscles wrapped around him, tighter than a fist, and she let out a strangled cry. A stab of apprehension almost killed the mind-numbing pleasure that ripped through him as they became one.

"Juliet?"

"What?" she gasped.

"Did I hurt you?"

She swiveled her hips and a shock of electricity sizzled from his pelvis outward. "Yes," she said in a throaty whisper, "do it again."

Apprehension was replaced with bone-melting fire. Grant dropped down onto his forearms and groaned as his body took over. He lunged inside her, her slick heat massaging him, pulling him deeper. The rhythm he set was slow and steady, but as her moans and gasps grew in frequency and pitch the pace increased. She wrapped those long, supple legs around his waist and tipped her hips, giving him full access. He felt the entrance to her womb and a shudder went through him.

He needed to kiss her, to breathe in her ragged groans. His tongue snaked inside her mouth, matching the movement of his body. Her nipples raked against his chest and her fingers dug into his shoulders as the tremors started. They were soft at first, as were her gasps, but with each measured thrust they grew and strengthened. The tingling started at the base of his shaft as he let the animal in him take over. There was no tenderness here, no gentleness. His hips hammered forward and she met each push with a fervor that matched his own. The pulses radiated outward from his groin, sharpening, penetrating, until he felt them to his core. He buried his face in her neck and fought it.

"God, Juliet," he groaned, "I don't know how much more of this I can take."

"Don't stop, Grant," she begged, "oh, please don't stop."

Her whispered plea strengthened his resolve, and the need raging through him. "Never, darlin'," he replied in a low voice, "not until you ask me to."

She moaned his name, her breath harsh and hot against his shoulder. His mind blanked as he felt the tide rise and he felt himself swell. His flesh burned against hers, her walls clinging to him, milking him until he couldn't stand it. It was too much, this fire that washed over him from head to toe, setting him aflame and driving him higher. He heard his own guttural groans, her fevered cries, the sound of their bodies melding in a bestial rutting the likes of which he'd never before experienced. His body wanted to give in, end this sweet agony in a primitive rush, but another part of him savored the torturous rapture of being one with her. It felt too good inside her, her flesh hot, slick, and so tight around him. Prolonging something this pleasurable was surely a recipe for insanity. A long, rasping groan exploded from his throat as he deliberately slowed his pace, and he didn't give a damn if he went crazy.

"Oh, Grant!"

She coiled up beneath him. He pumped slowly, fiercely into her, and her legs tightened around his ribs. He felt like he would disintegrate, sensations gathering and pulsating from his groin to the rest of him. Just when he didn't think he could go one more stroke Juliet let out a keening wail and her internal muscles clamped down on him *hard*. Her body shuddered violently and her nails raked his back as her hips slammed against him.

His entire body seized up as his orgasm hit the moon and heat surged. Scorching pleasure rocketed through him, stealing his breath, his strength, and what little sense he'd had left. Her name was dragged from his throat as he grabbed her derriere and drove himself to the hilt. One pulse, two, three, and then he collapsed on top of her with a deep moan. Fireworks crackled, the sharp snapping gradually fading and finally going to black.

When he was able to draw a full breath he leaned up on his elbows and framed her face. Her lips were swollen and slightly parted, her breathing rapid and shallow. Dark lashes arced above those high cheekbones, her eyes closed tightly. As his gaze wandered over her delicate features, something in his chest constricted to the point where it became difficult to breathe, and given his previous exertion he needed the oxygen. His thumbs stroked the satiny skin as he fought to inflate his lungs. Once he could finally inhale he willed her to look at him. As if he'd voiced a command her eyelids fluttered up and his heart vaulted into his throat. He almost didn't have the strength to swallow it down.

He whispered, "Juliet."

Her hands smoothed over his back and shoulders. "God, I love the way you say my name, all rough and raspy."

And I think I'm in deep shit here.

"I'm sorry if I hurt you," he whispered, "but once I got inside you . . . ."

She pressed a finger to his lips. "I know, and you didn't hurt me." Her expression turned wistful and she traced the outline of his mouth. "That was . . . *amazing.*" Finely arched brows drew together. "I've never felt anything like that before."

"Me either," he admitted.

Her eyes dropped to his chin and he saw the flush that rose in her cheeks. "I've also never . . . *ordered* anyone to . . . ."

Her voice trailed off. He had been too turned on to be surprised by her command, but as he replayed the scene in his head he realized that, up until that moment, he'd never heard her speak in such a manner. For some strange reason the idea that he'd driven her to that extreme, when it wasn't in her character, only sharpened his desire for her. He felt the familiar stirring low in his belly and gulped.

"Don't worry about it," he said softly, his fingertips grazing her jaw. "Anytime you feel compelled to demand what you want . . . go right ahead."

She bit her lip and he saw the flash of uncertainty in her eyes. Before she could speak he lowered his head and kissed her, her sigh of surrender lighting the fire. His lips played softly over hers, reassuring her, appeasing her doubts in spite of his own. When he sensed his libido was about to take over again, he ended the kiss and pulled back. The softly trusting look she gave him shot straight to his heart.

Yep, I'm in deep shit here.

He kissed the tip of her nose. "I'll be right back."

Juliet watched him stand, the fluid movements of his body both hypnotic and tempting. His warmth went with him as he walked away and she fought the desire to call him back. She wanted to touch him again, to have him touch her again, and the very thought sent desire thrumming through her. When he disappeared down the hall she rolled onto her side and stared into the fire.

Holy shit, Jules. Who'd have guessed the easy-going sheriff with the sexy smile and bedroom eyes would be such a stud? And you were certainly no shrinking violet. Way to go, sis.

"Oh, for God's sake," Juliet breathed, irritation rising at the unwelcome intrusion.

If I hadn't seen it for myself I never would've believed it. And here I was, wondering if you even liked sex. You've never spoken about it in particularly enthusiastic terms before.

The memory of the earth-shattering climaxes, all *three* of them, warmed her skin and she smiled. "I like it with Grant." Her smile widened and she felt the blush. "I like it a *lot.*"

"You like what a lot?" Grant asked.

She glanced up as he strode toward her, the long, powerful lines of his body outlined in stark relief by the firelight. A sharp twinge stabbed through her lower belly and her clit throbbed. The man was walking sex, and now that she'd seen and experienced just how potent a man he was she knew no one else would ever satisfy her like he had. Juliet took a deep, steadying breath and forced herself to look away from him. When he eased down behind her and spooned his body around hers, she sighed softly and closed her eyes.

"Nothing."

He chuckled and draped an arm over her waist, his fingers moving slowly over her belly. "E had some choice things to say about you, too."

"I think they should both shut up and mind their business."

His lips grazed the curve of her neck. "Ooh, someone's testy."

She tossed him a glare, but when their eyes met her annoyance disappeared. Juliet rolled toward him. "I'm not testy. I'd just rather *not* think about my sister and your Marine buddy watching us while we make love."

A soft smile flirted with his lips. "You know they're not really watching, right?"

Juliet huffed and dropped her brow against his chest. "I *know* that, but . . . you know what I mean."

His fingers fanned over her back and pressed her closer. "I do, and I'm sorry for making fun."

"You should be."

"I am."

"Don't do it again."

"Don't do what again?" He kissed the top of her head. "Make fun, or make love to you?"

Juliet groaned and tried to roll away from him, but he wouldn't let her. He lay on his side, his head propped in one hand, the other gripping her waist. She lifted her gaze to his and he scooted closer. Her heart started to pound as that sexy smile curved his lips, and when her breasts brushed his hard chest she sucked in a breath.

"I think if you told me not to make love to you again, that is one order I would have to disobey," he said. His head dipped and he kissed her quickly, then he smiled and nibbled on her lower lip.

Her throat tightened and her breathing quickened in anticipation of her airway closing off. When he released her lip a wicked gleam lit his eyes. Juliet knew she was lost.

"I think if I ever said anything so stupid you should slap me," she replied, breathless, "because I've obviously lost my mind." Her hands slid around his narrow waist, reveling in the supple play of his muscles as he breathed. His skin was surprisingly soft and smooth, and need burgeoned in her when she felt him harden against her belly.

"I'd never slap you," he said in a low, serious voice. Then a grin twitched about his mouth. "I might smack your ass, but only if you wanted me to." He wiggled his brows and planted another quick kiss on her mouth. "Aside from that I'd *never* raise my hand to you."

The thought of him spanking her sent a slew of strange flurries through her midsection. She discovered, to her surprise, that the idea of his hands slapping her bottom appealed to her in a delicious, naughty sort of way. Her previous sexual encounters had always been pretty straightforward. Oh, they had switched positions, locations, included oral sex and sometimes basic toys, but not once had she even entertained the notion of a little more physical play. Now that he'd broached the subject, sort of, she couldn't get the image out of her head.

Her thoughts must have registered in her eyes because his smile faded and sparks flashed in that penetrating gaze.

"Damn, girl," he breathed. "Don't look at me like that or I might think it's an invitation to warm that sweet ass of yours."

She exhaled sharply. "And if it is?"

He stared at her for a taut moment, and she couldn't decipher what she saw in his eyes aside from brazen hunger. The primal ferocity in his expression sparked her desire, and it curled hotly between her legs. She imagined what she was feeling was probably similar to what ancient cavewomen had felt after being dragged back to the cave: fear mingled with anticipation heaped upon burning need. His hand fanned over her backside and she tensed.

When he laid a resounding *smack* on her left cheek she yelped in surprise, both from the stinging and the raw lust that rifled through her. It settled with throbbing intensity in her clit and she gasped. It wasn't a cruel blow, more playful than painful, but still she felt it. *Everywhere.* He watched her carefully through narrowed eyes as he gently stroked her derriere, soothing the heated skin.

"Talk to me, Juliet," he whispered, edging closer. "I'll push it as far as you want to, but *only* as far as you want to."

She gulped. "Again."

She had firsthand knowledge of how powerful Grant was, so it was obvious to her he was tempering his strength. She knew he could seriously hurt her if he wanted to, but she also knew to her soul he didn't want to. Her nipples ached and her clitoris pulsated when he spanked her again, just once more, and then caressed the rounded curve. He was gauging her reactions, hesitant, but if the raging hard-on against her stomach was any indication, he was *really* turned on. And she was wet and panting.

He delivered another mildly stinging blow to her backside the same moment his mouth covered hers, his tongue spearing between her parted lips as she gasped. He devoured her and she ached to have him inside her again. She was so overwhelmed that she forgot to breathe, unaware until her throat and lungs started to burn. Desperate for air she pulled back just far enough to take a breath.

"Tell me you have more condoms," she said against his lips.

"I do," he replied in a husky voice. He rolled onto his back, pulled her on top of him, and smacked both cheeks lightly. "And this time . . . I think it's *your* turn to make love to *me*."

Her stomach clenched. A strangled sound caught in her throat as she found herself caught and held captive by those bedroom eyes. He was hard and throbbing beneath her, and she knew one shift of her hips would have him inside her again. She burned for it.

The slap on the ass he delivered sent a shudder of white heat through her and she closed her eyes with a moan.

"You really do like that, don't you?" he asked softly.

"Yes," she gasped out. "Just . . . no harder."

"I don't want to hurt you, darlin'," he breathed. "I just want you hot for me." His hand soothed her tingling skin. "Was that last one too hard?"

She shook her head. "No, it was perfect." Another smack and her head dropped back as her clit sang. "Oh, God." Something inside her clenched with need. There was a void there, and she wanted it filled.

With him.

Her eyes snapped open and she looked for his shirt. She clambered off him and grabbed the tangle of fabric, searching frantically for the pocket with the condoms. When she found one she held it up triumphantly, and then looked his way. Her breath caught. He had both hands behind his head, the lines of his musculature sharply accentuated by firelight and shadow. He looked like a reclining god. A shiver went through her and that need intensified. Damn. On a scale of one to ten he was pushing twenty.

Those sinful lips quirked up slightly. "You're giving me that look again, Juliet."

She gulped. "What look is that?"

"That hungry look."

"I *am* hungry."

One eyebrow shot up. "You didn't get enough dinner?"

Her heart hammered against her ribs. "I had enough dinner." She straddled his legs and slowly inched her way up until her thighs were pressed against his. The ache in her belly sharpened. She licked her lips and ripped open the foil packet. "It's more *dessert* I'm craving." The grin he gave her made her insides melt.

"I'm yours for the taking, darlin'," he crooned. "You can have as much dessert as you want, provided this old body can keep up."

Juliet slipped the condom over the swollen head of his erection and her womb contracted painfully as she anticipated their joining. "I have faith in you, Sheriff."

He closed his eyes and groaned as she slid her fingers down his granite-hard shaft, fully unrolling the condom. "Damn, girl, you are *killing* me."

"Don't die yet," she said, breathless. "I'm not finished with you."

His abdominals contracted as she stroked his hardness and straddled his hips.

"Come on then, darlin'," he bit out. "It's your turn to take what you want."

So she did. And this time when she came, she was sure her head did explode.

***

After she'd had her way with him, violently and explosively, and he'd warmed more than her rounded backside, he had his way with her. He took his time, savored every kiss, every caress, every sinuous joining of their bodies. He made slow, excruciating love to her, touched and explored every inch of her, until she begged him to let her come or let her go. Neither option had appealed to him. Her desperate cries of pleasure only fortified his determination, and when he finally allowed her release and took his own they were both so wrung out and replete they could neither move nor speak. After their muscles finally regained some strength she had rolled onto her side and he had curled his body around hers.

Grant ran his fingers over her arm and buried his face in her hair. Juliet lay on her side facing the fire, her back against his chest, and she sighed softly as he inhaled the scent of her shampoo. He didn't think he'd ever get tired of touching her. Her skin was soft and smooth, like warm satin, and she really did look awesome in firelight.

"You smell good," he said.

"So do you," she replied.

"I love touching you."

She turned her head toward him slightly, just enough so he could see the smile.

"I love it when you touch me."

I love you.

His heart seized up in his chest and something sharp catapulted into his esophagus. He knew he was treading on very precarious ground, potentially devastating ground, but he'd never been one to shy away from danger. Purposely stepping into the line of fire however? That was something even *he* would think twice about. Unfortunately, all he could think about was her, enemy bullets be damned.

Several minutes passed, the only sound the snap of logs. A melancholy sigh escaped her and he slipped an arm around her waist. "What's wrong?"

She was quiet for several long seconds. "What are we going to do about that guy with my picture?" she finally asked, her voice hushed.

And there's the damned elephant in the room. "We can't do *anything* until we know more about him and why he's here," he replied. "The best thing is to keep you out of sight." He felt her sadness. It pulled on him, made his gut ache uncomfortably, and he searched for something to say that would lighten her mood. He made lazy circles around her belly button and pressed a kiss to the curve of her neck. "Don't worry, Juliet. I'll keep you occupied."

She didn't respond to his attempt at humor, those tropical blue eyes fixed on the fire. Even though she was pressed against him, even though she laced her fingers through his, she wasn't there with him. It was as if her sorrow was taking her away, and his chest tightened as a glimmer of panic flickered to life.

"Where are you, darlin'?" he asked in a whisper, his chin on her shoulder.

She turned her head and looked at him, her expression solemn. "I'm right here."

"Physically maybe." His eyes narrowed on her face. "But mentally? I don't even think you're in *Montana.*" His fingers curled under her ribs and pulled her closer. "Talk to me, Juliet."

Her brows drew together and his throat constricted at the glimmer of tears in her eyes. He saw the convulsive swallow before she pulled away from him and sat up, presenting him with her back. She took a hitching breath and ducked her head.

"God, I don't want to be here again," she choked out.

Grant sat up and maneuvered himself around to her side. Her hair had fallen forward, like a dark, shining curtain between them, and he carefully tucked the strands behind one ear. He leaned over so he could see her face.

"Here where?" he asked. "Here with me?"

Her head snapped around and she inhaled sharply. "No. That's *not* what I meant."

He bit back a sigh of relief and dragged his thumb over her cheek. "Where don't you want to be?" She bit her lip and squeezed her eyes shut, silver tears trickling down, and he braced himself for the answer.

"I don't want to be in this place where I have no control over my life," she whispered. "I feel like . . . like a puppet, dancing on someone else's strings, like I can't do anything until *they* say I can." Her chin trembled and she hugged her knees to her chest. "I don't want to be back where I was before I left Seattle, watching, waiting for *something* to happen, as if I'm only a spectator."

He sighed softly and pulled her onto his lap. "What do you want to do, Juliet?"

She sniffed and tucked in beneath his chin. "What, you're not going to tell me to just stay put while you and Daniel sort it all out?"

"I'd like to," he replied, "but I know if it was me I sure as hell wouldn't be sitting around anticipating someone else's next move." He dropped a kiss on top of her head and kneaded the tense muscles in her neck. "So, what do you want to do?"

"What *can* I do?"

The pain in her voice sliced through him. "I wish I could answer that, darlin'." He closed his eyes against the onslaught of emotions that twisted his insides into tight, curling knots. "He hasn't done anything I can do anything about. All we have so far is a basic background and, unfortunately, we can't dig any deeper unless he does something to warrant a closer look. It's not a crime to ask questions, show a photo around, and eat all of Autumn's peach pie."

"It should be," she groused, "to eat all of Autumn's pie, I mean." Her arms slid around his waist and she settled herself against him. "I could use some sugar therapy right now."

"I'm not sweet enough for you?" he teased. He kept his tone light, but those knots wound tighter as he waited for her response.

She pulled back to look at him, her hand cupping his cheek. "You, Grant Donovan, are the sweetest man I've ever known." A faint smile flirted with her mouth. "And the naughtiest."

His brows shot north. "Me? I seem to recall it was *you* who invited me to spank you."

"I don't think so," she retorted. "*I* seem to recall *you* offered to spank *me*. I just took you up on it."

He laughed and she gave him a wicked grin. Seeing her smile made his heart swell until he thought he'd choke on it. He threaded his fingers into her hair and molded them to her head. "My mistake." He kissed her softly. "A mistake I will make a million times over if it can get you to smile."

"I can't help but smile when I'm with you," she told him. Her expression turned wistful. "Nice change of subject, by the way."

"Hey, *you* changed the subject," he pointed out, "so before we completely digress just promise me one thing."

"Anything," she replied in a breathless whisper, her lips a hairs breadth from his.

"Don't do anything reckless, dangerous, or crazy," he said, "or anything I can't get you out of."

She bit her lip and grasped his forearms. "Deal, on one condition."

"What?"

Her eyes searched his for a few seconds. "Make me forget about all this until tomorrow?"

The yearning in her blue-green gaze started heat burning through him once more. He scooped her into his arms and stood in one fluid motion. "I'll make you forget about it for as long as you want." He walked toward the bedroom with long, purposeful strides. "Just give me a chance."

Chapter Twenty One

Juliet watched Grant's sleeping face, wholly content and full for the first time in her life. Soft, golden sunlight found entrance through the cracks in the blinds, brightening the room just enough so she could see him. A flush warmed her cheeks. She had asked Grant to make her forget, and he had truly risen to the challenge. Literally. Before they'd fallen into an exhausted, sated sleep he'd made her forget her own name.

Three more times.

She brushed a lock of hair from his brow and memorized his features as her heart expanded inside her chest. He was so beautiful. In sleep she could see the handsome, mischievous youth he must have been, the charming adolescent Sherri had coveted, and the amazing man the woman had let slip away. On impulse Juliet eased away from him and reached for her duffel bag which lay on the chest at the foot of the bed. After retrieving her cell phone she took several pictures of him and then tossed the device back into the tote.

Don't do it, Jules. I know what you're thinking, but don't do it.

"I have to do *something*," she whispered. "Mayfield has taken everything else from me. I won't let him take Grant from me, too."

Cassie didn't reply to that.

She glanced at the clock. 8:23 a.m. The diner opened at seven, so Autumn was probably right in the middle of the breakfast rush. It was a Friday, payday, so the diner would be busy. Juliet thought about waiting a while before embarking on her chosen course of action. Then she decided not to. The longer she waited the more likely James Coulter would find someone willing to disclose that she was indeed in Evergreen and who she was with. Even if no one gave her up, with the modern technology available, it wouldn't take much for a skilled person to answer both those questions. She had no idea if Coulter was that skilled person, but if Mayfield was footing the bill the right minion was just a cash withdrawal away. Then again, if someone disclosed her location, her nemesis would need neither a skilled person nor technology.

With a sigh she left Grant's comfortable king-sized bed and walked around to his side. His cell phone sat on the nightstand. Guilt simmered in her belly as she picked it up. With one last look at him, she slipped into the bathroom and quietly closed the door.

It didn't take her long to find the text messages between Grant and Autumn. The last one read, "Yes, ma'am. Be there in five." She scrolled up a bit and read the other exchanges. Her finger hovered over the touch screen as she formulated a new message. That guilt bubbled a little higher but Juliet choked it down and started typing.

Morning, Autumn. Have you seen our new friend today?

She hit send and waited. When Autumn didn't immediately reply Juliet sat on the closed toilet lid and tapped her foot against the tile floor. The phone dinged a few seconds later and she jumped.

He just ordered a chicken-fried steak. What do you need me to do?

Just see if you can keep him there for a while.

I can do that. He's looking at me like I'm *peach pie.*

In spite of her misgivings Juliet chuckled at that. *Well, you are as sweet as one. Just remember to keep it light.*

Oh, I'll keep it light, Sheriff. I'll keep it fat-free.

Thanks. See you soon.

Juliet inhaled deeply, rose, and moved silently back into the bedroom. After putting Grant's phone back exactly where it had been she stood at his side and looked at him for a few moments. She reached out to touch him, pulling her fingers back just in time.

"I love you," she whispered.

She really wanted to kiss him, but she knew if she did he would wake up. Another sigh escaped her as she grabbed her duffel, left the bedroom, and walked to the other bath. After a quick shower she dressed and made her way outside.

It took her nearly 30 minutes to reach the town square, and she slid the Camry into a vacant spot in front of Casa de Mi Amigo. Her stomach was clenched into a warped ball of nerves and she felt mildly nauseous. There was a half-empty bottle of water in the drink holder, so she grabbed it and twisted off the cap. The liquid was stale and warm, but it helped ease her queasiness a bit. After taking another sip she put the bottle back and exited the car.

Instead of cutting through the park and heading straight for the diner, Juliet skirted the rolling green acreage. She passed in front of the Sheriff's Office and gulped as the nausea returned. Grant would be furious with her, at least she suspected he would. *She* would be furious if positions were reversed. Squaring her shoulders she continued walking.

She reached the end of the block where the diner was and paused on the corner, gathering her courage. She'd never considered herself a confrontational person, but she was no coward. To secure a spot at Juilliard and reach the level of principal dancer with the American Ballet Theater required not only talent but also guts and determination. The difference here was an audition couldn't kill you.

Please don't do this, Jules. Just get back in your car, drive back to Grant's, and get back in bed with that amazing, beautiful man.

Juliet ignored her sister's entreaty and walked toward the diner.

The bell jingled when she opened the door, just as it had the first time. The tinkle of spoons on mugs, the scrape of forks on plates, and the familiar sound of boisterous conversation washed over her. The diner was full, Autumn and two other waitresses, probably Kelly and Lucinda, intent on their duties. Shelby was nowhere to be seen. Juliet glanced quickly around the crowded space and her heart froze when she spotted him.

He sat in the corner booth facing the door, concentrating on lifting large scoops of chicken-fried steak into his mouth. In her periphery, she saw Autumn pause and turn toward her, but she ignored the shorter woman. Juliet sucked in a breath, clenched her teeth, and strode toward James Coulter.

When she slid in across from him he looked up and his dark, beady eyes widened slightly.

"I hear you're looking for me," she said in a low, fierce voice, anger warming her chest. "Congratulations. You just found me."

He said nothing, his jowls jiggling as he swallowed his mouthful. A cell phone lay on the table and Juliet grabbed it. She glared at him and thrust it into his face.

"Call him."

He blinked at her.

"Call him, you son of a bitch."

His expression shifted and hardened slightly. He snatched the phone from her hand and slipped it into his jacket pocket. "Morning, Miss Hall."

She ignored the greeting. "Why were you at the bistro that night?"

Coulter didn't reply. Instead, he continued eating. Juliet clamped down on the rage that wanted to erupt from the deepest part of her. Sensing a presence at her elbow she glanced to her right and met Autumn's dark, concerned eyes. There was also a gleam of understanding in those almond-shaped pools, and Juliet knew Autumn realized it wasn't Grant who had been texting her.

"Morning, Juliet."

"Not now, Autumn," Juliet bit out.

Autumn's brows drew together. "Juliet—"

Juliet fixed her with a hard stare. "Not. Now." Autumn blinked at her and retreated. Juliet turned her gaze back to Coulter. "What are you waiting for?"

He lifted one brow and cut into his over-easy eggs. "I'm going to finish my breakfast."

Before he could take another bite Juliet swept an arm over the table and sent the plate clattering to the floor. Chatter ceased and silence fell. This time both brows went up and his jaw went slack. Apparently, he hadn't expected *that*.

"You're done." She slid out of the booth and stood there. Anger rushed through her, as if her blood had been replaced by molten fury. She felt the heat of it to her scalp. Bracing her hands on the end of the table she leaned toward him. "Tell your boss I said hello, and when you speak to him . . . tell him to bring it. I'll be waiting."

Spinning on her heel she strode briskly out of the restaurant. Once the door closed behind her she paused, squeezed her eyes shut for a second, and took a deep, shuddering breath. Fear, anger, uncertainty, and guilt blended in her belly and expanded outward, pressing heavily on her heart. What was she supposed to do now? She hadn't planned this far out.

Unable to think she just started walking with fast, clipped steps. A breeze picked up and she felt the cold wetness on her cheeks. She imagined Autumn had already contacted Grant, and dread joined the mixture in her stomach. Her throat constricted and more tears stung. After she passed the Center Hotel, strong fingers snaked around her arm and jerked her to the right.

A surprised cry escaped her and she stumbled, her heart jolted into a gallop. Shadows loomed as Coulter dragged her halfway down the narrow alley between the hotel and the bookstore on the corner. Several seconds passed before her brain kicked into gear and she wasn't tripping over her own feet, but before she could react he growled and shoved her against the wall. Air whooshed out of her and her head snapped sharply against the bricks, sending bright spots of light across her field of vision.

"Bitch."

Juliet blinked and tried to focus on his face. The cold fury she saw in those dark eyes sent her heart into near cardiac arrest. His short, meaty fingers dug into her upper arms and she bit back a cry of pain. When she tried to twist away from him he jerked her forward and slammed her against the wall. Juliet gasped as pain rippled across the back of her skull.

"I've been tracking you halfway across the country," he said in a low, blistering voice, "for almost *three months* now." He leaned closer and she smelled the coffee on his breath. It was sour and unpleasant and hot on her cheek. "As much as I like Mayfield's money, I *do not* like living out of rat-trap motels and eating at truck stop diners for weeks on end."

Juliet got in his face. "So go *home.*"

As soon as she spoke the words she groaned inwardly. One thing she and Cassie had in common was a smart mouth, although she didn't use hers nearly as much as Cassie had. He laughed, and it was a sharp, bitter sound that chilled her.

"You know Mayfield. People do what he says, or they wind up like your sister."

That started a chain reaction in her. Her vision went red and rage exploded in the pit of her stomach. With a feral cry she drove her knee up into his groin. His eyes bulged and he hunched toward her but didn't let go. He pressed his forearm across her throat and leaned into her, cutting off her airway.

"You're going to pay for that," he ground out, his cheeks going ruddy and his jaw clenching.

"Let. The lady. *Go.*"

The voice was cold and angry. Juliet looked out of the corner of her eye and saw Mike standing there, a shotgun at the ready. Coulter was panting, veins throbbing in his temples.

"You're not going to shoot," the man said with a low, gravelly laugh. "You'd hit *her.*"

"*I* might not shoot you," Mike replied, his steely eyes like blue-tinged flint, "but *he* sure as hell will." He nodded toward the other end of the alley.

Her gaze shifted to the opposite direction as Coulter's head snapped around. Joy and sorrow welled up when she saw Grant standing there, his normally smiling eyes filled with dark fury. He was sighting down the barrel of a rifle, the weapon held as easily as if it was an extension of his arms. There was no trace of the gorgeous, easy-going man whose sexy smile had captured her heart. *This* man was every inch a killer.

"Get your hands off her or I will drop you where you stand."

His voice was low, but filled with a deadly undercurrent that carried well past them. A chill shivered up her spine. Juliet saw the flicker of fear in Coulter's eyes, but he tried to mask it with arrogant bravado as he turned a mocking smile on Grant.

"You sure you want to risk injuring your lady friend, Sheriff?" Coulter sneered.

Grant leaned into the stance just slightly. "I've taken out terrorists from more than a mile away with a single shot using this very rifle. From *this* distance . . . ?" His voice trailed off and a lethal smile lifted the corners of his mouth. "From *this* distance there is no way in *hell* I'll miss."

Coulter said nothing and Grant's brows drew down.

"You want to find out if I'm telling the truth . . . ? Knock. Yourself. Out. Your blood will wash right off her."

Juliet felt Coulter's frustration. He fairly vibrated with it, his eyes fixed on Grant with burning resentment. A feral growl reverberated through him and escaped his mouth. He released her, stepped back several paces, and thrust his hands high.

She took a great gulp of air and rubbed her throat as Daniel walked forward. The detective handcuffed Coulter and led him away without once looking at her, his expression inscrutable. Closing her eyes she slid down the wall until her backside hit the asphalt, her knees in her chest. She was panting, her diaphragm painfully tight and her airways fighting to inflate. When she felt Grant's presence she opened her eyes and looked up, dreading what she would see in his face. Harsh lines of anger bracketed his mouth, but she also saw the fear and relief in his expression. He extended a hand. She looked at those long, supple fingers for a few seconds, and then grasped them. He jerked her to her feet and against his chest.

Juliet clutched the back of his shirt as his arms closed around her. His body was taut, muscles tense and bunched. She was shaking, still struggling to breathe, and only now was her brain truly catching up. Fear rifled through her, followed by panic. A strangled sob caught in her throat. He seemed to sense her distress and tightened his embrace.

"Breathe, darlin'," he whispered, his cheek pressed to the top of her head. "Breathe."

"Is she okay?"

It was Mike's voice, and shame grated against the inside of her chest cavity. She hadn't intended to put her new friends in harm's way, but she also hadn't fully considered the implications of confronting Coulter. Self-reproach rose like bile.

"I think she's fine," Grant replied, "but I'm going to take her to the hospital and have her checked out anyway."

"Good idea," Mike said. His hand settled on her shoulder. "Grant will take good care of you, Juliet. We'll see you soon, alright? Nicole has some beignets set aside for you."

All she could do was nod and press closer to Grant. His warmth wrapped around her like a soft, soothing blanket. Mike squeezed her shoulder and walked away.

She and Grant stood together for several minutes, his hands rubbing up and down her back, her fingers fisted in his shirt. She was vaguely aware of hushed voices, knew the lookey-loos were eying the scene and talking amongst themselves. Grant, on the other hand, remained silent.

"I'm sorry," she finally whispered, unable to stand the quiet between them any longer.

He let out a long, slow sigh. "What the hell were you thinking?"

The question had no anger behind it, only confusion and what sounded like hurt and disappointment. The guilt was back, in spades, and suddenly she needed distance. She gently disentangled herself from his arms and forced her eyes up.

"You said he hadn't done anything you could do anything about." She waited for his agreement, but he just looked at her, his gaze shuttered. Pain blossomed beneath her sternum. She inhaled sharply, pressed her lips into a thin line, and fought the tears. "Well, now he has. And now you can do something about it."

She dropped her chin, stepped around him, and walked down the alley. There was a crowd of onlookers gathered, necks craning, whispers swirling like leaves caught in a windstorm. She ignored them. When she glanced at the redheaded, female deputy who was keeping the crowd back the woman gave her a slight smile. Juliet nodded once and walked toward Grant's Yukon.

Grant stared at the cracked asphalt, fists on his hips. His insides were pitching and heaving in familiar, painful waves that radiated outward from his chest until even his fingers throbbed. When he'd woken up to find Juliet gone he'd known in his gut what she was planning. A glance at his text messages confirmed it. He'd called his office, dressed, and broken several land speed records getting to town.

The rage that had detonated when he saw Coulter with Juliet against the wall still simmered inside him. He took deep even breaths and pulled hard on his inner reins. She was safe, Coulter was in custody, and Juliet was right. Now he and Daniel and Jack could do something about her situation. Part of him was mad as hell at her for putting herself, and others, in danger, but another part of him was impressed that she'd had the stones to face off with the man.

"Grant, are you alright?"

The familiar, honey-smooth voice penetrated his angry fog and he groaned inwardly. "I'm fine, Autumn. Go back to the diner."

"Grant—"

"Autumn, please." He glanced over his shoulder at her and sighed. "Not now. I have to take Juliet to the hospital."

A flicker of alarm brightened her dark eyes. "Is she hurt?"

He faced the petite beauty. "No. That asshole slammed her against the wall pretty hard, but I don't think she's injured. It's just a precaution."

"Okay." Autumn studied him for several long, taut seconds, and then put a hand on his arm. "Don't be too hard on her." She gave him a pointed look. "Or yourself."

Grant only nodded and walked toward his vehicle.

"Sheriff."

He paused and glanced at Sheridan.

She met his gaze, her expression solemn. "Do you want me to take Miss Hall's statement?"

He thought about it for a second then nodded. Given the fact he was directly involved in the confrontation, policy dictated that someone else should commence with the investigation. "Yeah. I'm going to take her to the hospital and have the docs look her over. Have Simmons start taking witness statements here and at the diner. Once the crowd moves on you can meet us at the ER."

"Will do." When he started walking again she touched his arm. He turned to look at her and she took a deep breath. "Nice work."

He rubbed his brow and forced a half-smile. "Thanks, Jessica. Just another day at the office."

When he climbed into the Yukon Juliet glanced at him and then turned her gaze out the window. The ten-minute drive to the hospital was completed in silence, which was fine with him. He was pretty sure if he opened his mouth right now the wrong thing would come out.

The triage nurse at Evergreen Springs Memorial Hospital, a woman named Patricia, took Juliet's vitals and entered her information into the computer. Aside from answering Patty's questions Juliet remained silent and kept her eyes downcast. Grant did the same, replying to Patty's inquiries with short, succinct sentences. Once Juliet was admitted Patty led them to a private room and left them alone.

Grant took a deep breath and shrugged his shoulders, willing away the tension in his neck. He pulled out a chair and eased down into it as Juliet lay back on the gurney. She bit her lip and her gaze focused on the ceiling, and then her eyes welled with tears.

"Please say something," she whispered.

He sighed and leaned his head against the wall. "What do you want me to say, Juliet?"

"Something, *anything*." She blinked and the tears ran slowly down the sides of her face. "Get mad, yell, reprimand me; *anything* but the silent treatment."

"I *am* mad at you," he said as he rubbed his eyes, "but I'm not going to yell at you. I don't own you, darlin', and I can't order you around." He planted his elbows on his knees and stared at the linoleum. "I just wish you'd have thought this through a little more."

"I knew Autumn would call you," she said in a small voice.

Grant let out an exasperated sound and lifted his head. "She did, but I was already in town. If I hadn't woken up when I did and realized what you'd done, I would still have been 15 minutes out when she called." He narrowed his eyes on her and tried to control the pain that swelled in a cold, cutting pool beneath his heart. "He could've done anything to you in that time; kidnapped you, raped you, beaten you, crushed your esophagus and left you to die." That picture danced through his brain and he had to pause as his insides recoiled. He inhaled deeply and pinned her with a look. "I asked you not to do anything reckless, dangerous, or crazy, or anything I couldn't get you out of. You almost did *all* of those things."

She covered her face with her hands, but he couldn't stop now. The memory of what he'd witnessed rushed through him, filling him with the same dread he'd tasted earlier. It was cold, bitter, and thick in the back of his throat. He *wanted* to yell at her, he *wanted* to reprimand her, but he kept his voice low and level as he continued.

"I *saw* him jerk you into that alley, which is the *only* reason Mike and I got there so fast." He thrust his fingers into his hair, rested his elbows on his knees, and closed his eyes. "I *wanted* to kill him, Juliet. I *wanted* to blow his fucking head off and watch his brains splatter all over those bricks. I have only felt that kind of anger once before . . . ." He paused and met her anguished gaze, ". . . and I *do not* like it."

"Grant . . . ." Her voice died and she choked back a sob.

He swallowed hard. "When I was in the Marines it was a job, it was war, and they were the enemy. It was never personal." He rose and move to the side of the gurney. "*This* was personal, and it can't *get* personal or I can't do my job."

"I never meant . . . ." She paused and sucked in a gulping breath. "I didn't want this."

Her tears ripped at the inside of his chest like claws. The pain was hot and sharp. He sat next to her, put a hand behind her neck, and gently pulled her to his chest. "I know, darlin'." He rested his chin atop her head. "I know."

She clung to his waist. "Please forgive me."

He sighed and closed his eyes. "Already done." The door whispered softly as it opened. Grant glanced over his shoulder and recognized Dr. St. Pierre. The man was a few inches shy of six feet, thin and bookish, with black hair and large, dark eyes. Grant kissed Juliet's brow and stood, turning to the doctor and extending his hand. "Hey, Dr. St. Pierre."

"Sheriff." They clasped hands briefly and then St. Pierre glanced at the clipboard he held. "So, what's going on with you, Miss Hall? I hear you've had some excitement this morning."

"I'll leave you two alone," Grant said. "I have a couple phone calls I have to make." Juliet looked at him in alarm and he gave her a reassuring smile. "I'll be right outside, Juliet. Dr. St. Pierre will take good care of you." He brushed a kiss over her forehead.

He left the room and leaned against the wall. The antiseptic smell of the ER wrapped around him and he tried not to breathe too deeply. He'd spent way too much time in hospitals in his life, and if he never saw the inside of one again it would suit him just fine.

Grant pushed away from the wall and walked toward the triage area, pulling out his cell phone as he went. He had Jack on speed dial, and he held the key down.

"Special Agent Vaughn."

"Jack, we have something to work with now."

"What happened?"

He let out a long breath. "Juliet got us the leverage we needed."

The line was silent for several seconds. "Is she okay?"

"Yes." Saying the word sent relief washing through him in a cool, soothing surge. "That Coulter guy I emailed you about went after her. Detective Riordan is questioning him now. That should give us enough to dig deeper and hopefully connect Coulter to Mayfield. We'll get all the information together and have it to you ASAP."

"I'll alert the team in Missoula." Jack went quiet again. "If this case is what you think it is, you're going to receive a lot of attention for cracking it open."

"I don't care. I just want this asshole put away . . . or dead."

"I know *exactly* how you feel."

Grant's voice failed him for a second. He cleared his throat. "Look, Jack, I understand why you and Bear did what you did to catch Ripley. I still don't like the fact that you used Laine as bait, but I get why you did."

"Grant," Jack began, "I didn't want to—"

"I know. Bear told me." He rubbed his brow. "I just want you to know that even though at the time I wished things were different . . . ." He paused and inhaled deeply, ". . . thank you for making her happy. I was worried the Laine I knew was gone, but you brought her back."

"She would have found her way back eventually on her own."

"I don't know about that," Grant said with a chuckle, "but thanks for not rubbing it in that *I* couldn't do it."

"Grant, that's *not* what I meant."

"I know. I'm just giving you shit. Take it at face value, Special Agent Vaughn. It means I'm warming up to you."

Jack laughed softly. "Laine will be happy about that."

Grant smiled. "Yes, she will."

"I have to admit . . . I don't mind it either. Guys like us need all the friends we can get."

"Yes, we do."

"Go take care of your girl, Sheriff," Jack said. "Get me whatever information you have as soon as you can. I talked to Bear last night and he said we can have the task force up and running by tomorrow evening."

"Good. The sooner we nail this guy, the better."

"Agreed. I'll talk to you soon."

"Yes, you will."

Grant hung up the phone and slid it back into his pocket. He walked toward Juliet's room, leaned against the wall across from her door, and closed his eyes with a sigh.

"How is she?" a familiar, female voice asked from beside him.

Grant met Sheridan's gaze. "The doc's in with her now. If I had to lay money I'd bet they'll want a CT scan and to keep her overnight for observation."

Sheridan nodded slowly. "Understandable if that guy smacked her head against a brick wall." Her gaze narrowed on his face. "How are *you*?"

"I'm fine."

She laughed. "Of course you are." When he glared at her she rolled her eyes. "Hate to break it to you, Sheriff, but you're not very good at hiding how you feel. You're pissed off, and hurt, and you have every right to be. But, then again, so does Juliet." An elegant shrug lifted her shoulders. "She felt cornered, and she fought back. I would think you of all people would understand that reaction to a perceived threat."

He *did* understand it, but he wasn't willing to let go of his anger just yet. It helped keep the pain at bay. "She should have told me."

"Maybe." Sheridan planted her hands on her hips. "But, think about it. She lost her sister, her career, and her family. Mayfield comes after her, she escapes, and just when she's got some breathing room the mountain comes crashing down again."

Grant straightened and faced her, feeling the frown. "You been reading her file?"

"No." A faint smile curved her mouth. "Detective Riordan gave me some of the details." She leaned against the wall next to him and looked at him out of the corner of her eye. "She's already lost everything else, Grant. I think the thought of losing you too was more than she could handle."

"Juliet can handle a lot more than you think."

A short laugh escaped her. "You just don't get it, do you?"

He looked at her, brows drawing down, and she stared back, eyes wide and incredulous.

"Grant, you are one of the smartest men I know, but when it comes to women you make an inbred hillbilly look like a Mensa member." She pointed at Juliet's door. "That woman is head over heels in love with you, and if you can't see that, you might want to get your eyes checked before you pick up that rifle again."

Chapter Twenty Two

Grant watched Jessica Sheridan spin on her heel and walk away with brisk strides. It was the first time since he'd met her that she'd spoken so frankly to him. They were friendly, but their relationship was primarily a professional one and didn't often extend out of the office.

He mulled her words, and two separate, distinct emotions shot through him: cold fear and the warm lightness of hope. Was she right about Juliet's feelings? Part of him was ecstatic at the thought, while another part of him didn't even want to go there. He had acute memories of how it felt to love and lose, and he would rather stay a bachelor than ever go through that again.

His head snapped around when Dr. St. Pierre left the room. "Is she okay, Doc?"

St. Pierre clasped his hands in front of him, the clipboard flat against his stomach. "She has a bump on the back of her head, but I don't see any signs of concussion. Her vitals are good, she's healthy, but she seems a little . . . *dejected* . . . ." His gaze turned speculative. "I imagine that's more for personal reasons than it is injury-related."

Grant didn't bother to reply. St. Pierre sighed.

"I've ordered a CT scan and I'd like to keep her overnight for observation."

"That's up to you and her."

"She doesn't want to stay."

He wondered briefly where she wanted to go and then pushed the thought aside. "Like I said, that's up to you and her."

St. Pierre stared at him for a moment, his expression unreadable. "Fine. An x-ray technician will be by shortly to take her to CT."

"Fine." Grant gave the doctor a tight smile. "I'll wait with her."

St. Pierre nodded. "Good. If her CT is clear, she'll be discharged within the hour."

"Thanks, Doc."

"Anytime, Sheriff."

Juliet closed her eyes as the door opened and she felt Grant's considerable presence enter the tiny 8' x 10' room. She heard the soft scrape of metal on linoleum, as he sat down in one of the chairs against the wall, and the sigh that escaped him. Her heart lurched violently against the inside of her chest. She wanted to touch him, lose herself in his embrace and forget about everything she'd done. She wanted him not to be angry with her.

She'd felt the irritation coming off him in waves as he'd spoken, though his voice hadn't betrayed that emotion. A thick, black clot of remorse clogged her throat.

"Are you okay?" he asked softly.

No, she wasn't. "Physically, I'll be fine," she replied in a hushed voice. "I really didn't want to come here, but I figured I'd better not argue with you."

He was silent for a few moments. "And otherwise?"

"Otherwise . . . ." Her voice caught and she bit her lip as tears stung. She blinked them back. "Grant, I am so—"

"Forgiven, forgotten, don't apologize again," he interrupted. "I know you didn't intend for this to happen, so let's just move on, shall we?"

She wanted to curl up and disappear into the foam pad on the gurney. "But you're still angry with me."

"Not really." He let out another long, deep sigh. "It's the adrenaline," he explained in a calm, level voice. "Once it gets pumping, and believe me it *was*, it takes hours for it to wear off. Until it does, *everything* is heightened . . . senses, emotions, reactions." He paused and she chanced a glance at him. He sat with his elbows on his knees and his head in his hands. When he spoke next his voice was low, barely audible. "You scared the hell out of me, Juliet. I was in the middle of some crazy shit in Iraq and Afghanistan, but I don't think I've ever been as frightened as I was today." He looked up then and her chest tightened at the concern she saw in those usually smiling eyes. "I have lost . . . *too* many people I care about." He paused and took a shuddering breath. "I don't want to lose you, too."

Juliet sat up and tears welled. Grant left his chair, sat down on the edge of the gurney, and gathered her in his arms. She curled up against him and inhaled his scent, his warmth leaching into her.

"Will you promise me something?" he asked.

"Anything," she replied, "and this time I *really* mean it. Scout's honor."

He chuckled. "If you ever think of doing something that nuts again run it by me first. Give me the chance to help you . . . or talk you out of it."

She took a deep breath and pressed her face into the curve of his neck as she exhaled slowly. "I promise." Her arms wound around his waist, her hands moving slowly over his broad back. "And, if you can't talk me out of it . . . just kiss me and that should do the trick."

"Really? That's all it would take?"

"Mm hmm."

He kissed her forehead. "I shall remember that."

***

Grant walked into his office just shy of noon. Jackson glanced at him and Sheridan waved him over.

"I've finished Juliet's statement," she said. "It'll be on your desk in five. Simmons is still at the scene."

"Thanks, Jessica. Where's Detective Riordan?"

"Interrogation." Sheridan's brows drew together. "Where's Juliet?"

"I had Autumn take her to my place. She'll stay with Juliet until I get there."

"She living with you now?" Jackson muttered.

Grant ground his teeth together and spun to face the deputy. "*What* is your problem?"

Jackson colored slightly but met his gaze. "I already told you. Get her to move on, Sheriff. Don't fuck her."

White hot heat erupted in the pit of Grant's stomach and he hauled Jackson out of his chair. With one swift movement he had the shorter man pinned against the wall, much as Coulter had done to Juliet earlier. He pushed Jackson up the wall until they were eye to eye. The deputy's feet dangled several inches above the floor, his heels knocking against the wood paneling. Grant heard the scrape of chairs as the other deputies sprang out of their seats, but he was too focused on Jackson to care.

"You listen to me, you son of a bitch," he said from between clenched teeth. "I am *done* putting up with your bullshit. Like I said before, if you don't like how I do this job, run for sheriff next election. If you find it too difficult to do *your* job between now and then," he paused and jerked his head to his left, "there's the fucking door. Nobody is forcing you to work here and, to be quite honest, I'd *prefer* it if you walked."

Jackson stared at him with wide, bulging eyes, his face white.

"Grant, let him down." The voice was Roberta's, and he felt her hand on his arm. She didn't pull on him, she just touched him gently.

His chest was hot and heavy and the adrenaline was back in full surge. He glared at Jackson for another few seconds then shoved him aside. He fell against a desk and Sheridan was right there, helping the stunned deputy to his feet.

Grant fought to rein in his anger. "Mouth off like that again, deputy, and I don't care how much of a pain in the ass it is, I *will* fire you." His hands clenched and unclenched at his sides, his vision edged in red. "Are we clear?"

Jackson straightened his shirt and nodded once, his gaze disbelieving and fearful. "We're clear."

Grant turned and strode toward the interrogation room. As he left he heard Sheridan say, "What is the *matter* with you? You pick *today* to antagonize him?" She snorted. "I've always thought you were a half-wit, Jackson, but even *you* should know better than to poke an angry bear. You're lucky *I'm* not the sheriff. *I* would've put a fist through your teeth."

Grant almost smiled.

When he reached the hallway outside the interrogation room he paused and took several deep breaths. His neck was tight, his shoulders bunched, and he knew he had to pull himself in. If he didn't, what had started out as a very bad day could quickly go from bad to worse.

"Grant?" He glanced over his shoulder at Roberta who watched him with worried eyes. "Are you okay?"

He was really getting tired of people asking him that question. "No, Roberta, I'm really not." He hung his head. "I wake up and Juliet has taken off, Coulter attacks her, I almost have to kill the guy, and for some reason Jackson thinks *now* is the best time to get lippy." He looked at her out of the corner of his eye. "How much vacation time do I have stacked up?"

She chuckled. "A lot."

"Maybe I should take some of it."

"And maybe you should start the paperwork to get rid of Jackson." When he lifted his head and met her gaze she grinned. "You're going to have to do *something* about him, Grant. He undermines you at every turn, and that doesn't play well with the other deputies. I have a feeling if he sent out a call for assistance, that assistance would *not* be in a hurry to get there."

He squeezed his eyes shut and pinched the bridge of his nose. "I know, but I have more important things to worry about right now."

"I know you do." She walked up to him and patted his arm. "I'll start the paperwork so when you *do* decide to kick him out, it'll already be done."

"Thank you."

"You're welcome."

She turned to go and he grasped her arm lightly. The older woman paused, looked at him, and he released her.

"Before you do that, start the paperwork for a concealed carry permit for Juliet."

Roberta's silver brows drew together. "Doesn't she have to be a legal resident for six months first?"

"Technically." Grant wiggled his eyebrows at her. "But, since I'm the Sheriff, I can bend the rules on that one. If Mayfield comes after her, or sends another one of his underlings, I don't want there to be any question as to whether or not she had the legal right to carry the weapon that put them down."

Roberta's expression sobered and she nodded slowly. "Right. I'll do it now."

Again she tried to walk away, and again he grasped her arm. She frowned and looked at him in silent question. Grant sighed and took her hand, his chest tightening. "Thank you, for *everything* you do. I don't say it enough, and I want you to know . . . I couldn't do this job without you."

She squeezed his fingers and smiled. "Yes, you could, Sheriff. You'd just have to spend a lot more time behind a desk doing paperwork."

He grinned and the tension in his middle released. "And that's why I couldn't do it without you. You know how much I *love* sitting behind a desk."

"I do." She patted his cheek and walked away.

Oddly enough, he felt much calmer now, but Roberta had that effect on people. He rubbed his neck absently, took several steps down the hall, and glanced through the one-way glass. Coulter was handcuffed to the table facing the window. Daniel was just pushing his chair back, so Grant waited for him to enter the hall. When they made eye contact, a light entered the detective's eyes Grant hadn't seen there before, and hope sprung to life in his chest.

"Tell me you have something," he said.

"Well, our friend hasn't said much," Daniel replied, "but we have his cell phone and one outgoing text timed shortly after Juliet left the diner reading Evergreen Springs, Montana."

Grant rubbed his chin. "So, he let Mayfield know where she is."

Daniel nodded. "Probably, which means we can get ready for him. Let's go to your office and get Steve on the phone, see if he's managed to find anything else out."

When Grant and Daniel walked through the main workspace Jackson was nowhere to be seen. Grant paused and looked at Sheridan.

"He decided to go on patrol," she said, reading his mind.

"Good."

They stepped into his office and he closed the door behind them.

"Problems?" Daniel asked as he eased down onto one of the chairs facing Grant's desk.

"Always."

"I guess being the guy in charge isn't always fun."

Grant gave him a bored look and sat in his chair. "Nope."

Less than a minute later they were chatting live via webcam with Steve.

"Give it to me, brother," Daniel said, his chair pulled up next to Grant's.

The handsome Asian man grinned. "Well, we've executed warrants on Coulter's home and office, seized his computers and records, and I'm working on getting his financials now." He gave them a grim smile. "If there's a link to Mayfield there, I'll find it."

"Good," Daniel replied.

"How is Juliet?"

Daniel glanced at him. Grant propped his chin in his hand, his elbow on the armrest. "She's fine. A little shaken up, but he didn't have a chance to hurt her."

"Thank God."

"Any luck with that cell phone?" Daniel asked.

Steve shook his head. "Call went to a burner, so no, although we do know the receiver is in downtown Seattle, and Mayfield's office is in the call radius of the cell towers activated. But, I have something else." There was some typing and then a document appeared on Grant's computer screen. "The document you're looking at is the paperwork for a legal name change. James Coulter was born James Callaghan of Olympia, Washington. There were some sealed legal records pertaining to the name change that I just managed to get unsealed."

"And?" Daniel asked.

"James Callaghan has a record, my friend, a fairly lengthy one. He has convictions for robbery, check fraud, assault, extortion, et cetera, et cetera. Served time at several different county facilities around Washington, and one two-year stint at FDC SeaTac. He also spent a year in Brookstone Psychiatric Hospital."

When Daniel sucked in a breath Grant looked at him.

"The same hospital George Mayfield was committed to after he killed Wendy Braxton."

"Exactamundo, my friend." Steve lifted one narrow eyebrow. "The name change was submitted about six months after Coulter was released, which was about two months after Mayfield was released. Looks like our friend, Coulter, or Callaghan, chummed up to the right people." A dark chuckle escaped him. "But, wait, there's more."

Daniel straightened in his chair. "What did you find in Wonderland?"

"I did some checking on Mayfield senior, tracked his movements over the past decade, and boy, oh boy." His expression sobered. "I have a feeling we're going to be closing a *lot* of missing persons' cases, Danny."

"What do you mean?"

"Well," Steve paused and started typing, and moments later a map appeared on their screen, "Mayfield senior travels all over the US for business, all over the world, really. I have calls in to more than a dozen different law enforcement agencies, including Interpol, and I've already gotten some hits."

Grant rubbed his brow. The map was dotted with dozens of red markers, obviously indicators of where Gregory Mayfield had been. The sheer number made his insides clench and started a dull throb at the base of his skull. He had a sneaking suspicion he wasn't going to like what came next.

"I cross-referenced reports of missing slender, blue-eyed brunettes with Mayfield's known whereabouts . . . ." Steve paused and took a deep breath. "Within 48 hours of his arrival in each of the cities marked there is at least one woman reported missing who matches Juliet's description."

Daniel's eyes widened slightly. "Could it be a coincidence?"

"Statistically?" Steve shook his head. "Not a chance."

Grant closed his eyes and ran his hand over his face. Sometimes he really *hated* being right. "Did you get anywhere with Mrs. Mayfield?"

"I did." More typing. "I spoke with Carla Mayfield's sister and her best friend. Both women told me that after Carla married Mayfield, what contact they had with her was little, far between, and often monitored by dear hubby."

"Textbook abuser," Grant mused, his mood dropping like a stone. "He isolated his victim, cut her off from anyone who could possibly help her."

"Exactly," Steve agreed. "Both women also told me that shortly before she died Carla confided she was going to divorce Mayfield. She said she was frightened not only of her husband . . . but also her son."

Grant and Daniel looked at each other.

"Any chance we can get an exhumation order," Daniel asked, "so our coroner can take a harder look?"

"Not yet," Steve answered, "but maybe our mutual friend at the FBI can help with that. I spoke with Special Agent Vaughn yesterday. Looks like we're going to be task-forcing it, Danny boy."

"Looks like it."

"And it looks like this thing is bigger than *any* of us thought it would be." His eyes narrowed into mere slits. "Nice job, Sheriff. The FBI estimates there are close to 300 active serial killers in the US. Thanks to you . . . we might be pulling one, or two, of them out of active rotation."

"I just noticed the pattern. If we make any headway it'll be because of you guys and the FBI." Grant sighed heavily, the familiar weight of responsibility pressing hard on his shoulders. "Let's just get this asshole, or both assholes, before any more women wind up dead."

"I'm with you, Sheriff," Steve said.

"Me, too," Daniel agreed. "Let's catch these sons of bitches."

***

"So, girlfriend, did you take notes?"

Juliet almost choked on her mouthful of Coke. Autumn laughed and bumped Juliet's shoulder with hers.

"I told *you* I was going to want details. Did you *not* hear that?"

Juliet's cheeks flamed and she closed her eyes as she put the can of soda aside. The river rushed over her feet but the cool water did nothing to lessen the heat fanning across her skin. "*Autumn.*"

"Oh, come on, girl! There are a lot of women in this town who wonder if Grant is as delicious in bed as he looks in those jeans." When Juliet turned mortified eyes to the petite women Autumn shrugged one delicate shoulder. "I'm just sayin' . . . ."

"I don't know if I'm as delicious in bed as I look in these jeans," Grant said from behind them with a chuckle, "but I stopped counting after orgasm number four. You, Juliet?"

Juliet pulled her knees to her chest and dropped her forehead on her knees as Autumn shot to her feet. The shorter woman took several deep, gulping breaths.

"Grant Donovan, you could give a girl a heart attack sneaking up on her like that!"

A chuckle rumbled in his chest, and Juliet felt the vibration of it from where she sat. She snuck a glance at him. He stood at the other end of the dock, thumbs hooked in his gun belt, looking incredibly sexy, totally at ease, and thoroughly amused.

"I'd rather give a girl a heart attack using *other* means."

Juliet groaned and closed her eyes, her brow pressed to her kneecaps as embarrassment flooded her face with heat.

"I'll bet you *can*, too." Apparently Autumn had recovered. "Oh, if I wasn't married." There was a brief pause. "Four, huh? Did you really stop counting after that, or are you just being modest?"

He laughed. "What do *you* think?"

"I think you know the *exact* number, Sheriff," Autumn replied in a saucy tone. "Ooo, I always *knew* you were an overachiever."

Juliet thought briefly about jumping into the river. She'd be swept downstream and probably drown, but right now that was okay with her.

"There are . . . certain activities I like to put extra effort into," Grant said.

"Mm hmm. I wonder what *those* are."

The water looked more inviting with each passing second.

"Juliet can fill you in."

Juliet ground her teeth together. "Leave me *out* of this."

Autumn and Grant both laughed. Juliet kept her head on her knees.

"Thanks for staying with her, Autumn. I can take it from here."

"You are welcome, Grant." There was a brief silence. Juliet jumped when Autumn slipped an arm around her shoulders and squeezed, her lips close to Juliet's ear. "Congratulations, girlfriend. And don't worry about taking notes. You can give me a verbal account later, because I know you probably remember *every* minute."

Juliet's head snapped up. "*Autumn!*"

Autumn giggled and rose. Without another word, she hugged Grant and then sauntered toward the house. When she disappeared from view Grant walked toward Juliet. Juliet pressed her head back to her knees, her stomach swirling with a disconcerting mix of embarrassment and anxiety. She *wanted* to look at him, and yet she was afraid of what she might see in his eyes. Was he annoyed with her and Autumn's "girl talk"? Was he still angry with her for earlier? She wanted to wipe away everything that had happened and see his sexy grin again.

He eased down beside her, his gun belt creaking softly. Several moments of heavy silence passed and Juliet dared a quick look at him out of the corner of her eye. She blinked and lifted her head. She had expected him to still be smiling but he wasn't. His expression was vague, introspective, those bedroom eyes staring at the whitewater. Her heart sank.

"Are you still mad at me?" she asked in a whisper.

He shook his head slightly but his expression didn't change. "No, darlin'."

The endearment lifted her spirits somewhat, but not enough to completely banish the uncertainty swirling in her middle. "Then what's wrong?"

"Too much to talk about." He removed his boots and socks then rolled his pants up. Stretching his long legs out in front of him he dipped his feet in the water and leaned back on his hands. "Let's just say your case has gone from stalking to a full-blown Federal investigation, complete with Federal agents and a Federal task-force."

Her eyes widened. "What?"

"Yeah." His brows drew together. "Sometimes I forget that the world outside Evergreen can be a pretty screwed up place, and a lot of the people aren't much better."

"Can I help?"

He looked at her then and a faint smile flirted with his mouth. "You already have, Juliet. You opened the door a crack. Our job is to kick it down." He took her hand and pressed a kiss to her fingers. "I want you to stay out of it and let us do our jobs." He pulled her closer. "Can you do that for me?"

"Yeah," she replied. "I can do that." The relief she saw in his eyes made her throat tighten. She dropped her forehead on his shoulder. "Are . . . *we* . . . okay?"

He laid his cheek against her hair. "We're fine. We're better than fine."

She couldn't stop the relieved sigh. He released her hand and wound an arm around her shoulders, drawing her closer to his side. Juliet drank in his essence and his fresh, clean scent. All the doubt, all the self-reproach, all the apprehension, fell off her and she settled against him.

The sound of the river washed over her and she felt his tension drain. When he'd first pulled her close his muscles had been taut, his posture stiff, but as the minutes passed he eased up. She smiled when he let out a soft sigh and brushed his lips over her brow.

"How are you feeling?" he asked softly.

Her arms wound around his waist. "Right now? Perfect."

"You up to doing something with me?"

"Hmm." She kissed his neck. "What did you have in mind, Sheriff?"

"Nothing to tell Autumn about," he replied with a velvety chuckle. "At least . . . not right *now*."

She made a disappointed sound. "Aw, why not?" Her tongue darted out to taste his skin and she nibbled his earlobe. He sucked in a breath. He pulled back and she met his dark and smoky eyes. Butterflies hummed against her insides. "You tired of me already?"

He threaded his fingers into her hair and molded them to her head. "I don't think I'd ever get tired of you."

Her body sang when his mouth crashed down on hers, every nerve alive and tingling with anticipation. He demanded entrance to her mouth and she gave it freely. His tongue explored, caressed, savored her, and everything else ceased to exist. Pulsing warmth started a slow, steady spinning in her nether regions, her nipples pebbled and ached for his touch. Then, just as suddenly as the kiss had started, it ended. He stood in one fluid motion and took several steps away from her.

"Damn, girl, you could make a man forget his own name."

Her blood rushed in her ears, her breathing fast and shallow, and it took her brain a couple of seconds to catch up.

"I hate to be a bucket of cold water," he said in a hushed voice, "but this thing isn't over, Juliet, not by a long shot."

She closed her eyes and took several deep, slow breaths, willing away the ache that throbbed low in her belly. When she had herself somewhat under control she stood and faced him. He stared over her head, his fists on his hips.

"Before Coulter came after you he sent a text," he said. "It was just three words. Evergreen Springs, Montana."

That hit her below the belt and her diaphragm spasmed.

"It's not a matter of *if* Mayfield is going to show up here, it's *when*," he said. "When he does, I want you to be prepared."

He was still staring over her head, so she framed his face and forced him to look at her. "What do you want me to do?" Grant slid an arm around her waist and gently pulled her to him. He studied her, and the tenderness she saw in those chocolate-brown eyes made her tremble.

"Shooting is a perishable skill," he replied in a low voice. "If you have to face off with this guy, I want you to be confident in your ability to hit your target."

"Okay." She nodded and flattened her hands on his chest. "So, we'll go to the range."

The corners of his mouth moved up just a bit. "And then I'll take you to the fair, if you're up for it." He cupped her neck. "After all, I *did* promise you a funnel cake."

"You *promised* me *ten*," Juliet corrected him.

One brow quirked up. "Which you turned down because you were worried about growing out of your toe shoes."

She pressed a little closer and saw the flash in his eyes. "Yes, well . . . that was before I discovered the Grant Donovan horizontal workout program."

An amused grin twitched about his mouth and the flame in his gaze burned a little hotter. "I seem to recall we weren't *always* horizontal," he said in a low growl.

That ache between her legs returned, slamming into her with full force, and her heart somersaulted. She loved the husky edge in his voice. It sent shivers through her, curling fingers of need that reached into the deepest parts of her and fueled her arousal.

His smile widened. "You're giving me that look again, darlin'."

She moved her hands up and over his shoulders, her fingers winding into the soft curls at the nape of his neck. "That bucket of cold water isn't working."

Grant splayed his fingers over her back, lowered his head, and brushed her lips softly. "Yeah, well maybe we have time for a quickie before hitting the range."

Juliet's breath caught when his tongue caressed her bottom lip and then stole into her mouth. He kissed her deeply, thoroughly, until she couldn't breathe, didn't *want* to breathe. A low moan escaped her when he broke the kiss to trail fire over her jaw and down her neck.

"Quickie," she gasped out, "do you even know the meaning of that word?"

"Nope," he replied, his tongue leaving a hot, wet trail over her collarbone, "but I'm willing to learn."

She yelped in surprise when he tossed her over his shoulder and headed for the house.

"C'mon, darlin'," he said, his voice filled with hidden promise. "We have things to do, and the first thing on that list . . . is each other."

Chapter Twenty Three

Grant smiled as the carnie handed over the enormous stuffed penguin, a sour look on his pock-marked face. Juliet grinned, her eyes dancing, as Grant turned and passed the penguin to her.

"Nice job, Sheriff," she said. "I thought those target-shooting games were fixed."

He draped an arm around her shoulders as they started walking down the midway. Around them neon flashed, carnies called to passersby, the sights and sounds and scents of the fair filled the night with garish lights, delighted shrieks from ride-goers, and the mouth-watering aromas of fried everything.

"They are," he replied, "but if I can hit someone in the eye from 1000 yards, obliterating that little red star from three feet isn't even a challenge."

She giggled and wrapped her arms around the three-foot-tall animal, holding it to her chest as she snuggled against his side. There were quite a few familiar faces at the county fair, and he smiled and nodded at each friendly greeting tossed their way. They had ridden all the rides, except the Gravitron which Juliet absolutely *refused* to get on, and now that he'd procured the obligatory stuffed animal for his date they were headed for the food court. It would be their second, and final, funnel cake of the evening before they headed home.

He'd had misgivings about the fair after the incident with Coulter, but Juliet insisted she wanted to go. The doctor gave the okay, but that had done little to assuage his reservations. Looking at her now, those Caribbean blue eyes twinkling and a relaxed smile curving her mouth, he was glad that he'd acquiesced.

"You holding up all right?" he asked.

"I'm *wonderful*, Grant," she replied, beaming up at him.

His chest tightened, her expression melting his insides. Warmth radiated out from beneath his sternum, a familiar, terrifying emotion following close behind. He wasn't doctor material, like Laine, but he was a pretty smart guy and he fully recognized what was happening. He was falling in love with Juliet, and as much as he *didn't* want to feel what he felt, he *did* want to feel it. He *craved* it. She ducked her head and slipped an arm around his waist, hooking a finger through a belt loop.

"I haven't had this much fun in a long time," she said.

"Really?" He dropped a kiss on the top of her head. "What about before the range?"

Pink bathed her cheeks and she gave him a sinful look. "Different kind of fun, Grant."

He chuckled. "Yes, it is."

"Although, now that I think about it . . . ." She stopped walking and faced him. "You *are* my favorite ride so far."

His groin throbbed. "I am?"

She dropped the penguin and stood on tiptoe. "Absolutely."

He fanned his fingers over her back as her lips brushed his, and heat burst inside him like a solar flare. Her arms snaked around his neck and she pressed against him. Grant deepened the kiss and lifted her up, her feet dangling above the ground, her breasts crushed to his chest. That heat started to throb and surge as her tongue met his with a fearless need that made him burn.

"*Way* to go, Sheriff."

He had no idea who had spoken and he didn't care. The noise of the fair softened as he lost himself in her. That familiar citrus and floral scent reached his nostrils and he remembered with acute clarity the last time he'd encountered that particular perfume. Her kiss was rapidly escalating to something that could very well embarrass both of them. Even though he didn't want to release her he did. He gently put her back on her feet and ended the kiss, his heart thrumming forcefully against his ribs.

Before he could say a word his phone rang. He thought about letting it go to voicemail, but given what was going on he knew it was probably wiser not to. Juliet tucked in beneath his chin, her arms around his waist as he pulled his phone from his pocket. When he saw Jack's caller ID his heart thumped.

"Yeah, Jack. What's up?"

"Where is Miss Hall?"

"She's right here. Something wrong?"

"Probably." Jack huffed. "I put our suspects on a no-fly list so we'd be alerted if they tried to flee or head your way. Only problem . . . that doesn't cover private charters."

Something cold and hard dropped into his stomach. "Okay."

"I have a friend at the FAA. He just called me to say a private charter out of Seattle filed a flight plan to Missoula. The plane landed in Montana about an hour ago."

"Shit." Grant took a long, slow breath. "I'd like to think that's coincidence, but that would just be naïve."

Juliet's head came up.

"I called the charter service but all they would say is the customer paid in cash," Jack said. "They're not giving out any other information without a warrant and we don't have enough to get one right now. I'm working on it, but it may take a while."

"He's going to need a way to get from Missoula to Evergreen." Grant's brain was firing. "Check all the small plane and helicopter charter services in and around Missoula. There can't be that many." He could hear Jack scribbling on the other end of the line as he continued. "He's obviously anxious to get here, and there's nowhere around here to land anything other than a small plane or a helo."

"Y'know, Grant, you're pretty good at this."

He grunted. "This ain't rocket science, Jack." He pressed Juliet's head back into the curve of his neck and then laid his free arm around her shoulders. "Then again, he may *drive* in from Missoula; be much less conspicuous if he does and a lot easier to get in and out."

"I'll check all the rental agencies and limousine services."

"Check car lots, too," Grant said. "He has the means to buy a vehicle without blinking, and a cash transaction is probably the way he'll go, which should narrow the list some. And he'll probably want an SUV, a van, or a large sedan. He's going to need space if he thinks he's taking someone with him when he leaves here."

"That's still a lot of checking, my friend."

"Well, I'd help you but computers are *not* my forte. Steve would be a better choice."

Jack let out a grim chuckle. "I'll call him now. Hope he doesn't like to sleep."

A stab of guilt skewered him and Grant rubbed his brow. "Tell Laine I'm sorry for adding to your workload. I know that between your respective jobs y'all don't have a lot of time to spend together."

"She gets it, Grant." Jack paused. "And, I think she'd be the first to tell us to get this asshole off the streets."

"She would."

"Well, I'd better get to work. I'll keep you updated, Grant, and you keep Juliet and yourself safe."

"Thanks, Jack. I will."

"Oh," Jack said, "one more thing. I called in a favor and I should have Mayfield's juvenile record in the morning. A judge friend of mine is signing the subpoena now."

"Great. Keep me in the loop."

Jack chuckled. "Will do."

Grant hung up and slid the phone back into his pocket. Juliet's body was tense, but her head was still on his shoulder.

"Was that about what I think it was about?"

Her voice was low, almost pained, and he pulled back. He cupped her neck, used his thumbs to nudge her chin up, and pressed his brow to hers. "Mayfield is on his way, darlin', but don't you worry. I am *right* here, and I'm not going anywhere."

Her breathing quickened and she closed her eyes. "When will he be here?"

"No way to know for sure," he replied. He kissed the tip of her nose. "It doesn't matter, baby. I'm ready for him, and so are you."

"So, we're back to waiting for the puppet master to start pulling strings."

His brows drew down. "No, Juliet, we're not. We're going to live, *love*, and go forward with our lives while staying prepared and vigilant." Her lashes fluttered up and he looked into her eyes. "He is *not* going to win this one, I promise you that." His gaze wandered over her face and his gut clenched. "I *will not* let him hurt you."

A pensive smile curved her mouth. "I know, Grant." She curled her fingers around his forearms. "I know."

He kissed her slowly, and then pulled back. "C'mon darlin'. Let's get another funnel cake and head home."

"Only one?"

He bent over, grabbed the penguin, and tucked it under one arm as the other went around her shoulders. "I'll buy you as many as you want, but if I buy 'em, you have to eat 'em."

She chuckled and settled against his side. "So . . . one *each* then."

"That'll work." He grinned down at her. "Wasn't planning to share with you anyway."

***

Juliet woke to the smell of bacon and rolled over, stretching and yawning. Grant's side of the bed was empty, which would account for the heady aroma, and she burrowed beneath the covers. She smiled as she remembered their lovemaking the previous evening. As always, Grant had performed flawlessly, and heat quickly blossomed in her middle, rolling outward in a languid wave.

So, how does it feel to be in love?

"It feels wonderful," she replied in a whisper.

You're not arguing with me? I guess that means you've finally admitted it to yourself.

"It does," Juliet said. She pulled a pillow to her chest. "What's the point in fighting it?"

There isn't a point. You're so far gone. And, as usual, you're the last one to know.

"What does *that* mean?"

It means everyone else already knows you're head over heels for the handsome sheriff, including the man himself.

Juliet sat up in bed and rested her chin on her knees. "How? I haven't said anything, especially not to *him.*"

Don't worry, sis. He's got it as bad as you do, maybe worse. And, before you ask, no, he hasn't said anything either.

"So how do *you* know?"

Let's just say things are a lot easier to see from here.

Cassie went quiet after that, and Juliet had no desire to pursue the conversation further. The idea Grant knew how much she cared for him started a chilling wave of butterflies that brushed against the inside of her chest cavity like hard, bouncing snowflakes.

"Morning, beautiful."

Juliet lifted her head and her heart leapt. He stood in the doorway, shirtless, pajama bottoms hanging low on his hips, those bedroom eyes looking at her with blatant male appreciation. What a magnificent animal he was. She couldn't stop the smile or the twinge of desire that settled in low in her belly.

"Damn, you look good in the a.m.," he said as he walked forward. He knelt on the edge of the bed and then crawled toward her, pushing her until she was flat on her back and he was on all fours over her. "Almost makes me want to have *you* for breakfast."

Juliet's throat tightened and that twinge sharpened. She sucked in a breath when he tugged the covers down to expose her breasts to his hungry gaze. He devoured her with his eyes then lowered his head and swirled his tongue around one dusky aureole. He suckled, nibbled, and teased her until she couldn't hold back the moan of pleasure.

"Yep, much rather dine on you," he said, his breath hot on her skin.

"But what—"

His mouth covered her other breast, his fingers plucking at the first. Juliet pressed her head back into the pillow and groaned as fire shot through her.

"About . . . breakfast?" she finally managed to gasp out.

"It'll keep," he replied in a low, silky voice that only stoked her desire. "I hadn't started the eggs yet, the pancake batter won't go bad, and the bacon is in the oven on low, so it'll still be a while before it's done." He slid his hand over her belly and between her legs, and when he found that engorged cluster of nerve endings she jumped. "We have time."

"Oh, God . . . ."

By the time he finished with her she was nothing but a mass of quivering flesh with only slightly more spine than Jell-o. She was wrapped around him, breathing ragged, limbs boneless and heavy.

"Now *that* is the breakfast of champions," he said as he nibbled her earlobe, his breathing just as ragged as hers. "Sorry, Folgers, but you are *not* the best part of waking up." He captured her mouth in a slow, deep kiss that had her gasping for air, but when he pulled away she decided that breathing wasn't all that important, as long as he kept kissing her.

"C'mon, darlin'. It's time to get moving."

Once her muscles regained some strength they showered, scrubbing each other's back and splashing playfully. Grant was done first and left her to finish up. She poured conditioner into her palm and started to work it through the long strands when he tapped on the glass enclosure. Juliet turned to look at him.

"I'll be in the kitchen," he said. "C'mon out when you're done." He pressed his lips to the glass, made a loud smacking noise, and then gave her a boyish grin before turning and leaving the bathroom. She chuckled and finished bathing.

He was just flipping the pancakes when she strolled out into the main room dressed in jeans and a t-shirt. She walked over to the breakfast bar and hopped onto a barstool. Resting her elbows on the granite surface, she watched as he moved around the kitchen with skillful ease, as if he was a short order cook instead of a small-town sheriff. He checked the pan filled with a pile of fluffy scrambled eggs, turned off the burner, and then opened the oven.

"Perfect," he said. He grabbed a pair of oven mitts and pulled out a sheet cake pan. There was a cookie rack settled neatly in that pan, crispy bacon sizzling on top.

"Wow," Juliet said. "That's actually a really smart way to cook bacon."

He put the pan aside, grabbed a spatula, and flipped several pancakes onto a plate. "Yep. It's a lot less messy, and all the bacon is cooked evenly, no flipping required." He passed the pancakes to her and grinned. "Saw it on the Food Network."

She smiled and reached for the bottle of maple syrup. "You watch the Food Network?"

"How do you think I learned to cook?" he asked as he turned off the oven. "I don't have time to sit down and read recipes." He poured more pancake batter. "Paula Deen is my culinary hero, and that Rachael Ray has some pretty great meal ideas, too."

She poured syrup over her pancakes and picked up her fork as Grant scooped a healthy serving of eggs onto the plate. "Do you eat like this all the time?" She gave him a once over. "I don't know how you keep that body if you do."

He gave her a wicked look. "I told you, I go running every morning . . . *almost* every morning." He started peeling bacon off the cookie rack. "But since I haven't been able to do that recently, I guess my horizontal workout program will have to suffice."

Heat bloomed in her cheeks and she turned her attention to her food. She'd had more sex in the past two days than she'd had in the previous two years, and the memory of what she'd experienced with Grant made her ache for more. She'd never considered herself a very sexual person, but damned if he wasn't turning her into one. All she could seem to think about when he got within arms' reach was kissing him, touching him, having him inside her.

"You're blushing, darlin'."

Juliet jumped, his words a breathy caress against her ear. Somehow he had managed to leave the kitchen without her noticing and stood at her back. Heat started to build in her belly as he kissed the curve of her neck. He chuckled softly and slid a bowl of fresh fruit next to her plate, his fingers grazing her arm as he pulled back. Tingles radiated outward from beneath his touch and she closed her eyes.

"Is someone's mind not on food?" he asked in that sexy, husky voice.

"Oooh . . . what have you done to me?" she moaned. "I'm not this person, Grant."

His lips feathered over her ear, his tongue trailing behind. "Who are you?"

"I'm just . . . a woman." Juliet gulped. "I'm not . . . some . . . sex kitten."

"Bullshit."

She melted as he nibbled her earlobe, the food forgotten. "I'm too level-headed for this sort of thing."

He slipped an arm around her waist and she leaned against him. His tongue flicked against her throat and her body betrayed her, her head turning to give him better access.

"What sort of thing?" he whispered.

Juliet ground her teeth together and pulled away from him. Her knees wobbled as she slid off the barstool and she grasped the counter for support. Steeling herself, she faced him. "*This* . . . thing." She gestured between the two of them.

One corner of his mouth curled upwards, his eyes glinting with laughter. He sat down on a barstool. "And what sort of thing is *this*?"

His amusement sparked her temper, something else out of character for her. She'd always considered herself to be quite even-keeled, but with Grant her emotions see-sawed violently from one end of the spectrum to the other.

She planted her fists on her hips. "The sort of thing where I can't form a coherent thought when you give me that look." He lifted one brow and that sexy smile blossomed. She pointed a finger at him. "Yep, *that* look, *right* there." Her heartbeat increased until she could feel it pattering against her sternum. "A man isn't supposed to make me feel like this."

His expression didn't change. "Feel like what?"

"Like I have no control over my own body," she shot back. "You look at me like that and I get all warm and . . . breathless. You . . . *touch* me, and I *dissolve* . . . like butter in a hot frying pan." She took a shaky breath, walked over to the sliding glass door, and rested her brow against the cool glass. "When we got home from the fair we didn't even make it to the bedroom, Grant. We had *sex* in the *foyer* against the *wall*."

"That's because the front seat of the Yukon isn't made for sex and the *back* seat . . . ." His voice trailed off and he chuckled. "Well, that seems a little too much like high school."

Juliet squeezed her eyes shut. "The *point* is . . . I wouldn't have cared."

She heard his footsteps as he walked up behind her. Nevertheless, she still jumped when his hands dropped gently on her shoulders. His thumbs worked the taut muscles in her neck and he kissed the back of her head.

"Juliet," he began in that velvety voice that made her insides clench, "right here, with me, is the one place where it is completely safe for you to lose control." He rested his forehead against her hair. "Go ahead and fall, darlin'. I'll catch you."

Her throat tightened to the point she could barely breathe. He released her and she turned toward him. A wistful smile curved his mouth and he dragged a finger over her cheek.

"I know exactly what you're going through." He took her hand and pressed it to his chest. "Do you feel that?" His heart pounded beneath her palm. "That's what *you* do to *me*, darlin', and although it scares the heck out of me . . . I'm not going to run away from it because *not* being with you . . . ?" He tucked her hair behind one ear, his fingers trailing lightly down her throat. "That scares me even more." His gaze focused on her mouth. "I'm falling for you, Juliet, something I didn't think would ever happen to me again."

Juliet's heart leapt into her esophagus, a throbbing clog that cut off her breath with each beat. *Oh, my God, is this really happening?* She'd thought she'd been "in love" before, but if the seismic activity in her chest was any indication, she'd been wrong.

See, Jules? I told you so.

"Shut up, Cassie," she whispered.

She stood on tiptoe and pressed her lips to his. Their tongues met in a slow, sensual dance and his embrace tightened slightly. When she started to feel the familiar lightheadedness Juliet ended the kiss and pressed her face into the crook of his neck.

"You may be falling, Grant," she whispered, "but I've already landed."

She thought briefly about forgoing breakfast and taking him straight back to bed, but then her stomach rumbled loudly.

Grant chuckled. "Your stomach is saying it's not me you're hungry for."

"My stomach is an idiot."

He laughed and kissed her temple. "C'mon, darlin'. Let's get you some food, and then we'll decide what to do with the rest of our Saturday."

She made a disappointed sound but allowed him to lead her back to the breakfast bar. After pouring more syrup on her pancakes she dug in. The first fluffy bite of pancake hit her tongue and she moaned.

"Oh, my goodness," she said. "These are amazing. Is that . . . *lemon* I taste?"

Grant's fork paused in midair. "Yep. It's the way my mom made them, simple Bisquik recipe with fresh lemon juice, a little sugar, and a couple teaspoons of baking soda." He gave her a wink. "Gives them a little tang and sweetness."

Juliet lifted one brow. "Kind of like you."

"Are you comparing me to pancakes?"

"No. Pancakes are flat and round and fluffy." She gave him a sidelong glance and quirked her lips when she saw the mischievous glint in his eyes. "You . . . ." She paused and took a deep breath, ". . . are *none* of those things." He chuckled and she took another bite, savored the velvety hotcakes, and sighed. "Lemon pancakes with maple syrup. Who knew?"

They finished the rest of their meal in silence, and Juliet groaned when she was filled to the gills. She put her fork down, wiped her mouth, and planted her elbows on the counter.

"So, any idea what you want to do today?" Grant asked as he sipped a glass of milk.

Juliet pursed her lips and gave him a lusty look. To her surprise, a faint hint of color rose in his cheeks, and both her brows shot skyward.

"Are you . . . *blushing?*"

"No," he replied with a shake of his head. "It's just . . . when you look at me like that my body temperature tends to rise."

"Along with something else, I hope."

A smile flirted with his mouth and when he turned those bedroom eyes on her, her insides liquefied.

"Want to sit on my lap and find out if something else is rising?"

She gulped.

His smile widened. "Maybe we should put that on the back burner, for now, and make a trip into town instead."

"Why?" She hated the breathlessness in her voice but there was nothing she could do to stop it. The corners of his eyes crinkled as his smile turned into a grin.

"Because I'm almost out of milk, eggs, beer . . . and condoms."

"Then let's go. And maybe this time you should buy the max-pack." The words fell out before she even thought them. She stood, spun on her heel, and made it across the living room before her brain decided to kick into gear.

Damn it.

She stopped in her tracks and slowly turned back to face him. "You can't buy condoms."

He gave her an indulgent look, the sort of look usually bestowed on petulant children. "Actually, I'm pretty sure I *can*. After all, I bought the first box."

A flicker of annoyance warmed her chest. She planted her hands on her hips. "And how long after you spring for a box of Trojans do you think it'll be before it hits the front page of the Evergreen Gazette?" She crossed her arms over her chest. "Hell, it would probably make the local *news*." His soft laughter pushed her straight from irritation to anger.

"Darlin'," he began, his eyes glinting merrily, "you've spent the last two nights here, and everyone knows it. Do you really think they haven't figured out we're sexually involved?"

She narrowed her eyes on him and took a deep breath. "It's one thing for them to *suspect*. It's a completely different thing for us to flat-out *announce* it."

His expression turned thoughtful. "Is there a particular reason you want to keep this under wraps?" He chuckled again. "No pun intended."

Heat rose in her cheeks and fanned over her neck and chest as her insides tightened. "Oh, I don't know, Grant, maybe it's because I don't want the entire town thinking I'm some slutty city girl."

A laugh escaped him. "They won't think that."

Juliet pursed her lips. "I've known you since *Tuesday*," she pointed out. "I think we both know in *Mayberry* . . . that's slutty." She ran a hand over her brow then planted her fists on her hips. "I usually play a *little* harder to get. I've only dated about a dozen different men in my *entire* life and I've only gotten intimate with four of those dozen . . . *not* including you. I don't *have* sex with some guy I've just met." She glanced at him. He was watching her with an amused smile, arms over his chest. Juliet sighed and turned her back on him. "I know, that's what they always say. I wouldn't believe me either."

"I didn't say I didn't believe you."

"You didn't have to."

"*I* don't *care*, and I'm just wondering why it's so important to *you*." He walked up behind her and slipped his arms around her waist. "We're both adults, Juliet. The people who matter won't mind and the people who mind . . . don't matter."

Juliet closed her eyes and leaned her head back against his well-muscled shoulder. "I've just never done this before . . . fall for a guy I haven't even known a week." She turned her head and pressed her face into his neck. "My last boyfriend . . . we knew each other for a *year* before we started dating. Once we started dating it was *still* more than a month before we slept together, and *that* was only because he . . . because he told me . . . ." Her mind flew back over the few serious relationships she'd had, and what had precipitated the first intimate encounter with each of those men. She groaned. "Oh, my, gosh, I'm a walking cliché, a living, breathing Lifetime Movie." Heat surged into her cheeks.

"What did he tell you, Juliet?"

His question broke into her thoughts and it took her a moment to find her voice. "He told me he loved me, which is *exactly* how the three before *him* finally got in my pants."

He chuckled and brushed a kiss against her temple. "Is *that* all it takes?"

"*You* didn't need to use that line," she observed with a growl.

Grant laughed softly and turned her to face him. One hand fanned over her lower back and pressed her closer while the other cupped her chin and tilted her face up. "Actions speak louder than words, darlin'." A pensive smile rounded that sinful mouth. "I love you."

Her heart launched into a full gallop and she sucked in a breath as she pushed away from him. She stared at him, jaw hanging slack, but all she saw in those beautiful brown eyes was amusement, warmth . . . and love.

Her brows drew down. "That is *not* funny," she said in a fierce whisper.

"Am I laughing?"

She pulled in another deep breath and held it until her lungs burned. Chills and heat rippled through her as fear and joy battled in her chest, neither seeming to best the other. Her heart drummed violently against her sternum and she blinked at him.

As if sensing her uncertainty he stepped closer, cupped her head, and kissed her. Her knees wobbled and he wound an arm around her waist to steady her while the fingers of his other hand threaded through her hair. His mouth demanded nothing, playing over hers lightly, teasing, coaxing, reassuring. He outlined her lips with his tongue and she moaned softly.

"I love you, Juliet," he whispered against her mouth.

Her brain was short-circuiting but the words somehow found a way out. "I love you, too," she breathed.

She felt his smile as his mouth covered hers again, not so lightly this time. He was demanding, insatiable, and her bones turned to rubber. As if they had a life of their own her arms crept around his neck and her body bowed closer to his. He growled in his throat and the sound sent shivers over her skin. Need pulsed through her and she broke the kiss.

"Hold that thought," she said in a breathless rush. He looked at her in surprise. Laughter bubbled up in her and she grabbed his head, kissed him hard and fast, and then spun away. She ran to the bedroom, scooped up her purse, and then jerked open the drawer on the nightstand. The nearly empty box of condoms was there. She picked it up, looked inside, and put it back. An expectant flush warmed her cheeks as she walked back to Grant. He was texting, so she waited until he finished before saying:

"Come on, Sheriff, we have some shopping to do."

One corner of his mouth lifted. "We do?"

"Yep." She stepped close and looped her arms around his waist. "You're almost out of milk, eggs, and beer and you have two condoms left." Giving him a wicked grin she pressed closer. "I seriously doubt that will last us the weekend, much less until Shelby's wedding."

Her statement got the desired reaction when his eyes widened and he blinked at her. "You're . . . you're staying for Shelby's wedding?"

"I am." She stood on tiptoe and kissed him. "Anything after that . . . we'll just have to negotiate."

Chapter Twenty Four

Grant glanced at Juliet, but her eyes were closed, her hair grasped tightly in one hand as air through the open window of the Yukon rushed past, wind pulling several long, dark strands to whip in its wake.

"Are we going to the range today?" she asked, turning her face toward the sun.

"Yep. We'll go every day that we can until you're safe. Why?"

She looked at him, her expression thoughtful. "Could you do something for me?"

The reply was automatic and completely true. "Anything."

"Could you teach me some self-defense moves?" she asked. "If another man puts their hands on me like Coulter did yesterday, I want them to regret it even if I don't have a gun."

Grant smiled and reached for her hand. He laced his fingers through hers and pressed a kiss to her knuckles. "You bet. There are some training mats in the classroom at the range." He wiggled his eyebrows at her. "And after I'm done teaching you a few moves, we could even use those mats for something else."

Color rose in her cheeks and she gaped at him. "Grant!"

"What?" He gave her an innocent look. "We'll have more condoms by then."

Before she could reply his phone rang, or more appropriately, the song on the radio was interrupted by his Bluetooth equipped stereo. He hit the button and waited a second. "Hello?"

"Grant, it's Daniel. Could you and Juliet come by the office?"

Juliet's head snapped around and he glanced at her.

"Yeah, why?"

"I'll tell you when you get here." He paused. "There aren't any new developments and it's nothing bad, so don't worry."

"Okay, we'll be there in about 20."

"See you then."

Grant pushed the button to disconnect the call.

"What do you think he wants?" Juliet asked.

"You heard him. He wants us to come by the office."

A wariness entered her turquoise eyes. "I wonder why."

Grant squeezed her fingers. "He said it's nothing to worry about." He gave her a reassuring smile. "Guess we'll find out when we get there."

Daniel was leaning against Roberta's desk when he and Juliet walked into the Sheriff's Office. Sheridan was at her computer, Sheila, the weekend dispatcher, was in Roberta's chair, and Jackson, thankfully, was nowhere to be seen.

"He's on patrol," Sheridan said when she glanced his way and saw his face. She gave him a jaunty grin and returned to whatever she was working on.

Grant scowled. "Maybe I should threaten to fire his ass more often," he said with a growl. He gave Juliet a grim smile and faced the detective. "All right, we're here. What do you need?" Daniel held a small box in his hands, the kind usually used for jewelry, and something in Grant's gut twisted.

"Can we go into your office?" Daniel asked in a low voice.

He and Grant battled visually for a moment and then Grant gave a terse nod. He had a feeling he wasn't going to like this. When Daniel and Juliet were both in his office he met Sheila's curious gaze and shut the door firmly. He took deep, even breaths as he walked around the desk and eased down into his chair. Leaning back, he tried to look unconcerned.

"What is it, Daniel?" Juliet finally asked.

Instead of replying Daniel opened the box. He pulled a long, gold chain from inside, and when the distinctive pointe shoe pendant was revealed Grant heard Juliet suck in a breath. He glanced at her. Her cheeks had gone pale and she clutched her own pendant in one hand, her eyes wide.

"Is that . . . ?" She blinked and stared at the glittering toe shoes.

"No," was Daniel's immediate reply.

Grant's mind flew back through the case file and he remembered the only thing missing from the scene of Cassie's murder was a necklace belonging to Cassie, a necklace that matched Juliet's own. The serial killer's trophy.

"She gave me mine when I graduated Juilliard," Juliet whispered, "and I gave her hers when she joined the company. They're exactly alike." She turned disbelieving eyes to Daniel. "Where did you get that?"

Daniel sighed heavily and held the necklace toward her. "We made it." Juliet reached out shaking fingers and he dropped it onto her palm. "Cassie let us borrow hers a few weeks before she was killed. My techs and a jeweler worked together to fashion an exact replica, but it took a little longer than we thought." He glanced at Grant and then looked at her. "The jeweler had trouble configuring the pointe shoes around the GPS tracking chip we wanted installed."

Her eyes widened and she stared at him.

"We didn't finish it until after Cassie died," Daniel continued in a low, sorrowful voice, "and you took off before I could give it to you." He rubbed his brow. "If I'd given it to you as soon as we got it from the jeweler maybe you wouldn't have been out here on your own all these months."

"Yeah," Grant began dryly, "which means Mayfield would've found her long before now. Or have you forgotten his subordinate followed you *here?*"

Daniel jumped to his feet and Grant also stood, but more slowly, his motions tightly controlled.

"Look, I *know* I've done a shitty job of protecting her," Daniel bit out, teeth clenched, bright spots of color in his cheeks, "but I did *everything* I could. And I'm going to do everything I can *now* to make sure Juliet doesn't end up like Cassie."

"Take a number," Grant growled.

"Please stop," Juliet whispered.

Both men went quiet and turned to her. Tears shimmered in her eyes but her expression was resolute as she continued to stare at the pendant.

"We're all on the same side here," she said in a low voice. She blinked, the tears fell, and she wiped them away with her empty hand as her other hand closed around the necklace.

Grant's stomach twisted and he looked at Daniel who was looking anywhere but at her. Grant saw her move and turned toward her as she took off her pendant and placed it on the edge of his desk. Then she put the necklace with the tracking chip on and folded her hands in her lap.

"There." She met both of their eyes and smiled, but Grant sensed it was forced. "Now, if he manages to take me you can find us."

Daniel turned anguished eyes to her. "Juliet—"

"It's okay, Daniel," she said. She shrugged. "I'm what he wants, I'm the bait. That's just how it is." She closed her eyes briefly and then straightened her spine. "Is there anything else?"

Bait. Grant's gut heaved. *Now you have an idea what Jack went through.*

"Have you told her your theory?" Daniel asked.

It took Grant a second to realize the detective was speaking to him. He met Daniel's eyes and shook his head.

"You should." Daniel's expression sobered. "She deserves to know what she may very well be up against."

Grant eased back into his chair as she turned to him.

"Grant?"

He rubbed his eyes and pulled in a long, slow breath. "I think George Mayfield is a serial killer," he said after a brief silence, "and I think Daddy is teaching him the ropes."

Juliet looked at Daniel. "And what do *you* think of this theory?"

Daniel glanced at him and then turned to her. He sat in the chair next to her and took her hands. "I think, *we* think, he's right. We've started digging and the evidence is leaning that way." He sighed. "I talked to Steve earlier and he said he'd started looking into Mayfield senior's background. Mayfield senior's mother died when he was 18." He looked at Grant. "She drowned . . . in the bathtub."

Something icy, sinister, and jagged raked against the inside of Grant's chest. "Just like his wife, George's mother."

"Yeah." Daniel nodded and rose, walking to the window overlooking the square. "All of the evidence is circumstantial, but it's starting to pile high, *really* high. Steve thinks we have enough to get search warrants *and* exhumation orders for *both* Mayfield wives." He faced them and leaned against the heavy glass. "George may be a third generation killer. Hell, if we had better records, who knows how far back this particular family trait goes. I've heard rumors there was a Mayfield with the Donner Party who survived and then headed into the Oregon territory. Maybe that's where it started."

Grant laced his fingers over his abdomen and looked at Juliet. She was pale, her fingers clasped around the pendant, a muscle twitching in her cheek. He wanted to comfort her, take her in his arms and protect her from all this, but he couldn't. And, he wouldn't do that in front of

Daniel. He knew the detective's pain ran deep, and even if he and the Seattle cop weren't the best of friends, he had no desire to add to the man's sorrow.

"So, you think . . . ." Her voice trailed off and she took a deep breath. "You think if George comes after me, he won't come alone."

Grant didn't bother to lie. "That's *exactly* what I think."

"And Cassie was . . . what?" She released the pendant and shoved her hands into her hair. "She was a . . . trial run, an *experiment*?"

Grant chose his words carefully. "I think she was a . . . a final exam, to see if he could pull it off without leaving any evidence behind, to see if he could handle the fact it wasn't *you*."

She stared at him. "You think George's father taught him this." When Grant nodded she rose and leaned on the edge of his desk. "How many?" He didn't reply right away and he saw the flash of anger in her eyes. "How many women, Grant? How many before me?"

Grant glanced at Daniel and rubbed his eyes again. "I don't know for sure, Juliet, but between the two of them . . . ? Possibly dozens."

Juliet blinked at him and sank back onto her chair. She took several deep breaths. "Am I naïve to hope you two have a chance of stopping these maniacs without me having to die first?"

Grant left his chair, came around the desk, and crouched in front of her. "That will *not* happen."

She looked shell-shocked, pale, her eyes wide and disbelieving. "How can you know that? Has anyone *else* ever escaped? If you're right and George and his father have gotten away with this . . . *dozens* of times . . . how can you *possibly* know that?"

"Because we know where he's headed," Daniel said softly, "and we'll be there to catch him." He pushed away from the window. "Have a little faith, Juliet. I promise I won't let you down again."

Grant took her hands and laced his fingers through hers. Her skin was cold and he rubbed gently. "I'm sticking close to you until we catch him. So, I hope you weren't lying this morning, because if you were you'll be sick of my face by the time this is over."

"It could be over *tomorrow*," she pointed out.

"And I'm pretty much all you're going to see . . . until it *is* over."

Juliet took a deep breath, held it for a second, and then exhaled slowly. "Well then, I guess we'd better get to the range. We want to make sure I'm prepared if I run into George or his daddy, right?"

"Juliet," Daniel began, stuffing his hands in his pockets.

She rose fluidly and faced him, a faint smile on her mouth. "Grant said he'd teach me some self-defense moves, so that's what I'm going to do . . . learn to defend myself." Grant saw the convulsive swallow, and she fisted her hands at her sides. "George Mayfield has already taken too much from me. I'm not letting him take *anything* else . . . not without a fight."

Pride warmed Grant's chest and he straightened. Juliet met his eyes as she picked up her pendant from the edge of his desk and held it out to him.

"Keep this for me," she said softly. "You can give it back when this is all over."

Grant only nodded. He opened his hand and Juliet dropped the pendant into his upturned palm. He glanced at Daniel, but the man was stone-faced. The detective caught his gaze and tossed him the empty jewelry box. "Thanks," Grant said as he dropped the necklace inside.

"Don't mention it," Daniel replied in a level voice. "Keep it safe for her."

He slipped the box into a pocket of his jacket. "I will."

"Mind if I go with you to the range?" Daniel asked. His voice sounded flat, devoid of life, and Grant saw Juliet's concerned expression. When she faced him the detective smiled, but it seemed forced. "You're going to need someone other than your instructor to practice on. I can be your training dummy."

Juliet took a step toward him. "You don't have to—"

"I know," Daniel interrupted her. "But I can't do much more from here right now, and I could use the fresh air." He gave Grant a look. "I'm sure you'd rather have her kicking *my* ass than yours."

Grant didn't really care one way or the other, but he gave the detective a shrug. "I don't mind, as long as it's okay with her." They both looked at her. She simply nodded. Grant nodded in return and looked at Daniel. "Fine, we'll meet you at the range in an hour. Sheila can give you directions. It's just past the city limits and you shouldn't have any trouble finding it."

"Alright." Daniel stole a glance at Juliet and then dropped his chin. "I'll see you there."

Grant watched the detective as he turned and left the office without another word. What had started out as a beautiful day was veering sharply off course. Juliet sank back into a chair and sighed heavily.

"You alright?" he asked.

Instead of replying she rose and pressed herself against him. His arms immediately wrapped around her and he laid his cheek against her hair.

"Now I'm alright," she whispered.

They stood like this, quiet and unmoving, the clock ticking loudly on the wall and muted conversation drifting in from the main office. He closed his eyes. Sheridan said something and Sheila burst into laughter, but none of it really registered. The scent of her hair drifted up to him, her heart beating a steady rhythm against his chest.

"I suppose we should go," she said softly.

Grant glanced at the clock. Three minutes had passed. He pulled back and framed her face with his hands. "Probably. Groceries aren't going to buy themselves, and if we don't get moving we'll be late meeting Daniel."

Dark brows rose. "If we go *shopping* we're going to be late anyway."

He shook his head and pursed his lips. "Nope. Texted in my order while you were checking to see how many condoms I had left." When he saw her surprised look he smiled. "Wes Greenaway owns the Evergreen Mercantile. I often call in orders and he bags everything up for me so all I have to do is pay and pick it up."

She blinked at him. "And when he saw condoms on your list?"

His smile deepened. "He didn't. Autumn is getting those for me."

Pink surged into her cheeks. "What?" she squeaked.

He looked into those aquamarine eyes and toyed with a lock of her hair. "You were right about one thing. If I buy the crate of condoms it will be the top story on the six o'clock broadcast because Paulette's husband owns the pharmacy." He shrugged. "Condoms are Autumn and her husband's preferred method of birth control, so no one will blink if *she* buys some."

Her color deepened and she squeezed her eyes shut. "I would ask how you know that but I think I'd better not."

Grant chuckled. "One day after the lunch crowd cleared out Shelby asked Autumn why she and Landon didn't have any kids yet. Autumn popped off with 'Because Trojans are 97% effective, and Landon and I don't *have* sex on those other days.'" His fingers sifted through her hair, enjoying the cool silkiness against his skin. "You should've seen her expression when she realized I'd overheard. First time I've ever seen her flustered."

A soft knock on the door separated them and Grant walked over to open it. Sheila stood there, a white take-out bag in her hand.

Sheila Gerard was a single woman, 35, with dark, graying hair and intelligent hazel eyes that were a mix of grey and blue. She stood just shy of six feet tall but probably barely hit 150, with a straight, boyish figure. Grant didn't know her very well, she'd only been in town a few years, but she was good at her job and seemed to get on well with everybody, even Jackson. What he *did* know was that she worked part-time for him as a weekend dispatcher, part-time for Miss Nicole as a night auditor, and part-time for Paulette as a bookkeeper.

"Tom Cullen just dropped this off," Sheila said, handing the bag to him, "two pieces of peach pie." A smile warmed her otherwise austere features. "And he brought two more for Sheridan and me, said Autumn sent them over at your request. Thanks for thinking of us."

Grant immediately understood Autumn's ruse and hoped Tom, or Sheila, hadn't mixed up the bags. He glanced inside the white paper container and gulped when he saw the Styrofoam boxes. He took one out, peeked inside, and handed it to Juliet. Two pieces of peach pie had been stuffed into that single container. A glance in the second box almost made him smile. No peach pie in that one.

"Thanks, Sheila. You know I'd never have food delivered without some for you and whoever else is on duty." Grant made a mental note to send Autumn a thank-you. "Enjoy it."

Sheila nodded pertly, spun on her heel, and closed the door behind her.

He turned to Juliet and grinned when he saw her crimson cheeks. She sat on the edge of his desk, the peach pie in her hands, her gaze focused on the wall.

"I'm never going to be able to look Autumn in the eye again," she said with a slow shake of her head.

He chuckled. "Why not, darlin'?"

She put the pie aside and covered her face with her hands. "Between her request for written notes on your sexual prowess and *this* . . . ?" She peeked between her fingers. "Seriously?"

A laugh escaped him and he hooked an arm around her neck. "She won't say anything."

"Of course she won't," Juliet shot back, her brows drawing down.

"Why talk when she already *knows* everything?"

He leaned in to nuzzle her ear. "She doesn't know *everything*."

Juliet made an annoyed sound. "Might as well."

"Just be thankful it's Autumn and not Paulette," he teased. "Then *everyone* would know *everything*."

She pulled away and glared at him. "If I didn't know better, I'd say you're enjoying my embarrassment."

"Would I do *that*?" He gave her a slow smile. "I like your cheeks to be pink for *other* reasons . . . *both* sets of them." He saw the convulsive swallow and her eyes widened. She stared at him for several long, silent seconds, and then she chuckled.

"Again, only *you* could make me laugh in the middle of something like *this*." Her gaze wandered over his face. "I love you, Grant Donovan."

"I love you, too, darlin'." He kissed her quickly. "Now, let's get out of here. We have some groceries to take home and some ass to kick."

***

Juliet struggled to breathe as the arm around her neck tightened.

"Daniel, that's enough," she heard Grant say in the background.

Daniel's reply was harsh in her ear. "Mayfield isn't going to treat her with kid gloves if he gets his hands on her. She needs to know how to fight back, against a real threat."

Juliet's vision started to gray around the edges and she knew if she didn't do something she would lose consciousness. Instead of fighting harder she diminished her struggles, slowly, and after several seconds of waning activity allowed her body to go limp. Daniel held onto her.

"Let her go, damn you," Grant growled, "or *I'll* kick your ass."

Juliet's arms hung at her sides, flaccid, and she tried to inhale slowly against the pressure on her windpipe. Sparks of exultation glimmered to life when Daniel loosened his hold. She kept her body slack until he eased up some more, and then she struck.

She jerked out of his grip and dropped to a knee. Whirling, she drove her right fist into the center of his chest, hitting the solar plexus as Grant had shown her. Daniel's eyes widened as air was forcefully expelled from his lungs. She brought her left fist up in an uppercut that had Grant saying, "Yikes," and then kneed Daniel in the groin. A strangled cry caught in his throat and he dropped to his knees. Even though he wore protective padding and a cup, she had put everything she had behind the offensive. In all it took less than five seconds. Daniel fell onto his side, curled into a ball, and it wasn't until her breathing slowed that the pain registered. She flexed her fingers several times then shook her aching hand and glared down at him.

"Guess I took off the kid gloves," she said flatly.

Grant coughed loudly, grinning from ear to ear, and then he walked over to help Daniel to his feet. Juliet moved to grab her water bottle, took a long drink, and watched the detective, her insides vibrating with anger.

Daniel rested his hands on his knees, lines of pain bracketing his mouth, but he managed a smile. "Good." He groaned and straightened. "That's what I was going for." He cast a wry glance at Grant. "I guess you told her cheating was okay."

Grant crossed his arms over his chest and gave her a wink. "The only fair fight is the one you win."

Juliet took another drink and turned away from the two men, her heart still throbbing and adrenaline still surging. She walked to a window in the portable building and looked over the range. Movement out of the corner of her eye drew her gaze and she straightened as a black Cadillac Escalade pulled into the gravel-covered lot. It parked next to Grant's Yukon, clouds of dust swirling around it before the breeze finally dispersed them.

"Grant."

He was at her side almost instantly. His eyes narrowed and he turned, walking toward the door with long strides. "Stay here."

Juliet watched through the window as Grant stepped outside and strode down the ramp, his right hand resting on his gun. Her heart pattered uncomfortably in her chest, and she glanced at Daniel as he moved to her side, his brows drawn together. Her gaze was pulled back to the Escalade as the driver's and passenger's doors popped open.

She sucked in a breath as the driver stepped out, his blonde head towering over the top of the SUV when he straightened. Grant stood about 6'4" and this man was several inches taller, much broader, and more muscular. He looked like a human tank. "Holy cow, that's a big boy."

"That's an understatement," Daniel said under his breath.

The passenger came around the front of the SUV to stand at the blonde man's side. The second man was just a hair shorter than Grant with dark hair and an athletic build. Her eyes widened when she saw both men were armed.

Panic glimmered to life in her chest and she ran for the door. She pushed through the panel and rushed to Grant's side, her fingers wrapping around his bicep. Grant turned and she blinked when she saw his smile. He patted her hand.

"The FBI is here, darlin'," he said. "Come on, I'll introduce you."

Grant started walking and she traipsed along behind, her vocal chords frozen. The two men moved toward them and the taller one extended a hand when they came together.

"Afternoon, Grant," the blonde said as they shook hands briefly.

"Bear," Grant said. He pulled Juliet forward. "Juliet, meet Special Agent Ted Bristol, FBI."

Razor-sharp blue eyes rested on Grant briefly and then scanned her with laser-like intensity before a faint smile softened his harshly chiseled features.

"Miss Hall," he drawled, extending his hand toward her. "My friends call me Bear, for obvious reasons, and that will include you now if you would do me the honor."

She didn't remember grasping his fingers and she blinked, surprised, when her hand disappeared in his much larger one.

"Nice to meet you," she said when she found her voice. She cleared her throat as heat crept into her cheeks and she craned her neck to look up at him. "Call me Juliet."

Grant's hand was warm in the small of her back and he half-steered her toward the other man. "This is Special Agent Jack Vaughn," he said.

Juliet glanced at Grant. His expression was neutral and she turned to Jack Vaughn. Laine's Jack. Grant's Laine's Jack. Her heart thumped uncomfortably.

"Special Agent Vaughn," she said in a hushed voice.

Silver eyes returned her stare directly, the corners crinkling attractively as he smiled.

"Call me Jack," he said.

Someone cleared their throat and both she and Grant turned. Daniel stood there, hands clasped neatly in front of him. Grant stood to the side and the detective strode forward.

"Gentlemen," Grant began, "this is the man y'all have been spending so much time on the phone with, Detective Daniel Riordan, Seattle PD."

Juliet backed up, feeling oddly excluded as the circle of law enforcement officers greeted one another. And then they all turned and looked at her. She couldn't help but smile. If the situation weren't so serious, she'd think she was witness to an Abercrombie and Fitch cattle call.

Damn, Jules. Wish I was in your shoes right now. Talk about a veritable buffet of gorgeousness. There's blonde, brunette, short hair, curly hair, blue eyes, brown eyes, grey eyes, hazel eyes, and muscles, muscles, and more muscles. I thought I was the one who was supposed to be in heaven.

She ignored her sister's voice, but she had to agree. A veritable buffet, indeed. A tingle ran up her spine when she noticed Bear's sharp gaze traveling between her and Daniel, and she realized the detective was still wearing his protective padding.

"Training?" Bear ventured.

"Yeah," Daniel replied, a sheepish smile warming his features. "She was actually kicking my ass, but if you want to call it training I'm cool with that."

Bear's eyes narrowed on her and she gulped.

"Want to learn some top-secret FBI moves?" He glanced at the others. "Why don't you all get caught up while I teach Juliet how to kill someone with their own thumb?"

Bear grinned and she was momentarily taken aback by the change. Straight-faced he was intimidating, his features sharply carved and stone-like with a gaze that was cutting and precise. However, when he smiled his features were transformed from menacing to a level of attractive that would make women sigh with adoration. Then there was the matter of his size. He towered over her by at least a foot and outweighed her by an easy hundred pounds, if not more. Daniel she had been able to get away from, but *this* guy? She doubted many escaped the FBI agent's grasp once he got hold of them. Juliet blinked and nodded as he gestured toward the portable building. A flutter of uneasiness danced through her middle and she glanced at Grant.

He seemed to sense her anxiety and a smile curved his mouth. "Go on, Juliet. You're in good hands." He looked at Bear and his smile widened. "Don't be fooled by her delicate looks, Bear. She had Daniel on his knees not two minutes ago."

"She's definitely a fighter," Daniel agreed. He looked at her and the warmth in his gaze made her stomach cramp. "Underestimate her at your own peril, Special Agent Bristol."

"It's *Bear*," Bear said with a growl and a grin. "And thanks for the warning, gentlemen, but if a beautiful woman has me on my knees it's because I want to be there."

"And you'd *still* be taller than me," Juliet muttered. At 5'7" she wasn't *tall*, but she'd never before felt like a dwarf. It bothered her down to the very bottom of her XX chromosome.

Bear laughed. "I'm taller than almost everyone, Juliet. But, I promise I shall not use my size to my advantage." He cupped her elbow and nodded toward the building. "Shall we? I want to see what you've got."

Juliet rolled her eyes and started walking toward the building. Bear fell into step beside her.

"So, I'm guessing they have things to talk about I shouldn't hear?" she ventured as they walked up the ramp to the door.

"Not at all," Bear said. He opened the door and held it for her. "I just want all of them on the same page, and since *I've* read all the pages, *I* don't need the update."

She let it go and paused at the edge of the mat. "Are you really going to teach me how to kill someone with their own thumb?"

One corner of his mouth lifted in a smile. "No. That's a trade secret that would violate my non-disclosure agreement. However, I can teach you several other things that will help you put down an opponent should you have need to. And then, I'd like to talk."

That flutter of uneasiness was back, and it had grown. "About what?"

He rubbed his chin. "Well, I've read all the case files and police reports, but what I'm more interested in is what *isn't* in those reports." He kicked out of his shoes, moved to the center of the mat, and gestured for her to come closer. "I want to hear about Mayfield from you, *after* I teach you how to put him down."

Chapter Twenty Five

Grant entered the building and was surprised to see Juliet and Bear sitting in the middle of the mats talking. Jack and Daniel were right behind him, and a look at them told him they were as surprised as he was. He glanced at his watch and saw less than 30 minutes had passed since the arrival of the FBI's finest.

"Hey," he said, "I thought you were going to teach her how to kill someone with their own thumb."

Bear rose in one fluid motion and helped Juliet to her feet. "I did. How long do you think it takes?"

Grant chuckled and shook his head. "Not long I guess."

Bear shrugged. "When you're a great teacher and you have a great student lessons go much faster." He gave her a grin. "She's a quick learner."

"I know," Grant said. He gave her a sidelong glance and was rewarded by the flush that rose in her cheeks. "You don't reach her level in the dance world without that type of skill."

Bear gave him a wry smile and Grant knew the taller man had noticed her blush and had guessed the reason behind it. Then again, Laine had probably told Jack, who had probably told Bear. It was a simple equation to finish.

"True," Bear agreed. "Now, why don't Jack and I head over to the hotel and get a couple rooms. Special Agents Fellowes and Vargas should be here in a couple of hours with our mobile command post."

Grant was surprised. "I thought you were headquartering in Missoula."

"We have a field office there," Bear confirmed with a nod, "but since this is where the action is . . . ?" He shrugged. "We'll coordinate with Missoula, but we have this great RV with all these federally funded bells and whistles that make the International Space Station look like a Ford Pinto." He gave Grant a wry look. "Unless you think we're stepping on your toes here."

Grant rolled his eyes and fought a smile. "Really?"

Bear studied him for a few seconds, and Grant knew most would be intimidated by that pointed look. But, not only was he friends with the hulking FBI agent, he also didn't intimidate easily, and he knew Bear was only messing with him. He returned Bear's stare. Finally, a faint smile softened the taller man's features.

Bear's gaze slid to Riordan. "How about you, Detective? Many of the relationships I have with local cops are contentious at best. They worry about the Feds swooping in and stealing the spotlight. You concerned about not making the collar?"

Grant looked over his shoulder at Daniel and grinned when he saw the man's scowl.

"Are you fucking kidding me?" Daniel asked. "I don't give a damn where the credit goes. I just want to make sure no more women wind up dead." His eyes narrowed to mere slits. "Why? Do *you* need the attention?"

Bear's face went absolutely expressionless, as blank as a slate that had been washed clean, and Grant felt the chill from where he stood.

"I didn't get into this line of work for the accolades," Bear began in what Grant knew was a deceptively mild voice, "and if you did you picked the wrong career path, my friend."

Jack stepped forward. "Down, gentlemen." He gave Bear a warning look and then tossed a benevolent glance at the detective. "Forgive him, Detective Riordan. Although he's not interested in who gets credited for any arrest, Bear *is* accustomed to being in charge."

"That he is," Grant agreed. "But he's very good at it, so I think you're going to have to cut him some slack, Daniel. At least on *this* case."

Daniel's scowl lightened a bit, but he didn't back down. "I can handle it. He's not the first bossy guy I've worked with."

"Good." Grant glanced between the three men. "Now that we've agreed none of us care about anything *other* than bringing the Mayfields to justice, can we get on with it?"

"Well," Bear began, "we can, but that's up to you, Sheriff." One blonde brow rose. "This is your county and you are the head honcho here."

Grant should've known. Bear was nothing if not by the book. "You want my permission to take charge?" Grant asked.

"I will not take charge otherwise," Bear replied. "Like I said, this is *your* county. You supersede even the Federal Government in this neck of the woods."

"Fine," Grant said with a chuckle. "This show is yours, but I expect for all of us to be in the loop, or I will kick you right out of my county."

"Absolutely." Bear chuckled and strode forward, hand extended. Grant immediately grasped the taller man's fingers. Bear grinned. "I have a feeling I'm going to enjoy working with you, Sheriff." They shook briefly before Bear glanced at Jack. "Let's get this show on the road."

"I'll call Fellowes," Jack said. "There's a KOA just outside of town. He and Vargas can park the RV there, and it's clear of trees so they'll have access to the satellite feeds."

"I'll get a couple of rooms at the hotel," Bear said. He looked at Riordan. "Detective, why don't you go back to Grant's office and coordinate with your partner in Seattle. I want our offices hooked up and communicating as soon as the rest of the team gets here."

"Will do," Daniel said with a nod.

"Grant."

"Yeah, big man?"

"Looks like it falls to you to look after Miss Hall," Bear said. He tried to hide the smile, but Grant saw it twitch about his mouth. "Unless you'd prefer otherwise? I could call in a team from Missoula to protect her."

Grant slid his gaze to Juliet, who had watched this scene unfold in wide-eyed silence. "It's alright with me, as long as it's alright with her."

Three more pairs of eyes turned her way and Grant smiled as her blush deepened. She chewed her lip for a couple seconds and then shrugged.

"Fine with me."

"Alright then," Bear said, rubbing his hands together as a grin flashed, "let's do this."

***

Grant watched the whitewater as it churned over the rocks, enjoying the familiar, soothing sound and the feel of Juliet at his side.

"That must have been hard for you."

He glanced to his left. Juliet had her elbows on the deck railing, hands clasped, her eyes focused on the river. He turned toward her. "What?"

"Seeing Jack."

"Ah." He thought about it for a few seconds. "Not really. But it would've stung a lot more if he'd shown up before *you* did."

Her gaze was questioning as she faced him. "What do you mean?"

His heart started a steady *ka-thump* as he looked into those impossibly beautiful eyes. "I mean . . . love has a way of healing old wounds." He gave her a small smile and traced the line of her collarbone. "That's what Jack did for Laine, and that's what you've done for me."

Her brows drew together. "I don't understand."

He wasn't sure how to explain it to her. The subject of Laine was one he'd avoided for a long time, for good reason. There had been a point not so long ago in which even the thought of his best friend brought with it a familiar pain, the sort of heart-rending ache he'd felt each time he lost someone he loved. The worst part about surviving a war was living with the bruised, throbbing wounds left by the absence of those who didn't make it home. The worst part of loving someone was when they couldn't love you back.

"Jack is Laine's second husband," he finally said in a low voice. "Her first husband, Nick, was a detective with the Chicago Police Department."

"Oh, Grant," she whispered. "You had to go through that *twice?*"

A wry chuckle escaped him and he wound his fingers through hers. The contact made telling the story much less painful for some reason, and he pressed his lips to the back of her hand. "I did."

"I'm so sorry."

He shrugged. "That's life. And Laine got the worst of it, believe me."

"How so?"

"Nick and Laine had been married about seven years or so when he was killed in the line of duty. She was working the ER when they brought him in." He glanced at her. Her expression was stricken and she took a deep breath. Grant sighed. "She was devastated, of course, and she came back to Evergreen for a little while before heading to California for a few years. Eventually she returned here, but she wasn't the Laine I knew. She was . . . a *shell,* and nothing I did seemed to help."

A pained smile curved Juliet's mouth and she blinked rapidly. "I can relate."

"Yeah, well, Jack brought her back. His love is what it took to heal those wounds." He held her hands to his chest. "And *that* I can relate to." His heart swelled until he felt like he was choking on it. He tried to swallow it down, but it took several attempts before he managed to speak. "*You* brought *me* back, Juliet. I never thought I'd fall in love again, didn't really want to, and then *you* danced into my life." His voice caught as familiar, long-avoided warmth spread through his chest. It permeated to the core of his being and his throat tightened with emotion. He took a shaky breath, pressed his lips to her fingers, and whispered, "You saved me."

Tears shimmered in her eyes and she shook her head slowly. "No, Grant," she said in a hushed voice. She disentangled her hands from his, stood on tiptoe, and cupped his neck. "We saved each other."

Grant pressed his brow to hers for several seconds, then tilted his head and covered her mouth with his. His arms stole around her slender form and pulled her closer. This wasn't a possessive kiss or a prelude to passion. Rather, it was an expression of his feelings for her, an intimate caress meant to assure her, to illustrate the esteem he had for the bond growing between them. It was as much a promise of allegiance and protection as it was a melding of mouths and souls.

He ended the kiss slowly and then rested his chin atop her head as she pressed her face against his neck. She sighed and settled against him.

"So," he began, "what do you think of our FBI agents?"

"Well, I didn't get to speak to Jack, but I really like Bear. I think he could intimidate or charm a confession out of a suspect, depending on the mood he's in."

Grant chuckled. "Yeah, Bear's a good guy. Jack, too. And they're both *really* good at their jobs." He kissed the top of her head. "You're in good hands with them."

She pulled back and looked up at him. "I'm in good hands with you."

He smiled. "And my hands certainly like having you in them."

Color stained her cheeks but she grinned at him. "You are terrible."

"You weren't saying that this morning." He brushed his lips over hers.

She melted into him. "No, I wasn't."

He buried his face in her hair and tightened his hold on her. Her cheek rested on his chest, her fingers stroking lazily over his back. He knew he would be happy to just hold her like this forever, provided he was allowed to kiss and make love to her also.

"What do you want to do with the rest of our Saturday?" he asked softly.

She was quiet for several seconds. "Hmm. I don't know." Those turquoise eyes met his. "What do *you* want to do?"

"How about something normal? Something regular people do."

Her brows drew together. "Normal? Like what?"

"Like . . . ." His voice trailed off, his train of thought derailing as his eyes drifted to her mouth. He shook himself. "Like a picnic at that spot by the river. I'll make us some sandwiches, throw in some fruit and cheese, and we can eat and watch the sunset." He paused and ran a finger over her cheek. "Just downstream is an eddy where the water is deep and calm. It's perfect for skinny-dipping."

Patrician brows rose and a smile flirted with her mouth. "Are you trying to get me out of my clothes, Sheriff?"

He pursed his lips and pretended to think about it. "If I'm to take you at your word, all I have to do to get you out of your clothes is tell you I love you."

She blinked at him and then gave him a wry grin. "So, do you?"

"Want to get you out of your clothes, or love you?"

"Both."

His heart seized up and his throat tightened. He let his gaze wander over her face slowly, memorizing the delicate bone structure, the lush mouth, the sweeping brows, and the Caribbean blue eyes. Warmth expanded from beneath his heart until it permeated his fingers and toes. The realization he'd never felt like this before, not even with Laine, both startled and frightened him.

He'd had an idea what the relationship between him and Laine would be like, what he would *want* it to be like. However, the reality of what he felt for Juliet was quickly overshadowing what he'd imagined he'd have with Laine. Apparently, someone somewhere knew better, and for the first time in his life he was thankful he and Laine weren't together. There were no guarantees with Juliet but, despite the uncertainty in what lay ahead of them, the one thing he did know was how deeply he cared for this woman. This was the moment where he decided if he played it safe or stepped into the line of fire. *Well, looks like it's onto the battlefield I go.*

The seriousness of his thoughts must have registered on his face because her smile faded and he saw the convulsive swallow before he caught and held her blue-green gaze. "I love you," he whispered, "more than I thought I could love anyone." He framed her face, fought a smile, and added, "*And* I want to get you out of your clothes."

She closed her eyes and a short sigh of relief escaped her. She bent her head and pressed her brow against his chest, clutching the back of his shirt as she chuckled. "Whew. For a second there . . . ."

He nudged her chin up with his knuckles. "What?"

She bit her lip, her expression pensive. "I don't know. You just looked so serious all of a sudden." Her fingers plucked at the buttons of his shirt and her eyes focused there. "I thought maybe you had . . . changed your mind."

"Changed my mind about saying I love you?" he offered.

Pink surged into her cheeks and she closed her eyes. "We all say things we don't mean, Grant. Sometimes words just fall out when we don't want or plan for them to." She shrugged. "It happens."

"Not to me," he replied in a low voice. A cold, dark knot of uncertainty coiled tightly in his belly. "Is that what happened to you?" He swallowed hard. "Did you say something you didn't mean?"

Her head snapped up and she looked at him in dismay. "No."

Relief surged through him and he closed his eyes for a second. "Thank God."

Her fingers slid up his chest and twined around his neck. "Even if I didn't *plan* to say it, I *did* mean it." She stood on tiptoe and moved close. "I love you, Grant Donovan."

His heart somersaulted and inside he was dancing a jig. He had the sudden desire to toss her over his shoulder, run down the deck steps into the grass, and spin around until she was laughing hysterically and they both collapsed from dizziness. Instead, he lowered his head and captured her mouth.

Juliet's body arched toward him and warmth fanned over every nerve-ending, making them stand up and pay even more attention to the hardness and blatant masculinity of the body pressed to hers. His nearness overwhelmed her, his taste, his scent, the strength that shielded her and the tenderness that melted her. When he ended the kiss and pulled back she made a disappointed sound and rested her brow against his chest. His heart pounded against her forehead, and she smiled when he dropped a kiss on top of her head.

"C'mon, darlin'," he said softly. "Let's go have us a picnic, and then I'll see if I can't get you out of your clothes again."

Oh, that won't be much of a fight, trust me, Sheriff.

***

Juliet sighed and smiled. Her head rested in Grant's lap as he leaned against the same fallen tree they'd sat beside a couple of nights ago. The river sang its soothing, liquid song. The remains of their early dinner had already been packed up and put away, the picnic basket sitting nearby like a squat, voiceless sentry. The sky overhead was cast in fiery neon ribbons of red, fuchsia, and gold as the sun fell behind the mountains. Even though she knew Mayfield was on his way and that a confrontation would probably happen sooner rather than later, her body refused to feel anything other than relaxed, safe, and content, more content than she'd ever been. Grant's hand rested on her chest, his finger absently tracing the line of her collarbone.

"You look happy," he observed, that sexy smile curving his mouth. "Thinking about skinny-dipping?"

"No," she replied, looking askance at him, "but now that you mention it . . . ."

He laughed. "What *were* you thinking about?"

She narrowed her eyes on a snippet of cloud that slashed across the darkening sky in a blaze of yellow-gold. "Shouldn't I be afraid? I mean, I spent more than a year being terrified of him and I never knew *when* he might show up." She turned her face toward him, her cheek against his flat stomach. "Now, I *know* he's coming, but at this moment I could care less."

He pursed his lips and toyed with a lock of her hair. "Maybe it's because you're prepared. You *know*, and it's not going to be a complete surprise. Not to mention you're armed and know how to kill someone with their own thumb."

She chuckled. "Yeah, between you and Bear I feel *way* more confident about what will happen if I run into him." A thought popped into her head. "Y'know, I really think the only reason I got away from him when he came after me in that parking garage was because I fought back. He didn't expect that, and it surprised him."

Grant's brows drew together. "What do you mean?"

Juliet sat up and faced him. "The whole time he was stalking me everyone, including the police, told me not to engage him, not to antagonize him, ignore him and maybe he'll just go away on his own." She snorted softly. "For more than a year I skittered around like a frightened mouse, and it turned me into one." Her gaze wandered to the river. "I wonder if he'll be taken by surprise again, or if he'll expect me to fight back and be prepared for it."

"Maybe," Grant replied, running a hand down her arm and lacing his fingers through hers. "You just have to surprise him again. Remember, if you ain't cheating you ain't trying." He kissed the back of her hand and narrowed his eyes on her. "Listen to your gut, Juliet. Many times people ignore that little scratch on their spine because they're more concerned with being polite and not offending someone. You hear all the time from people who survive an attack that they knew something was off or they had a bad feeling, but they convinced themselves they were imagining things." He flattened her hand over his heart and covered it with his own. "*Don't* do that."

"I won't. You've taught me too well."

She leaned forward and kissed him. One of his hands tangled in her hair while the other fanned over her back and pressed her closer. A sultry ache swirled in her midsection and furled outward, and when his tongue demanded entrance to her mouth it started to spin. Her skin tingled, demanding to be touched, her nipples taut and throbbing.

"Grant," she said against his mouth.

"Hmm?"

"Take me home," she said. A moan caught in her throat as he deepened the kiss and she curled her fingers into his hair. Her insides liquefied and heat pulsed through her like a drug. Without breaking contact she straddled his hips, and a shock of desire flamed to life. He was hard beneath her, and she dragged her mouth from his. "Take me home *now*."

Without waiting for an answer she got up and grabbed the picnic basket, her knees wobbling. She paused, trying to steady her legs, and glanced at him. A languid grin flirted with his lips and he grabbed the blanket from the ground.

"Yes, ma'am."

He extended a hand to her and when his fingers wrapped around hers the strength in her legs returned. He pulled her against his side, draped an arm around her shoulders, and they walked back to the Yukon. The sun gave up its fight to shine and she almost heard it sigh in resignation as it sank behind the mountains. Juliet opened the rear passenger door and put the basket on the floor behind her seat, then closed it and leaned against the vehicle. The last vestiges of solar illumination flickered and she paused to admire the show as waves of navy and indigo chased the light into the west. Grant walked up behind her and rested his chin on her shoulder and she leaned against him.

"I love it here," she said softly.

"Me, too." He turned his head and kissed the curve of her neck. "And I'll never be able to come back here without thinking of you."

Juliet faced him and was caught by those beautiful bedroom eyes. "Why not?"

"This is where I realized I was falling in love with you." He cupped her neck, his thumb stroking over the line of her jaw. "When you jumped so quickly to my defense, it hit me how much your opinion mattered to me, and how happy I was that you thought more highly of me than I deserved."

"I think the *world* of you," she said as she pressed a hand to his cheek, "and so does everyone else, as they should." Warmth radiated outward from her heart and she smiled at him. "You, Grant Donovan, are one of the finest men I've ever known and a credit to your gender. And," she paused and gave him a wicked look, "if you take me home right now, I will show you just how much you mean to me."

"Get in and buckle up." He kissed her hard and fast and then jogged around to the driver's side. "Let's see how fast we can get there."

Despite his statement Grant drove home at a pace only a few miles over the posted speed limit. Juliet leaned her head back against the headrest, wind through the partially open window caressing her with cool, nature-perfumed air. She smelled pine and water and earth and inhaled deeply. Grant's fingers brushed hers and she smiled at him as he grasped her hand. He grinned at her and all was right with the world, her heartbeat speeding up as she imagined what the next few hours would bring. As if reading her mind, he gave her a wink and turned his attention back to the road.

The Bluetooth once again interrupted the radio and Grant shook his head as he pushed the button near the volume knob.

"Donovan."

"Evening, Grant." It was Jack. "Just calling to see how you're doing before Bear and I head to the hotel."

"We're fine," Grant replied. "Just finished an early dinner and are on our way back to my place now. Anything new on your end?"

"Got a look at Mayfield's juvenile record," Jack replied. "Am I on speaker?"

Grant glanced at her and she rolled her eyes. "I've seen firsthand what George Mayfield is capable of, Jack," Juliet said. "I don't think anything you say will shock me."

"Fine, but the following presentation contains mature subject matter not suitable for younger viewers. Just so you know."

"Go on," Grant said, squeezing her hand. "Give it to us."

"Well," Jack drawled, "less than a year after his mother's death, George Mayfield was charged with sexually assaulting a classmate. She said he tied her up, raped her, and cut her." Jack paused and Juliet met Grant's gaze. "Two more girls came forward after that, but before the case could go to trial they recanted and dropped the charges. The original complainant stuck to her guns, but the night before opening arguments she died in a car accident."

Grant exhaled slowly. "Aw, hell."

"Police report says they found broken vodka bottles in the wreckage, and she had alcohol in her stomach. Her death was ruled an accident."

"Did they run her blood?" Grant asked.

Jack clicked his tongue and she heard the flipping of pages. Her nerves stretched taut as she waited for Jack to reply.

"Not that I can find," Jack said at last. "It looks like this was one of those 'hurry-up-and-close-the-investigation' jobs." He sighed. "Without a complaining witness there was no case, so the charges were dismissed and George Mayfield's records were sealed when he turned 18. Helps to have a powerful father with powerful friends, I suppose."

Grant flexed his fingers on the steering wheel. "Wonder what the chances are we could get an order to re-examine her blood sample, see if she was *actually* drunk, or the accident was staged to make it *look* like she was."

Juliet's throat started to burn and she realized she was holding her breath.

"Sorry if I ruined your night," Jack said, "but you *did* ask."

Grant squeezed her fingers again and gave her an apologetic look.

"Thanks for the update, Jack," Grant said. "By the way, I made reservations at the hotel for Sunday brunch. Let's meet in the lobby at 11:30. I want to introduce you to Deputy Sheridan. She's going to be stepping into my shoes temporarily, so I want her in the loop."

"Sounds good. You two have a lovely evening, if you can, and we'll see you tomorrow."

Grant disconnected the call and wound his fingers through hers again.

"Are you alright?"

Something dark and clotted churned in her belly. "No, Grant, I'm not." She closed her eyes when they started to sting. "He's been doing this since he was . . . a *teenager*, and they knew. They *knew*."

He sighed. "I don't mean to play devil's advocate, but it's not what you know, darlin'. It's what you can *prove*."

The shriek of rending metal suddenly tore through the serene night, followed by the high-pitched, almost musical shower of shattering glass. Then the impact registered. The world teetered crazily as the Yukon spun in tight circles, rubber squealing and air rushing past in what felt like a gale force wind. Juliet's seatbelt pulled her back sharply, cutting across her chest and shoulder. Her fingers dug into the armrests as time seemed to slow. She saw the individual squares of safety glass as they danced crazily through the cabin of the SUV, and each strand of hair as the long tresses were caught up in the centripetal force and fanned out like dark, delicate spokes on a wheel. Grant yelled for her to hold on, but each word was drawn-out and distorted. Then, just as suddenly as it had started their wild ride came to an abrupt, bone-jarring end. There was a hiss, an explosion of hot air and unseen pressure that seemed to engulf her and push her even further into her seat, and then her world went black.

Chapter Twenty Six

The darkness started to recede and Juliet bit back a moan. What the hell was going on? The last thing she remembered was . . . the accident. Her eyes snapped open and she looked for Grant. When she realized she wasn't in Grant's Yukon her heart nearly jumped out of her chest and then continued beating fast and heavy.

A glance around revealed the inside of a vehicle, but what kind she couldn't know other than it was some sort of SUV. She lay in the backseat. She started testing body parts and stiffened when she realized she was bound. A glance down revealed coarse rope wrapped around her hands, and when she tried to move her legs she discovered her ankles were tied as well. A gasp escaped her.

"I think someone is back with us," a deep, masculine voice said.

"I'll take care of it, Father."

Ice rushed through her, turning her blood cold and freezing her lungs. She knew the second voice all too well, and although Gregory Mayfield wasn't as familiar, she still recognized his dulcet, diplomatic tones. *You were right, Grant. George didn't come alone.*

Juliet shrank back against the cushion as a form loomed in front of her, a silhouette outlined by the lights on the dashboard. Even though she couldn't discern the features, his face was too clearly visible in her mind's eye.

Come on, Jules. Keep your head. It's really great here, but it's not time for you to join me yet.

Then another voice registered in her quickly overloading brain.

"You just have to surprise him again. Remember, if you ain't cheating you ain't trying."

How could she fight both of them, and bound no less?

Just don't panic, sis. The right time will present itself, unless you're too freaked out to see it.

Before she could reply to that a hand clamped around her throat and pushed her into the seat. Then a damp cloth covered her nose and mouth. Juliet struggled as best she could with her hands and feet bound. She held her breath, but Mayfield had the positional and physical advantage, and as the seconds dragged on her lungs and throat started to burn. Finally, her body demanded air and her diaphragm spasmed violently, forcing her to take a breath. The fumes from the cloth burned as they traveled through her nostrils into her lungs on her sharp inhale, and seconds later the blackness returned, encroaching softly inward from the edges of her vision. She fought it, but she knew it was a losing battle. Finally, with a whimper, she succumbed.

***

Jack knocked on Bear's door. The big man opened it a few seconds later, his mouth full of toothpaste. He glanced at his watch and then gestured for Jack to come in. As Jack closed the door behind himself Bear went into the bathroom, rinsed his mouth, and reappeared.

"It's 8:30, Jack, and we're not supposed to meet Grant and the others for another few hours," Bear said. "What's up?"

"Does anything feel wrong to you?" Jack asked. He met Bear's laser-like gaze. "Mayfield landed in Missoula night before last. He should've made an appearance by now."

Bear's eyes narrowed. "He's not dumb, Jack, or he wouldn't have been getting away with murdering multitudes of women for only God knows how long." He tipped his head. "Why? What's your gut telling you?"

"I don't know." Jack planted his hands on his hips and stared at the floor. "I tried to call Grant last night but he didn't answer."

Bear chuckled softly. "I'm sure he and Miss Hall had, um, *other* things to do besides answer your call."

Jack glared at him. "And I talked to Laine a little while ago and she said she's tried to call him. He might not answer *my* calls, but Laine's?" He shook his head. "There's no way he lets *those* go to voicemail."

Bear's brows drew together. He pulled out a phone, dialed, and put it to his ear. After about fifteen seconds he hung up and dialed again. A scowl darkened his brow. He dialed a third time and then a fourth. Someone answered on the last call.

"Yeah, Miguel, get me GPS coordinates for Sheriff Donovan and Miss Hall's cell phones and call me back once you have a lock on the locations. Jack and I are heading out." He hung up his phone and grabbed his gun.

"What's up?" Jack asked.

"Well, I just called Grant's cell, his house, *and* Juliet. No answer." He started walking toward the door. "Let's get over to Grant's office and talk to Daniel." He paused at the door and tossed Jack a glare. "You always did like to stir up hornet's nests."

"What the hell is *that* supposed to mean?"

"It means now *my* gut is telling *me* something is wrong, and I haven't even had breakfast yet."

They walked into the Sheriff's Office ten minutes later and found Daniel in Grant's office. When he saw them his brows drew together and he rose from the chair.

"What's going on, guys?" he asked. "Brunch isn't for another couple of hours."

"Have you heard from Grant or Juliet?" Bear asked flatly.

"No, why?"

"Because I've called both of their cell phones and Grant's house and no one is answering at any of those numbers."

Daniel's eyes widened. "I haven't talked to either of them since the range yesterday."

Jack met Bear's gaze just as Bear's phone rang.

"Bristol." He listened for a few seconds and nodded. "Got it. Send it to my phone." He hung up and faced the other two men. "We've got a hit on Grant's phone. Juliet's phone is either off or someone disabled the GPS."

"Shit," Daniel said.

Jack and Bear turned as Daniel thrust his hands into his hair. "What?" they asked in unison.

"Juliet has a tracking chip in her pendant." He ran around to the other side of the desk, found a yellow sticky pad, and ripped the top page off. "This is the frequency number."

Jack took the note and a precautionary step back when a storm cloud gathered on Bear's face.

"And you're just telling us about this *now?*" Bear's features were absolutely granite-like. "I'm beginning to see why you guys in Seattle couldn't put this bastard away in the *first* place."

Daniel's eyes glittered angrily and he took a step toward the taller man. "I just gave her the pendant yesterday and we hadn't even tested it yet to see if it works." His brows drew down. "Instead of tearing into me about what a shitty cop I am, why don't you have your guys in that high-tech RV locate the pendant?" He got in Bear's face, or at least as close as he could given Bear was a good six inches taller than the detective. "If you want to go toe to toe after this is over I'm fine with that, but right now we have more important things to worry about."

Jack was already on the phone with Vargas, giving him the frequency for Juliet's GPS tracker. He glanced at the men, and while he didn't know Detective Riordan well enough to know what the shorter man would do, he knew Bear. Bear wouldn't waste time fighting Riordan, and if Riordan swung first Bear still wouldn't waste time fighting. One punch and the fight would be over, and Detective Riordan would be on the ground, most likely unconscious.

"Jack," Bear said through tightly clenched teeth.

"Yeah?"

"I'm going to take Deputy Sheridan with me and find Grant. You and the detective follow that tracker once Vargas gets a bead on it." He broke eye contact with Riordan long enough to toss him a look. "Keep in touch and let me know the second you have anything."

"Roger that, big man. Now, if you two gentlemen are done with the pissing contest, can we get on with this?"

Bear didn't even look at the detective again. He spun on his heel and left Grant's office.

Jack hung up his phone as Daniel turned to him.

"Is he always like that?" Daniel asked.

"When things start to go south," Jack began, "yeah. Bear doesn't like it when things go south."

"I take it that doesn't happen to him very often?"

Jack shook his head. "No. No it doesn't, and I'm not exaggerating. He's just that good." His phone rang and he hit the speaker button. "Go ahead, Miguel. What do you have?"

"Well, I have good news and bad news. Which do you want first?"

"Good news."

Miguel sighed. "Well the tracker's not moving."

Jack frowned. "And the bad news?"

"It's located in northeastern Washington."

"What?" Jack asked.

"Close to a Lake Heron."

"Nice work, Mig. Send the coordinates to my phone and Bear's, and then coordinate with Missoula and pull in Seattle. We may need more backup."

"You got it, Jack."

"Aw, hell." Daniel ran around the desk and started shuffling through papers. When he found the file he flipped through the pages. "The Mayfield family has lake property in northeastern Washington on . . . ." His eyes scanned the page and then he paled and said in a whisper, ". . . Lake Heron."

Jack watched as the man's sails visibly deflated and he sank down on Grant's chair.

"Daniel—"

"If the pendant is there that means one of two things." Daniel ran a hand over his face and then lifted anguished eyes to him. "Either Juliet is there . . . or just the pendant is."

Jack knew exactly where the detective's mind was headed. "You can't think like that," he said. "Get up, Detective, *now*. I'm going to call Seattle and have them send a tactical team that direction while we start that way from here. Let's go."

***

"Grant, buddy can you hear me?"

Grant lifted his head, pain rippling across his brow. Every inch of him was sore and stiff, and it took what seemed superhuman effort just to open his eyes. The first thing he saw was the shattered windshield, two windshields actually, and when he shifted his gaze to the left two of Bear's concerned face slowly merged and came into focus. The flaccid remnants of the front and side airbags fluttered in the light breeze.

"What the . . . ." He groaned as a pounding started behind his eyes. "What happened?"

"Looks like someone ran you off the road, Sheriff. Don't you have Onstar on this thing?"

His mouth was dry but he worked up enough saliva to swallow and find his voice. "We did for the first six months, until the free subscription ran out." He tried to move his legs but they wouldn't budge. "We let it lapse because of budget cuts." A steady pounding started behind his eyes and he grimaced. "I should've fired Jackson and kept the Onstar."

Bear gave a mirthless chuckle. "Are you hurt?"

"My head is pounding but otherwise . . . ." Grant's voice trailed off and his head snapped to the right. Panic glimmered when he saw the open passenger door. "Juliet?" He looked at Bear, and what he saw in the taller man's eyes made his heart twist.

"She's not here," Bear said. "I have guys combing the woods to see if she got out and wandered away, but there are several sets of boot prints on that side of the vehicle. The person who crashed into you left their ride so he, or she, probably had a follow car . . . and help."

Grant's heart plummeted to the ground and a cold, dark wave of despair washed through him. "Oh, God, it had to be Mayfield."

"Do you remember what happened?"

Grant squeezed his eyes shut and thought for a few seconds. "We were just heading home after dinner when the collision came out of nowhere. I didn't see any lights or vehicles. One second we were talking and the next all hell broke loose."

"When?"

"It was about a minute after I got off the phone with Jack. My phone's probably in here somewhere."

Bear looked around and spotted it on the floorboard on the passenger side of the Yukon. He ran around to the other side, grabbed it, and started pushing buttons. "Okay, that means the accident happened about . . . 7:40 p.m. Are you sure you're not hurt?"

Grant started testing his limbs. "I think I'm okay, but my legs are pinned."

"EMS and fire should be here any minute," Bear told him. "As soon as we had a lock on your cell phone I gave them the code three." He reached through the cab of the SUV and rested a large hand on Grant's shoulder. "We'll have you out before you know it."

"Juliet's wearing a tracker," Grant said suddenly.

Bear nodded. "We know. Jack and Daniel are working that angle, and Jack just texted me that they're on their way here."

Grant's internal sensors went off and another chill filled him. "What are you *not* telling me?"

Bear studied him for a moment and dropped his chin as he sighed heavily. "The crash was more than 12 hours ago, bud."

Grant looked around, surprised that he hadn't noticed the bright daylight until now. His throat tightened and he closed his eyes. "Where is she?"

"Washington."

Something black and cold bubbled up inside Grant, filling his chest cavity and pressing heavily on his heart and lungs. "Get me out of this fucking car, Bear."

"I can hear the sirens now. Fire should be here any minute."

"And then we're going to Washington, right?"

"You need to go to a hospital."

Grant skewered him with a glare. "No. Juliet is out there. She needs me."

Bear gave him a level look. "We'll get her back."

"There's no way I'm going to a hospital while you guys go look for her." His eyes stung and he squeezed them shut. The thought of what she might be going through made nausea burgeon and he whispered, "I promised her I wouldn't let Mayfield hurt her."

"Grant, you've been in and out of consciousness for hours. You probably have a concussion, maybe more serious injuries—"

"If I had more serious injuries I'd already be dead, Bear!" Grant shouted, panic swelling and expanding through his abdomen. "Now get me the fuck out of this car so we can find her before Mayfield does to her what he did to Cassie!" When Bear didn't answer Grant looked at him and his anger evaporated, drowned by unadulterated fear mixed with a chilling swirl of despair that threatened to overwhelm him. "What would *you* do if it was Beth out there, or Laine?"

Bear closed his eyes briefly and sighed. "Fine. But you know if anything happens to you Laine will kill me."

Grant swallowed hard. "If anything happens to Juliet . . . it won't matter."

***

"Remember, if you're taken and knocked unconscious try to remain as still and silent as possible when you start to come to." Grant smiled at her. "Try to gather as much information as you can by using your ears and other senses before you let your captors know you're awake."

Juliet smiled back at him and then his face faded and dissipated, like fog in the wind. That's when memories gradually surfaced and noises started to register. She remembered waking up several times and each time that same damp, noxious cloth had sent her straight back to unconsciousness. This was different. She could tell they were no longer in the car, and she was laying on something much softer than the backseat of an SUV. Probably a bed. She heard birds chirping and the muffled sounds of music, the way it sounds when you hear it through a closed door. The tune was an old classic, "...*I kissed her and she kissed me ...*" Ah, Dean Martin. A clock ticked nearby, and there was a rhythmic creaking. It was oddly familiar, and she concentrated on breathing deeply and evenly as she tried to identify the noise. She almost shouted in triumph when she realized it was a rocking chair. Then fear surged through her. That meant she was not alone.

Panic bloomed slowly and she fought to rein it in.

"Whatever you do, do not *panic,"* Grant had said. *"You panic, you can't think. You can't think you're as good as dead."*

Juliet continued her blind assessment.

She was still bound, and it was probably early morning given the amount of time it felt like she'd been out and the light she could detect through closed eyelids. Aside from that and the continued creak of the rocking chair, there wasn't much else she could discover without opening her eyes.

Suddenly there was a rattling and then a soft squeal. Hinges.

"Has she woken up yet?"

She recognized Gregory Mayfield's voice, George's father. She remembered meeting him several times at the ballet, and the time he'd introduced her to his son. That night had been the beginning of this terrifying, devastating odyssey. She'd wanted to stay home that particular evening, but the ballet director had insisted. The cocktail parties/fundraisers the company often put on to lure in more supporters and more money bored her to death, and thankfully she was rarely asked to attend. Juliet didn't drink much and flirting to coerce patrons to pull out their checkbooks had never been her strong suit. Cassie was a much better choice, but since Juliet was a principal dancer duty called. Apparently one of the company's primary patrons had asked to meet her, and thus her perilous journey had begun. If only she had refused.

"No, not yet, Father. I told you I'd let you know when she came to."

"She's been out too long. Did you give her too much?"

"I did just as you showed me. Now, relax and go back downstairs. I'm sure she'll wake soon."

There was a brief, taut silence.

"Very well. Just remember everything I taught you, and *do not* underestimate her. That's what landed you in a psychiatric hospital for four years."

George laughed softly. "I won't, Father. And I think I got off rather easy. Four years at Brookstone is nothing compared to life in prison, don't you agree?"

Juliet could barely repress a shudder. She waited until the door closed again, waited another minute or so, and then pretended to wake up.

The room was bright and cheerful, so *not* what she had expected. She had expected something dour and depressing, but the whitewashed walls, the yellow curtains, the simple, country-style furniture would look more at home in a romantic comedy than the horror movie she was in. The place looked old, but it was obviously well maintained, the paint bright, the curtains clean, cheerful quilts tacked to the walls. There was a door and window to her left and a window in front of her, and finally her gaze fell on George Mayfield. He sat in a rocking chair to her right, that familiar intensely apathetic gaze locked on her, a wicked-looking knife in one hand. He tapped each of his fingers on the point of the blade and then reversed the motion, but he never once looked away from her. After several seconds he smiled, rose, and approached her.

Juliet rolled toward the edge of the bed but he was faster. Before she could blink he tossed her back onto the mattress, straddled her waist, and clamped his free hand over her mouth. He pressed her head into the pillows and slowly brought the blade to her throat. Juliet braced herself for the first of what she knew would be many cuts.

She stiffened when the knife dragged lightly over her neck, but there was no pain involved. Her fear and surprise must have registered on her face because an understanding smile curved his beautifully shaped mouth.

"Ah, my love," he cooed. "I'm not going to kill you, not yet. There are rules we follow, procedures. Everything must be done in order." His smile widened. "Now, promise me you will be quiet, and I will take my hand from your mouth. No one will hear you scream but my father and Leopold, and it will only anger my father. Leopold won't care."

The chill in her belly grew colder and fanned outward.

"Do you promise to be quiet?" Juliet nodded once. George grinned and moved to sit on the edge of the bed. "That's my girl." He brought the blade toward her and she cringed. His smile faded and a strange light entered his eyes, a light that actually seemed to darken the blue rather than illuminate it. He dropped his chin and said in a low voice, "I already told you I'm not going to hurt you right now." He closed his eyes, took several deep breaths, and then looked at her again. "I'm going to cut your ropes, because you've been out for a very long time and I'm sure you have certain . . . *needs* that must be tended." His head tipped to the side. "You will behave, will you not?"

Juliet nodded again and a second later the knife sliced through the ropes binding her hands and feet with nauseating ease. He gently removed the coarse strands and she rubbed her wrists.

"There now, isn't that better?" He reached behind his back and her eyes widened when she saw the pistol in his hand. He leveled it at her, and the way he gripped it said he knew how to use it. "Get up, darling. The bathroom is right through that door, but before you get it into your head that you can escape, the outer door has been nailed shut and the window is barred from the outside." He ticked the gun toward the door and then pointed it at her. "Go on. Relieve yourself, brush your teeth, and take a shower. After that you can have something to eat."

Juliet slowly stood, her heart like a jackhammer against her ribs and her lungs vibrating with fear. She moved toward the indicated door and grasped the antique knob tightly, her eyes locked with his. The door opened easily and she stepped into the small room with its ball-and-claw tub/shower. As she pulled the door closed she paused, swallowed hard, and whispered, "Thank you."

George beamed at her and sat down in the rocking chair. "You're welcome, my love. Now, go on, get cleaned up. Your breakfast is almost ready."

She closed the door and backed away from it, dropping down onto the closed toilet lid. About a second later a shadow darkened the narrow opening beneath the door and there was a scraping in the lock. Realizing her mistake too late, Juliet grasped the knob and turned. It didn't move. He'd locked her in from the outside. She immediately dropped to her knees and looked through the keyhole just in time to see George exit through the only other door she could see. The familiar scraping noise told her he had locked that one, too.

Air rushed out of her lungs in a gasp of hopelessness and she plopped down onto her derriere, her back against the door. A look around the bathroom revealed nothing she could use to help herself. The window was indeed barred from the outside. A medicine cabinet was recessed into the wall above the standalone sink, but the door had been removed and the removable shelves taken out. The toilet tank lid was gone and she scrambled across the floor to inspect the toilet seat. A desperate whimper escaped her when she realized it was securely bolted on. Her eyes flew around the room. A towel and washcloth were draped over the shower enclosure because there was no towel bar. Gaining her feet she inspected the polished metal from which the shower curtain hung, but one jerk on that rail made her heart sink. It was bolted into the ceiling, and she doubted even Bear would be able to budge it. She sank to the floor.

Don't panic, sis. Breathe, just breathe and keep your head on straight. By now they know you're missing, and you know Grant is doing everything he can to find you.

A cold surge of despair clogged her throat. "If he's still alive," she whispered, dropping her head onto her knees.

He is. At least, he's not here, *which means he's not dead yet.*

The flash of relief was short and not nearly enough to counteract the panic that threatened to consume her. Then Juliet gasped and touched her neck. The pendant was still there, which meant they could find her. Hopefully the cavalry would arrive before he killed her and not after.

"So, what do I do now?"

Just play along, Jules, and keep your eyes open. Do what Mayfield asks until the opportunity presents itself. You'll know it when you see it.

"How do you know?"

You've always been the strong one. Now is not *the time to chicken out.*

Juliet lifted her head.

Yes, I heard you that night, big sister. Despite how scared you were you came for me.

Her eyes brimmed. "But, I didn't get there in time."

And I'm glad you didn't, because then we'd both be dead. Now stop with the guilt and start using your head. Grant is coming, and if you can stay alive until then everything will be fine.

Juliet dashed a hand over her eyes and took a huge gulp of air. "Okay. I can do this. I *have* to do this."

She stood and took another deep breath. After relieving herself and brushing her teeth with the travel-sized toothbrush she stripped and stepped into the tub. With a jerk she pulled the plastic curtain closed. Travel-sized bottles of shampoo, conditioner, and liquid soap sat in the cutout for the soap dish. With a dispirited sigh she turned on the water, let it heat up, and activated the shower head.

Standing under the water the tears started. She desperately hoped Cassie was right, that Grant was indeed okay. The idea that he could be hurt or worse sent her emotions spiraling. The possibility of him not being there if she survived this ordeal was almost more than she could bear. She remembered the rending pain from the night she'd found Cassie. It had felt as if her heart was being torn in half, slowly and deliberately. She crouched beneath the flow, hugging her knees, and tried to choke back the sobs that clogged her throat.

A knock on the door startled her and she slipped, plopping onto her backside. Moments later the key scraped in the lock and the door popped open. Juliet scrubbed her face quickly, carefully gained her feet, and peeked out of the shower curtain. George stood there, a pile of clothes, additional toiletries, and hair care tools in his hands.

"These are for you. When you're done your breakfast is in the other room." He put the stack on the toilet lid and turned to go.

"George?"

He paused with his hand on the knob and looked at her. "Yes, my love?"

"Why?"

His brows drew together. "Why what?"

"Why are you feeding me?"

He looked bemused. "Aren't you hungry?"

Food was the last thing on her mind, and she wasn't sure she'd be able to swallow anything if she wanted to. "What's the point? If you're going to kill me, why bother?"

Understanding dawned and he nodded slowly. "Everything happens in its time, Juliet, and right now it's time for breakfast." As if that should be explanation enough, he gave her a small smile and left the room. She stared at the door, her heart pounding and her mind spinning. What the heck did *that* mean? *Now it's time for breakfast.* So, when is *killing* time, *after* lunch? She heard the key scrape in the lock and closed her eyes. Since shortly after meeting him she'd known George Mayfield was crazy, but this was a level of crazy she couldn't wrap her mind around. Juliet let the curtain fall back into place and stuck her head back under the water, fighting the panic growing inside her.

"Okay, Juliet," she said to herself, "get it together."

Yeah, or I might not get to see my nieces and nephews. I wonder, will they look like Grant or you? It won't matter. Either way they'll be gorgeous.

Cassie's voice, even though she knew it wasn't really Cassie's voice, calmed her. She quickly showered then dried off before slipping the curtain back and stepping onto the thick rug. After wrapping her hair in the towel she looked through the items George had brought. On top of the clothes was a small bottle of moisturizer, deodorant, facial lotion, as well as a brush and comb. She put the toiletries and styling tools aside and fingered the items of clothing: undergarments and a simple cotton sundress in a shade that nearly matched her eyes. They were new, still had the tags attached, but they were all her size and of similar styling to what she usually wore, down to the lacy bra and matching panties. He'd obviously done more than just wait for her the two times she had found him in the cottage, the two times he'd decorated her bedroom as he had the night he killed Cassie. Her stomach rolled and she took a deep, steadying breath.

After an application of lotion and a swipe of deodorant she removed the tags, then dressed and combed out her hair. With that she was done. Dread curled through her like thick smoke. Now what? In an effort to stall, she straightened the room. Once all the toiletries were lined up on the bottom shelf of the medicine cabinet, the towel and wash cloth hung up, and her dirty clothes folded, there was nothing else she could do except exit the bathroom. She gripped the knob, but for some reason she couldn't turn it. It wasn't locked, but her muscles refused to function. Panic returned, and it was more than a glimmer this time. She felt it pulse through her veins, as if it had been injected into her bloodstream.

Pull it together, Juliet.

Cassie sounded angry.

You do not *get to panic, do you hear me? Remember what Grant told you. You* have *to do this, Jules. You* cannot *die here today. You said you wouldn't let him take anything else without a fight, so* fight.

Juliet closed her eyes and took several deep, steadying breaths. "Okay, Cassie. Better take notes, little sister. This is going to be the performance of a lifetime."

Chapter Twenty Seven

Juliet put the now empty glass of orange juice back on the wicker breakfast tray and pushed the tray away. "I can't eat anymore." She glanced at George, who had returned to his seat in the rocking chair. "I'm sorry. It's delicious, but I'm full."

A warm smile curved his mouth, and she was astounded that such a beautiful face covered up such wickedness, and so effectively. To look at him one would never know what he truly was.

"That's fine, my love. I'm glad you enjoyed it." He stood and lifted the pistol. "Back into the bathroom with you."

Juliet calmly retreated to the bathroom and when the door closed and locked behind her, her knees buckled. She was shaking, and nausea threatened. Deep breaths did nothing to quell her stomach's unease, and once his booted feet had retreated she lunged for the toilet. She vomited as quietly as she could then leaned against the wall beneath the window taking in enormous gulps of air.

She was waiting for the opportunity to use some of her newly learned skills and try to escape, but the moment hadn't presented itself as of yet. While she'd eaten he'd sat in the rocking chair with the pistol aimed at her, talking all the while like they were a loving couple chatting over Sunday brunch. His eyes had never left her, and neither had the pistol's muzzle. And he was careful to keep enough distance between the two of them to give himself time to react should she attack. She couldn't believe it, but she was praying for him to get closer.

Gripping the edge of the sink she pulled herself upright, her knees wobbling dangerously. She turned on the water, scooped a mouthful to her lips, swished, and spat. Then she splashed her face and leaned her elbows on the porcelain as water dripped off the end of her nose. She reached for the towel and heard the familiar grating of the key as she dried her face. After putting the towel aside she took several deep breaths, left the bathroom, and pulled the door closed behind her. George stood on the other side of the bed. He gestured to the bed with the pistol.

"Lay down."

Fear burst upwards like a geyser, threatening to choke her. Juliet blinked at him, cleared her throat, and whispered, "Why?"

A tolerant smile moved the corners of his mouth just a bit. "Just do it, my love, else I shall have Leopold force you down. Trust me. He won't be gentle."

She eased down on the edge of the bed and scooted into the middle of the full-sized mattress. Her heart rate picked up when she saw the colorful scarves attached to each corner of the bed frame. A flashback from the night of Cassie's murder threatened to suffocate her. George obviously recognized the fear in her face because his smile widened.

"Ssh, my love," he cooed, the pistol still aimed at her chest. "It's not time yet. Now, lay down."

It dawned on Juliet what he was doing. He was like a cat, mercilessly toying with a mouse until it was too frightened and demoralized to fight back. Then, finally, the helpless creature would be put out of its misery. That sparked something inside her, something that resembled anger, although it was too faint for her to be certain. All she knew was she wasn't nearly as frightened as she'd been a few seconds ago.

She lay down and waited.

"Leopold."

The door swung open and a man of indeterminate age walked in. His hair was silver, but his face was smooth and unlined. He was just short of six feet tall and on the thin side, with high cheekbones and a sharply carved nose and jaw. Sharp black eyes roved over her once, and then he looked at Mayfield. They were the eyes of a shark; flat, emotionless, and cold.

"Tie her now," George said.

"Very good, sir."

"Now, Juliet, please don't struggle. I won't like it, and Leopold certainly won't like it. Trust me, darling, it will go much easier for you if you cooperate."

Now frustration started to simmer. She was pretty sure she could take out Leopold, but with an armed Mayfield standing there what would be the point?

Hold on, Jules. Just hold on. Your moment is coming, I know it.

She stared at the ceiling as Leopold grasped one of her ankles and bound it securely with the scarf. He then did the same with her other leg and both her hands, until she was spread out on the bed. The somber man tested all the knots, twice, and then stood aside and clasped his hands neatly behind his back.

"That's all, Leopold. Tell father I'll be down later. I'm going to take my time with her."

"Very good, sir."

"Oh, and take this." He held out the gun and Leopold grasped the weapon firmly. George smiled lovingly at her. "I don't need it anymore."

Hope burst through the terror clawing at her insides and she tried to keep it off her face. Although he was still physically more powerful than she, the absence of the gun considerably lessened his advantage.

Wait for it, Jules. Be smart. Grant and Bear taught you well, but you need to wait for the right moment. You cannot blow this.

"Very good, sir."

Juliet wondered if those three words were the extent of Leopold's vocabulary.

After the door closed behind the thin man George eased down on the edge of the bed. He reached out a hand and Juliet fought not to flinch when he dragged a finger over her cheek.

"So beautiful," he whispered.

She jumped when she felt him touch her chest. He gently picked up the pendant and his expression turned pensive, almost loving.

"Soon, this pendant will be my most treasured possession." He looked at her. "I remember the first time I saw it, the first time I saw *you*. You were . . . *breathtaking*. You still are." He paused and his expression brightened. "I want to show you something."

He stood, moved to a dresser, and returned with what looked like a jewelry box in his hands. The deep, red wood was delicately and whimsically carved, the surface shining like glass. He sat on the edge of the mattress and put the box in his lap, the front facing her.

"This belonged to my mother." A brief frown flitted over his brow, and then he opened the lid and tipped it so she could see the red, velvet lined tray inside. It was filled with dozens of pieces of jewelry, and he picked up a beautifully wrought butterfly pendant. "This is all I have left of her, this and my memories."

He replaced the butterfly and lifted a delicate gold chain. Juliet held her breath and her stomach cramped when Cassie's pendant was revealed. He glanced at her and held the necklace aloft.

Grief ravaged through her as it had that night, sharp, hard, and cutting. Tears obscured her vision and she blinked them back.

"Soon, this beautiful piece will have company, just as your sister will have company." He sighed. "I am sorry she had to die, but she shouldn't have been home."

"If you had Coulter watching me how did you *not* know she was home?"

A gentle smile curled his lips. "Coulter works for my father, not me." He sighed. "When he realized you were going to the bistro in Cassie's place Coulter called my father. My father told him to stay with you and keep you occupied, let things play out. He wanted to ensure I could handle any curveball, deal with the stress, and he was very proud."

Her throat clogged with tears. "I'll bet."

"My love, had you not gone to work in her place I had a plan to get Cassie out of the house so we could be alone. Therefore, her death is actually *your* fault, but I suppose that's unimportant now."

Juliet couldn't have said anything else if she'd wanted to. Her chest was so tight she could barely breathe. Her lungs fought to inflate against the enormous, growing pressure.

Don't listen to him, Jules. He killed me, not you.

"So, what happens now?" Juliet finally managed to whisper.

He slid the necklace back into the box, closed it, and returned it to its spot on the dresser. There was a CD player next to the jewelry box, and after he pushed a couple of buttons romantic music poured from the speakers. "Now, we consummate our union." He started to undress, his fingers working the buttons of his shirt. After draping the garment over the rocker he went to work on his shoes.

Juliet swallowed the lump that materialized in her esophagus. "Did you rape Cassie, too?"

George's head snapped up and he paused in the untying of his loafers. He straightened and looked at her strangely. "I didn't rape her, Juliet. I made love to her, just like I'm going to make love to you." He bent over and continued to pluck at the laces.

"But she was tied up, gagged," Juliet said. "How is that *not* rape?"

He glanced at her as he slipped off the first shoe. "It was for her protection. If she had fought me I might have hurt her prematurely, and that's not how this works."

This is it, Jules. This is your chance.

Juliet squeezed her eyes shut and took a deep, steadying breath. "I won't fight you, George." She forced herself to meet his gaze.

His brows drew together and he looked at her as if she'd said something in Swahili.

"You don't have to tie me, George," she repeated. Her voice sounded breathless, but because of the sheer terror compromising her airways, not because she was trying to seduce him. She hoped *he* didn't realize the difference. "I won't fight you, but afterward you'll have to bind me again . . . because of the pain. I won't be able to lie still for that."

His expression was surprised at first, and then his features hardened. "Don't lie to me, not today. Today is supposed to be special, and you're lying so you can try to get away."

"No, I'm not." She blinked rapidly against the stinging in her eyes. "If you don't trust me, and I understand why you wouldn't, then just untie my ankles. That way when you come inside me I can wrap my legs around you." She bit her lip and gave him an earnest look. "Don't you think that would be far more pleasurable than having me splayed out like this, unable to move with you, make love *with* you?"

That's it, Jules. Work it.

More tears gathered behind her eyes, but instead of fighting them she let them rise and then fall. "If I'm going to die tonight, then I want to enjoy the time I have with you, however long or short that time may be."

He looked taken aback. "Juliet—"

"*Please*, George." Her breath hitched, and she closed her eyes briefly, sending more tears sliding down her cheeks. "Let's be together . . . *really* together."

"But . . . my father won't like that." His brows drew down. "He's always told me this is how it has to be."

She gaped at him and her stomach twisted. "Is he going to *watch* us?"

A patient smile flirted with his perfect mouth. "Of course not, Juliet, it's just—"

"So don't tell him." She pleaded with her eyes. "After we make love you can tie me back up. He'll never find out, unless you say something." He seemed to ponder her words and she sensed she was winning. "Kiss me, George."

His brows shot skyward. "What?"

"Come here and *kiss* me."

He stared at her for a moment then slowly walked toward her. Juliet swallowed hard and prayed she could pull this off. The last thing she wanted was his lips on hers, but if it meant she might survive the day she was willing to do much more than kiss him.

Just imagine he's Grant, Jules. Focus on your man and do what you need to do, which, hopefully, won't involve much more than a little tonsil hockey.

Her eyelids fluttered as he eased onto the bed and straddled her hips. Juliet took a slow, deep breath. Her heart was racing so fast and hard the individual beats were indistinguishable, and her sternum ached from the rapid, steady pounding. He gazed down at her and if she didn't know who he was and what he was capable of she could almost believe he loved her.

"Ask me again," he said in a low voice.

It was obvious he wasn't accustomed to his victims *wanting* to participate, and it was even more obvious the idea turned him on. "Kiss me, *please*," she whispered.

Mayfield lowered his head and she closed her eyes as his lips brushed hers. Chills radiated outward from the point of contact and fanned over her skin, goose bumps following behind. Good. This physical response could easily be misinterpreted as desire rather than cold revulsion. He kissed her again, a little more firmly. After several seconds he pulled back slightly and she looked at him. He watched her, gauging her reaction, and she forced a tentative smile to her mouth.

"You call *that* a kiss?" she asked. "You can do better."

His expression was disbelieving for a few seconds, but then his mouth crashed down on hers, his tongue spearing inside. Juliet pictured Grant, which helped temper the nausea. There was no comparison between the two men, but thankfully her brain was able to convince her body not to totally revolt at his assault. It was as if her very DNA realized how tenuous the situation was. Her stomach calmed, her pulse eased down, and even though his kiss disgusted her she managed to return it with an enthusiasm that was surprising. The next time he pulled away his eyes were aflame with desire, his breathing rapid and shallow.

Without a word he leapt off the bed and reached for the knife on the dresser. She stiffened and fear exploded beneath her heart, sending icy, jagged shrapnel through her chest. He grabbed the hem of the sundress, and with one swift swipe, cut it up the middle, pulling a gasp from her startled lungs. Pushing the shredded material back, his gaze turned hungry as his eyes roved over her nearly naked form. She saw the flush that rose in his cheeks and the rapid rise and fall of his muscled chest.

"My God, you are perfection." He looked at her uncertainly, as if he wasn't sure what to do next.

Almost there, Jules. Almost there.

The front of his half-open pants were tented over his erection. He ran one hand slowly up the length of her right leg to the juncture of her thighs and his breathing hitched.

"Wouldn't you rather have that wrapped around your waist than tied to the bed?" she purred. "It'll feel so much better, George. Let me show you." She saw the inner debate, the anxiety in his cobalt eyes, and then his features hardened. Two more swipes of the knife and her legs were free, and then he made quick work of her panties. She gave him an inviting smile and slowly placed her right foot on his chest, deliberately baring herself to his gaze. Licking her lips she dragged her toes down his torso. She brushed his erection and he sucked in a breath.

He stared at her sex and then turned heated eyes to her. "Juliet—"

Her name was a guttural whisper and his groin swelled beneath her touch. Her gaze never left his as she slid her foot over his erection. She caressed him for a while, noting the dilated pupils and the labored breathing. When she was relatively sure she had him at her mercy her foot trailed back up and rested on his left shoulder.

"You can't make love to me from there," she said, beckoning with her sexiest voice. "Imagine how much deeper you can come inside me with my legs over your shoulders." Her left foot resumed the stroking of his erection. "It will be better than anything you've *ever* experienced."

"How do you know?" His eyes narrowed. "Is that what you did with the sheriff?"

She saw the spark of jealousy in his eyes, heard the undercurrent of anger in his voice. "Yes, but I was thinking about you, wishing it was you instead of him." She licked her lips slowly, sensuously. "Make love to me, George. Let me show you how good it can be."

He regarded her for another taut, silent moment, fire flashing in his eyes. Suddenly the knife clattered to the floor and he shed his pants and shorts. The bed dipped as he clambered onto the mattress and knelt between her thighs. Sending a silent prayer heavenward she did what she did before every audition and performance. She visualized the choreography in her mind's eye, saw each step from start to finish in a flash, and then let her body take over. Giving him a seductive smile she slid her right foot slowly up his chest.

After the back of her knee rested on his muscled shoulder she moved her left leg into the same position on the opposite side. Then she locked her ankles behind him. He was practically drooling, his head turning so he could kiss the inside of her leg. Juliet forced out a soft moan, inhaled deeply, and then jerked her knees together.

She squeezed as hard as she could, her back arching off the bed and her thighs clamping down on his neck. His eyes widened, and another second or two passed before he seemed to realize what she was doing. He started to struggle but she closed her eyes, gritted her teeth, and squeezed tighter. A scream was cut off as her leg pressed on his esophagus and then she twisted her hips sharply to the left. A choking sound escaped his wide-open mouth but he continued to struggle, his hands digging into her thighs. Sharp pain burned her legs as he raked his fingernails over her skin, but that only made her tighten her grip. She twisted her hips farther to the left in a sharp, jerking motion, nearly taking herself and him off the edge of the bed. Her right wrist and shoulder protested the overextension. Suddenly a crisp *snap* bounced off the cheery, whitewashed walls.

Juliet froze, her chest heaving, her muscles twitching as she kept her legs clamped around Mayfield's neck. She didn't know how long it was before she realized he wasn't struggling anymore. Glancing down she gulped at the sight of his bulging eyes fixed on the ceiling, and the memory of Cassie's face flashed in her mind's eye. She bit the inside of her cheek and forced the image down.

Uncertain she'd been successful, she kept her thighs locked together until several minutes passed. After all, she'd managed to fool Daniel the previous afternoon by playing possum. She wasn't about to take the chance Mayfield was using that same trick. Her right hand was numb and the shoulder joint ached, but she didn't move, her eyes intent on his face. He neither blinked, nor twitched, nor made a sound, and she couldn't feel a pulse. By the time she loosed her hold on him her breathing and heart rate were almost back to normal.

She stared at him for a few seconds and then kicked him away. He rolled onto his belly, his head at an angle that was *not* normal or natural. A few more seconds passed, and then her heart launched back into a gallop. Now she had to get out of her restraints and out of this house.

She swung her hips the opposite direction and prayed the knife was close enough to the edge of the bed for her to reach it. Her foot moved slowly and carefully over the floor, and then pain lanced through her big toe.

"Yikes."

Using her foot she felt for the handle of the knife. She had always had the ability to pick things up with her toes, a weird skill she used primarily for grossing Cassie out.

Eew. I always hated it when you did that, but bravo, Jules. You won.

Unbidden, Juliet smiled. "Not yet," she said softly. "I still have to get loose and get out of here. There are two more to deal with."

She lifted the knife onto the mattress, slowly and painstakingly, and wiggled her toes to get a better grip. Then, using her innate flexibility, she lifted her right leg up and across her body. She had to cut carefully, because she knew too much pressure would make her lose her grip on the blade. It seemed to take forever as she slowly sawed at the vibrantly colored silk. Gradually, a gash appeared in the fabric and excitement started to bubble up in her. She twisted her wrist as she continued to gently slice, and the material finally gave way with a soft *riiiip*.

Juliet stared at her hand for a moment, as if she didn't believe she was truly free.

Move, sis.

Her lungs spasmed and she inhaled sharply, taking the knife in her left hand. She made quick work of the scarf on her right hand and rubbed her bruised, chafed wrists as she moved to a sitting position. Shrugging out of the shredded dress she rested her hands on her thighs for a moment. Something warm and sticky coated her fingers and she looked down. Her legs were criss-crossed with angry, bleeding scratches, and only now did they start to sting. She blinked, wiped her hands on the patchwork quilt, and jumped to her feet. A brief check for Mayfield's pulse told her what she already knew, the man was dead. Oddly, that knowledge brought her no joy. In fact, as she looked at his face she felt nothing.

Move it, Jules!

Juliet slipped into the bathroom and pulled on her t-shirt and jeans, a pained gasp escaping her as the denim scraped over the angry red furrows on her thighs. Once dressed, she returned to the bedroom. The knife went through her belt, and after a quick search of Mayfield's pockets she found the ring with the antique key. She looked at the door as her heart rate steadily eased up. With a deep breath, she knelt, looked through the keyhole, and then pressed her ear to the same.

The music she'd heard earlier was still playing, but she also detected two male voices. Anxiety gripped her and she looked for another way out, but these windows were also barred. Then her gaze landed on the jewelry box and an idea sprang to life.

She lifted the lid and stared at Cassie's pendant for a few moments. With shaking fingers she removed her necklace, put it in the jewelry box, and picked up Cassie's chain. Her fingers shook even more as she tried to fasten her sister's pendant around her neck, and she dropped it twice. Cursing, she sucked in a breath and fought to rein in the panic.

What the heck are you doing? Get out *of here, for Pete's sake!*

"When Mayfield senior leaves this place, he's going to take his son and his trophies with him." Juliet finally fastened the clasp and closed the lid. "If for some reason I don't make it, I want to make certain the FBI can find him and finally put him away."

Ah, I see what you're doing. You always were the smart one, Jules.

Juliet knelt in front of the door and pressed her ear to the keyhole again. The muted voices from below sounded normal. Sending another silent plea to the Creator, Juliet slid the key into the lock as quietly as she could. She grimaced as she turned the key, the tumblers scraping and clacking softly. A loud click signaled the lock was open and she froze. Pulling the key from the keyhole she put it in her pocket and stood. After wiping clammy palms on her thighs she gripped the doorknob. She held her breath as she slowly turned it and pulled the door open about an inch. Pressing her eye to the opening, she looked down the long, narrow hall.

The downstairs conversation continued. Her heart vaulted into her throat as she opened the door a little further and it squeaked softly. Juliet froze. Apparently the noise hadn't traveled to the first level of the house because Mayfield and the man named Leopold continued to speak. She heard the tink of metal against glass and realized Mayfield senior was probably having breakfast. Wow. His son was upstairs *making love* to a bound, captive woman who would be murdered after coitus, and he was stuffing his mouth with Eggs Benedict.

She squeezed through the opening and stepped into the hall, her sneakers whispering over the wood floors. Moving slowly, she walked toward the stairs. When she got closer to the landing she pressed herself against the wall and inched forward. Pausing at the head of the stairs she took a deep breath, closed her eyes briefly, and then peered around the corner.

The stairs went straight down into the foyer. A laugh drew her eyes and she saw the feet of a long, elegant dining table only partially visible through an arch across the foyer from the foot of the staircase. Mayfield had to be sitting at the other end of the carved monolith, hidden from her view. She drew back as Leopold entered her field of vision when he came around the end of the table and then disappeared as he walked back in the other direction.

Can't go that way, Jules. Too exposed.

"No shit, sis," Juliet said under her breath. A pool of despair gathered in her belly. She pressed her back into the paneling and stared at the opposite wall. Her thoughts were spinning when movement out of the corner of her eye drew her gaze and she turned her head. At the opposite end of the hall was a large window, which was open, the curtain fluttering lazily. From here it didn't appear to be barred and hope broke the surface of the despair pool. She glanced down the stairs again to see if the coast was clear, and then moved quickly toward the window.

She was about halfway there when a voice from the foot of the stairs made her freeze. Backing against a closed door she listened intently.

". . . check on him."

"But, sir, he said he was going to take his time with her." Leopold sighed. "This is his final test, sir. Perhaps you should give him a little latitude."

Juliet grimaced. She hadn't bothered to close the door behind her and it would take Gregory Mayfield all of ten seconds to reach the room and realize what she'd done. Panic bloomed and raced up her throat, clogging her airways.

MOVE IT, JULIET.

Her sneakers barely touched the floor as she flew to the window. Mayfield's footfalls grew louder as he mounted the stairs, and she knew if she wasn't through that window before he reached the landing he would see her. Thankfully, the roof for the first floor was outside the window instead of a sheer drop, but she had been more than willing to make the jump if need be. She plopped her rump on the sill, swung her legs over, and glanced backwards. Mayfield had just reached the landing.

His head turned her direction. Juliet inhaled sharply and immediately dropped into a split, flattening out on the first floor roof.

She crawled forward, making sure to keep her head down. She reached the edge of the roof, grasped the edge, swung her legs around and over, and lowered herself down. She hung there for a few seconds, and then her heart nearly exploded. Directly in front of her was a window, and looking out that window was Leopold. The man's eyes went wide and his mouth fell open.

That was all Juliet saw before she dropped to the ground and sprinted for the forest. Then a feral howl split the air.

"Juliet!"

The anguish in Mayfield's voice was evident as the mournful sound reverberated off the trees. She pumped her arms faster and stretched out her legs. Another anguished cry followed her into the forest. Goose bumps fanned over her skin and a chill raced up her spine.

"I will kill you, Juliet! *I will kill you!*"

***

"Wait," Jack said, "something's happening. Pull over."

"What?" Bear asked as he eased the SUV over to the shoulder and stopped.

"The tracker is moving."

Grant's heart dropped as he leaned forward and looked over Jack's shoulder at the computer screen. They were only a couple of miles from the turnoff for the Mayfield's lake property, and his muscles were pulled so tight he felt like he was going to snap in half.

Once Grant had been freed from the crumpled Yukon and the paramedics had given him a cursory once over, he, Bear, Jack, and Daniel had raced to his house where a chopper was waiting in the field across the road. The flight to Spokane had been uneventful. After meeting up with the Washington State Police and a team from the FBI, a caravan of half a dozen police SUVs started the circuitous journey north on a two-lane stretch of state highway. About ten miles out from Mayfield's property they had crossed into a state park and picked up a trio of rangers familiar with the area. Air support was on the way, and teams from Seattle were positioning themselves to intercept Mayfield if he managed to escape them. Border security was aware and on high alert. The noose was tightening, but all Grant could think about was Juliet, and all he could do was pray.

"Oh, my God," he breathed. He closed his eyes briefly and then looked back at the screen.

"Don't go there, Grant," Jack said, reaching back to clap a hand on his shoulder.

"You know what that probably means."

"No," Bear said flatly. He met Grant's eyes in the rearview, his gaze sharp and angry. "You start letting yourself believe anything other than she's alive and we're going to get her then I'm leaving you here on the side of the road." He turned in his seat. "We are going to get her back, Grant, *alive*, and then we'll all be expecting our invitations to that wedding."

Despite the circumstances a faint smile tugged at his mouth. "Laine sure does talk a lot these days."

Bear shrugged and turned to Jack. "Which direction is it heading?"

"North, northwest," Jack replied.

Grant closed his eyes and started taking deep, even breaths, clearing his mind. It was a practice he'd gotten into during his time in the Marines, and many times it had proven very useful. It seemed to sharpen his instincts, hone his senses. He had to check the house. If Juliet was gone, he wanted to be the one to find her and not some stranger. Ice invaded his chest and he tried *not* to imagine what he might discover.

"Daniel and I will take two of the park rangers and one team and check out the house," Grant said after a few seconds of taut silence. "You and Jack and the rest of the men follow that tracker." He opened his door and then hesitated. Turning back to Jack, Grant grasped his shoulder. "I'm counting on you and Bear, Jack. Please . . . don't let him get away."

Jack's steely gaze met his. "No way, brother. No way in hell."

After a brief conversation with the rest of the team, Grant and Daniel hopped into an SUV with the Park Rangers and the convoy pulled back onto the road. When they reached the turnoff Bear stuck a hand out the window and waved as he and the others kept going. Grant waved back as he and one additional tactical team left the highway.

The gravel covered road was narrow, just big enough for the SUV. Tall trees covered the lane in a canopy of green. The house was roughly three miles from the highway and sat on nearly 20 acres of lakefront and forest.

"You're familiar with this area," Grant said to the driver, Ranger

Forbes. The dark-haired, green-eyed man nodded.

"Born and raised around here," Forbes replied.

"Don't pull up to the house. Stop about a quarter mile out and we'll hoof it in."

"You got it, Sheriff."

The front passenger, Ranger McFadden shook his head. "The Mayfields have been a fixture up here as long as I can remember. They spend most Christmases here, a lot of Spring Break seasons, and they usually come up three or four times each summer."

Daniel snorted. "Be thankful they didn't come here more often, or your female population might be considerably smaller."

McFadden looked askance at him over his shoulder, but said nothing and faced forward again. Grant glanced at the detective and knew he felt the cutting fear and barely contained dread just as keenly as he himself felt it. On impulse, he put a hand on Daniel's shoulder.

"We'll get her back," Grant said with quiet conviction. "Believe that."

Daniel didn't even look at him. "Yeah, but will she be breathing?" The last word was half swallowed by a sharp intake of breath and the detective turned his face away.

Grant closed his eyes as his throat tightened and his lungs constricted. "God, I hope so."

"Here we are, Sheriff," Forbes said as he eased the SUV as far to the side of the road as he could. The follow vehicle did the same and four heavily-armed men got out. The eight of them gathered in a circle.

"All right," Grant began, "let's fan out and surround the house." He glanced at the driver of the follow vehicle. "Jensen, you and your guys take the front while we go around back." Jensen nodded. "Remember, we have at least two suspects and the victim, so proceed with caution. I *do not* want this guy getting away, and I don't want him hurting the victim before we can get to her, so keep it swift and silent. Any questions?" He glanced at each grim face, but no one spoke. "Move out."

The four from the follow car melded into the forest walking in the direction of the house. Grant opened the back of the SUV, grabbed his rifle, and slung it over his shoulder. Forbes' eyes widened when he saw the weapon.

"Nice rifle," he said.

"Yeah," Daniel said in a subdued voice, "and if you piss him off he can shoot you from the next county."

Forbes chuckled, looked at Daniel, and when he saw the detective's expression he turned a wary eye back to Grant. He studied him briefly. "Military?"

"Marine sniper," Grant said. "Let's go."

Chapter Twenty Eight

The men kept in contact with headsets as they surrounded the house, staying hidden in the bushes. Just as Grant was about to signal for them to converge on the house, air support arrived and the pilot chimed in:

"Spotted two individuals headed west from your location on the River Gorge trail."

Grant's heart somersaulted and he keyed his mike. "Did you get a look at them?"

"Negative," the pilot replied. "Too much cover, but it looks like one is chasing the other. They're roughly a klick west from the house."

"Roger that. Keep circling and see if you can get a better look."

"Will do."

"Jensen."

"Go ahead, Sheriff."

"You and your team clear the house and outbuildings. The rest of us will see if we can catch up to our runners."

"Roger that."

Grant checked his rifle. "Form up on me Team One." Moments later Daniel and the rangers materialized out of the brush. He met Forbes' eyes. "Do you know where that trail goes?"

"Yeah, it goes to the river gorge."

"Terrain?"

"The trail is easy, but it dead ends at the river." Forbes' expression darkened. "It's more than 100 feet down to the water and 10 feet across at the narrowest point. If one of those two runners is the victim, she'll be trapped once she hits the end of the trail, and there's nowhere else to go but back . . . or down."

A distant scream tore through the quiet afternoon and Grant's head snapped around the same time his pulse jumped. It was definitely a woman's cry, and the fear that reverberated through him made his throat close up. He waited a second. His airway opened up, his pulse dropped, and that otherworldly calm enveloped him, just as it always did. Taking a deep breath he turned to Daniel. "You and McFadden take the trail and catch up."

"You got it."

Daniel and McFadden started out at a full-on sprint, their running forms quickly obscured by the thick woods. Grant turned to Forbes. "Can you find me a spot that overlooks the gorge, someplace I can get a clean shot?"

"Absolutely," Forbes said with a nod. "Follow me."

***

Juliet screamed as she was tackled from behind. Air whooshed out of her and she was momentarily dazed. The knife she'd taken from George's body skittered across the dirt and into the bushes, but her brain and muscles were still communicating. She tried to scramble away and screamed again when Mayfield's hand snagged her ankle. She flipped onto her backside and kicked viciously, rewarded when her heel made contact with his face. There was a crunch and blood flowed, but she didn't stick around to enjoy her triumph. Jumping to her feet she darted down the trail and continued to run.

The trees started to thin and she skidded to a stop as the ground fell away before her. Her arms did large circles at her sides as she teetered on the edge of the ravine, but she wasn't a prima ballerina because she lacked balance. She jumped backward and heaved a sigh of relief, but then the fear returned in a cold rush as she spun to look back down the trail. The thrashing told her Mayfield was coming. Looking around her heart sank as she realized there was nowhere to go. She turned to face the ravine and looked across to the other side, gauging the distance.

Jules, don't, it's too far.

Juliet looked over her shoulder. "Don't have much choice, Cass." Gathering every ounce of her nerve she ran about twenty feet back down the trail, then turned and sprinted toward the ravine, trying to build up as much speed as she could. She pictured the choreography in her head, saw herself sailing over the ravine and landing safely on the other side, and then she hit the edge of the cliff. Blocking out the scenery she imagined herself back in the studio, the wooden floor beneath her, the music coming from the speakers, and the other dancers cheering as she propelled herself up and forward through the air. After all, as Cassie had reminded her recently, she'd never once lost a jump competition.

Time seemed to stop and it felt like she was suspended in mid-air, aloft but unmoving. Then reality stormed back in. Her eyes widened and started to tear as the wind rushed past and she saw the ground on the other side of the ravine rush up to meet her, or at least she prayed it would. Her heart hammered against her ribs and her eyes widened as she realized it was going to be close, *very* close. A gasp of surprise escaped her when her toes hit the edge of the ledge, but before the exultation could emerge her foot slipped. Juliet screamed and fell forward, reaching for something, anything. She felt herself slipping backward just as her hand wrapped around the base of a squat, thorny bush. Sharp spines dug into the soft flesh of her palm and her fingers but she tightened her grip, gritting her teeth at the pain. It halted her digression long enough for her to roll her hips and pull herself sideways onto the edge of the ravine.

A shot split the air and she curled into a ball as the dirt near her head exploded, peppering her with rocks and sand. Her gaze flew to the opposite side of the ravine. Gregory Mayfield stood there, face contorted with rage, sighting down the barrel of the pistol. Damn it.

Juliet scrambled backwards, but the brush was too thick. She was trapped.

"Drop it, Mayfield!"

Her breath caught as the sound of Daniel's voice echoed across the chasm. He approached Mayfield from behind, pistol drawn, eyes glowing with rage. Certainly it had to be over now. Mayfield glared at her across the gap and she felt his rage as if she'd been hit with it. She shrank against the fury in his eyes, pressing as far as she could into the underbrush. Thorns stabbed her back and hands, but she didn't care. She would eat them all if it meant survival.

Mayfield lifted his hands but the pistol was still tightly gripped.

Daniel scowled. "Give me a reason to end you. I won't bother with an arrest this time."

Mayfield stared at her for several long, taut seconds and then dropped the weapon. Juliet watched as another man, dressed in the uniform of a park ranger, strode forward with a pair of handcuffs at the ready. Just as the ranger reached Mayfield the man pulled another pistol from beneath his shirt, spun, and fired point blank. The ranger flew backwards and a scream clogged her throat as Mayfield fired again. Daniel fired almost simultaneously and Mayfield staggered, dropping to his knees. Juliet's eyes widened in horror as Daniel catapulted backwards from the force of the blast. He landed flat on his back, arms and legs splayed.

"Daniel!" she screamed, scrambling to the edge of the ravine, tears welling in her eyes. Anguish scored the inside of her chest, and then she realized Mayfield had gained his feet. There was a growing stain on his left shoulder, his arm hung limply at his side. Unfortunately for her, he was right-handed. Juliet turned and tried to push through the wall of brush, but all she did was get tangled in the prickly plants.

"You killed my son," Mayfield said, his voice carrying.

Juliet faced him, her knees trembling and her heart fluttering wildly. "And you killed my sister."

"She'd still be alive if you hadn't gone to work in her place."

Anger blossomed like a sunflower, large, bright, and warm. "She'd still be alive if you and your son weren't *psycho*." The thought of her sister fanned the flames, and the temperature went up. "So would dozens of other women."

A slow, menacing smile curved his mouth, transforming his perfectly carved features into a mask of evil. "It's a rather exclusive club, one which you shall join shortly."

A cold, dark surge snuffed out her rage as he lifted the pistol. Juliet raised her chin in defiance and blinked back tears. "Sorry, little sister. I tried."

Her body jerked as the shot split the air and she dropped to her knees. She looked down at her chest, expecting the burgundy flow to darken her t-shirt, and then she realized she felt nothing. And, her shirt remained white. Her head snapped up and she watched in disbelief as Mayfield collapsed sideways. The gun skittered over the edge of the ravine and ticked off the rocks as it made its way to the river. He stared at her, unblinking and lifeless, his brains splattered across the ground, and then his body rolled and dropped off the edge of the cliff into the ravine, following the gun. The dull thud of his body hitting the rocks was far more unpleasant than the clicking noise the pistol had made. Juliet grimaced, clapped her hands over her ears, and fought a wave of nausea.

The soft *splash* from below brought her back to reality and she leaned one hip into the ground. Grant. She closed her eyes and took in great gulps of air, and then the laughter started. At first it was soft, but then it overwhelmed her and her ribs began to ache. She was alive. *Alive.* Both Mayfield men were dead. A wave of relief roared over her, so strong it would have buckled her knees had she been standing. The laughs turned to tears at some point and she wasn't sure when. Juliet covered her face with her hands and rocked slowly back and forth, sobs wracking her.

You did it, Juliet. You won.

"Juliet."

Her head snapped up and her jaw dropped when she saw Daniel standing on the opposite side of the ravine. He had his hands on his thighs, a pained expression on his handsome face. The ranger stirred, and Daniel reached to help him up. Her eyes went wide. When Daniel saw her expression he gave her a wan smile.

"We're wearing vests." He lifted his shirt briefly to display the bullet-resistant vest. "Wasn't sure there'd be gunplay, but it's better to be safe than sorry." He met her gaze. "Are you okay? Did they hurt you?"

She shook her head and slowly stood, her energy depleted and her muscles nearly limp with relief. It was over. *Really* over. And just like that, the shadows that had dominated her life for a year and a half were gone. Juliet closed her eyes and turned her face to the sun.

"George is dead," she said. She basked for another couple of seconds and then met Daniel's gaze. "I killed him."

His expression was somber as he stared at her. Then he nodded once. "Good girl."

"Are you *out* of your *ever-loving* mind?!" Grant shouted across the ravine.

Juliet turned and her heart soared as he stalked to the edge of the ravine, his eyes dark and his brow drawn down in a fierce scowl. His rifle hung over his shoulder and he shrugged it off, propping it against a nearby tree.

"What the *hell* were you thinking, leaping over that ravine like you were on stage somewhere?" He planted his fists on his hips and glared at her. "Are you *trying* to get yourself killed?"

She didn't care that he was angry. She was so happy to see him that all she could do was grin. In spite of the abrasions and lacerations on his face, no doubt from the accident, he was the most beautiful man she'd ever seen. Her grin widened. "I was trying *not* to get myself killed, in case you hadn't noticed."

He dropped his chin and took several deep breaths. When he finally lifted his eyes to hers, those amazing bedroom eyes, the concern and relief she saw there made her heart spin and flutter like *it* was dancing.

"Are you okay?" he asked in a low voice.

Juliet smiled and bit her lip. "Yeah," she replied with a nod. "I'm just not sure how to get back across." She pretended to gauge the distance and shrugged. "I guess if I made it once I can make it again."

Grant's eyes widened and he held his hands in front of him. "No, no, no, just stay there. Chopper's coming." He pushed his hat back on his head and rubbed his brow. "You are going to be the death of me."

"At least you'll die smiling."

***

Grant plopped down on the edge of the queen-sized bed in the nondescript hotel room, exhausted and so drained he was sure he could sleep sitting up with his eyes open. Now that the adrenaline was wearing off the aches and pains started to manifest, and his muscles grew stiffer with each passing minute. No doubt after-effects from the car accident were contributing to his discomfort. He rubbed his neck absently and sighed. His debrief was done, and Bear and Jack were seeing to Juliet's debrief at the local state police office. When they were finished the three of them would be checking in. He guessed he had two to three hours before he saw her again.

The memory of her leaping across that gorge flashed in his mind and he squeezed his eyes shut with a grimace. His heart had literally stopped, his lungs pressing against it until he thought it would pop out of his chest, and when she had slipped he almost dropped his rifle. After she found a handhold and pulled herself onto the ledge relief had sucked the bones from his limbs. Then Mayfield had started shooting.

Fear had roared through him in a seismic wave, his insides vibrating with the force when Mayfield had aimed the pistol at Juliet. Thankfully, the shot impacted the ground near her head, but he knew Mayfield wouldn't miss again, not from less than four yards. Then the sound of Daniel shouting had drawn his gaze. In the next three seconds the ranger and Daniel went down. Grant's finger slid to the trigger as Mayfield turned toward Juliet. A couple seconds slogged by with unnatural slowness, but when Mayfield raised the pistol again that was all it took for him to take aim and end the man's life. As soon as Grant saw Mayfield's head explode he jumped to his feet, shouldered the rifle, and sprinted for the ravine with Forbes on his heels.

And so, Juliet's ordeal was over. *Which means she can move on now.*

Grant opened his eyes and looked at his reflection in the mirror hanging on the wall across from the bed. Something cold and thick snaked through his insides, winding around his heart and squeezing. He took a deep breath and held it until his lungs started to burn. Letting it out slowly, he chided himself. No use in worrying about something that couldn't be changed. With a sigh, he stood, dropped his hat and gun belt on the bed, and then strode into the bathroom. Maybe a shower would help dissipate the chill in his middle. He doubted it, but there was nothing else he could do at the moment except wait.

***

Juliet trailed behind Jack as he walked down the hall. Despite her exhaustion, with each step her excitement grew. A glance at the numbers on the doors told her they were almost to her room, which meant she would see Grant shortly. Jack stopped in front of a door, took the keycard from his breast pocket, and opened the nondescript panel. He spun to face her and handed the key over.

"Your suite, my lady," he said with a wink and a quick grin.

Juliet walked into the room and dropped the two plastic bags she held onto the bed. After Jack had finished her debrief he'd taken her to Walmart to purchase toiletries and clothes. She didn't want to like the handsome FBI agent with the steely silver eyes, but it was hard not to. He was sweet and funny and considerate, much like Grant.

Her head came around when she heard knocking. Jack stood at the door across the hall, tapping lightly. Moments later the door swung open and Grant's body filled the frame. He met Jack's eyes and when Jack jerked his head in her direction Grant's gaze swung toward her. He exhaled sharply and strode across the hall.

Her heart slammed against the inside of her chest and her eyes stung as he enveloped her, his arms tightening around her and his cheek pressed to the top of her head. She squeezed her eyes shut.

"I'll leave you two alone," Jack said.

"Thanks, Jack," Grant whispered.

"I didn't do anything, bud, but you're welcome," Jack replied. "Talk to y'all in the morning."

Juliet clung to him as the door closed. His muscles were taut and bunched, his breathing sharp and shallow. She buried her face against his chest, clutched the back of his shirt, and suddenly her body reacted. Even though it had been hours since the incident with the Mayfields, it was as if her brain was just realizing what had happened. She started to shake and her lungs refused to inflate.

"Breathe, darlin'," he whispered. "Breathe."

Fear chilled her, and then panic washed over her in an even icier wave. Grant pulled her closer, cupping her head in one hand, but she still couldn't inhale. Dizziness spun her.

"You're safe, baby," he said. "I'm right here."

Her chest was heavy and her throat burned, tears squeezing out from beneath tightly closed lids.

"I'm so sorry, darlin'," he choked out. "I promised you I wouldn't let him hurt you, and I let you down."

The self-reproach she heard in his voice sparked something angry and indignant inside her. Heat devoured the chill, and the crushing weight in her chest disappeared. Suddenly free, her lungs spasmed and she sucked in a breath.

"You didn't let me down," she said softly, pulling back enough to look him in the face. "*You* saved me, Grant." Regret bubbled in her midsection and she dropped her chin. "I'm just sorry you had to kill someone to do it."

"I'm not."

His voice was flat, devoid of emotion. Juliet shook her head and gulped. "I see the hurt in your eyes when you talk about your time in the Marines, Grant." She laid her brow against his sternum. "You try to hide it, but I can tell you feel more than you let on."

"Hey." He released her and cupped his hands around her neck, using his thumbs to tip her face to his. "I *do* feel more than I show, but not in the way you think." His brows drew together. "I don't regret the lives I had to take, Juliet. I regret the lives I couldn't save in spite of the lives I took." He studied her for several long, silent moments. "I'm sorry I couldn't keep you from following in my footsteps, but I am *so* glad you did it anyway." He sighed, shook his head, and pulled her back against his chest. "I didn't save you, darlin'. You saved yourself."

"I would never have known how if not for you," she whispered. "Thank you."

He chuckled and the tension seemed to fall off him. "Thank Bear. He taught you how to kill Mayfield with his own thumb. I just taught you how to cheat."

And you were an excellent student, Jules. I'm proud of you, big sister.

Now I'll get to see my nieces and nephews.

Juliet smiled at Cassie's intrusion but didn't bother to reply. She relaxed against him and inhaled his scent, letting it wrap around her. He was warm, strong, and solid, like an impenetrable fortress of flesh and bone.

So, what are you going to do now, sis? That decision I told you you'd have to make is looming.

Juliet frowned. "Grant?"

"Yes, darlin'?"

"Make me forget all about this?"

Chicken. You're only postponing the inevitable.

"Please?" she added.

Grant pressed a kiss to her hair. "Yes, ma'am."

***

"So, are we going back to Evergreen tomorrow?" Juliet asked. Grant's heart beat steadily against her cheek, his fingers running absently up and down her arm. They lay in the middle of the king-sized bed, naked, limbs entwined. She flattened her hand on his stomach, his skin was warm and smooth beneath her fingers.

He inhaled deeply and sighed. "That's something we need to talk about."

She leaned up on one elbow and looked at him, a flutter of uneasiness brushing her heart. "Why?"

Those amazing bedroom eyes met hers and she saw the flash of anxiety in their chocolaty depths. "I talked to Miss Nicole earlier." He looked away from her and frowned. "Somehow the media found out about my involvement, and the vultures have descended. The hotel is booked solid, all the local campgrounds and rentals are full, and there are news vans clogging up downtown and all the secondary streets." He grimaced and met her gaze. "Nicole says there are almost as many reporters in town as there are residents."

Juliet groaned and put her head back on his chest. "Great."

He was quiet for a few seconds. "Do you have somewhere you can go, someone you can stay with for a while, until all this shit blows over?"

That flutter of uneasiness sprouted full-blown wings and started swooping around her chest cavity. A lump hurtled into her throat and she swallowed hard as she sat up and faced him. "You want me to leave? Why?"

Suddenly she wished she'd kept her mouth shut, because she wasn't sure she wanted to know the answer. Had his feelings changed? Maybe he'd realized that what he thought was love wasn't. A bolt of cold pain punched through her and she felt the tears sting behind her eyes. As if sensing her turmoil he pressed a hand to her cheek.

"No, darlin', I don't want you to leave," he replied, a small smile flirting with his mouth, "but this isn't a fixed spotlight. You thought having *Mayfield* stalk you was bad? Think how bad it will be with every media outlet from L.A. to New York following you around." His thumb rubbed slowly over her lower lip. "Apparently they're already camped out in front of my house, both houses actually."

"*Both*?" Juliet stared at him. "You have more than one?"

He shrugged. "I have a two-bedroom ranch just outside the county line."

"Two houses *and* the studio?" She blinked at him. "Being Sheriff must pay well."

"Well, when you're receiving combat pay, special-duty pay, re-enlistment bonuses, and have nowhere to spend anything, all that money adds up fast." He gave her a smile. "I've always been more of a saver than a spender."

Juliet let that sink in, realizing how much she *didn't* know about him. She wrapped her arms around her legs and rested her chin on her knees. Grant twirled a long strand of hair around his finger.

"Where were you headed when you left Seattle?" he asked softly.

She shrugged. "I told you. I didn't really have a destination in mind."

"You had to have at least *considered* a final stop," he coaxed. "Most people don't just take off without having an idea of where they're going to land."

Juliet chewed her lip for a moment. "Well, before George attacked me in the garage I was thinking of visiting my friend, Amanda." She glanced at him. "We danced together in New York until she blew out her Achilles. Now she choreographs for the Chicago Ballet."

"Would she mind you staying with her for a few weeks?"

A few weeks? Her throat tightened but she shook her head. "I don't think so. She's asked me to visit a dozen times if once. I was always too busy to go."

Grant sat up and slid his fingers around the back of her neck, but she couldn't bear to look at him. His thumb traced her cheekbone and she closed her eyes against the onslaught of emotions that crawled determinedly up her throat.

"You can call her in the morning and find out for sure," he said. "If she's okay with that, we'll put you on the next plane out of Spokane to Chicago."

Juliet clenched her teeth and closed her eyes. "Okay."

"Juliet."

"Yeah?"

"Look at me, darlin'."

Juliet swallowed convulsively. She looked into his smiling brown eyes and her heart seized up. When she saw the concern on his face she knew she wasn't fooling him at all. A pensive smile curved his mouth and he leaned toward her.

"My feelings haven't changed," he said softly. "If you want to brave the journalistic gauntlet I will shield you as best I can." He rested his brow against hers. "I just wanted to spare you that."

Juliet closed her eyes. She wanted to be selfish, stay with him, but the thought of reporters shoving microphones in her face and photographers screaming her name made her stomach curl up and knot. And if Grant got in trouble protecting her? She shuddered.

"I'll go visit Amanda," she said, lacing her fingers through his. "And then, when the dust settles and the predators lose interest . . . ." Her voice trailed off and she opened her eyes. "I will be knocking down your door."

"You won't have to knock it down, darlin'," he said with a chuckle. "It'll always be open for you."

He covered her mouth with his and her body sang. Warm tingles spread through her as he explored her mouth. She wound her hands into his hair and straddled his hips. His arms snuck around her waist and pulled her tightly against his chest, and tension coiled in her belly.

"Are you going to ask me to make you forget again?" he asked against her mouth. "I'd be more than happy to do that for you." He trailed his lips over her jaw and down her throat.

Juliet gasped, that ache coiling tighter as he hardened beneath her. "No. I want you to give me something to remember you by, so I'll have the burning desire to see you again."

He laughed softly. "I can do that, too."

Chapter Twenty Nine

Juliet stared at the contract in her hands, her insides pitching and twisting.

Holy crap, Jules. That decision you've been avoiding has just plopped itself in front of you, and there's no more putting it off.

"Isn't it exciting?" Amanda asked, her green eyes dancing. She had just returned from rehearsal, her black hair put up in a soft French twist and her dancewear hidden by the large overcoat. She bounced up and down on the balls of her feet and clasped her hands beneath her chin.

The gesture reminded her of Cassie, and Shelby, and the thought of Shelby reminded her of Grant. Her heart joined her other internal organs in their spinning dance and for a second she thought she'd be sick.

"I don't understand," Juliet said, her throat so tight she could barely form the words.

Amanda toyed with the scarf around her neck. "Well . . . remember when I asked you to fill in during technique class last week, and then the company talked you into doing one of your solos from Cinderella?"

Juliet gulped and nodded.

Amanda shrugged and looked at the ceiling. "Well . . . Ivan was watching."

Juliet stared at her.

Amanda grabbed her hands. "He *really* loved you, Juliet. He told me he hasn't seen anyone dance with passion like that in a very long time. Why else would he offer you a principal contract mid-season?" Amanda pleaded with her siren eyes, a practice that usually got the petite beauty whatever she wanted from almost anyone. "You have *no* idea how pissed some of the corps are going to be when they find out he bypassed them for you. He just doesn't *do* that."

"Which is even more reason to turn it down," Juliet pointed out.

"This is an opportunity anyone wearing pointe shoes would *kill* for," Amanda replied as her perfectly arched brows pulled together, marring her alabaster forehead with a deep frown line. Juliet almost laughed because she knew if Amanda could see herself she'd be horrified. Her next move would've been a call to her cosmetic surgeon demanding Botox.

"I'm not staying here, Mandy," Juliet said. "I *told* you that."

Amanda eased onto the barstool next to her, her expression somber. "Are you *really* planning to go back to that little-bitty town in the middle of nowhere? They don't even have a *Starbucks*, Jules."

Juliet's eyes stung and she pulled her cell phone from a pocket. She opened the photograph she'd taken of Grant while he was sleeping and stared at it, warmth filling that space in her chest and calming her inner upheaval. She'd given Amanda a brief, non-detailed synopsis of where she'd been and what had happened the past several months, but she'd left out the part about falling in love with Grant. Why, she didn't know.

"You're right, Mandy, they don't have a Starbucks." She looked at the picture for a few more seconds, then placed the phone on the counter and slid it toward her friend. "They have something *much* better than overpriced coffee." With a sigh she stood and walked slowly to her room. After closing the door she threw herself across the bed, rolled onto her side, and pulled a pillow to her chest.

It had been three weeks since she'd seen him, and the media furor had yet to die down. Bear and Jack had caught Mayfield's man, Leopold, at the Canadian border with George's body in the cargo area under a tarp and the jewelry box in the front passenger seat. With the Mayfield men both dead, Leopold and Coulter had volunteered all the information they knew, especially when the Feds threatened to charge them with capital crimes. Between confessions from the minions, the jewelry box, and evidence found at the Mayfield's home, nearly ten missing persons' cases had been closed, and nearly twice that number were connected to the father/son duo and under investigation.

She and Grant talked almost every night and Skyped every few days, but it wasn't the same as being encompassed by her big, beautiful sheriff. She missed him, his laugh, that sinfully sexy grin, and those bedroom eyes that saw her more clearly than she saw herself. No matter how much she missed him, she knew he had been right to send her to Chicago. The move had kept the media attention off her, and for that she was thankful. Every time another case was linked to Gregory or George Mayfield, Grant's name inevitably came up and they started hounding him again. She actually saw more of him on the news than she did via webcam. Tears stung and she squeezed her eyes shut.

A soft knock drew her attention and Amanda peeked in the room. "Can I come in?" she asked.

Juliet nodded and rolled onto her side facing her friend. Amanda sat on the edge of the bed and handed back her cell phone.

"I'm so sorry, Jules." She shrugged gracefully. "At least now I know where you've been since you got here, because your mind *definitely* hasn't been in Chicago." Her expression turned inquisitive. "He's the one who broke open the father-son serial killer case, isn't he?"

All Juliet could do was nod. Her throat was tight, her chest heavy and throbbing.

"I recognize him from the news reports you keep watching, although I must say, he looks *much* better shirtless." An impish grin curved her rosebud of a mouth, but it faded when Juliet didn't react. Amanda sighed. "So, the question is . . . ." She paused and tipped her head to the side. "Which one are you going to choose?"

Aaaand, thanks to Amanda for asking the $64,000 question. Have I mentioned how much I don't like this woman?

Juliet grimaced and barely stopped herself from telling Cassie to shut up. She bit her lip, pulled the pillow closer, and buried her face against the soft cotton. Her move to Seattle had been precipitated by a growing dislike for the big city, and the need to be closer to her family. Correction: closer to Cassie. Now, she had no family to speak of, not really, and while Chicago wasn't New York it was still a big city.

Be honest, Jules. You didn't think you'd have to make a choice, did you? You thought this shit-storm would just blow over, you'd go back to Grant, and you'd live happily ever after. Thank you, Life, for throwing a monkey wrench into the works. AGAIN.

"I'm done dancing," Juliet said, her voice muffled against the pillow.

"Are you *kidding* me?" Amanda asked, her tone rising with the question and disbelief. "Y'know, you're the kind of dancer that dancers like *me* hate."

The venom in Amanda's voice startled her. Juliet lowered the pillow enough to look at her friend. Amanda's green eyes were narrowed and spitting fire.

"Exactly what kind of dancer am I that you're not?" Juliet asked.

"I'm one of those dancers who actually have to work, sweat, and practice," Amanda shot back, her color brightening. "Unlike *you*, to whom dancing is as easy as breathing. You're one of the gifted ones, Jules, and you're passing on an opportunity like this? For a *man?*"

Anger sparked in Juliet's chest and she jackknifed to a sitting position. "*Why* do people keep saying I don't practice?" She raked her hands through her hair. "I practice *all the time.*"

That seemed to deflate Amanda's indignant sails a bit. "I know you do," she said with a small sigh. She trailed her fingers over the bedspread. "But, you don't *have* to." Her shoulders drooped. "You have no idea how easy it is to dislike you, Juliet. When you first started in New York I sort of hated you, but then I got to know you." Amanda gave her a quick, ashamed glance. "You're one of my closest friends now, but I still envy your talent if you want to know the truth."

Juliet couldn't contain her surprise. Envy was common in the performing arts world because there *were* those who had a natural ability and didn't have to work as hard at some things, but Amanda had never indicated she felt that way. The fact her friend had hidden how she truly felt stung.

Bitch. I never liked her, Jules. Even though I never spent any real time with her, I never liked her, and now I know why. She was a suck-ass friend anyway. You know she'd stab you in the back in a second if it meant getting one of your roles, if she was still dancing of course.

"When did you start lessons, Mandy?" Juliet asked point blank. Although she and Amanda were friends, Juliet hadn't belabored the facts of her upbringing. Complaining about how she'd been raised would only garner another label, one less positive than *gifted.* "How old were you when you started taking formal lessons?"

Amanda blinked at her. "I was seven, I think. Or eight. Why?"

"I was in pointe shoes by the age of eight," Juliet said softly. "I was *three* when I started taking lessons, and when you were just starting I was already enrolled at the San Francisco Ballet's School of Ballet."

Hurt blossomed in her chest, and she knew it was only partly because of Amanda. She'd been raw and aching since leaving Grant, and knowing one of her only friends envied her just added to the constriction in her chest. She stood and walked to the door. "Until you've danced in *my* shoes, don't *ever* say I have it easier than you do." Amanda's voice stopped her as she left the room.

"If you didn't come here to dance, why did you come to Chicago at all?" her friend asked.

Juliet thought about it for a moment. "Great question, Mandy. I've been asking myself that for days now."

***

"The Chicago Ballet offered me a principal contract," Juliet said in subdued tones.

Grant's heart lurched uncomfortably and started to throb against the inside of his chest. He forced a smile and gripped the phone a little tighter. "Really? That's great, Juliet. They'll be lucky to have you."

The line was silent for several seconds, and when she did speak again he heard the quiet indignance in her voice.

"I'm not taking the job."

"Maybe you should."

Where the *hell* had that come from? Grant ground his teeth together and tried to take slow, deep breaths despite his racing heart.

The silence stretched out longer this time.

"Why would you say that?" she asked in a whisper.

He mentally kicked himself, but his brain still didn't pay attention and for some reason his mouth kept going. "Do you really want to pass up an opportunity like that?"

"I didn't come here for that *opportunity*," Juliet argued.

Grant rubbed his brow. "And yet, there it is."

"Just like *you* were."

He went silent this time. This entire scene was too familiar, too painful, and too close to home. The memory started to play.

"If you want me to stay, I'll stay," Laine said softly, her hand pressed to his cheek. "I'll go to MSU, become a vet, come back here, and open up my own practice. I don't have to go to Harvard."

"You've wanted to be a doctor all your life, Lainey," Grant replied. As he said the words his heart shattered. "You've worked so hard and turning down a full-ride scholarship would just be stupid. As much as I want you to stay, you

have *to go. You* know *that.*"

Telling Laine to pursue her dream had been more painful than ingesting broken glass, until she'd actually left for Harvard. *That* had been like breathing, swallowing, and swimming in the razor-like shards, and it had also solidified his decision to enlist. Although he regretted that he and Laine had never been together, he had never once regretted telling her to go to medical school. He had taken leave from the Marines to attend her graduation, and no one had been prouder of her than him.

"I won't keep you from pursuing your dream, Juliet," he said softly but with full conviction. "I care about you too much."

"I've already achieved my dream," Juliet said. "When I was a little girl all I wanted to be was a ballerina. I've *done* that."

"And you're still living it," he said, hoping the words didn't sound as forced as they felt.

"I *was*, until the company let me go and Mayfield killed Cassie." She paused. "Now, I have a new dream, and it doesn't involve putting my toe shoes back on in Chicago."

He squeezed his eyes shut and fought for breath. "I don't want to be the reason you stop dancing, Juliet."

"I can dance *anywhere*, Grant," she replied.

"Then I don't want to be the reason you stop *performing*," he bit out. "You can't *perform* in Evergreen."

"Why not? There's that great gazebo where we *performed* after our first date. And if that isn't enough attention for me, I'll just go to the health club and use the aerobics room. I won't be ten minutes into Giselle before Eric and half the bodybuilders leave their weight room to watch me dance."

He made an exasperated sound. "You're not done yet, Juliet. You're too good to quit now. You'd only miss it and end up resenting me."

"How could I resent *you* for a decision *I'm* making?" The disbelief in her tone was obvious. "And of course I'll miss it, just like I will if I keep dancing until I hurt myself or age out. I have another five to seven years in this particular career, barring any serious injuries, but eventually I *will* have to retire. When I do, whenever that is and for whatever reason, I *will* miss it, even if you're *not* part of the equation."

"I don't want to *be* part of *that* equation."

"But you already are." She took a deep breath and exhaled slowly. "I left New York for a couple reasons, Grant. One, I was tired of living in the big city and two . . . I missed my family. Everyone told me taking a position as principal with Ballet Northwest was a mistake, a step down, but I didn't care. I was at the pinnacle of my career in New York, but I just wanted to be around Cassie again. The fact I could do that in Seattle and *still* dance was just icing on the cake. Then Cassie was taken from me and my parents disowned me."

Grant wished his heart would stop pounding so mercilessly against the inside of his sternum. The bone was starting to ache and he absently rubbed his chest. "Juliet . . . ."

"Then *you* entered my life," she said, the hitch in her voice hinting at tears barely contained. "My heart isn't in performing anymore, Grant, because it's in Evergreen with you and Autumn and Miss Nicole and everyone else who welcomed and befriended me without even *knowing* I was a dancer." She laughed shortly, but the sound held only hurt, not humor. "Outside of my father and Cassie, you're the only relationship I have that isn't somehow based on ballet. You liked me for *me*, not because I was a ballerina. Correct me if I'm wrong."

That last sentence was laced with accusation, daring him to correct her, and although he wanted to he couldn't. He'd felt the pull the second they'd made eye contact that first day. It didn't matter one bit to him what she did for a living. She was his Juliet, the foil to his frustrated Romeo, the woman who had captured his heart when he wasn't entirely sure he'd had any semblance of a heart left. Now that she'd proven he did, it hurt like hell.

"You're not wrong," he whispered, rubbing his brow as an ache gathered there.

"Then I'm going to say one more thing," she said in a rush. She paused. "Okay, two more things before I hang up."

He couldn't speak, his throat was too tight with anxiety, his vocal chords caught fast in a death grip of uncertainty.

"First thing." She cleared her throat. "I *love* you, Grant Donovan, more than I thought I could love anyone."

I love you, too.

"Second thing: if you don't want me back in Evergreen then send me a text saying so because I couldn't bear to hear you say the words. *But* . . . you have to base your decision to send me that text on *you*, not *me*."

"What do you mean?"

"If you don't want to see me again it has to be because you don't have feelings for me and can't even imagine a future with me. *Do not* send me that text because you think you're doing me some sort of favor."

"Juliet—"

"I mean it, Grant." Her tone was flat but serious. "I'm not a young Laine who hasn't had a chance to chase her dreams. I'm a grown woman and I've lived my dream. I achieved more by the age of 16 than most people do in an entire lifetime and I want something else now. If you don't want that same thing . . . ."

Her voice caught and he knew if he could see her she'd be fighting tears. The thought he was causing her pain made his insides curdle and his protective instincts roared to the forefront.

"If you don't want the same thing," she continued in a hushed, tear-filled voice, "*that's* why you should tell me to stay away, *not* because you want to be a martyr."

It took him several seconds to realize she'd hung up. He couldn't move, the phone still pressed tightly to his ear, as if by doing so he could will her back onto the line. His chest was so taut his lungs couldn't inflate, and a pounding at the base of his skull worked quickly upward and outward. *I love you, Grant Donovan.*

Frustration curled through him like a hot, venomous serpent. It coiled and rippled, scalding his insides as it wound tighter around his internal organs. Then, that emotion that he despised above all others rose in a cold, invading rush. Guilt. How could he ask her to turn down what others dancers would kill each other to get? She was being handed a golden ticket and even though he had no right, all he wanted to do was beg her to come home.

Home. The word sent him off balance for a second. He'd only known her a few weeks, but the time she'd spent in his house had never once felt awkward. It felt like she belonged there, with him. He briefly imagined a future with her, waking up to her every morning, dancing with her, falling asleep with her each night. The sudden, unwelcome image of Juliet, her belly rounded with child, flashed in his mind and a strange warmth and contentment filled him. She would look glorious pregnant. He steeled himself and quashed the thought like a bug. No. He couldn't do that to her.

A growl coiled in his throat and he clenched his teeth. He pulled up his text menu, highlighted the conversation with Juliet, and started typing.

Stay in Chicago. It would never work between us. His finger hovered over the send key, but he couldn't press it. With a growl he stuffed the phone in his pocket. *Later*, he thought to himself. *This is one battle I'm going to have to work up to.*

*****

Juliet lifted the hood of the rental car and stared at the engine, silently cursing it a thousand ways from Sunday. It wasn't the radiator hose this time, and she had no clue what she was looking for. A glance up and down the road confirmed what she already knew; she was alone and she doubted anyone would be driving by anytime soon. This was the road to Evergreen, after all, and the only people who traversed it were heading to see relatives, on their way to Canada, or were just plain lost. She was none of those things.

The chill burrowed through her thermal leggings and heavy jacket, snow whirling in the softly keening wind like mini-tornados. It was getting colder by the second and visibility was shrinking. The other side of the lonely highway was barely visible now. She pulled the hood of her jacket over her hair and slid back into the driver's seat, closing the door a little more forcefully than was necessary. The window shuddered but remained intact. Oddly, that disappointed her.

She waited nearly an hour, the temperature dropping rapidly inside the car now that the damn thing was dead and she had no heater. Pulling her cell phone from her purse she stared at it. The car wasn't the only thing that was dead.

Juliet put the phone aside and hugged herself as the chill from outside fully invaded the car and started to burrow through her. Her breath turned into frothy puffs of condensation with each exhale. The cold burned her lungs. Snow had been piled high on both sides of the two-lane stretch of asphalt, yet she couldn't see anything now through the fogged up windows. The realization hit her that she could die of hypothermia if help didn't get to her soon, but death was actually the least of her worries on this little road trip. At least it had been.

She closed her eyes as weariness overcame her. Part of her understood that drowsiness was part of the process when one's core body temperature dropped. Another part didn't care. Minutes continued to creep by and she realized she could no longer feel her fingers or toes. Oh, well, there was nothing she could do about it. She had donned all her cold-weather gear after the engine gave out, but apparently her idea of cold-weather gear and the kind of cold-weather gear one needed in Montana during a snowstorm was vastly different. She yawned and closed her eyes as the sleepiness overcame her.

Wake up, Jules! Don't you dare go to sleep, do you hear me?

Cassie was yelling at her and she tried to open her eyes, but she couldn't.

Damn it, Juliet Hall! WAKE THE HELL UP!

She jolted upright at the shouting in her head.

Do something, Jules. You can't just sit there.

Juliet scrubbed her face with her hands, sighed, and got out of the car. "Well, here goes nothing."

She started walking, staying close to the edge of the highway. Falling snow was actually one of her favorite things, but not like this. She pulled her scarf up over her face and tucked her hands in her armpits. It was going to be a long walk to Evergreen, if she made it that far . . . .

***

Grant's phone rang and he put it to his ear without looking at the caller ID. "Donovan."

"Sheriff Donovan?" a soft, female voice asked. It was a voice he was unfamiliar with and he sat up in his chair a little straighter.

"That's me. With whom am I speaking?"

"My name is Amanda Penner. I'm the woman Juliet's been staying with."

He was mildly puzzled. Juliet had told him that her estimation of the depth of their friendship had been overly optimistic, and wasn't holding up under scrutiny, so he wondered why Amanda was calling *him*. "Afternoon, Miss Penner, how can I help you?"

There was a long pause and a shiver tingled up his spine. It was a familiar feeling, a feeling that told him something was about to go horribly wrong.

"Have you heard from Juliet?"

Now those tingles turned into a full-on buzzing. He was hit with the sudden, chilling knowledge that he wasn't going to like this conversation. "No, why?"

"Well," she began, sniffling, "she was on her way to see you. Her plane should've landed in Helena hours ago, and she said she'd call me when she got to Evergreen, but I haven't heard from her and all of my calls are going straight to voicemail."

It felt like a hand fisted itself around his throat. A glance out the window made that hand squeeze until his esophagus ached. He'd decided to sleep in the station's bunk room because, as familiar with driving Evergreen's roads as he was, going home in near white-out conditions didn't really appeal to him. Better to wait it out at the office than risk driving off the road. His new Yukon had OnStar with a prepaid two-year subscription, but if something happened to him even emergency vehicles would be hard-pressed to help.

Grant closed his eyes and concentrated on clearing his mind until the stress inoculation kicked in. Then he said, "I want her flight number, flight details, and the name of the car rental agency. *Now.*"

***

Juliet continued to put one booted foot in front of the other, though she knew her pace was seriously flagging. She'd started keeping track of the mile markers after she left her car, and the one she had just stumbled past told her she'd traveled about seven miles. She had no idea how long she'd been out in the snow, but her entire body was numb. A glance at the sky didn't reveal the time, other than the light seemed to be waning.

Keep going, Jules. Someone is bound to drive by soon.

Although she wanted to believe her sister, she wasn't sure Cassie believed herself. The road to Evergreen was not a busy thoroughfare, and with near blizzard conditions, the chances of someone venturing out and inadvertently coming to her rescue were almost zero. Juliet's teeth chattered, snow clung stubbornly to her eyelashes, the wind stinging over the exposed skin of her brow and temples. She wore thick, winter gear, but it wasn't made for prolonged hikes through the snow and it was nowhere near waterproof. Hell, she wasn't sure it was water *resistant.* Her winters in New York had been spent indoors, or clothed in just enough outerwear to keep her warm from the door to the cab and back.

Her vision started to gray on the edges. She focused on what she thought was the apex of the road, but with the snow she couldn't be sure. She kept walking. Until she stumbled. Air whooshed out of her as she landed face first in the snow. She was so cold she felt brittle, as if her bones had been flash-frozen and would shatter.

Get up, Juliet. Get up NOW.

But, she couldn't. She'd been frozen with fear before, but until this day she'd never actually been *frozen.* It pretty much sucked as far as she was concerned. Her muscles refused to cooperate, and just breathing was exhausting. She closed her eyes, planning only a second or two of rest, her eyelids unnaturally heavy.

JULIET!

Her sister was shouting again, but soon even that faded to nothingness as drowsiness sent her toward the brink of oblivion. In the back of her mind she thought she heard sirens but chalked it up to her brain seizing up from the cold. If only she could've seen Grant one more time . . . .

Grant scanned the road, his windshield wipers jumping frantically back and forth. No one had heard from Juliet since she'd left for the airport, more than eight hours past, and the dread in his belly was colder than the North wind howling outside.

He came around a curve and something in his periphery caught his eye. Slamming on the brakes, the Yukon yawed wildly, but he'd already thrown it in park and jumped out. He only hoped he was in time.

They didn't usually have such frigid temperatures in mid September, but a freak cold-front had moved down from Alaska through Canada, blanketing much of the area in snow and sending temperatures plummeting. Even those in Evergreen, who were accustomed to harsh winters, had been caught off guard by the sudden shift. He and his deputies had spent the better part of two days doing welfare checks on the older citizens in town, and more than half of them had been unprepared for the cold snap. He had fired up more fuel oil furnaces in the past day and a half than in the previous two years.

He ran to the odd shaped, snow-covered mound on the side of the road. It was the size and silhouette that had caught his eye. It just didn't look natural. As he knelt a gust of wind blew away the top layer of snow, revealing a bright red patch of material. A jacket. The material was dark with moisture, probably soaked through. The chill in his gut turned into an Antarctic wasteland. He brushed the rest of the snow away and rolled the person onto their back. Relief and fear exploded simultaneously, sending a wave of nausea through him.

"Juliet?"

Her lips were blue and she was unresponsive. Without thinking about it he lifted her into his arms, opened the passenger door on the Yukon, and bundled her into the seat. After clicking on her seatbelt he ran around to the driver's side and slid behind the wheel. The engine roared, the heater came on full-blast, and he angled the dash vents so the warm flow hit her in the chest and not her feet and legs. Sending cold blood from her extremities to her heart could cause cardiac arrest, so he needed to heat her core first. Grant stomped on the accelerator. Even as fast as the SUV accelerated, which was impressive in spite of its size, he couldn't outrun the stark, biting dread that threatened to choke him.

He thought about taking her to the hospital but his house was closer, and he was Montana-born-and-bred-familiar with hypothermia. What the *hell* had she been doing out here? Silently cursing the rental company for loaning her an unreliable vehicle, he reached out to grab her glove-covered hand. Her fingers were so cold he felt the chill from underneath the insulated mittens, and he was afraid they would snap off if he held too tightly.

"Come on, darlin'," he said softly, gently holding the freezing digits. "You've fought too hard to live to quit now."

When he reached his house he almost skidded into the garage door. Grant didn't bother to go around to Juliet's side. He clicked off her belt, pulled her gently into his arms, and then left the SUV. Unlocking and opening the front door was a little harder because his hands were shaking, but once he was inside he kicked the door shut and headed straight for the master bedroom.

Juliet mumbled something incoherent as he carefully put her on the bed. His heart was racing, but he pulled in several deep breaths and then his stress inoculation kicked in. With quick, efficient movements he cut her out of her clothes, discarding the freezing wet garments in a sodden pile. Then he slid her beneath the sheets, and pulled the thick comforter around her shivering form as he turned the electric blanket on low. He grabbed his cell, dialed 911, and told Roberta to get an ambulance headed his way. Tossing the phone aside he leaned in close and laid his cheek against hers, her skin felt like ice.

"Come on, darlin'," he crooned, his lips near her ear. His heart rate started to climb when she didn't respond. Her skin was still tinged with blue and the earth opened up beneath him again as cold, unadulterated fear cut through his chest with an icy blade. This was different than combat. In Iraq and Afghanistan he hadn't had emotions to cloud his thinking, and the stress inoculation didn't seem to be working nearly as well as it usually did. He didn't have an enemy, or Coulter, or Mayfield, to concentrate on. His sole focus was Juliet. *His* Juliet. He felt the tears sting and closed his eyes.

"God, please don't take her from me," he whispered. "Please."

With that prayer he stripped out of his clothes and slipped into bed beside her. He sucked in a breath as her skin contacted his with a shock of cold, and then he pulled her on top of him. As the bed started to warm he sent fervent, silent prayers heavenward.

Juliet gradually became aware of heat. At first it burned, but the stinging soon faded and she wanted more. Never in her life had she been so cold. Even her heart seemed nearly frozen, and each beat labored to push the slush of icy blood through her veins. Then she became aware of something else: strong arms. She was being cradled against a chest and she reacted instantly. She didn't know how she knew it was Grant, she just did. He was the man she'd given her heart to, the man who hadn't texted the dreaded rebuff, and the same man who hadn't answered any of her calls or responded to any of her attempts to contact him for nearly a week. None of that mattered now. Right now she was in his arms, she was safe, and she was getting warmer with each passing second.

"Fight, darlin'," he said in a low, fierce voice. "Come back to me, damn you."

I told you, Jules. I told you he wanted you back. Forgive him for trying to be noble. It is part of why you love him, after all.

"Shut up, Cassie," she thought. She realized she'd spoken the words when he jerked back.

"Juliet?"

He pulled her close again, his embrace tightening. Juliet sighed softly and her hands slowly slid up his body to rest on his chest.

"Baby, are you with me?" he asked.

She heard the trepidation in his voice and pressed her face into the curve of his neck. Her vocal chords were still stiff with cold, but she managed a croaky, "There's no place I'd rather be, Sheriff."

He let out an explosive breath and cupped her head with one hand while the other fanned over her lower back and pressed her closer. "Thank you, God. Thank you, thank you, thank you."

They lay like this, silent and unmoving, until the shivers left her body. She drank in his heat, relished the feel of his skin against hers. Unbidden, her thoughts started to wander from warmth to something else as the fog of hypothermia receded a bit and her awareness of his body beneath hers sharpened. A familiar ache sprang to life in her belly only to be snuffed out as the high-pitched whine of a siren pierced the silence. She heard the front door crash open.

"Sheriff?"

"Back here!" he shouted.

Seconds later, people rushed into the room. She wanted to protest as she was wrapped up in the blankets, gently lifted, bundled onto a gurney, and wheeled out of the room. She didn't even have the strength to open her eyes. Just as the gurney was loaded into the ambulance she managed to rasp out, "Grant, where is Grant?" When there was no response panic flared inside her, which helped to strengthen her voice. "Where is Grant? I want Grant!"

Strong fingers wrapped around hers. "Hush, darlin', I'm right here."

The swirl of panic receded as warmth and light enveloped her and she felt herself smile. She tightened her grip on his hand, but she only had the strength to give his fingers a light squeeze. He squeezed back, let out a long, slow breath, and then pressed his lips to her brow in a lingering kiss.

"Rest, baby," he whispered, his breath fanning over her face. "Just rest."

Juliet smiled again and gave up the fight to stay awake. She felt the paramedic working on her, taking her vitals and communicating with the driver, but he, or she, wasn't important.

Now you can sleep, Jules. Grant will take excellent care of you.

Chapter Thirty

Grant sighed, rubbed his eyes, and stretched his legs out in front of him. He *hated* hospitals. Dr. St. Pierre was taking care of Juliet and had asked him to wait in the waiting room. That alone communicated the seriousness of the situation. He had refused to leave the ER, and so he'd been relegated to the hall outside of the room where they were treating her. The back of the chair scraped against the wall as he adjusted his position and tried to get comfortable. Minutes turned into hours. He leaned his head back, his eyes closing as the aftermath of adrenaline left him worn-out and drained. When the door finally opened and the doctor stepped out of the room Grant stood and stuffed his hands in his pockets.

"How is she?"

St. Pierre glanced at the chart and gave him a faint smile. "She'll be fine. It was good you got to her when you did, and you did all the right things, Sheriff."

Grant grunted. "I've had a little experience with hypothermia in my life."

St. Pierre lifted one dark eyebrow. "I've heard tell of some of your youthful misdeeds, so I have no doubt about that." His expression sobered. "Her core temp is still well below normal, but we're using heated saline to bring it up slowly. Had you not found her when you did, she might have been beyond help."

The same cold, dark fear filled him but he pushed it back. Juliet was safe. He hung his head and sighed again. "I know."

St. Pierre patted his arm. "You can sit with her now if you like, but there will be no early checkouts this time. She's staying at least until tomorrow."

Grant nodded. "I'll make sure she stays."

A wry smile curled the shorter man's mouth. "You may have to stay yourself to make that happen."

"I know," Grant replied, rubbing his brow. "Not a problem, unless it is for you."

St. Pierre shook his head. "No problem at all. We'll get a room set up for her . . . and you."

"Thanks, Doc," Grant said, extending his hand. The two men shook briefly.

"You're welcome." St. Pierre grinned. "Besides, I know if I don't take good care of you and yours Dr. Wheeler will hear about it and then *I* won't hear the end of it." He chuckled and turned. "I'll check back with both of you in a little while."

"Thanks again, Doc."

Grant stood in the hall and stared at the closed door for a minute. Juliet's presence was having a distinctly unsettling effect on his emotions, sending them heaving in two different directions at the same time. He was overjoyed to see her, warmth radiated through him, and yet cold waves of guilt rushed in to dampen the heat. No doubt she had traveled here because of his inability to send that text, and she'd almost frozen to death as a result.

E had been insulting him in spectacular language almost daily since his last phone call with Juliet, extolling to him about the futility of martyrdom and guilt. As Grant added his personal responsibility for Juliet's current condition into the mix the friend in his head went nearly ballistic. But, he wasn't in the mood to argue with E, especially since E wasn't really there. He stood unmoving until his friend finished his current tirade, and he could almost see E stalk off to a corner of his brain, hands clenched and eyes narrowed dangerously, his famous Latin temper simmering hotly. It wasn't the first tiff they'd ever had, but it was the first where Grant had been unable to argue back.

When his brain once again went quiet he pushed open the door and stepped into the room. Juliet was dozing, her lashes a dark arc above her delicate cheekbones, her breathing deep and even. She was covered in blankets and although she was still a little pale, she was no longer blue. Grant eased down onto a chair against the opposite wall and sent up another silent prayer of thanks.

He ached to touch her, but as he sat there the recollection of her cold skin against his made him wince. His mind drifted to when the shivers had finally stopped, allowing some of his anxiety to leach away as he happily gave her his body heat. Then he'd felt a change. He'd sensed her gradual rise to consciousness, and the brief stirring of awareness before the paramedics had dashed onto the scene. The way her hand had caressed his chest, the slight hitch in her breathing, her raspy words told him she was not only happy to not be frozen, she was also happy to be where she was, naked, on top of him. The very thought made his groin twitch and he frowned at the inappropriateness of his reaction.

"Grant?"

His head snapped upright and he made it to the side of her bed in one long stride. Easing down on the edge of the gurney he took her hand and pressed a kiss to the back of it.

"I'm right here, darlin'." A small smile rounded her lush mouth and before he knew what he was doing he cupped her cheek and allowed his thumb to stroke the plump lower lip. Her smile deepened and her eyelids fluttered up. When he looked into those searing turquoise pools his heart did a double flip into his throat and it took considerable effort to swallow it down. "How are you feeling?"

"Better . . . now that you're here."

She shivered and his reaction was immediate. "You still cold, baby?" he asked.

Juliet bit her lip. "If I said I was, would you climb up here and help me not be?"

The hopeful note in her voice turned his insides to mush. His thumb rubbed over her lip again. "Don't you know by now that I'd do just about anything for you?" He shrugged out of his jacket, spread it over her torso, and then kicked off his boots and tossed his hat aside before spooning himself around her. Careful of the IVs, he slipped an arm beneath her head and nestled it in the crook of his elbow as his other arm draped over her waist, his fingers tucking in beneath her ribs. A soft sigh escaped her and she snuggled back against him.

"What the hell were you thinking?" he asked. He wasn't angry with her, and he kept his tone carefully neutral.

"You didn't send that text," she said softly. "But you stopped taking my calls. I've been on pins and needles since I hung up on you, and I couldn't stand it anymore."

He sighed softly and pressed a cheek to her hair. The faint scent of her shampoo wrapped around him and he felt the familiar stirring. "Juliet—"

Her next words came out in a rush. "I decided enough was enough, and I was going to get the information I needed straight from the horse's mouth, so to speak."

She went still and silent, her body tensed and poised for flight, most likely in anticipation of rejection. Grant tightened his hold on her and inhaled the scent of her hair once more. There was no way he was letting her go again.

"I wrote the text, but I couldn't send it," he admitted.

"What did it say?"

"It said stay in Chicago, we would never work out."

Her body remained stiff and a dark chuckle escaped her. "Thank you for not sending that." Her brows drew together and she shifted toward him slightly so she could look at his face. "If you couldn't send it, why wouldn't you take my calls? I've been driving myself crazy for a week, Grant."

He dipped his chin and brushed a kiss over her temple. "I was afraid that if I talked to you I'd say what I'd written, and even though I wouldn't have meant it, once those words are out there you can't take them back."

"So . . . ." Her voice trailed off and she slowly turned until she lay facing him. "If you didn't mean it *that* means you don't *want* me to stay in Chicago, right?"

She bit her lip again and Grant smiled as he recognized her nervous tell. Instead of replying he lowered his head and kissed her. She didn't respond at first, but when he traced the outline of her mouth with his tongue a soft gasp escaped her and he took full advantage. He angled his head to get a better seal and delved deeper. Her fingers curled into the front of his shirt, her body arched toward him, and that familiar heaviness settled in his groin. A growl rumbled in his chest and she sighed.

When he'd had his fill he ended the kiss and pulled back, but one look in her eyes had his tank on empty again. "No, darlin'," he whispered, brushing his nose over her cheekbone, "I don't want you to stay in Chicago."

"I'm not sure I believe you," she said in a whisper.

He nuzzled her ear. "What do I have to do to convince you?"

A soft laugh escaped her. "I'm sure you'll think of something. After all, it'd be a shame to waste this *semi-private* room."

"No, it wouldn't." He pulled back and met that turquoise gaze. "We'll be moved to a *private* room shortly, and they already know I'm spending the night."

She blinked at him. "They do?"

"Mm hmm," he replied. His tongue traced the curve of her ear and she shivered, but the faint hint of pink in her cheeks told him it wasn't hypothermia related. At least her circulation was returning to normal. "Doc figured it'd be the easiest way to make sure you stayed put."

"So . . . ." Her voice trailed off and she inhaled sharply when he bit down lightly on her earlobe, and then sucked the same. Her blush deepened and she was quiet for several seconds before she cleared her throat. "So, we can't get naked until after we change rooms?"

A chuckle rumbled in his chest. "Here you've just survived almost freezing to death, and all you can think of is getting me out of my clothes." He clicked his tongue several times. "That's highly inappropriate."

"So is nibbling on my ear."

"Touché." He rested his chin atop her head and pulled her closer. "I guess I'll have to wait until later to take your internal temperature."

"*Now* who's being highly inappropriate?" she asked, her breath warm on his neck.

He laughed softly and closed his eyes. "Sorry, darlin'. That's what you do to me."

"Maybe the doctor won't mind."

He pulled back slightly and looked down his nose at her. "Excuse me?"

"Well," she began, toying with the buttons of his shirt, "you are *really* good at getting my circulation going." She gave him a slanted look. "Maybe a little temperature taking would be a *good* thing."

He shook his head and cursed his body for its ferocious and enthusiastic reaction. "Sorry, darlin'. Hypothermia can damage the heart, so my clothes are going to remain on until the doc gives the all clear, no matter how much I hate it." Her sound of disappointment made him smile and he tightened his embrace. "Don't worry, Juliet. As soon as the doc says you're okay I'm all yours. In fact, you may not make it home fully clothed."

When she was released two days later, she didn't. And the back of the Yukon was *nothing* like high school.

***

Eight months later . . . .

Juliet leaned back in her seat and sipped champagne as she absently rubbed her feet. Grant danced with Miss Nicole, the older woman's face beaming as he whirled her around the floor. Bear and his new wife, Beth, were dancing slowly despite the upbeat tune, and the look in their eyes as they stared at one another made Juliet smile. Daniel and Jessica Sheridan were deep in conversation, but their close proximity told her there was more going on there than heated debate. Juliet glanced around the idyllic scene and realized the only thing missing was her parents. The invitation she'd sent them had been returned unopened, but her father had sent a separate card asking for forgiveness and wishing her nothing but happiness. Their absence still hurt, but her dad's request lessened the sting. Grant had said they'd stop in San Diego on the way back from their Hawaiian honeymoon for a face-to-face. If her parents still refused to see her, that would be that, and she and Grant would go on with their lives with no regrets.

"Here," Autumn said, her voice breaking into Juliet's thoughts as she handed her a pair of white satin ballet flats. "Thought you could use these."

Juliet smiled and slipped the comfortable shoes on. "Oh, you're amazing. I love you."

Autumn pursed her lips, lifted one elegant brow, and crossed her arms over her ample chest. "Girlfriend, there is a *reason* I'm your matron of honor. That *is* my job, to take care of the things you *can't* remember because you're so head-over-heels in *love.*"

Juliet's gaze slid to Grant and her heart started to thud. "Is it that obvious?"

"You forgot your *dress* this morning," Autumn said flatly. "What *bride* forgets her *dress*?"

The petite beauty was about to say something else when her eyes shifted and her expression brightened. Juliet followed the direction of her gaze and watched as Autumn's husband, Landon, strode toward them. He was tall, well-built, and incredibly handsome in his navy-blue tuxedo, blonde hair glinting beneath the warm lights that hung inside the enormous white tent.

"My lady," Landon said when he reached Autumn's side, his grass-green eyes sparkling, "may I have this dance?" He offered his arm and Autumn giggled like a school girl.

"Excuse me, girlfriend," Autumn said without looking at her. "I'll be back soon."

Juliet watched her go and sighed happily. She gazed out over the crowd of wedding-goers, nearly overcome by the sense of belonging and contentment that welled warmly inside her. The entire town was here. How much her life had changed in such a short time!

Movement out of the corner of her eye drew her gaze and she turned slightly. Across the broad lawn behind the reception area, near the river, a lone figure walked. Juliet knew exactly who it was. Only one woman at the reception wore a navy blue dress.

She'd met Laine a week ago when she, Jack, Bear, and Beth had arrived in Evergreen in advance of her and Grant's wedding. At first Juliet had been cool to the woman, holding a grudge for Grant's sake, but it hadn't lasted long. Laine had responded to her chill with warm understanding, and Juliet had even seen regret and what resembled shame in the woman's eyes when she thought Juliet wasn't looking. The wistful looks Laine gave Grant showed Juliet that Grant wasn't the only one hurt by what had happened, or what *hadn't* happened, in their relationship. Juliet took another sip of champagne, then put the flute aside and rose.

Her feet whispered through the grass and she lifted the hem of her dress. Laine's back was to her, one shoulder leaning into the trunk of an aspen tree, her gaze locked on something past the river. Juliet approached slowly, so as not to startle her.

"Laine?"

Laine looked over her shoulder then quickly looked away, dashing a hand over her cheeks. "Juliet. What are you doing over here? Shouldn't you be dancing with that incredibly sexy husband of yours?"

Though she'd tried to hide it, Juliet saw the tears behind the forced smile. "I needed a breather." She took a step closer. "Are you alright?"

"Fine," Laine replied with a nod. "I always cry at weddings, even my own. Just ask Jack."

Laine wouldn't look at her, and Juliet sensed her turmoil from three feet away. "Laine, what's wrong?"

"Nothing." Laine dropped her chin and wiped her cheeks again.

"Sorry, not buying it." Juliet paused for a few seconds. "Talk to me. I know I'm not your husband or your best girlfriend, but I'm willing to listen." She sighed. "Look, I know I didn't give you the warmest welcome, but . . . I *like* you, I really do. I'd like for us to be friends, and *not* just because of Grant."

Laine glanced at her. Tears shimmered and she smiled a genuine, cheery smile. "I'm so happy for the both of you." She blinked and the tears fell as she turned her gaze back to the river. "I guess it just hit me when I was watching the two of you that, even though I've known Grant all my life, you know him better than I do."

"Just in the Biblical sense," Juliet joked with a chuckle. "Complete strangers get to know each other that well all the time, so don't give *that* too much credence."

"Don't." The vehemence in her tone made Juliet's eyes widen. Laine faced her, a scowl furrowing her brow. "Don't make light of what you two share in an attempt to make me feel better, because it doesn't." The frown faded, she looked at the ground, and twisted her fingers together. "I suppose . . . part of me wishes I'd gotten to know that side of him when I had the chance."

Juliet was thunderstruck. She'd always assumed Grant and Laine had been intimate, but if what she was hearing was true, she was wrong. "You and Grant never . . . I mean, you two didn't . . . ?"

"No," Laine said with a sigh and a soft, poignant smile. "I mean, we made out like *crazy* in high school, but after that . . . between medical school and the Marine Corps the opportunity never really presented itself. At least, it didn't at a time either of us was inclined to do anything about it." Her head snapped up and her eyes widened. "Please don't think that I want to do that now, because that's *not* what this is." She ran a hand over her face and leaned against the aspen. "To be honest, I'm not sure *what* this is, but I know it's not *that.*"

"I get it, Laine," Juliet said softly. "It's like when you turn down a really nice guy for a date, and then wonder what might have happened if you'd said yes. We all have regrets."

"My biggest regret in life is hurting him in the first place." Laine wrapped her arms around herself, a hint of a breeze picking up as the sun started to sink behind the mountains to the west. "He deserved better." Laine gave her a sidelong glance and a wistful smile. "And he finally got it."

"I'm not *better*, Laine," Juliet argued, "I'm just . . . the right one." Laine's head turned and her eyes narrowed slightly. Juliet felt like she was being studied, or examined by a doctor.

"Yes, you are," Laine agreed, her smile widening just a bit, "and that man *loves* you . . . more than he *ever* loved me."

Juliet laughed. "I don't know about *that*—"

"I do." Her expression sobered. "He'll always be my best friend, aside from Jack, and I'll always be his best friend, now aside from *you*." Laine laid a hand on her arm and leaned closer, a warm light filling her eyes. "But *you* are the air he breathes, Juliet, and I have *never* seen him happier. Thank you."

"For what?"

"For getting him to fall in love again," she replied, tipping her head to the side. "Now I don't have to worry about him anymore, at least not in *that* department."

Grant sidled up to Jack, who was getting a beer from the bar. Jack turned and gave him a smile as he put the bottle to his mouth and took a long drink.

"What do you think is going on over there?" Grant asked, nodding in the direction of his new bride and his old flame. "Isn't it a bad thing when two women go off to be alone and *talk*, especially at an event like *this*, and especially *those* two?"

"I don't think we have to worry about a catfight, if that's what you're asking," Jack said with a chuckle.

"Good." Grant shook his head, turned, and asked for a beer. "Because I have a feeling those two would be pretty evenly matched."

"As do I."

The two men looked at each other.

"Maybe we should head on over there and see what's happening," Grant suggested.

Jack took another swig of his beer, put the bottle on the bar, and straightened his lapels. "Yeah, that might be a good idea."

They strolled, their eyes locked on their wives.

"Grant, can I ask you something?"

Grant looked at Jack out of the corner of his eye. "Sure. Not going to guarantee an answer, but ask away."

"If you weren't married, and something happened to me, do you think you and Laine would wind up together?"

Grant slowed his steps. "I've never really thought about it," he replied, watching Jack's face carefully. "Why?"

Jack shrugged. "Just curious. In our line of work that's something we have to think about more than the average Joe." He glanced to where the women were standing. "It's just . . . I think this whole thing with you and Juliet is bittersweet for Laine. It kind of . . . closes the book on the two of you."

"*That* book closed when Laine fell in love with you," Grant said. He chuckled. "And it was sealed shut when she *married* you."

Jack studied him as they walked slowly. "I guess you probably know better than anyone what she's feeling right now."

Grant rubbed his chin. "Probably."

Jack's eyes narrowed. "Being her man of honor must've been hard, but you did it anyway. *Twice.*"

The memory didn't hurt anymore. "I love her," Grant replied simply. "I want her to be happy even if that's not with me." He gave Jack a sidelong glance. "You make her happy. Enough said."

"And Juliet makes *you* happy." Jack chuckled. "Even Ray Charles could figure *that* out."

"That obvious, eh?"

"Absolutely. The air temperature is several degrees warmer around the two of you." Jack stopped walking and faced him. "I'm really happy for you, Grant, and I'm glad that we're at least speaking to each other."

"We're more than just speaking to each other, Jack." Grant sighed and stuffed his hands in his pockets. "Laine forgave you that night, and I should have followed her example, but it's taken me a while to deal with it. Now I have, and I've forgiven you too, as long as you'll forgive me for being an asshole and holding a grudge."

"Done." Jack smiled, held out a hand, and the two men shook. "Friends?"

"You bet," Grant agreed with a quick grin. "Now, let's go get our women before they start sharing things we'd rather they didn't."

"I have a feeling it's too late for that."

"Probably."

Juliet stood at Laine's side, gazing out over the river. She felt the woman watching her.

"What are you going to do about the offer from that Ivan guy?" Laine asked. "He must really want you to dance for him if he's willing to start a company in Helena just for you."

"I don't know," Juliet answered. "Grant thinks I should do it since Helena is only a few hours away, but we both know he'd say that even if he hated the idea."

"Yep," Laine agreed. "That's Grant. He's always putting others' welfare and wishes ahead of his own." She shrugged. "I guess that's part of the reason he was such a good Marine, and why he's such a popular sheriff." Laine put a hand on her arm. "My recommendation is to talk about it and make a decision together, one you can both live with."

Juliet nodded, not wanting to think about the proposal from the head of the Chicago Ballet. That was something they could deal with later. Right now, there was something else pressing on her heart. "Do you wish things were different between you and Grant?" she asked, almost dreading the answer.

"No," Laine said immediately in a soft voice. "I love Grant, but there was always something that seemed to keep us apart." She gave Juliet a sidelong glance. "Now I know why." She paused, and then added, "Jack always says that the Big Guy upstairs knows what He's doing, and I'm starting to think my husband is right."

Juliet tipped her head. "What do you mean?"

A graceful shrug lifted Laine's shoulders. "Could Grant and I have had a good life together? I think so. Could Grant and I have the sort of life and relationship *Jack* and I have? I'm not sure." She extended a hand and the women laced fingers. "I mean, look at what all of us – you and Grant, Bear and Beth, Jack and I – look at what we went through to find love. I guess somebody up there somewhere really knows which people belong together." A grin lit her face. "That, or they have one *hell* of a sense of humor."

Warmth filled Juliet and she realized she'd just found a true friend. "I think you're right on both counts."

"Right about what?" a deep, sexy male voice asked.

Butterflies took to wing and Juliet released Laine's hand to face her husband. He looked delicious in his black tuxedo, the jacket tossed over one shoulder, the neck of his shirt open just a little bit. He gave her that sensual grin and stepped forward to drape his jacket around her bare shoulders.

"What is Laine right about?" he asked again.

Juliet walked into his embrace and wound her arms around his waist as her head dropped onto his chest. She looked at Laine out of the corner of her eye as the woman moved into Jack's arms. They exchanged a look and smiled at each other.

"She's right about everything," Juliet replied.

Grant chuckled and rested his chin atop her head. "Well, that's par for the course."

"Hey," Laine protested.

"What?" he asked in an innocent voice. "Am I wrong? Because if I am that just makes you right, *again.*"

Juliet laughed, Jack grinned, and Laine scowled, but soon she was chuckling too.

"You're lucky I love you, Grant Donovan," she said with narrowed, twinkling eyes.

"Yes, I am," he replied in a low, sincere voice. He pressed a kiss to the top of Juliet's head. "I am a *very* lucky man." Juliet looked up at him and her throat tightened at the love so evident in those bedroom eyes. He gazed down at her, a slight smile curling his lips, his hold tightening just a bit. "I have been blessed with more luck than any one man should have."

"Come on, Jack," Laine said softly. "Let's give the newlyweds some privacy. Besides, you owe me a dance."

"You bet, Doc." Jack chuckled softly and Laine tucked in beneath his arm as they strolled back toward the reception. Juliet and Grant watched them for a few moments, and then locked eyes again.

"Is everything alright?" Grant asked, cupping her neck and rubbing his thumbs over her jaw.

Juliet swallowed hard, tears stinging. She bit her lip. Her vocal chords knotted in her throat, words to express her feelings just a jumble of meaningless nothing in her head. The depth of her love for this man bound her to him forever, and those bonds, oddly enough, freed her. No matter how high she flew, she knew he would catch her if she fell.

His brows drew together. "What is it, darlin'? What's wrong?"

A smile blossomed and the tears trailed slowly down her cheeks. She framed his face with her hands and stood on tiptoe, her heart beating so hard she was sure he would feel the vibration.

"*Nothing* is wrong," she finally managed to whisper. Her eyes welled and her chin trembled. "I just never knew I could be *this* happy *off* stage." She kissed him and his arms snuck around her waist, lifting her off the ground and pulling her tightly against him. "I love you, Grant Donovan. You are the one partner I know I can dance with for the rest of my life."

"Yes, ma'am, you can," he agreed. "Why don't we get started on that?"

He put her feet back on the ground, then bent down and tossed her over his shoulder. Juliet cried out in surprise.

"What are you doing?"

He started walking toward the reception with long, confident strides. "Asserting my husbandly rights," he replied with a sound smack to her bottom.

A thrill of anticipation went through her and she sucked in a breath. She stopped herself just before asking him to spank her again. "And what *rights* are those?" she asked.

"I have the right to dance with my wife, and then watch her toss the bouquet so we can get on with the rest of our night."

She laughed softly, noting the even and level pace he kept to avoid digging his shoulder into her ribs. "We have two more hours here, Grant."

He shifted his grip and moved her until she was cradled in his arms. She wrapped her arms around his neck and the familiar tingles started. The look he gave her was dark and smoky and her pulse responded accordingly by jumping several notches.

"I have plans for the next two hours that *do not* involve the waltz or a conga line." His eyes called to her, and she found herself leaning toward him almost against her will. Just before their lips touched he said, "I want to start the honeymoon *now*, darlin'. Can you handle that?"

"What makes you think I can't?" she asked, breathless.

A grin twitched about his mouth. "Oh, I don't doubt you, but I can pretty much guarantee the only sleep you're going to get is on the *plane* to Kauai." His smile widened and a devilish sparkle lit those chocolate pools. "That's *after* we join the mile high club on the way there, of course."

"Of course," she whispered as his mouth claimed hers. A small moan caught in her throat and she wound her fingers through his hair, relishing the feel of his hard body against hers, and the sensation of soft, crisp curls against her palms. Alternating waves of hot and cold washed over her and her insides went all gooey. Suddenly the wedding dress was too confining, too constricting, and in the way. Juliet pushed out of his embrace, grabbed his hand, and started walking quickly toward the reception.

"Juliet?"

She glanced at him and gave him a wicked look. "The guests can stay, but it's time to throw the bouquet and get out of here." She paused and lifted one brow. "Can you handle that, Sheriff Donovan?"

He caught up to her, lifted her in his arms, and set off at a run, grinning like the devil. "I can, Mrs. Donovan. I most *definitely* can."

Epilogue

Cassie's fingers wound through hers, waves lapping at their feet and a soft, ocean breeze ruffling their hair. Juliet looked at her sister, pride welling up inside her, and when Cassie glanced at her they both broke into a smile. It was early, the sun rising behind them in a glowing golden orb, brilliant discs of color dancing on the water.

"It's time for me to go, Jules," Cassie said softly.

It took several seconds for that statement to register, and the joy that had been so snugly wrapped around her fell away like a discarded quilt.

"What?" Juliet gaped at her. "You can't leave me."

Cassie faced her and grasped her hands. "I'm not my sister's keeper anymore, Juliet. That's Grant's job now, and I have every confidence that he will do a much better job than I ever could." She dropped her chin and looked at the sand. "Live your life well, sister, and be happy with him." Cassie met her gaze and Juliet's gut knotted when she saw the sheen of tears in her sister's eyes. "He is one *hell* of a man. *Never* forget what you went through to be with him, and never let him go. *Never.*"

"I won't," Juliet choked out, tears obscuring her vision. She tightened her grip on her sister's hands. "Where . . . where are you going?"

A poignant smile curved Cassie's mouth. "This place was only temporary, Jules, until I could make sure you were taken care of." A lone tear trickled down her cheek. "Now I know you will be taken care of. Tell Grant I said thank you."

Cassie hugged her and Juliet clung to her tightly. "Please don't go, Cass," Juliet whispered. "Please stay."

"I can't, big sister," Cassie replied, her voice tear-filled. "But I'll always be in your heart, just like you're in mine. Whenever you think of me, know that means I'm thinking of you, too. We're sisters, Juliet. Not even death can sever *that* bond." Cassie rubbed her back and then pulled away. "Now, I have to go." Her gaze slid down the beach, and a shy smile lifted the corners of her mouth.

Juliet followed the direction of her gaze and her brows rose when she saw a man standing about 30 feet away. He was roughly six feet tall, well-built, with dark hair and skin and a smile that would put Shelby's to shame. He lifted a hand in greeting, but stayed where he was.

"Who's that?" Juliet asked in a low voice.

Pink bathed Cassie's cheeks. "He's a friend." She leaned in for another quick hug. "Don't worry, Jules. *He's* going to take care of *me*." She pulled away, took several steps toward the man, then spun back and grabbed hold of her again. "I love you, sister. Always remember that."

And with that she was gone. Juliet watched as she ran down the beach toward the man, who opened his arms and caught her as she leapt into them. She heard her sister laugh, and tears welled as he spun Cassie several times. They kissed, and then he put her feet back on the sand. The two of them turned and waved before clasping hands and walking away from her. Juliet covered her mouth and tried to hold back the sobs.

"Juliet."

She turned at the sound of Grant's voice, but she couldn't see him. A look over her shoulder started the tears afresh as Cassie and her friend faded from view.

"Juliet?"

Her eyes fluttered open and she looked into Grant's face, his eyes dark with concern. He was sitting up in bed, gripping her shoulders gently. Even though her mind was cloudy with sleep she felt a distinct absence, as if someone who had been standing close to her for a very long time was suddenly gone. And just like that she knew. Cassie was no longer there. Juliet covered her face with her hands, tears squeezing out from beneath tightly closed lids.

"It's okay, darlin'. You were just having a dream."

Sorrow welled up in her and she threw herself against his broad chest, her fingers clutching at his back. Tears clogged her throat and cut off her airway. The room dipped and spun as she wept, his arms closed around her protectively.

"Breathe, baby. Breathe."

"Sh-she's g-gone," Juliet choked out. "C-Cassie is . . . gone."

Grant lay back, pulling her on top of him. "Oh, darlin'. She's not *gone*, she's just not *here*. She'll always be part of you, Juliet, *always*."

"No," Juliet wailed, "her v-voice is g-gone. Th-the one in my head. It's not th-there anymore. It's just . . . *gone*."

He put a finger under her chin and tipped her face to his. His brows were drawn together. "What do you mean *gone*, baby?"

Juliet fought to hold onto the dream and relayed the details to Grant between sobs. He listened quietly, his hands moving slowly up and down her back. When she was done she took a deep shuddering breath and pressed her face into the curve of his neck. His pulse pattered against her cheek but he said nothing, and after a few moments of silence she lifted her head to look at him. His expression was thoughtful, his gaze focused on the ceiling, and Juliet's heart sank.

"I'm not crazy, Grant," she said, dropping her head back onto his shoulder.

"I know, darlin'," he replied. "It's just . . . weird."

She sighed. "I know."

"No, that's not what I meant."

She lifted her head again.

He pursed his lips and continued to stare at the overhead. "I woke up a few minutes before you and E decided to pop off. He told me he was out, that since I had you I didn't need him anymore." He shifted his gaze to meet hers. "He said he had a date with a hot blonde."

Juliet gaped at him, her insides spinning and twisting like a Tilt-a-Whirl.

Grant ran a finger over her cheekbone. "Even weirder . . . I was sure I heard waves and seagulls, like he was at the beach." He eased her off him and sat up. "What did the guy in your dream look like?"

"He was tall, but shorter than you, Hispanic, and he had a smile brighter than Shelby's."

Grant stared at her for a few seconds and she saw the convulsive swallow. He blinked rapidly several times, then hopped out of bed and started rooting through his duffel bag. After about ten seconds he pulled out a 5"x 7" photo album. He looked at the cover for several long, heavy moments, then flipped through it until he found what he was looking for and handed it to her. "Is that him?"

Juliet pressed shaking fingers to her mouth and blinked back tears. The man from her dream who had twirled Cassie around and kissed her so tenderly stared back at her from that photograph. The megawatt smile was unmistakable. He wore desert camouflage, his face dirty and smudged, and he had an arm around Grant's neck. The American flag snapped in the background as they leaned against an armored transport.

"Yes," Juliet rasped out, her voice breaking. "That's your friend?"

Grant eased down on the edge of the bed and rested his elbows on his knees. "Yeah, that's E." He pressed his thumb and forefinger into his eyes and took a shaky breath.

Juliet looked at his broad back for several moments, tears welling and her throat so tight she couldn't swallow. Her own pain was bad enough, but feeling his was more than she could bear. Her heart broke for him, for her, for Cassie, and for E. Lives drastically altered by circumstances completely out of their control. And then she had an epiphany. She pressed herself against his back and wrapped her arms around him. Resting her chin on his shoulder, her tears plopped onto his skin.

"You know what this means, don't you?" she asked, barely able to summon a whisper with the obstruction in her esophagus.

Grant wrapped his fingers around her forearm. "What, darlin'?"

"It means we're going to be okay," she replied. She kissed his neck. "They wouldn't have left us otherwise."

Grant was silent for a few moments. "I've gotten so used to hearing him."

"He's been there a long time," Juliet said, her eyes filling yet again. "And he'll always be a part of you, like Cassie is with me. But . . . you know what else this means?"

He turned to face her and tugged her onto his lap, his arms looping around her waist and pulling her in close. His eyes were unnaturally bright and when he blinked a single tear fell. Juliet pressed her lips together to keep from crying.

"What else does this mean, baby?" he asked in a hushed voice.

She sniffled and framed his face. "It means they're going to be okay, too." A smile burst forth despite her grief, because in her heart she knew what she'd just said was the truth, all of it. She and Grant were going to be okay, and so were Cassie and E. She looked deep into those bedroom eyes she loved more than life itself. "They found each other, just like we did."

She kissed him then, and as their mouths melded and the seconds passed the hurt dropped off, much like the ice over her heart that Grant had determinedly shattered. She pictured Cassie, the happiness in her bright eyes, the way E had kissed her, as if she was irreplaceable and priceless. Peace suddenly filled her, a warm-water spring seemed to erupt in the bottom of her soul. It flooded her, permeated her, enveloped her, penetrating to the deepest parts of her until not only her body but her mind and psyche were tingling and relaxed.

"We're going to be fine, Grant," she whispered against his mouth. "We're all going to be just fine."

He flipped her onto her back on the mattress and covered her body with his, leaning up on his elbows to avoid crushing her. The intensity in his chocolate-brown eyes made her heart flutter wildly. It was as if the visual connection they now shared transmitted the tranquility she felt directly to him. The hurt left his eyes, his beautifully carved features relaxed and a pensive smile curved those sinfully sculpted lips. He studied her intently, his thumbs caressing her cheeks as he cupped her head.

"God, I love you, Juliet," he whispered. "Lucky doesn't *begin* to cover what I am."

"And I love you," she replied through a haze of happy tears. "I never knew what I was missing, until I met you." She ran a hand over his stubble-covered jaw, her heart somersaulting in tight, frantic circles. "This is the first day of the rest of our lives, Grant. Let's not waste a minute of it."

He pressed his brow to hers and smiled. "Yes, ma'am."

THE END

About the author

Leslie McKelvey has been writing since she learned to write, and her mother still stores boxes of handwritten stories in the attic. Her debut novel, Accidental Affair, was published in 2012.

Leslie is a veteran of the Gulf War who served with the U.S. Navy, and she was among the first groups of women to work the flight deck of an aircraft carrier.

Leslie lives in California with her husband and has three sons.

Also by Leslie McKelvey

Accidental Affair

Jack Vaughn is sure his life is over as he tumbles down the wooded hillside onto the deserted two-lane stretch of asphalt. Years of work ended with a single gunshot. Yet, it's not over.

A good Samaritan stops to help him, despite the danger he poses to her.

Laine Wheeler knows better than to stop for strangers on the rural Montana highway near her home, but her conscience won't allow her to leave an injured man behind.

What she doesn't know is the man is an undercover ATF agent tasked with infiltrating a domestic terrorist group. His cover has been blown and helping him will put her life in danger.

Though there is an instant attraction, Jack knows that beginning a romantic relationship with Laine would be both unfair and unwise. Yet the farther they run, the harder it gets to ignore the feelings surging between them.

Latest titles from Black Velvet Seductions

Playing for Keeps by Glenda Horsfall
Playing by His Rules by Glenda Horsfall
The Love She Wants by Mila Winters
Holly's Big Bad Santa by Starla Kaye
Cowboys in Charge by Starla Kaye
Punished! by Richard Savage, Nadia Nautalia & Starla Kaye

See more of our titles at
www.blackvelvetseductions.com

Our titles are available from:
Amazon
Smashwords
LuLu
Nook
and other retailers